The Overlords

The Wild Ones

FIGHTING BACK . . .

Durant's instincts kicked in from the war. He sought cover, dodging behind a telephone pole, and pulled the Luger from his waistband. The two gunmen fired almost simultaneously, one shot nicking the telephone pole and the other whistling past his ear. He crouched, arm extended at shoulder level, and caught the sights in the reflection from the streetlight. He ripped off three quick shots.

The first shattered the car's windshield. The second plucked at the sleeve of the man by the passenger door. The man by the rear door grunted with surprise, a starburst of blood covering his shirt front from the third slug. He lurched sideways, his legs collapsing, and slumped face-down on the curb. The driver shouted a curse.

The other man jumped on the running board as the Buick roared away. Durant rose from behind the telephone pole, glancing at the dead hoodlum, and decided to make tracks. The cops, given the opportunity, would charge him with murder.

PRAISE FOR SPUR AWARD-WINNING AUTHOR
MATT BRAUN

"Matt Braun is head and shoulders above all the rest who would attempt to bring the gunmen of the Old West to life."
　　　—Terry C. Johnston, author of the Plainsmen series

"Matt Braun has a genius for taking real characters out of the Old West and giving them flesh-and-blood immediacy."
　　　—Dee Brown, author of *Bury My Heart at Wounded Knee*

ST. MARTIN'S PAPERBACKS TITLES
BY MATT BRAUN

WYATT EARP
BLACK FOX
OUTLAW KINGDOM
LORDS OF THE LAND
CIMARRON JORDAN
BLOODY HAND
NOBLE OUTLAW
TEXAS EMPIRE
THE SAVAGE LAND
RIO HONDO
THE GAMBLERS
DOC HOLLIDAY
YOU KNOW MY NAME
THE BRANNOCKS
THE LAST STAND
RIO GRANDE
GENTLEMAN ROGUE
THE KINCAIDS
EL PASO
INDIAN TERRITORY
BLOODSPORT
SHADOW KILLERS
BUCK COLTER
KINCH RILEY
DEATHWALK
HICKOK & CODY
THE WILD ONES
HANGMAN'S CREEK
JURY OF SIX
THE SPOILERS

The Overlords

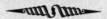

MATT BRAUN

St. Martin's Paperbacks

This is a work of fiction. All of the characters, organizations, and events portrayed in this novel are either products of the author's imagination or are used fictitiously.

THE OVERLORDS / THE WILD ONES

The Overlords copyright © 2003 by Matt Braun.
The Wild Ones copyright © 2002 by Winchester Productions, Ltd.

For information address St. Martin's Press, 175 Fifth Avenue, New York, NY 10010.

ISBN: 978-1-250-19628-6

Our books may be purchased in bulk for promotional, educational, or business use. Please contact your local bookseller or the Macmillan Corporate and Premium Sales Department at 1-800-221-7945, ext. 5442, or by e-mail at MacmillanSpecialMarkets@macmillan.com.

Printed in the United States of America

The Overlords St. Martin's Paperbacks edition / January 2003
The Wild Ones St. Martin's Paperbacks edition / January 2002

St. Martin's Paperbacks are published by St. Martin's Press, 175 Fifth Avenue, New York, NY 10010.

10 9 8 7 6 5 4 3 2 1

To
My Classmates
Oklahoma Military Academy
Those Were the Days

Author's Note

Galveston was the Las Vegas of the Roaring Twenties. There were casinos, nightclubs, Broadway entertainers, bookmaking parlors, and a red-light district with over a thousand ladies of the evening. The Roaring Twenties was also the era of the Volstead Act, a federal law prohibiting the sale of alcoholic spirits anywhere in America. The Island, as Galveston was called by locals, was nonetheless home base to the largest rumrunning operation west of the Mississippi.

Overlooking the Gulf of Mexico, and located off the coast of Texas, Galveston was controlled by modern-day mobsters. A triad of gangsters, crooked politicians, and unscrupulous businessmen transformed the Island into a paradise of sun-and-surf resorts, with a nightlife that rivaled New York and Paris. Millions of tourists flocked to the Island, and tens of millions of dollars were siphoned off by an underworld empire that lasted more than fifty years. There is nothing remotely similar to Galveston in all of American history.

The Overlords is historical fiction. Literary license has been taken with names and places, dates and events, and a large part of the story is pure invention. In fact, *The Overlords* bears testament to the hoary adage that truth is stranger than fiction. The historical reality of Galveston Island often beggars belief.

The Roaring Twenties was an era of booze, jazz, and "let the good times roll." Galveston Island was a microcosm of a people and a nation involved in a decade-long party orchestrated by the mob. *The Overlords* is their story.

The Overlords

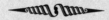

Chapter One

A horseman in a black hat thundered over the hill. Not an instant later a rider in a white hat topped the rocky crest and spurred his barrel-chested stallion. He closed the gap with a burst of speed.

Off to the side, not twenty yards away, a Ford truck barreled along in a sputtering roar. The back of the truck was rigged with a wooden platform, enclosed by a sturdy metal railing. A cameraman fought to maintain his balance, his camera mounted on a tripod and the legs of the tripod bolted to the platform. He furiously cranked the handle on his camera, tracking the action.

The horseman in the white hat leaped from his stallion. He slammed shoulder-first into the black-hatted desperado and drove him out of the saddle. The men tumbled to the ground in a gritty cloud of dust.

The director yelled, *"Cut!"*

The command was amplified through a megaphone held by the director. He was standing behind the cameraman, gripping the metal railing to steady himself. The truck lurched to a halt as the two horsemen levered themselves off the ground. The director looked pleased.

"Good job," he said. "Someone get Tom and Tony in there while we still have sun. Earl, move your horse out of camera."

Earl Durant was the stuntman who doubled for Tom Mix. His white stallion doubled for Mix's famed movie horse, Tony. He dusted himself off, nodding to the black-hatted stuntman, and led his horse behind the truck. A wrangler led Tony into camera.

The sun dropped steadily toward the Pacific Ocean.

The motion picture, titled *The Drifter*, was being shot in the tree-studded hills north of Hollywood. The crew had been at it since early that morning, and the director was fearful of losing the sun. He waved his megaphone.

"People, *please!*" he said in an agitated voice. "We need Tom *now!*"

Tom Mix stepped out of a Dodge touring car parked in the shade of a tree. He was handsome in the way of matinee idols, with hawklike features, dark flashing eyes, and a muscular build. At forty-six, he was still in good shape, though he seldom did his own stunts these days. He stopped beside Durant.

"How about it, Earl?" he said quietly. "Did our great leader get the shot?"

Mix didn't trust directors. He was particularly at odds with Reave Eason, who had little experience at directing Westerns. Eason strutted around in breeches and riding boots, with all the airs of a Prussian cavalry officer commanding a regiment. He wielded his megaphone like it was a baton of power.

"I reckon he got it," Durant said. "Just be careful with the fight scene. He doesn't know a right cross from an uppercut."

"How would you handle it?"

"Let Dusty knock you down. Then get up and trade punches even-steven. Show the audience it takes grit to win a fight."

"Yeah, that's the ticket," Mix agreed. "Give 'em a real knock-down-drag-out."

For all his success, Mix was never hesitant to seek advice. He had fought in the Spanish-American War, following Teddy Roosevelt in the charge up San Juan Hill. Some years later he'd caught on as a bronc-buster with the Miller 101 Wild West Show, which toured out of Oklahoma. Then, after being discovered by a movie producer, he went directly from the rodeo arena to the silver screen.

There were other popular motion picture stars who

made Westerns. William S. Hart, Ken Maynard, Buck Jones, and Hoot Gibson all had a loyal following. But Tom Mix was billed as the "King of the Cowboys," and by 1926, he earned a staggering $20,000 a week. He was the highest paid actor in films, eclipsing such luminaries as Douglas Fairbanks and Charlie Chaplin. Some thought the better billing would have been the "King of Hollywood."

By contrast Durant made fifty dollars a day for risking his neck in death-defying stunts. Yet stuntmen were the daredevils of Hollywood, relying on nerve and finely tuned reflexes to deliver action scenes that amused and amazed audiences. They were the gladiators of the motion picture amphitheater, and even the stars accorded them their due. None was more respected than Earl Durant.

Mix always insisted that Durant work on his pictures. Durant was slightly taller, lithely built, with chestnut hair and gray eyes. He was in his late twenties, broad through the shoulders, athletic in appearance. But he had a chameleon quality on film, and he easily doubled for such diverse actors as Mix and Fairbanks, and the master of illusion, Lon Chaney. Mix looked at him now.

"Told you before, you ought to be a director. You know more about pictures than Eason and that artsy crowd. When are you gonna take the leap?"

Durant smiled. "One of these days."

"Don't wait too long."

Eason was fussing about losing the sun. Mix rounded the truck and walked to where Dusty Miller, the black-hatted stuntman, was waiting. Durant listened as Eason set the scene, a climactic moment for any Western, the big fight. He thought he would have staged it differently, and wondered if perhaps Mix was right. Maybe it was time to take a shot at directing.

Durant's journey to Hollywood had been one of chance rather than purpose. In 1918, like many young idealists, he had joined the army in the belief that he was off to fight the war that would end all wars. Yet he had

soon discovered there was nothing chivalrous about the
poison gas and machine guns found in the trenches of
France. Instead there was something in the killing which
suggested humanity's end—and oblivion.

On the day Armistice was declared, over ten million
people had lost their lives. As quiet fell across the battle-
fields, there was little rejoicing in the trenches. The stench
of death was still too strong, and the men huddled there
felt the taint of barbarism deep within their souls. The
doughboys who survived were disillusioned, shorn of innocence. They had seen man at his worst.

For Durant, the revulsion of war was compounded
by personal loss. In 1918, while he was fighting in
France, what was called Spanish influenza ravaged continent after continent. Worldwide, in just nine months,
over 21,000,000 people died, and the toll in America
climbed above half a million. Among the dead were Durant's parents, and his only sibling, a younger sister.

In early 1919, after his discharge from the army, Durant came home to an empty house. His father had been
a cattleman, and the family ranch, located in the Texas
Panhandle, encompassed a hundred thousand acres and
almost ten thousand head of cows. Embittered, with no
purpose in life, he sold the ranch, banked the money, and
drifted from job to job, ever heading westward. He came
at last to Hollywood.

Western motion pictures were a staple of the film
industry. Durant, who had been raised on a horse, gravi-
tated to the studios and caught on as an extra. Stuntmen
were better paid, and he soon made the switch, unconcerned that a stuntman's life expectancy was a slim proposition. Defying the odds, he'd suffered only a concussion
and a broken leg during his six years in films. In the
process, he became a student of the men who were rev-
olutionizing motion pictures.

The film industry was born in New York City. Thomas Edison demonstrated a crude projection system in
1889, and a few years later, his newest invention, the Ki-

netograph projector, assured the future of motion pictures. *The Great Train Robbery*, the first film with a running storyline, was a one-reel Western made in 1904. By 1908, there were five thousand Nickelodeons across the country, a nickel being the price of admission. Vaudeville houses in many cities were swiftly transformed into theaters.

Hollywood, eight miles outside Los Angeles, was mostly farmland at the time. Moviemakers began migrating there, attracted by a Chamber of Commerce claim of 350 sunny days a year. By 1914, Hollywood had become the center of the motion picture industry, home to Paramount Pictures, Universal Films, Twentieth Century-Fox, Metro-Goldwyn-Mayer, and Warner Brothers. Neighborhood theaters and plush movie houses sprang up everywhere, with the Strand Theater in New York seating 3,300 patrons. The industry moguls were quick to brag that more people went to the movies than read books.

By the 1920s, motion pictures were big business. D.W. Griffith's masterpiece, *The Birth of a Nation*, cost $100,000 to produce and grossed over $50,000,000. Other directors readily imitated his style, and Earl Durant, in between doing stunts, was their keenest student. One way or another, his future lay in films.

"Earl."

Durant turned at the sound of his name. Neal Cushman, the assistant director, handed him a letter. "Forgot to give you this," he said. "It came addressed to you at the studio."

"Thanks, Neal."

The envelope bore the imprint of a law firm in Galveston, Texas. Durant tore it open and scanned the contents, his features suddenly grim. The letter was dated August 28, five days ago, and informed him that his uncle, Joseph Durant, had died of a heart attack. As the only living relative, he was the sole heir to his uncle's estate. The bulk of the estate was comprised of the People's Bank & Trust.

Durant slowly refolded the letter. He was reminded

that Uncle Joe's only son and his cousin, George Durant, had been killed at the Battle of the Marne in France. His Aunt Sarah, Uncle Joe's wife, had died in the same influenza epidemic that had killed his parents. The family, he reflected bitterly, was now gone. He was the last Durant.

"Cut!"

Eason's shout came as the sun tilted lower toward the Pacific. The fight scene was completed, good having again vanquished evil, and Tom Mix walked around the end of the truck. He saw the expression on Durant's face.

"What's wrong, pardner?" he said soberly. "You look like you've seen a ghost."

"Guess I have," Durant replied. "Just got word my uncle passed away."

"Well, hell, that's a damn shame."

"Yeah, I'll have to head out for Galveston in the morning."

Mix clapped him on the shoulder. "Get things squared away and hurry on back. We start another picture in a couple weeks."

"I'll be here in plenty of time."

Mix nodded sympathetically, then moved off toward the Dodge touring car. Durant looked down at the letter, struck by a hollow irony. He was the last of the line, and he wished he had made an effort to visit his uncle while there was still time. He hadn't been there since before the war.

He wondered what Galveston was like these days.

Galveston Bay was an immense body of water, seventeen miles wide and more than thirty miles long. The causeway, supported by concrete pylons, spanned the narrowest section of the bay. Three miles from the mainland to the Island, the two-lane ribbon arched skyward over marshes and bayous.

The headlights of a massive, four-door Buick slashed through the silty darkness of night. There were three cars in the convoy, the Buick and two Chevrolets, all bearing the emblem of the Texas Rangers. Captain Hardy Purvis, commander of the Houston district, rode in the shotgun seat of the Buick. He stared straight ahead as the causeway dipped back onto land.

Galveston Island paralleled the coastline, some fifty miles south of Houston. The Island itself was a thin sliver of sand, two miles wide and thirty miles long, and flat as a dime. It was part of a chain of barrier islands, running northeast to southwest along the coast, looking south into the Gulf of Mexico. To the east, at the tip of the Island, was a deep-water passage into Galveston Bay.

The causeway spilled out onto Broadway. The street bisected the Island, along an esplanade of palms and oaks, with a huge sign in electric lights touting *GALVESTON, THE TREASURE ISLAND OF AMERICA*. The town proper was located at the eastern end of the Island, and was alternately known as the "Sin City of the South" and the "Island of Illicit Pleasures." Gambling, bootlegging, and prostitution brought Galveston notoriety as well as prosperity.

"Take a right," Captain Purvis ordered the driver. "Head for the Seawall."

The Buick swerved off Broadway onto Twenty-first Street. Purvis glanced back through the rear window, assuring himself that the cars behind were still in line. There were five Rangers in each of the Chevys, and three in the backseat of his Buick. Tonight was the seventh time he'd raided Galveston, and he reflected all too bitterly that he had yet to arrest his first hoodlum. He told himself now that fifteen Rangers were equal to any job . . . even the Hollywood Club.

Twenty-first Street intersected Seawall Boulevard. A hurricane had devastated Galveston in 1900, and afterward the city had built a seawall seventeen feet high, sixteen feet at the base, and five feet across the top. Seawall Boulevard was a six-lane paved road fronting the wall, lined with luxurious hotels and tourist resorts. The wall was over ten miles long, and on the Gulf coastline, a

glittering strip of casinos, nightclubs, and pleasure piers
hugged the beaches. An access road bordered the strip.

The Hollywood Club was the swankiest nightspot in
town. Dining and dancing, along with top entertainment
and a plush casino, attracted thousands of people every
week. A pair of searchlights out front revolved in a flashing display that lit the sky and distinguished the establishment from others on the beach. The club was laid out
along a four-hundred-foot pier that terminated in a T-head
looking out onto the Gulf of Mexico. The casino was reportedly at the end of the pier, strategically located at the
head of the T, suspended over water. Purvis and his Rangers, despite their previous raids, had yet to find it.

The owners of the club, Oliver "Ollie" Quinn and
Edward "Dutch" Voight, were the acknowledged czars of
the rackets on the Island. A year ago, when Purvis had
been assigned to the Houston district, he'd undertaken an
investigation that quickly identified who controlled Galveston's underworld. He operated on the theory that to
kill a snake, you cut off its head, and he'd targeted Quinn
and Voight as the first step in routing the Island's vice
element. Having been stymied in the effort, tonight's raid
was being conducted in utter secrecy, with every Ranger
he could muster. He meant to have his snake.

A light breeze from the Gulf brought with it the tangy
scent of salt water. As the cars skidded to a halt before
the Hollywood Club, Purvis jumped from the Buick. He
marched toward the entrance at a brisk clip, the Rangers
formed behind him in a tight wedge. The doorman, who
was tricked out in a top hat and tails, gave them a snappy
salute. He rushed to open the door. "Good evening,
Cap'n," he said with a pearly grin. "Hope you enjoy the
show."

Purvis ignored the gibe. He went through the entrance, entering a hallway lined with exotic potted plants
and two doors. From previous raids, he knew the one on
the right led to a business office and the one on the left
led to dressing rooms for entertainers and band members.

A busty young blonde waved to him as he went past the cloakroom. Directly ahead were heavy swinging doors constructed of glass.

The doors opened immediately onto the nightclub. The decor was vaguely Spanish, with rattan furniture, intimate shaded lamps on the tables, and crystal chandeliers dangling from the ceiling. Off to the right was a dining room that seated five hundred, and to the left was a dance floor only slightly smaller than a football field. A raised stage with a twenty-three-piece orchestra overlooked the dance floor.

Ollie Quinn hurried forward. He was a man of medium height, attired in a tuxedo, with a square jaw and a humorous mouth. There was a certain Gaelic charm about him, and his eyes, blue as carpenter's chalk, seemed forever lighted by some secret joke. He stopped in Purvis's path.

"Well, Captain Purvis," he said genially. "Welcome again to the Hollywood Club."

"None of your nonsense this time, Quinn. I'm here to close you down."

Purvis brushed past him, followed by the phalanx of Rangers. Quinn smiled, turning toward the stage, and idly signaled the bandleader. A moment later, the orchestra, trumpets blaring, segued into *The Eyes of Texas*. The bandleader stepped to the microphone with a broad grin. His voice boomed out over the nightclub.

"And now, ladies and gentlemen, the Hollywood Club takes great pride in presenting, in *all* their glory— the Texas Rangers!"

The crowd, as though on cue, rose to their feet. All of them, from the tables and the dance floor, moved to block the aisle in the center of the room. Their voices swelled in merry abandon to the beat of the music.

> *"The eyes of Texas are upon you*
> *All the livelong day!"*

The Rangers, formed in a knot around Purvis, bulled a path through the revelers. But the crowd gave way by inches, laughing and singing louder, slowing their progress. Several minutes passed in a jolly little struggle before the Rangers emerged onto the opposite side of the nightclub. There, dressed in tuxedos, were two muscular bruisers, arms folded across their chests. They barred the way to another set of glass doors.

"Stand aside!" Purvis shouted. "Stand aside or be arrested!"

The bruisers patted their pockets, their faces a study in bogus consternation. Finally, one of them came up with a key and fumbled around unlocking the doors. One of the Rangers stepped forward, roughly pushing him aside, and held the door open for Purvis. They entered a hallway, which led to a bar and an elegant lounge, again decorated with rattan furniture and exotic plants. The patrons of the lounge greeted them with knowing smiles and polite applause.

Beyond the lounge was still another set of doors, fashioned this time from sturdy oak polished to a luster. The doors led to the T-head part of the club, which was supported by stout pylons over the waters of the Gulf. Dutch Voight, attired in a double-breasted tuxedo, stood before the doors as though waiting to greet the Rangers. He was short, his barrel-shaped torso solid as rock, and his features had an oxlike imperturbability. He nodded impassively.

"Back again, Captain?" he said in a voice like sandpaper on pebbled stone. "Thought you would have seen the light by now."

Purvis glared at him. "Out of my way, Voight. I intend to shut down your casino once and for all."

"You know we're not in the gaming business. We operate a private club, members only."

"I'm ordering you to move aside."

"Captain, you're just bothering our guests, and for no reason. There's nothing illegal going on here."

Purvis exploded. "Goddammit, get out of my way and do it right now! Otherwise I'll break down those doors."

"No need," Voight said with a sly smile. "Our doors are always open to the Texas Rangers."

The doors swung open as if by magic. A man with strikingly handsome features and alert green eyes waved them inside. Purvis and his Rangers charged through the doors, and then, abruptly, hauled up short. The room was massive, two hundred feet wide by a hundred feet deep, and lavishly appointed with teak paneling and lush wall-to-wall carpet. Tall windows offered a panoramic view of the Gulf of Mexico.

There were two hundred or more people scattered about the room. Some of the men wore suits and ties, others were formally dressed in tuxedos, and the women, dripping jewelry, wore fashionable evening gowns. Eight billiard tables dominated the center of the room, and men with cue sticks stood around watching while others pocketed balls. The onlookers were quick to call out "Good shot!" whenever a ball fell.

Along the walls were at least fifty backgammon and bridge tables. The dice cups rattled at the backgammon tables, and cards with the Hollywood Club logo were dealt to bridge players. At every table, people were gathered around, smoking and sipping champagne, watching with rapt interest. Some turned as the Rangers barged into the room, looking at them with the bemused curiosity normally reserved for acrobats and dancing elephants. Others, as though absorbed in a pleasant social pastime, simply ignored them.

"Disappointed, Captain?" Voight asked wryly. "As you can see, things haven't changed since your last visit. Billiards and backgammon, same as usual."

"Horseapples!" Purvis barked. "You're not fooling anybody, Voight. There's gaming rigs here somewhere."

"Be my guest, search the place to your heart's content. We're a legit operation."

"There's icicles in hell, too!"

Purvis ordered a search. From previous raids, he knew it was a waste of time, and he ground his teeth in frustration. However it was managed, the gambling paraphernalia and slot machines had disappeared from the brief interval between the front door and the moment he'd stormed into the room. He wondered how the hell they pulled it off.

The Rangers conducted a thorough search. They tapped walls, kicked at the flooring with their high-heeled boots, even looked under the billiard tables. At the rear of the room were two offices and an employees' lounge, and they combed through these as well. They found nothing; no gaming chips, no roulette wheels, no sign of a slot machine. Their search was swiftly concluded.

"You're slick," Purvis fumed when it was over. "But don't think you've seen the last of me. We'll get you yet—and damn soon!"

Voight appeared unimpressed. "Captain, you and your men are welcome at the Hollywood Club anytime. Have a nice ride back to Houston."

Purvis and his Rangers passed Ollie Quinn as they went out the door. Voight walked forward to his partner, watching as the lawmen marched back through the nightclub. The orchestra accompanied their retreat with another rendition of *The Eyes of Texas*. The audience merrily chimed in with the lyrics.

Quinn wagged his head. "Dutch, I've never seen such a determined man. I just imagine he'll be back."

"Wouldn't surprise me," Voight agreed. "Nothing worse than a Texas Ranger with egg on his face."

"Yes, too bad we can't buy him off. Honest men are a burden, aren't they?"

"You and your fancy talk, Ollie. Why not just say he's a pain in the ass?"

"Oh, that's much too coarse for an impresario like myself. You have to remember I'm a *showman,* Dutch."

"Yeah, and I'm a magician. Now you see it, now you don't."

Voight turned to their lieutenant with eyes the color of emeralds. "We're losing money, Jack. Let's have some action."

"Whatever you say, boss."

Jack Nolan signaled the housemen. He walked off through the crowd, flattering the women and nodding politely to their husbands. All the while he was checking his watch, herding the patrons this way and that as the housemen went about their business. Not quite three minutes later, the whirr of a roulette wheel and the rattle of dice on a craps table sounded throughout the room. Dutch Voight and Ollie Quinn looked on with approval.

The Hollywood Club Casino was back in action.

Chapter Two

Austin was situated along the banks of the Colorado River. Like ancient Rome, the town was built upon seven hills and spread northward from the rugged shoreline. The surrounding countryside was a pastoral setting of rolling prairie and limestone mountains.

Congress Avenue, the main thoroughfare, rose gently from the river to the state capitol grounds. Early on the morning of September 4, Sergeant Clint Stoner of the Texas Rangers parked his car and walked toward the entrance. A ray of sunlight glinted off the dome as he mounted the sweeping steps to the capitol.

Stoner wondered again why he'd been summoned to the statehouse. He was assigned to the Headquarters Detachment, located on the outskirts of Austin, and worked in the investigative division. When he signed in for duty that morning, his commander, Captain Fred Olson, told him that he had been ordered to report to Colonel Homer Garrison, head of the Texas Rangers. Olson seemed put out that he himself hadn't been informed as to the reason.

On the second floor, Stoner turned down a long corridor. A moment later he entered the reception room of the state headquarters. The secretary was an older woman, her hair pinned back in a severe chignon, and she asked him to have a seat. She wrote his name on a slip of paper and moved to a thick oak door leading to an inner office. Shortly she returned, nodding to him without expression. She ushered him through the door.

Colonel Homer Garrison was seated behind a large walnut desk. His chiseled features and brushy mustache gave him an appearance of solidity and iron will. The office, like the man, was utilitarian, with two leather chairs positioned facing the desk. The sole decorations were the Texas state flag and the national flag, draped from standards anchored to the floor. His greeting was brusque.

"Good morning," he said. "Have a chair."

Stoner seated himself. "Captain Olson told me I was to report to you, sir."

"I suspect Olson was burned at being kept in the dark."

"The captain didn't say one way or the other."

"No, he wouldn't." Garrison opened a folder on his desk. "I've been reading your file, Stoner. You have a commendable record."

"Thank you, sir."

Stoner had been in law enforcement for nine years. He began as a deputy sheriff, later joined the highway patrol, and four years ago, he'd been recruited into the Texas Rangers. In that time, he had killed two men in gunfights, a bank robber and a murderer, and steadily advanced in rank to sergeant. He was thirty-one, the most highly decorated officer in his Ranger company.

"I'm looking for a volunteer," Garrison said, closing the folder. "How would you feel about working undercover?"

There was no question in Stoner's mind that he'd already volunteered. When a superior asked, there was only one acceptable response. "I'm your man, Colonel."

"Excellent," Garrison replied. "Are you familiar with the situation in Galveston?"

"Well, sir, I know it's a hotbed of vice."

"Actually, it's somewhat more complicated, Sergeant."

Garrison went on to explain. The town and the county were controlled by two mobsters, Oliver Quinn and Edward Voight. By all accounts, they operated casinos, a fleet of rumrunners, and were so powerful they collected tribute from lesser gangsters. Their limitless source of funds allowed them to bribe the police chief, the sheriff, the county attorney, and any number of judges. The Island was so corrupt that it had become known as the Free State of Galveston.

Humbling as it was to admit, Garrison noted, the Rangers had conducted seven raids, all to no effect. Captain Hardy Purvis, the Houston District commander, had reported the most recent failure only late last night. Yet Purvis was correct in his assessment of how the war should be waged against Quinn and Voight. The way to bring them down was to dismantle the flagship of their empire—the Hollywood Club.

"The raids simply haven't worked," Garrison concluded. "So I want to send you in there undercover. Plainclothes, a fake identity, a cover story that will withstand scrutiny."

Stoner nodded. "Just exactly what is it I'm looking for, Colonel?"

"The assignment is more difficult than it sounds. Quinn and Voight somehow—mystically, it seems—make their casino disappear."

"Pardon me, sir?"

"Quite literally, Sergeant, the casino vanishes before our raiding party can make their way to the rear of the club. I want you to determine how it's done."

Stoner's eyes narrowed. He was just shy of six feet, whipcord lean, with weathered features and sandy hair. He survived as a lawman on sharp instincts and quick reflexes, striking first and fastest. He sensed a pitfall in the assignment.

"Way I hear it," he said in a level voice, "Galveston's a pretty rough place. An undercover man might get himself killed if he was found out."

Garrison steepled his fingers. "Do I detect a condition in there somewhere, Sergeant?"

"I'm requesting that I report directly to you. Loose talk has a way of getting to the wrong ears."

"In other words, keep Captain Olson in the dark as to your assignment. And neglect to tell Captain Purvis he has an undercover agent operating in his district. Is that about it?"

"I'd feel easier, Colonel," Stoner told him. "Quick as I turn up anything, I'll let you know. Time enough then to plan a raid."

"Point well taken." Garrison was silent, thoughtful a moment. "Your file indicates you're a single man. Is that correct?"

"Yes, sir."

"You'll need a woman along, to complete your cover. Someone to act as your wife. Any ideas?"

Stoner smiled. "Colonel, I've got just the girl. She'd jump at the chance to play detective."

"Known her long?" Garrison asked soberly. "Would you trust her with your life?"

"Well, sir, in lots of ways, she'd be trusting me with her life. I guess it'd be a fair trade-off."

"Very well, I'll accept your judgment in the matter. As of today, you are reassigned to my office. Get to work on your cover story and keep me advised."

Stoner got to his feet. "I'll come up with something airtight. Shouldn't take more than a couple of days."

Garrison thought he'd picked his man well. The Rangers was an organization of long tradition, founded before the Civil War and carried on to the present day. Looking at Stoner, he was reminded of the adage that underscored the tradition: One riot, one Ranger. He felt confident one Ranger was adequate for Galveston.

"A final thought," he said forcefully. "You have but one assignment in Galveston. Bring me the secret of the Hollywood Club."

Stoner grinned. "Colonel, I'll deliver it with bells on and a red ribbon. You've as good as got it."

The train slowed at the top of the causeway. Earl Durant, who was seated at a window, stared down at the bay, which was almost twenty feet below the monolithic arch. He saw oceangoing freighters docked at the city wharves.

A car overtook the train as it started down the grade. Durant always marveled at the engineering feat of the causeway. The concrete span was wide enough to accommodate train tracks, a two-lane highway for automobiles, and an electric interurban railway. The interurban whisked back and forth to Houston on the hour.

The train pulled into the Santa Fe station shortly before noon. Durant collected his suitcase from an overhead rack and followed the other passengers off the coach. His trip from Los Angeles had taken two days, with changes of trains in Albuquerque and Dallas. He felt grungy and soiled, ready for a hot shower.

From previous trips, Durant recalled that the Tremont was one of the better hotels in the downtown area. He walked east on the Strand, which was Galveston's main business street, crowded with shops and stores and ornate Victorian office buildings. A block north, on Water Street, he saw sea gulls floating lazily over ships berthed at the docks.

Durant was reminded that Galveston was a place apart. The Islanders lived by their own values, their own measure of morality, and prided themselves on being different from mainlanders. There was a mystique about the town that flaunted *joie de vivre* and a zestful wickedness, tolerance for the risqué. Life was meant to be a celebration, a somewhat naughty party that never ended.

The hotel was on Mechanic Row, a block south of the Strand at Twenty-second Street. Durant engaged a room for an indefinite stay, and once upstairs, quickly shed his soiled clothing. He unpacked, took a scalding shower and shaved, and then changed into a fresh suit, starched white shirt and striped tie. Downstairs again, he ate lunch in the hotel dining room.

Shortly after one o'clock, he entered the Hendley Building, on the corner of the Strand and Twentieth Street. On the second floor, he found the law offices of

Grant, Kline & Shapiro. After announcing himself, a secretary showed him into the office of Walter Kline, a lanky man with gray hair and sad eyes. Kline offered him a chair.

"Please accept my condolences," Kline said. "Your uncle was a fine man, salt of the earth. We were friends for over thirty years."

Durant shook his head. "Doesn't hardly seem real just yet. Wish I could have been here for the funeral."

"Yes, of course. There were two hundred people, perhaps more, at the services. Your uncle was very highly regarded in the community."

"I'll visit the cemetery while I'm in town."

"Hmmm." Kline's sad eyes appeared sadder. "However sudden his death, his will expresses the wish that you take over the bank. Do I infer you have other plans?"

"Mr. Kline, I work in moving pictures," Durant said equably. "Even if I knew how, I've got no interest in running a bank. I figured to put it on the market." He paused. "Maybe you could help me find a buyer."

"May I make a suggestion?"

"Sure thing."

"Ira Aldridge is the vice president. He was your uncle's right hand for many years, a very capable man. Talk to him before making any hasty decisions."

Durant nodded. "Sounds like he'd be the one to buy the bank."

"Nooo," Kline said slowly. "I'm afraid Ira hasn't the resources."

"Then what's to be gained by talking?"

"Perhaps you owe it to your uncle, Mr. Durant. He held Ira Aldridge in great esteem."

"Yeah, I suppose you're right. I need to find out what's what with the bank anyhow."

"By the way," Kline said, "will you be staying at your uncle's home? He owned a very nice house on Twenty-ninth Street—and it's yours now."

"No, I took a room at the Tremont. I'll probably go

by the house tomorrow. See about Uncle Joe's personal effects."

"Do let me know if I can be of assistance."

"Thanks, I will."

Some five minutes later, Durant walked into the People's Bank & Trust. A Victorian stone structure, the bank was on the Strand, between Eighteenth and Nineteenth Streets, in the heart of the business district. Aldridge's secretary, an attractive young woman who introduced herself as Catherine Ludlow, escorted him to an office at the rear of the bank. She smiled as she closed the door.

"Well, well!" Aldridge said, hand extended in greeting. "I certainly see the family resemblance. Joe spoke of you often, and with great pride, I might add."

Ira Aldridge was a portly man, amiable in manner, somewhere in his early fifties, with a shock of salt-and-pepper hair. They chatted a few minutes about the late Joseph Durant, and Aldridge expressed his deepest sympathy. His eyes went moist as he spoke of the loss of his closest friend.

"But no more of that," he said with an open smile. "We've laid Joe to rest and you're here now to take his place. I know he would be pleased, very pleased."

Durant cleared his throat. "Well, the thing is, I plan to sell the bank. I'm a movie stuntman, not a businessman. It'd never work."

"Of course it would," Aldridge protested. "I'll be right by your side, and banking is far less difficult than people think. You'll catch on in no time."

"Sorry, but it's not a matter of catching on. I've got a motion picture waiting on me in Los Angeles."

"You don't understand, Earl. May I call you Earl?"

"Wish you would."

Aldridge appeared agitated, his hands darting like birds. "Your uncle devoted his life to the People's Bank & Trust. He thought of it as a bank for the common man, the little people. Unless you stay on, it will all have been for nothing."

"You lost me there," Durant said, an eyebrow lifted quizzically. "What've I got to do with anything?"

"William Magruder is the only man in Galveston with money enough to buy this bank. And he was your uncle's mortal enemy. The man's an out-and-out scoundrel!"

"Who's William Magruder?"

"One of the two richest men in town," Aldridge said. "He owns the Galveston City Bank and half the Island. He's old money, and lots of it."

Durant shrugged. "Then he's the man I need to talk to. Sounds like a hot prospect."

"Good God, you can't do that! Magruder tried every underhanded tactic imaginable to force us out of business. Your uncle fought him tooth and nail, just to keep the doors open."

"Not my fight," Durant observed. "How much is the bank worth, in round figures?"

Aldridge sighed wearily. "A hundred thousand, perhaps a little more."

"No kidding!"

"Earl, do you understand what I'm saying? Magruder would shut down the bank and foreclose on every poor soul who's struggling to buy a home or keep from going under in a small business. The man has no scruples. None!"

"Look, don't get me wrong," Durant said uneasily. "I've got nothing against the common man, and I respect what Uncle Joe tried to do. But any whichaway, I wasn't cut out to be a banker. That's it in a nutshell."

"I see." Aldridge deflated back into his chair. "So you plan to contact Magruder?"

"Unless you'd like to buy the place yourself."

"I regret to say I haven't the means."

"Then I guess Magruder's the only game in town."

"Joe Durant would be disappointed in you, Earl. Very disappointed."

"I reckon I'll have to learn to live with that."

Durant walked out the door. A moment later Catherine Ludlow stepped into the office. She was a wholesome young woman, in her early twenties, with a shapely figure, auburn hair, and eyes the color of larkspur. Aldridge was slumped in his chair, and she moved closer to his desk. She gave him a look of concern.

"Are you all right, Mr. Aldridge?"

"I'm afraid not," Aldridge muttered. "The heir to our little kingdom took the wind out of my sails."

"Mr. Durant?" she asked uncertainly. "What did he do?"

"I fear it is what he plans to do."

"Pardon me?"

"Catherine, he intends to sell the bank to William Magruder."

"Omigosh!"

"Yes, indeed."

Ira Aldridge thought he heard the faint knell of doomsday.

The Gulf sparkled with silvery starlight. The moon was down, and apart from the luminous iridescence of the stars, the water spread onward into an infinity of darkness. High clouds scudded northward on a gentle breeze.

The *Cherokee,* a twenty-six-foot Chris-Craft with twin Liberty engines, appeared out of the starlit swells. A salty spray laced off the bow as the sleek mahogany hull sliced through the surface chop. The course was south by southwest out of Galveston.

Diamond Jack Nolan stood in the cockpit. His gangland moniker stemmed from the diamond ring he wore on his pinky finger, and tonight his chiseled features were a study in concentration. Whizzer Duncan, his second in command, stood beside him cradling a .45 caliber Thompson submachine gun. A man of slight build, with wispy hair and pale eyes, Duncan was dangerous as a pit viper.

To the rear, in the *Cherokee*'s wake, was a fleet of fifteen wooden lugger boats. The luggers rode low in the water, powered by twin 100 horsepower engines, and in the dark resembled nothing more than large rafts. Aboard the boats were Nolan's rumrunning crew, hard men armed with Winchester 12-gauge pump shotguns and 1918 A1 Browning Automatic Rifles. Their eyes strained southward into the inky waters.

The dim glow of a lantern appeared off the port bow of the *Cherokee*. The pilot, on Nolan's order, quickly throttled down, the hull of the speedboat plowing roughly through the troughs. A three-masted schooner, the *Shark*, loomed ahead, ninety feet at the waterline and painted a dull black. The ship swayed at anchor against rolling swells, armed men stationed at her gunwale. She was all but invisible except for the guttering lantern.

The *Cherokee* swung in under the lee of the schooner. The weathered rigging of the ship creaked in the breeze, audible over the rumbling growl of the speedboat as it throttled down to idle. The fleet of luggers stood off a hundred yards out, bobbing in the swells, armed crewmen at the alert. Nolan clambered up a rope ladder thrown over the side of the ship and nimbly hopped onto the deck. Whizzer Duncan covered him with the tommy gun.

Captain Rob McBride, master of the *Shark*, waited amidships. He was powerfully built, with a red beard, and in the swaying lamplight, he looked every inch the pirate. He greeted Nolan with a crushing handshake and a booming laugh. "Jack, my darlin' boy, it's good to see you again!"

"That goes double for me, Rob. I take it you found fair winds along the way."

"Aye, laddie, we did indeed."

Nolan and McBride were business associates, not friends. Their relationship was one of wary neutrality, mutual respect underscored by guarded watchfulness. Smuggler and rumrunner, brothers in a dangerous trade, neither of them ever chanced being robbed by the other. Their truce was maintained by parity in firepower.

"I'm bearing a load," McBride said with his pirate's

grin. "Fifteen hundred cases, all as you ordered, Jacko. Scotch, gin and bourbon."

Nolan handed over a fat manila envelope. "Sixty thousand, just as we agreed. You can count it."

"Why, of course I will, no offense intended."

McBride riffled through the cash, all in hundreds. On his signal, one of the crewmen waved the lantern back and forth over the side of the ship. The lugger boats motored in one at a time, idling in the lee of the black schooner. The crew hoisted nets out of the hold, loaded with crates wrapped in burlap, and lowered them to the waiting boats. The rumrunners worked with quick efficiency to stack the crates.

Captain Rob McBride was but one of hundreds of skippers smuggling illegal spirits. The Volstead Act, enacted by Congress in late 1919, had ushered in the era of Prohibition. A decade of campaigning by temperance leaders, who decried the evil of strong drink, was the moving force behind the law that took effect in 1920. Evangelist Billy Sunday cursed the influence of demon rum, arguing that "whiskey would make the world a puking, spewing, staggering, bleary-eyed, tottery wreck." He and his fellow temperance leaders turned off the spigot.

Yet little could they have foreseen that banning liquor would plunge America into the wildest, most turbulent time in history—the Roaring Twenties. Mobsters throughout the country were quick to grasp the potential, and tens of thousands of speakeasies sprang up across the land. Smugglers routinely sailed from Cuba, Jamaica, and the Bahamas, anchoring offshore in international waters, and provided a steady source of booze for the rumrunners. Prohibition backfired, to the tune of millions of dollars in illicit trade.

Jack Nolan, for his part, thought it was laughable. Galveston, with Quinn and Voight at the helm, became the conduit for bootleg liquor throughout Texas, Colorado, Oklahoma, and other states across the Southwest. The Federal Prohibition Agency headquartered in Houston was on the pad, and in six years, there had never been a raid on the bars and nightspots in Galveston. The good times rolled, and with it an avalanche of untraceable cash. The shipment being transferred to lugger boats would later be off-loaded to bootleggers at a deserted beach on the mainland. Tonight's haul, at a return of five for one, would net a cool $250,000.

A veteran of the late war, Nolan looked upon Prohibition as kid's stuff. In France, at Chateau-Thierry and Belleau Wood, he'd been brutalized by the sight of death. The generals on both sides pitilessly waged war by pitting massed strength against massed strength, and victory fell to those who demonstrated a superior ability to bleed. After the armistice, he was awarded the Distinguished Service Cross and the French Croix de Guerre. The medals meant nothing; he was merely thankful to be alive.

Upon returning from the Western Front in 1920, his cynicism was matched only by his ruthlessness. Through a friend, he caught on with Quinn and Voight, and slowly moved through the ranks to become the lieutenant of Galveston's underworld. He often thought the work he did for them was mild compared to the war, and he was sometimes amused that the trenches in France had prepared him well for the life of a gangster. He was head of the rumrunning operation, the mob's chief enforcer, and on occasion, a killer. He did good work.

Shortly before midnight, the lugger boats were finished loading. Nolan shook hands with Captain Rob McBride and went down the rope ladder to the *Cherokee*. By now, after years of running illegal booze, the operation was conducted by a standard drill. The men in the luggers had their orders; and they knew which beach had been selected on the mainland for tonight's delivery. The bootleggers would be waiting with trucks, and Nolan would join them in time for the payoff. He first had to attend to the Coast Guard.

The fleet of luggers turned northeast for the mainland. The *Cherokee* came about, motors rumbling, and took a heading due north. The Coast Guard station was located on the northeastern tip of Galveston Island, and they routinely patrolled the southern waters, searching for rumrunners. Nolan's immediate mission was to intercept the patrol and decoy them west, away from the lugger boats. He felt a rush of adrenaline at the prospect of action.

Twenty minutes later he spotted the silhouette of CG-204 from the Galveston station. The cutter was seventy-five feet long, armed with .50 caliber machine guns and a one-pounder cannon mounted on the forward deck. Intended for pursuit, the cutter was capable of speeds up to thirty-five knots. But Nolan was unconcerned about being overtaken, for the *Cherokee,* powered by Liberty aircraft engines, could outrun any vessel on the Gulf. His purpose was to lure them into pursuit.

Whizzer Duncan snapped a 100-round drum magazine into his Thompson chopper. The magazine was loaded with incendiary rounds, and when he opened fire, a stream of white-hot tracers spewed across the water. Nolan's standing orders were to engage the Coast Guard, rather than kill seamen, and the tracers fell short of the cutter. The response was immediate: a blinding flare soared skyward, illuminating the night, and the one-pounder cannon roared. A geyser of water exploded off the bow of the *Cherokee.*

The Liberty engines thundered and the speedboat took off on a westerly course. The *Cherokee* planed across the water, skimming the surface, its wake pocked by slugs from the machine guns on the cutter. CG-204 gave chase just as the flare died out and the sleek little boat zipped away at fifty knots. The cutter throttled up, her massive screws churning astern, but it was no contest. The *Cherokee* disappeared into the inky waters of the Gulf.

Later that night, Diamond Jack Nolan walked into the Hollywood Club. His smile was that of a cat with a mouthful of feathers, and he carried a satchel stuffed with three hundred grand in cash.

He thought Ollie Quinn and Dutch Voight would be pleased.

Chapter Three

The Strand was one of the major finance centers between New Orleans and San Francisco. From the Civil War to present times, the port of Galveston was also one of the busiest shipping points in the world. The wharves along Water Street handled more exports than any harbor in America except New York. The language spoken along the Strand was the language of commodities and exchange, and money.

High in a windless sky, the sun was a white orb as Durant crossed the Strand the next morning. Yesterday, after leaving the bank, he had called and made an appointment with William Magruder for ten o'clock. He regretted the hard feelings with Ira Aldridge, but he had no qualms about dealing with one of the Island's wealthiest men. Business, after all, was business.

The Magruder Building was a ten-story brick structure at Twenty-second and the Strand. The lobby opened onto a vaulting atrium, towering upward to a domed ceiling limned by a massive skylight. Durant took a birdcage elevator to the tenth floor, the marble corridors flooded by the skylight and the warmth of the sun. A suite of offices for William Magruder & Company occupied the entire floor.

A secretary ushered him into Magruder's lavishly appointed office. Overlooking the wharves, it was furnished with wing chairs and a couch crafted of lush morocco leather. The walls were lined with nautical oil paintings, and at the far end of the room, framed between windows with a view of berthed ships, was a broad desk that looked carved from a solid piece of ebony. The room seemed somehow appropriate to the man behind the desk.

William Magruder was a figure of considerable girth. His hair was plastered to his head like black paint on a boiled egg, and wattled jowls hung from his fleshy features. His beady eyes and stern, scowling countenance left the impression of a man who brought sighs of relief whenever he departed a room. He extended a meaty hand.

"Good of you to come by, Mr. Durant. This is my son, Sherman."

A younger man, somewhere in his early thirties, rose from the leather couch. The resemblance was uncanny, though the son was taller and his puffy, ruddy face was that of a hard drinker. After a round of handshakes, Sherman settled back onto the couch and Durant took one of the wing chairs. Magruder lowered himself into a throne-like judge's chair behind his desk.

"Allow me to offer our sympathies for the loss of your uncle. We never saw eye-to-eye, you understand, but he was a good man. Solid as they come."

"Yes, he was," Durant said. "I appreciate the sentiment."

"So you're here to sell his bank, is that it?"

"Are you a mind reader, Mr. Magruder?"

"Why else would you be here? Matter of fact, who else would you sell it to?"

Durant had done his homework. Last night, over drinks in a bar, he'd talked with a garrulous man who turned out to be a native of Galveston. He learned that the Magruders and the Seagraves were the two aristocratic families of the island. For all practical purposes, they controlled the economic lifeblood of the community. They were, in a very real sense, like feudal lords of old.

William Magruder owned the Galveston City Bank, the Galveston Cotton Exchange, several hotels, and the largest insurance company in the Southwest. George Seagrave, the other financial lion, owned the *Galveston Daily Chronicle*, the largest sugar mills in Texas and Louisiana, and the Gulf Railroad, which had merged with the Atchison, Topeka & Santa Fe, and added several million to his empire. Together, they owned the Galveston Wharf Company, which encompassed the entire waterfront. Galveston was the only deep-water harbor in Texas, and that gave them control of all shipping, domestic and foreign. They extorted a ransom in dockage by virtue of their monopoly.

"So, young man," Magruder said without expression. "What's your proposition?"

Durant spread his hands. "A hundred thousand dollars and it's yours. Ira Aldridge says it's worth that and more."

"Aldridge is a nitwit and everybody in town knows it. I'll give you twenty-five."

"I'm not here to horse trade, Mr. Magruder. A hundred's my price."

Magruder laughed a blubbery roar. "I like a man who sticks to his guns. Let's say fifty and call it a deal."

"No, sir," Durant said, poker-faced. "A hundred, take it or leave it."

"You're out of your league here, bub. Nobody in a thousand miles would buy that ten-cent bank and butt heads with me in Galveston. Your uncle learned that the hard way."

"Maybe so, but I won't be blackjacked into a fast sale. You've heard my price."

"Mr. Durant," Sherman interrupted smoothly. "We had you checked out and we know you're a stuntman in moving pictures. Be prudent, take fifty thousand and consider it a windfall." He paused with an oily smile. "You'll never get a better offer."

Durant knew something about Sherman Magruder as well. Last night he'd learned the heir to the throne was a Yale graduate, considerably more urbane and sophisticated than the old man, and some thought he was even shrewder. He was jokingly referred to as "the bootlegger's friend," a man who loved his sauce.

"The answer's the same," Durant said stubbornly. "I won't let it go for less than market value."

"Market value?" Magruder snorted. "Your uncle was a fool and it appears to run in the family. The market value is what I'm willing to pay. Not a nickel more!"

Durant stood. "I reckon I'll just have to put it on the market and find out. Thanks for your time."

"You listen to me, bub. You won't get an offer between here and Chicago! Nobody would dare come into my town."

Durant walked out the door. When it closed, Sherman slowly wagged his head. "Nice going, Pop. You insulted the man and drove him off."

"Goddammit, Sherm, don't you tell me how to run my business. I know what I'm doing."

"You've missed the point, Pop. We can't tell him we're after the deed to the property his bank holds. He might find out the property is worth more than the bank. Then he'd never sell."

"You're wrong," Magruder said sullenly. "He'll be back."

"I don't think so," Sherm insisted. "Mr. Durant has a stubborn streak, and we're the ones who need the deal. We have to buy his bank."

The tourist and convention trade was immensely profitable in Galveston. The Magruders were deep into secretive plans for a large hotel resort overlooking Seawall Boulevard and the Gulf. Too late, they had discovered that property contiguous to their project, property they needed to complete their hotel resort, was owned by the People's Bank & Trust. The bank and the property were now owned by Earl Durant.

Magruder's brow knotted in a frown. "Durant bought into the wrong game. We'll persuade him to sell."

"Oh?" Sherm arched an eyebrow. "And how will we accomplish that?"

Magruder lifted the receiver off the phone and jiggled the hook. "Central. You there, operator?"

"What number, please?"

"Give me 3154."

"Ringing."

The line buzzed and a man answered. "Oliver Quinn's office."

"Put him on. This is William Magruder."

A moment later Quinn came on the line. "Bill, always a pleasure. What can I do for you?"

"Ollie, I need to see you on a matter of business. The sooner, the better, here at my office."

"I'm booked solid today, Bill. How about tomorrow morning."

"All right, ten sharp and don't be late."

Magruder rang off. He sat for a moment, nodding absently to himself, and then looked across at Sherm. His mouth widened in a gloating smile.

"We'll teach young Mr. Durant some new tricks."

Blanco County was situated in the Hill Country. Johnson City, the county seat, was nestled in the hills some forty miles west of Austin. A ranch community, small but prosperous, it was a dogleg turn south of the Pedernales River.

Sergeant Clint Stoner drove into town under a bright forenoon sun. He circled the courthouse square and found a parking place in front of a hardware store. The car was his own, a Chevrolet sedan, and he was dressed in civilian clothes. He walked across to the courthouse.

The office of Sheriff Frank Shelley was on the main floor. Stoner and Shelley were old friends from the days Stoner had served with the highway patrol. He'd called Shelley yesterday afternoon, requesting a meeting as quickly as possible. His manner had been cryptic, sparse on details.

Shelley was heavyset, in his late forties, the sheriff of Blanco County for the past decade. His view on crime and criminals was that a man who stepped out of line deserved hard time, all the law allowed. He looked up from his desk as Stoner came through the door.

"Well, well," he said with a broad grin. "If it ain't the pride of the Rangers himself."

"Frank, good to see you," Stoner said, exchanging a warm handshake. "Putting on a little weight, are you?"

"The missus says I eat regular, too regular. Have a seat and tell me why you're tricked out in civvies. Your phone call was a mite shy on particulars."

"Not too much I can say at this point. I'm working a case undercover and I need a new identity. Thought maybe you could lend a hand."

Shelley chuckled out loud. "Hell, a crime-fighter like yourself, how could I say no? What d'you need, just exactly?"

"A name," Stoner said. "Somebody legitimate, in case the name gets checked out. It'd help if he was well fixed financially."

"Christ, why don't you ask for the moon, too?"

"I'll also need the credentials to go with the name."

Shelley leaned back in his chair, which creaked in protest under his weight. He stared out the window for a time, his features thoughtful. He finally looked around with a crafty smile.

"Bob Eberling," he said. "Bob won't mind if we borrow his name. Known him all my life."

Stoner nodded. "Who's Bob Eberling?"

"Just the biggest rancher in Blanco County."

Shelley went on to explain. Robert Eberling owned the Lazy E ranch, a hundred-thousand-acre spread along the Pedernales River. He ran a herd of ten thousand cows, and was reportedly worth more than a million dollars. Equally important, Eberling and his wife were on an extended trip to England. The ranch was being managed by Eberling's longtime foreman.

"Off buyin' Hereford bulls," Shelley concluded. "Told me he wants to add a new bloodline to his herd. Won't get home till late September."

"Sounds good to me," Stoner said. "I'll have the case wrapped up long before then."

Shelley proceeded to brief him on Eberling's history in Blanco County, Eberling's wife, who was named Olive, and salient details about the Lazy E Ranch. They had lunch at a café on courthouse square, and Stoner continued to draw out more information about his new persona. They parted shortly before one o'clock.

"Frank, I owe you," Stoner said with genuine warmth. "Nobody else I'd trust to set me up with a cover story."

Shelley laughed. "Folks you're after likely don't care no more about the law than a tomcat does a marriage license. You put 'em behind bars and that's payment enough for me."

"I'll surely do my damnedest."

By early afternoon, Stoner was back in Austin. Colonel Garrison had assigned him a new, canary-yellow Packard touring car, confiscated by the Rangers from a San Antonio bank embezzler. Garrison, calling in favors as chief of the Rangers, had also made covert arrangements with the head of the State Motor Vehicle Department. In short order, Stoner had auto license plates matching those of the car owned by Robert Eberling and a driver's license with his photo in the same name. All that remained was to find himself a wife.

Late that afternoon he called on Janice Overton. She was a part-time legal secretary and a full-time party girl. A dazzler at twenty-three, she was tall and sensuous, with long lissome legs, high full breasts, and skin like alabaster. She could be bawdy or ladylike, as the situation demanded, and she turned heads wherever she went. She had been Stoner's steady girl for the past four months.

Janice listened raptly as Stoner described his assignment. Until she accepted the proposition, he skirted any mention of Galveston. But he embellished on the undercover nature of the assignment, and the fact that it involved mobsters who operated an illicit empire built around gambling and rumrunning. He felt obligated to end on a cautionary note.

"I won't kid you," he said solemnly. "These are tough cookies, and they play for keeps. It could get dangerous."

"Oooo!" Her hazel eyes went round with excitement. "I like dangerous."

"Don't jump too quick. One slip and we'll be dead ducks. I want you to know what you're getting into."

"Are you trying to frighten me?"

"Damn right I am," Stoner said. "There's no second chances when you're working undercover. You'll have to be on your toes all the time."

She went up on her toes and kissed him. "I will, honeybunch. I promise."

Janice Overton was a thoroughly modern girl. The climate of the Roaring Twenties was one of ballyhoo and whoopee, a time when all traditional codes of social behavior were under assault. Hemingway and Fitzgerald, and other expatriate writers, were particularly influential in shaping the attitudes of the younger generation. But the greater revolution was stimulated by a radical new science emanating from Vienna.

Sigmund Freud, and to a lesser extent, his disciples Carl Jung and Alfred Adler, were the new messiahs. A generation devoted to "let the good times roll" began exploring introversion, inferiority complexes, and joyously, with open abandon, their libidos. To be happy and well, according to this liberated doctrine of self-expression, one must obey atavism, the pull of deeper instincts. The stairway to emotional bliss was an uninhibited sex life.

Janice found the new creed of intellectualism boorish and somehow pretentious. She was intelligent, with a mind of her own, and perfectly capable of formulating a philosophy of a more practical nature. So she discarded all the pseudo nonsense about the psyche, and adopted what seemed to her the salvation of liberated women, the libido. She loved making love, and never so much as with the Tarzan of lovers, Clint Stoner. A night in bed with him was a dangerous experience; the thought of it gave her goosebumps.

Undercover work sounded like an adventure too delicious to be missed. She put her arms around his neck. "We'll make a good team, sweetie. You wait and see."

Stoner held her closer. "You'll have to take off from your job. Any problem with that?"

"Oh, foo!" she said lightly. "Jobs are a dime a dozen."

"All right, consider yourself officially sworn in and deputized. You are now Mrs. Olive Eberling."

"Olive?"

"You'd better get used to it."

"Ugh!" She pulled a face. "What a dippy name."

"You'll get to like it," Stoner said with a grin. "Especially when I take you shopping."

"We're going shopping?"

"We have to look the part of ritzy swells. They gave me a thousand dollars to outfit ourselves in sporty fashion. We'll blow the whole wad."

"Godfrey!" she yelped gaily. "Just call me Olive."

"Well, Olive—" Stoner consulted his watch. "Too late to shop tonight. Got any ideas?"

"You naughty man. I just love you to death."

She led him into the bedroom. The late afternoon sun was in the west, flooding through the window with golden, shimmering light. She didn't mind in the least.

She knew he liked to watch her undress.

The nightglow of Galveston marbled the sky with shadow and light. A soft breeze floated in off the Gulf as the swirling waters of the bay lapped at the shoreline. Stars blinked like fireflies high above wispy clouds.

Jack Nolan drove across the causeway into deepening nightfall. His car was a black Ford, indistinguishable from others on the road, and unlikely to draw attention. Seldom introspective, his mind was nonetheless on the man he was to meet in La Marque. He thought Arthur Scarett was another lost soul in a topsy-turvy world.

The universe seemed to Nolan in a state of flux. On

the opposite side of the Atlantic, Benito Mussolini and his
Fascist party had overthrown the old order in Italy. Joseph
Stalin had taken over as dictator in Russia, annihilating
his opposition in a series of purges. And in Germany an
ex-corporal named Adolf Hitler had presented his mani-
festo for the future entitled *Mein Kampf*.

Not to be outdone, America had spawned an original
all its own, the underworld mobster. A phenomenon
uniquely American, these homegrown gangsters, men like
Ollie Quinn and Dutch Voight, were brilliant capitalists.
The almighty dollar became the only ideology in a remarkable marriage of free enterprise and brass knuckles.

Prohibition had shifted a market worth tens of millions to a trade controlled exclusively by the underworld.
The rackets grew and diversified, proliferating amid a climate of tommy-gun violence, cheered on by Americans
who simply wanted a drink. Bootlegging and speakeasies
operated openly, and for the most part, law enforcement
officials turned a blind eye. The accommodation, but-
tressed by graft, was made easier by the fact that lawmen
were merely mirroring public opinion.

As Nolan came off the causeway, he reflected that
Galveston was typical of the country as a whole. The casino, along with the rumrunning operation and protection
payoffs from gambling dives and whorehouses, generated
illicit revenues of more than five million dollars a year.
Everybody in town knew that various city and county officials were on the payroll, and while no one spoke of it
openly, it was an accepted fact of life. The payoff that
hardly anyone knew of was the one that went to Arthur
Scarett.

A few miles north of the causeway, Nolan entered
the town of La Marque. On the outskirts of the business
district, he pulled into the parking lot of Big Jim's Roadhouse. The nightspot was popular along the southern
mainland, with dancing, liquor, and poker tables in the
back room. He was carrying a .38 Colt in a shoulder holster, and as he stepped out of the car, he adjusted it to a

comfortable position under his suit jacket. The gun, like a necktie, was part of his everyday attire.

The front door of the roadhouse opened onto a hallway. Off to one side was a room with a bar, where girls mingled with customers, and for a slightly higher tariff took them upstairs. On the opposite side was a larger room with a dance floor and a three-piece band. There were tables around the dance floor and cozy booths along the walls. The place was crowded, and waiters scurried back and forth serving drinks. The music, with a trumpeter blasting away, was all but deafening.

Arthur Scarett was seated alone in a booth. He was a squat, fat man with a pocked moonlike face and a gift for duplicity. Few people knew him on sight, even though he was the chief prohibition agent for Houston and the southern counties, including Galveston. His squad of agents routinely raided bootlegging operations and speakeasies that refused to share the wealth. All of which looked good for the record and allowed him to extend preferential treatment where it counted the most. Big Jim's Roadhouse was a longtime client.

Nolan scooted into the booth. "Evening, Art," he said. "Enjoying the music?"

"Music's music." Scarett waved a pudgy hand. "But, then, I'm not much of a dancer anyway. My wife says I have two lead feet."

"So how are things otherwise?"

"Never better, Jack."

A waiter took Nolan's order for bourbon and water. Scarett was drinking scotch on the rocks, and they made small talk until the waiter returned. Nolan sipped his drink, then slipped a thick envelope from his inside coat pocket. He placed it on the table.

"Mr. Quinn and Mr. Voight send their regards."

"The usual?"

"The usual."

The payoff was all part of the cost of operating an illicit business. The federal penalty for rumrunning was

$1,000 and six months in prison, and repeat offenders were fined $10,000 and sentenced to five years. The law also mandated forfeiture of all property, including boats, trucks and cash seized at the time of arrest. Bribing a prohibition agent was considered an investment in the future.

Scarett pocketed the envelope. "I got a call from the Coast Guard today. How many cases did you bring in last night?"

"Does it matter?" Nolan said. "You know our deal."

The deal was simple. Galveston Island, from the Hollywood Club to the lowest hooch joint, was immune to raids. The rumrunning operation was immune as well, at least on the beach, where smuggled liquor was transferred from boats to trucks. Once the trucks cleared the Galveston County line, the rules changed and bootleggers became fair game. Everyone understood the rules, including the bootleggers, who scattered like quail when they crossed the county line. Scarett was paid ten thousand a month to abide by the rules.

"I've been thinking," Scarett said in an exploratory tone. "Maybe we ought to up the ante."

"Why spoil a good thing?"

"Jack, you're running God knows how many cases a month. I deserve a bigger piece of the action."

Nolan's gaze was empty of emotion. "You wouldn't want to try that, Art."

"Are you threatening me?"

"Call it a word to the wise."

Their eyes locked and several moments elapsed in silence. Scarett blinked first, some inner voice telling him not to push too hard. "Well, like you said, why spoil a good thing?"

Nolan slid out of the booth. "Enjoyed our little talk, Art. See you next month."

Outside, as he pulled away in the Ford, Nolan thought there was no accounting for greed. But he didn't fault Scarett, or particularly think the worse of him. There was no great harm in throwing out a line and seeing if the fish took the bait. No harm if a man knew when to call it quits.

Nolan arrived back at the Hollywood Club shortly before nine o'clock. He found Quinn and Voight in the office at the rear of the casino. They were involved in a discussion about the astronomical salary needed to import Al Jolson from Broadway. Jolson was opening at the club Friday night, and Voight was still complaining about the price. Nolan thought the ongoing argument typified the differences between the two men.

Quinn was a polished gentleman, a bon vivant and raconteur with an easygoing manner. He was always impeccably dressed, his wardrobe tailored in London, and he frequently traveled to New York booking headliner entertainment for the club. Voight, apart from his tuxedo attire at the casino, wore off-the-rack suits and always appeared a little rumpled. His manner was polite but quietly sinister, no laughter in his eyes. He looked like he might hurt you, given the slightest pretext.

For all their contrasts, the partners ran a smooth operation. Gulf Properties, their holding company, employed over a thousand people, fully five percent of the adult population on the Island. They owned gambling clubs, bars, a restaurant and an amusement pier, and several other legitimate businesses. The Hollywood Club was nonetheless the jewel of their empire.

Yet, for all their gangland activities, they were astute businessmen. They realized that public relations were key to success and they allowed only wealthy Islanders inside the casino. Their patrons were drawn instead from the upper financial strata of Houston, Dallas and other cities throughout the Southwest. To show Galveston in the best light, they also maintained their own brand of law and order with a squad of hooligans known as the Night Raiders. No one feared to walk the streets after dark.

Quinn finally noticed Nolan waiting by the door. He broke off the argument about Al Jolson, and looked around with a quick smile. "Everything status quo with our friend, Mr. Scarett?"

"Went off fine," Nolan replied. "He tried to sandbag us for a raise, but he backed off when I spelled it out. He didn't like the options."

"Damned ingrate," Voight grumped. "We've made him rich as Midas. His only option is to go for a swim."

"I told him as much."

Quinn kept a blue macaw parrot in the office. The bird was named Cuddles and sat perched on a stand behind the desk. A master mimic, Cuddles often joined in the conversation. He cocked his head now and looked at them with a puckish glare.

"Oh, boy! Oh, boy! Take him for a swim. Kiss my ass!"

"See there, Dutch," Quinn said ruefully. "He's picked up all your bad habits."

Voight chuckled. "Smart bird."

Chapter Four

Ollie Quinn occupied the penthouse suite at the Buccaneer Hotel. The hotel was located on Seawall Boulevard, and the balcony of his suite offered a sweeping view of the Gulf. A morning sun, bright as new brass, reflected off waves lapping gently at the beach.

Breakfast, weather permitting, was always served on the balcony. Quinn was in shirtsleeves and tie, seated at a table covered with spotless linen, a napkin tucked into his collar. A waiter from room service fussed over him, setting out a ripe melon, bacon and eggs, and coffee. The breadbasket was filled with piping hot buttermilk biscuits.

Maxine Baxter wandered out of the master bedroom as the waiter left the suite. She was a honey blonde with a ballerina's grace and blue eyes the color of a tropical lagoon. Her hourglass curves amply strained a sheer peach peignoir and high-heeled satin slippers covered her dainty feet. She was small, a pocket Venus.

"Mornin', sugar," she said, moving onto the balcony. "Aren't you up early?"

Quinn spooned a bite of melon. "Today's a big day, Maxie. Al Jolson arrives this afternoon."

"Oh, sure, I guess I forgot. You're excited, aren't you?"

"The king of Broadway! Who wouldn't be?"

Quinn and Maxine were both native Texans. She began as a hatcheck girl at the club, and her lilting Southern drawl, as well as her other charms, quickly caught his attention. A little over a year ago she had moved into the penthouse, happy as a clam to be his only girl. Their lives were filled with luxury and interesting people, and languorous nights dreamily exhausted from love. Neither of them asked for any promises, and there were no strings attached. They lived it one day at a time.

Dutch Voight, by comparison, shunned the limelight. Apart from Quinn, who was occasionally invited to a modest house on Twenty-ninth Street, few people in the sporting world had ever seen Voight's wife. She was a deeply religious woman who lived in denial that her husband was a gangster. A great many people were unaware that Voight had two teenage children, a son and a daughter, who attended Galveston High School. He adroitly kept his personal life separated from his business affairs, and his gangland associates. Quinn often thought his partner needed a girlfriend.

"What a gorgeous day," Maxine said, pouring herself a cup of coffee. "Maybe I'll run downtown and do some shopping. What would you like to buy me, sugar?"

Quinn layered jam onto a biscuit. "Anything your little heart desires. Find a new dress for Jolson's opening."

"Why, I just believe I will! Won't you come help me pick it out?"

"Sorry, buttercup, I have a meeting at ten."

"Business, business, business. You're never any fun."

"That's not what you said last night."

"Oh, you wicked man!"

"I accept the compliment."

For all his cheery banter, Quinn's mind was on the day ahead. At ten, he had a meeting with William Magruder, and he was still wondering what that was all about. Yesterday, on the phone, Magruder had sounded harried, which was unusual. William Magruder was what he'd always thought of as collected, even a bit calculating. A cold fish.

Whatever it was, Quinn was determined that it wouldn't spoil his day. Early that afternoon, Al Jolson was arriving by train, and he meant to celebrate the major coup of his career as a showman. He kissed Maxine on the cheek, and left her to plan a shopping spree that would likely cost him a fortune. In the bedroom, he shrugged into his suit jacket, tilting his Panama hat at a jaunty angle, and hurried out of the suite. The elevator operator gave him an express ride to the lobby.

Turk McGuire, his chauffeur and bodyguard, was waiting outside. There was small chance of anyone trying to rub him out in Galveston, but he believed in playing the odds. McGuire was robust as an ox, his head fixed directly on his shoulders, with the vacant eyes of a man who spent his time contemplating deadly acts. More to the point, he was loyal, quick with his hands and fast with a gun, and seemingly robbed of fear the day he was weaned. No one messed with Turk McGuire.

Quinn's car was a Cadillac Phaeton with a V-16 engine. The body was gold, the teardrop fenders a rich maroon, with a gleaming silver grill and wide whitewall tires. The Phaeton was sleek and rakish, the only one in Galveston, and everyone in town knew it on sight. The day was bright and sunny, and the collapsible top had been folded down, which highlighted the car's lush leather interior. Turk McGuire kept the Caddy washed and polished, every ornament glittering in the sunlight, a rolling tribute to the impresario of the Hollywood Club. He held the rear door open for Quinn.

Some ten minutes later McGuire parked in front of the Magruder Building. The distinctive Cadillac was like a pronouncement of Quinn's presence, but he hardly gave it a thought. Galveston's biggest open secret was that the two reigning families, the Magruders and the Seagraves, occasionally worked with the mob for the civic and economic betterment of the community. Quinn strolled into the building with the brisk air of a man on important business and not a moment to waste. He took the birdcage elevator to the tenth floor.

A secretary escorted him into Magruder's office. The old man was behind his desk and Sherm was seated on the couch. Their relationship with Quinn was one of wary civility, for they preferred to distance themselves from mob activities on the Island. After perfunctory handshakes all around, Quinn was offered one of the leather armchairs. Magruder went straight to the point.

"We have a minor business problem. Your assistance would be most appreciated."

"Anything at all, Bill. How can I help?"

"People's Bank & Trust," Magruder explained. "Upon Joseph Durant's death, the bank was inherited by his nephew. The man's name is Earl Durant."

Quinn nodded. "I believe I heard something about the bank changing hands."

"A change for the worse, no question about it. Mr. Durant is a stuntman in moving pictures. Hardly a welcome addition to Galveston."

"I see."

"In any event," Magruder went on, "we wish to purchase People's Bank & Trust. Despite our generous offer, Durant refuses to sell. Therein lies our problem."

"These things happen," Quinn said equably. "What assistance may I offer you?"

"Joseph Durant was respected by a certain segment of our community. I daresay the townspeople would not have condoned violence in his case. On the other hand, his nephew is a stranger. . . ."

Magruder paused, underscoring the thought with weighty silence. Quinn saw now that he'd been asked here not as a fellow businessman, but rather because of his reputation as a gangster. He found it ironic that Galveston's guardian of morality and good taste would recruit him to join in a criminal conspiracy. He decided it might work to advantage at some later time.

"Let me understand," he said. "Do you want this Durant fellow killed?"

"Good God, no!" Magruder huffed. "We simply want him frightened."

"Roughed up, put on warning."

"Yes, that's it."

"I'm with you now," Quinn said without inflection.

"And is he to be told the reason? The purpose of the beating?"

Magruder exchanged a quick, somewhat startled glance with his son. Their bemused looks indicated they clearly hadn't thought that far ahead. Sherm finally lifted his shoulders in a shrug.

"Why not?" he said. "The purpose is to persuade him to sell us the bank. I think he should be told."

Magruder pursed his mouth. "All very discreetly, of course. Nothing that associates our names with violence."

"Naturally," Quinn agreed. "I'll see that it's handled with the necessary discretion. Durant will get the message."

"Fine, fine," Sherm said hurriedly. "We realize there are expenses involved in this type of thing. Let us know what you think is fair."

"No charge," Quinn said. "Call it a favor among friends."

"That's very decent of you," Magruder said. "I assure you we won't forget your courtesy."

Quinn couldn't have agreed more. On his way out of the building, he wondered why they were so interested in a nickel-and-dime bank. Whatever the reason, he told himself, it wasn't all that important. Today's transaction, with the debit on their side, was what counted most.

Somewhere down the line, he intended to call in the chit.

The train chuffed to a halt with a belch of steam. Several people waited on the cobbled platform outside the Santa Fe depot, there to greet passengers. The stationmaster, pocket watch in hand, noted the train had arrived at 12:59, one minute early.

Quinn was almost dancing with excitement. He wore a smartly tailored linen suit, creamy beige in color, topped off by his Panama hat. As passengers began debarking the train, he moved through the crowd, his expression eager and alert. Then, with a sudden laugh, he hurried forward.

Al Jolson stepped onto the platform. He was a man of medium height, with broad features, snappy electric eyes, and a perpetual moonlike grin. He was attired in a blue tropical worsted suit, an exotic silk handkerchief draped from his breast pocket, the brim of his fedora rolled at a natty angle. The effect was one of casual elegance, faintly continental.

"Mr. Jolson!" Quinn bugled, pumping his hand. "Welcome to Galveston. I'm Oliver Quinn."

"Glad to meet you, pal." Jolson wiped a trickle of sweat off his brow. "Never expected a heat wave in September."

"Well, it's not the heat, it's the humidity. We're right on the Gulf."

"You could've fooled me, sport. Feels like the equator."

"Then you'll like the club, Al—may I call you Al? We had it air-cooled."

"Thank God for small favors."

Quinn signaled a porter. The baggage car door slid open and the porter moved forward with a rolling handcart. Jolson's luggage included three suitcases and two large steamer trunks, which the porter manhandled off the train. He trundled along behind as Quinn led the way around the side of the depot.

"Traveling light," Jolson quipped, waving idly at the luggage. "I might decide I like it in California."

"No question about it," Quinn said. "Motion pictures are all the rage."

"Wait till you see my talky. We're gonna call it *The Jazz Singer*."

Jolson was on his way to Hollywood. Warner Brothers had signed him to star in the first talking movie ever made. Until now, motion pictures were silent, with sporadic dialogue displayed on-screen through subtitles. *The Jazz Singer* would have recorded songs, accompanied by live music.

Quinn felt very fortunate. He had been able to secure

a booking of one week only because Jolson was traveling to California. Jolson was in such demand on Broadway that he seldom made an appearance outside of New York. He was billed as "The World's Greatest Entertainer," and it wasn't mere hoopla. His was the rags-to-riches story of show business.

Al Jolson was the immigrant son of a Jewish cantor. His voice, a brassy blend of warmth with a sob, first made him the preeminent star of the vaudeville stage. From there, seemingly overnight, he catapulted to fame at the fabled Winter Garden Theater in New York. Millions listened to his weekly radio show, and he recorded a new hit record every two weeks. He was the brightest light on Broadway.

A renowned braggart, with a monumental ego, he was widely acknowledged as the musical comedy star of the century. Just within the last year, a New York columnist wrote: "Al Jolson is to show business what Jack Dempsey is to the ring and Babe Ruth to baseball." And now, he was to make the first talky film in motion picture history.

But first, he would play the Hollywood Club. Quinn was beside himself, for it would garner publicity from coast to coast. A phone call earlier had arranged the opening salvo; a reporter and photographer from the *Galveston Daily Chronicle* waylaid them as they crossed the platform. Jolson quickly took center stage, always at his best in front of a camera. He regaled the newsmen with stories of the one he loved the most, himself.

Quinn, meanwhile, had Turk McGuire call for a truck to collect the luggage. A suite was booked for Jolson at the Buccaneer, and he ordered that the luggage be taken ahead to the hotel. When the interview concluded, he steered Jolson to the Cadillac, explaining the band was waiting for them at the club. Jolson gave McGuire a casual once-over as they climbed into the car. He smiled knowingly when they pulled away from the curb.

"I see we're well protected. Dempsey himself wouldn't tangle with your driver."

"Al, we look after our guests on Galveston Island. You're in safe hands."

Quinn, playing the good host, acted as tour guide. He explained that the Strand, which took them east from the depot, was christened to honor London's famed thoroughfare of the same name. Farther uptown, he motioned to the bayside wharves, subtly easing into a point of interest. He knew the story of Jolson's heritage and he related that Germans, Czechs, and Russian Jews had immigrated to the new world by way of the port. Galveston, no less than New York, was a melting pot.

On Twenty-first Street, where they turned south, he pointed out the Grand Opera House. The immense baroque structure was modeled after the great opera houses of Europe during the time of the Renaissance. The elite of the operatic world, as well as Sarah Bernhardt and Anna Pavlova, the Russian ballerina, had all performed there. The auditorium seated 1,600 and was constructed without square corners, a marvel of perfect acoustics. Galveston, he noted, was a city rich in culture.

A few minutes later they crossed Seawall Boulevard. Quinn proudly recounted that the Hollywood Club was the only nightspot in the greater Southwest with top-notch entertainment, gourmet dining, and a plush casino, all under one roof. Dutch Voight met them as they entered the nightclub, and Quinn performed the introductions. Voight took Jolson on a tour of the club and casino, explaining that it was the first air-cooled nightspot in America. He kept the temperature at 69°, confident that gamblers who were cool didn't feel their liquor. Drunk gamblers, he observed, were happy losers.

Jolson, who had known many New York gangsters, recognized Voight as one of the breed. The menacing attitude, however carefully suppressed, was there in mannerism and tone of voice. He thought Quinn, who came off as a dapper devotee of arts and entertainment, was probably no less dangerous. Yet he was impressed by their club and casino, a grand nightspot literally at land's end, suspended over water. He was taken as well by the welcome comfort of air-cooling. He'd finally stopped sweating.

"Are you a gambler?" Voight asked as they left the casino. "We'd be happy to reserve you a table."

"I'm a gambler," Jolson said with an immodest grin, "but only on Al Jolson. I know I can't lose on myself."

Voight covered his disappointment. Entertainers were notoriously poor gamblers, and typically dropped a large part of their salaries at the tables. A few, the worst of the lot, left the Hollywood Club owing the casino money. He'd had similar hopes for Jolson.

Ben Pollack was waiting with his orchestra in the nightclub. Popular all across the country, and a draw in itself, the orchestra featured rising young musicians such as Glenn Miller and Benny Goodman. Jolson had met Pollack once before, in New York, and it was something of a reunion when he hopped onto the stage. They began talking music—particularly Jolson's kind of music—and it soon became apparent that there was a new leader of the band. Jolson, as he did anywhere he went, got it his way.

Quinn and Voight watched from the dance floor. Jolson was a star of the first magnitude, certainly the top entertainer who had ever played the Hollywood Club. Quinn felt as though he had capped his career as a showman, and he could hardly contain his excitement. He looked around at his partner.

"Dutch, do you believe in providence?"

"You talking about divine intervention?"

"Call it what you will," Quinn said. "Somebody was watching over us when he got the role in that moving picture. Otherwise we'd never have been able to book him into the club."

"Tell you what I believe," Voight said crossly. "The bastard's not gonna drop a nickel at the tables. He'll leave town with our ten gees in his pocket."

"Yes, but we'll get that back ten times over in publicity."

"Nobody sings that good. Not even Jolson."

"Wait a week, old friend. You'll change your tune."

"Not likely," Voight said. "I'm tone deaf."

Quinn smiled. "That's exactly why I hired Jolson."

The Turf Club was headquarters for mob activities on Galveston Island. The Hollywood Club was the showpiece, but all serious business was conducted at a three-story building on Twenty-third Street. Quinn and Voight operated their criminal enterprises from an office on the third floor.

A small sign over the main door identified the Turf Club. The building, constructed of white brick, was located between Market and Postoffice Streets, a few blocks from the Strand. The ground floor was a bookmaking parlor, where sporting men could wager on baseball, boxing matches, or horse races at tracks across the country. There were four betting windows at the back of the room.

The atmosphere was congenial and comfortable. A bar along the south wall looked over groupings of tables and leather club chairs, where customers could follow the action at their leisure. On the north wall was a tote board, posted with up-to-the-minute results from racetracks and various sports events. Two men, chalk in hand, constantly worked the tote board.

On the back wall, near the betting windows, was an elevator. The elevator operator took patrons to the second floor, where there were two lounges dispensing alcoholic beverages. The Western Room, done in a nouveau Texas motif, was appointed in leather, rodeo murals, and broad, spear-pointed longhorns affixed to the walls. The Studio Lounge, all modernistic Art Deco, was lights and mirrors and bright geometric designs. One lounge featured Country Western music and the other a jazz quartet.

The third floor was restricted to employees of Gulf Enterprises. On one side of a long hallway was a billiard room, with three pool tables and two snooker tables. On the opposite side was an athletic club, with a boxing ring, weightlifting equipment, and a steam room. Voight, in particular, believed the strong-arm boys and gunsels employed by Gulf Enterprises should be in tip-top shape. Every man on the payroll was required to work out three times a week.

The far end of the hallway was guarded by a gorilla in a pin-striped suit. There, on the street side of the building, was the central headquarters of the mob. Quinn and Voight, from an office paneled in dark wood and furnished in leather, directed the myraid aspects of their underworld empire. The proceeds, upwards of $100,000 a week, flowed from the casino, the rumrunning operation, and payoffs from their cohorts in crime. Entrance into their inner sanctum was by appointment only.

Late that afternoon Fred Crowley stepped off the elevator. He was short and lantern-jawed, attired in a sharkskin suit, spit-shined cordovans, and beige spats. A derby hat was perched atop his head and his eyes flicked left and right, to the billiard room and the athletic club, as he moved along the hallway. He prudently stopped in front of the gorilla.

"I'm Fred Crowley," he said. "Mr. Voight knows I was comin' by."

"Act like a gent in there or I'll break your legs. Take off the lid."

Crowley removed his derby as the gorilla swung open the door. Voight was seated behind a desk, and the man everyone knew as Diamond Jack Nolan occupied a leather armchair. Tall filing cabinets were aligned along one wall and a massive double-door safe was wedged into a corner. Bright sunlight splashed through a window that overlooked the street.

"Come on in," Voight said. "Grab a chair."

Crowley glanced at Nolan, who was paring his nails with a penknife. He seated himself in one of the armchairs, his derby balanced on his knees. "I appreciate you takin' the time to see me, Mr. Voight."

"Business is business," Voight said. "So you want to buy the Roseland?"

"Yessir, I've already worked a deal with George Napoli. He said I'd need your okay to buy him out."

The Roseland Supper Club was one of many joints spread around town. Despite its elegant name, the Roseland was a bar with a short-order cook, a dozen slot machines, and a poker room. All of the joints paid tribute on their gaming operations.

"You're new to town," Voight said. "Where are you from?"

"Spring Valley, west of Houston," Crowley replied. "I ran card games there for a couple years. Decided to move where there's more action. Galveston's the place to be."

"You know I'll have you checked out?"

"Yessir."

"You know what will happen if you don't check out."

Crowley fidgeted. "I'm clean, Mr. Voight. You got my word."

"Just so you understand," Voight said. "Did Napoli explain the rules?"

"Yeah, he did. I buy all my liquor from your boys, and I never welch on a bet with a customer. Always pay up."

"You pay up with us, too. We get ten percent off the top on slots and games. You get protection from the cops and the feds."

"Worth every nickel of it, Mr. Voight. Protection's the main reason I decided on Galveston."

"There's one last rule," Voight told him. "Never try to skim and short us on the grease. You skim and you're gone. You follow me?"

"Yeah, sure," Crowley said weakly. "I'm out of business."

"No," Voight corrected him. "You're gone, like forever. Got me?"

Crowley swallowed hard. He darted a glance at Nolan, who was reputed to be a stone-cold killer. He cleared his throat.

"I'll never hold out, Mr. Voight. You got no worries about me."

"Come see me in a week," Voight said. "We find you're on the up and up, you can close your deal with Napoli. You'll make good money with the Roseland."

"Thank you. Mr. Voight. I'll be here same time, next Friday. You can bet on it."

Crowley, hat still in hand, went out. When the door closed, Voight took a cigar from a box on the desk. He deftly clipped the end, struck a match, and lit up in a haze of blue smoke. He looked at Nolan.

"Make a few phone calls, Jack. Somebody we know in Spring Valley will likely know Crowley."

"Larry Hebert," Nolan said. "He's our bootlegger up that way. I'll get on it."

Ollie Quinn came through the door. He dropped into a chair with an exhausted look. "Jolson's a handful," he said. "I finally got him settled into the hotel. I think he would've gone on tonight without any rehearsal."

Voight grunted. "Why didn't you let him? We could've got eight nights for our money instead of seven."

"Dutch, it doesn't work that way. I have the newspapers coming from Houston and Dallas for the opening tomorrow night. We'll make headlines, believe you me."

"I'm surprised you're not playing nursemaid with Mr. Showbusiness. What brings you over here?"

"William Magruder," Quinn said. "You'll recall I met with him this morning."

"Now that you mention it," Voight said, puffing his cigar. "What'd he want, more charity donations?"

"Nothing quite so simple."

Quinn went on to relate the gist of the meeting. He outlined Magruder's designs on the People's Bank &

Trust, and the impediment of the heir, Earl Durant. He ended with a shrug.

"We've been asked for a favor we can't refuse. He wants the fear of God put into Durant."

"Fear of God," Voight amended, "or fear of Bill Magruder?"

"I suppose it's all one and the same. Anyway, we put him in our debt by doing the favor. So I told him we'd handle it."

"Christ, he could've called Western Union if he wants a message delivered. Sounds like small potatoes."

"Not to him," Quinn said. "I gave him my word, Dutch."

"Oh, hell, I'm not arguing with you, Ollie. How do you want it done?"

"We'll leave that to Jack." Quinn turned, nodding to Nolan. "Get a line on this Durant and take care of it. You know the drill."

"Shouldn't be too hard," Nolan said quietly. "I'll have a talk with him in private, put him on notice. He'll see the light."

"Velvet glove on a mail fist?"

"Usually works," Nolan said. "Time enough for the rough stuff if reason fails."

"You're a hot ticket, Jack." Quinn considered a moment. "All right, but make sure you scare the bejesus out of him. Let's fix it so Magruder knows who owes who for what."

Nolan bobbed his head. "I'll look after it."

"And no miscues," Voight added. "Lay it out in spades for him. Get the message across."

Quinn laughed. "What happened to Western Union?"

"Last time I heard, they don't break legs."

Diamond Jack Nolan thought that said it all.

Chapter Five

Saturday was the busiest day of the week in Galveston. Tourists there for the weekend swarmed the town sightseeing and visiting the amusement piers on the beach. Stores were crowded with shoppers and traffic jams were constant on the Strand. The police were hard-pressed to control the circuslike atmosphere.

The People's Bank & Trust, like other businesses, stayed open six days a week. A large segment of the bank's customers were workingmen, struggling to make ends meet, and rushed in on Saturday to cash their paychecks and catch up on mortgage payments. Long lines began forming at the cashier cages soon after the noon hour.

Durant was technically the new president of the bank. Yet he asked few questions and left daily financial operations to Ira Aldridge. After his meeting with Magruder, he had explained the situation to Aldridge, and hardly to his surprise, the older man's reaction was somewhat euphoric. Aldridge was clearly delighted with the turn of events.

"William Magruder is a scoundrel," he'd observed with obvious relish. "He'll try to steal the bank out from under you. He has all the ethics of a jellyfish."

"That won't happen," Durant had avowed. "I'll just have to find another buyer."

"Earl, I'd say your chances are somewhere between slim and none. No one wants to compete with Magruder in his own backyard. He's simply too powerful."

Aldridge had nonetheless put together a list of banks on the mainland. From thirty years in the business, he knew the executive officers of every financial institution in southern Texas. He allowed Durant to use his name as an entrée, and agreed to stay on if the bank was sold to an outside party. He expressed the opinion that the likelihood was on the order of snowballs in hell.

Today, as he had for the past two days, Durant was working the phone. So far, he had called bankers in the towns of Hitchcock, La Marque, Santa Fe, and Texas City. The response in each instance had been a polite but very definite lack of interest, and by now, he had spoken with the presidents of seven banks. Disappointed, though undeterred, he had exhausted the list of banks along the coastline. He was calling institutions farther inland this morning.

The man on the line now was Horace Taylor, president of a bank in Dickinson. "Look, Mr. Taylor," Durant said. "I'd be happy for you to audit the books and see for yourself. I know you'll find it fair value for the price."

"Not questioning value," Taylor said on the staticky line. "I've known Ira Aldridge most of my life, and he's honest as they come. If he says it's worth it, then it's worth it."

"Why don't I drive up there Monday and let's talk about it? I'll even bring Ira along if you like."

"Mr. Durant, it'd be a long drive for nothing. I'm not the first banker you've approached, am I?"

"No, sir, you're not."

"And I'd venture to say they've all told you the same thing. Nobody wants any part of Galveston because of that sorry bastard William Magruder. Am I right?"

"Well, most of them called him a son of a bitch. But that's been the general thought."

"You've got a tough row to hoe," Taylor said. "I suspect you'll have a deuce of a time finding a buyer. I wouldn't tangle with Magruder for all the tea in China."

The conversation ended with Taylor wishing him well. Durant hung up the phone and slumped back in his chair. He stared at the list of names on the desk, all too aware that it was growing shorter by the minute. Dickinson was twenty miles north of Galveston, and apparently that wasn't far enough. No one cared—or dared—to take on William Magruder.

The door opened. Catherine Ludlow stepped into the office carrying a cup of coffee. She was wearing a dark skirt and a white round-collared blouse, with a little blue grosgrain bow at the throat. The outfit showed off her figure without being obvious, and he thought she looked cute as hell. She placed the cup of coffee on the desk.

"Time for some java," she said brightly. "How's it going?"

"More of the same," Durant admitted. "You'd think they're all reading off the same script. Always ends with 'thanks, but no thanks.' "

"You must be getting discouraged."

"No, I'm a regular brute for punishment. I'll find a buyer yet."

She lowered her eyes. "I really shouldn't say this. Mr. Aldridge wouldn't like it. . . ."

"Go ahead," Durant coaxed her. "I'm the original Silent Sam."

"Well—" She looked at him, and he was suddenly aware of the larkspur blue of her eyes. "Mr. Aldridge truly, truly wants you to take over the bank. He says you're your uncle all over again." She smiled shyly. "And I think so, too."

"I appreciate the sentiment. But it wouldn't work out in a million years. I'm not interested in being a banker."

"Mr. Aldridge says you're a stuntman in moving pictures. That must be fascinating."

"Why, do you enjoy the movies?"

"Oh, do I!" she said engagingly. "I see every picture that comes to the Bijou. That's our movie theater."

"I saw it when I was walking around town."

"Do you know any of the—?"

A man appeared in the doorway. Durant's first impression was that he would be perfect for moving pictures.

He was unbearably handsome, with eyes so green they glittered like gems. Aldridge, flushed with anger, was right behind him.

"I tried to tell him he couldn't come in here. He just barged on past me."

Durant got to his feet. "What's the problem?"

"No problem at all, Mr. Durant. I'm Jack Nolan and I'd like to talk with you. In private."

"Jack Nolan, the gangster!" Aldridge shouted. "He's the hatchet man for the mobsters that run Galveston."

Nolan looked wounded. "Give a fella a break, old man. You might hurt my feelings."

"Ira. Catherine." Durant got their attention. "Would you mind stepping outside? I'll talk to Mr. Nolan alone."

Aldridge waited at the door until Catherine went out. He gave Durant a concerned look, clearly reluctant to leave, and then closed the door. Durant motioned to a chair.

"I've never met a gangster," he said as Nolan seated himself. "Or was Mr. Aldridge mistaken?"

Nolan rocked his hand, fingers splayed. "I work at the Hollywood Club. Hottest spot in town."

"I heard Al Jolson's opening tonight."

"Come on by and be my guest. I'll save you a good table."

"I get the feeling you're not here to talk about show business. What can I do for you, Mr. Nolan?"

"Let's talk about your bank," Nolan said casually. "The people I work for, they're friends of William Magruder. They think you ought to sell him the bank—at his price."

"Well, that's a twist," Durant said, openly surprised. "Magruder in bed with the mob. One hand washes the other, is that it?"

"Don't worry yourself about that. What's important here is your health, follow me? You need to put Galveston behind you."

"Are you threatening me, Mr. Nolan?"

"I'm delivering a message, and it's real simple. Take the money and run."

"And if I don't?"

Nolan eased his suit jacket aside. The Colt revolver, nestled in the shoulder holster, spoke for itself. "Save yourself some grief, chum. Nobody wants trouble."

"I'll give you a choice," Durant said with a hard stare. "Pull that gun and I'll take it away from you. Or you can hit the road. Which is it?"

"You ought to get your hearing checked."

"You're the one that's not listening. What'll it be?"

"I'll see you around, tough guy. Real soon."

Nolan rose with a tight smile and walked to the door. As he moved through the bank, Aldridge and Catherine hurried into the office. Durant gave them a funny look, shook his head. A ghost of a grin touched his mouth.

"Try this on for size," he said. "The mob's playing fetch and carry for Magruder. I've been warned to sell him the bank—or else."

"Or else what?" Aldridge demanded. "Are you saying Nolan threatened you?"

"Yeah, I think it qualified as a threat."

"Good Lord!" Catherine said on a sudden intake of breath. "What will you do?"

"Just what I intended to do," Durant said. "Sell the bank to somebody on the mainland."

Aldridge frowned. "I wouldn't take it lightly if I were you. These are dangerous men, very dangerous indeed." He paused, his eyes dark with fear. "They might well do you harm . . . great harm."

"Ira, I guess I'll have to take my chances. I never learned how to cut and run."

Catherine thought he was either incredibly brave or incredibly stupid. Then, looking closer, she saw something in the cast of his face. Something implacable and cold.

Her heart went out to him, and she wished he would

run and keep on running. Yet she somehow knew he wouldn't. Or couldn't.

She wondered if Diamond Jack Nolan knew it as well.

The Turf Club was packed. Saturday was a big day for the sporting crowd, particularly on the opening day of football season. The horse tracks were still open as well, and several important races were scheduled around the country. The betting cages were lined with men waiting to get down a wager.

Nolan paused halfway across the room. He ignored the hubbub of conversation, and stood for a moment studying the tote board. He saw that the Chicago Bears were playing the New York Giants in the Windy City that afternoon. The Bears were favored by five points, and he idly wondered if anyone would bet against Red Grange. But then, on second thought, he knew it was a bookmaker's dream. The suckers always took the long odds.

Joe Reed, the elevator operator, greeted him with a loopy grin. "How's tricks, Jack? Sleep late, did you?"

"Don't I wish," Nolan said. "Out and about on a little business."

"Well, business before pleasure, that's our motto. Gotta keep the gelt rollin' in."

The car lurched upward. The interior walls were mirrored in an Art Deco design, and Nolan's gaze was drawn to the older man's reflected image. Reed was in his late forties, with a lung condition, and he'd been retired to elevator operator. In his heyday, he had been a rough customer, one of many strong-arm boys for the mob. Time and asthma had sapped his strength.

Nolan thought it spoke well of Quinn and Voight. Rather than give Reed the boot, they had pensioned him off as an elevator operator. There were seven men on the payroll in the same situation, men who now ran errands, or answered telephones, or worked the betting cages. Still, while he respected the benevolence of his bosses, he was determined never to end up as an elevator operator. There were better ways to die, and quicker.

On the third floor, Nolan walked along the hallway. Elmer Spadden, the ape who guarded the office door, would never wind up on an elevator either. Of all the men in the organization, Nolan gave Spadden and Turk McGuire a show of respect. He feared no man, but he'd seen them in action, and he knew he couldn't whip either one in a fight. Before it came to that he would resort to a gun, and he liked them too much. They reminded him of overgrown boys with an aptitude for breaking bones.

Quinn and Voight were seated at their desks in the office. Saturday was their most hectic day, busy from morning until late at night with the action at the Turf Club and the crowds jamming the Hollywood Club. Earlier, he'd phoned and told them he planned to drop by the People's Bank & Trust. They were expecting results.

"How'd it go?" Voight asked. "Durant ready to sign over the bank?"

Nolan took a chair. "I'd have to say he surprised me. He's a cool one."

"What happened?"

"Well, for openers, he doesn't scare. I gave him the pitch and he never blinked an eye. Told me to hit the road."

"I'll be damned," Voight said, amazed. "Not losing your touch, are you, Jack?"

"You be the judge," Nolan countered. "You know how you accidentally-on-purpose show a man your gun? Just to put him in the right frame of mind?"

"Yeah, so?"

"I showed him mine and he threatened to take it away from me. How's that for brass balls?"

Voight and Quinn were shocked. Their years on the Island had made them masters of extortion and intimidation, overlords who were never challenged. What they'd just heard mocked their authority, insulted them. Their reaction was predictable.

"Does he know who we are?" Quinn said hotly. "Does he know we *run* this Island?"

"Aldridge told him," Nolan replied. "Followed me through the door and told him I'm the hatchet man for the mob. That got things off to a fast start."

"I'm sure," Quinn said. "You didn't let Aldridge stick around, did you?"

"Didn't have to lift a finger. Durant shooed him out of the office pretty as you please. Everything said was said in private."

"So you told him we represent Magruder and it's in his best interests to sell. Does that cover it?"

"More or less," Nolan said. "I dropped the hint it's not healthy for him on the Island. Told him to take the money and run."

"And?"

"He as much as told me to stuff it."

Quinn and Voight exchanged a look. Nolan knew what they were thinking, for he'd had the same thought himself. But it was not his place to point out the obvious, or step on their authority. He waited for them to speak.

Voight took the lead. "No way we can keep this from getting out. People are gonna hear a wise-ass nobody told us to go screw. We've got to turn that around."

"And quickly," Quinn added. "We gave our word to Bill Magruder. We have to deliver."

"Magruder's second on my list," Voight said. "Durant's made us look bad, and I won't have it. We'll send a message to the whole damn Island. Nobody fucks with the organization."

Nolan was always amused by the euphemism. Everyone on the Island, and the mainland as well, referred to them as the mob. The Texas Rangers, and the occasional reformer, labeled them gangsters and racketeers. Voight and Quinn, who considered themselves businessmen, opted for a more respectable term. Impervious to the irony, they called it the organization.

"Dutch, I think you're right," Quinn said. "What we

need here is an object lesson. One that will impress our associates."

Voight nodded soberly. "Hoods and bootleggers understand only one thing, and that's cracked heads. We'll give them a little reminder not to step out of line."

Nolan shook a cigarette from a pack of Lucky Strikes. He lit up with a gold lighter and exhaled a streamer of smoke. He looked at his bosses.

"Why go halfway?" he said, as though offering a suggestion. "Why not clip Durant and leave him dead on the street? That'll send the message loud and clear."

"No, I think not," Quinn said quickly. "Magruder has a weak stomach when it comes to killing. He was very definite on the point."

"The hell with him," Voight growled. "We're the ones with egg on our faces. Jack's got the right idea."

Quinn shook his head. "Dutch, it just won't do. I agreed to the terms with Magruder, and that's that." His expression was stolid. "We have to stick with the original plan."

Voight was reluctant to concede the point. But he would never compromise his partner's honor, and dismissed it with a wave of his hand. His gaze settled on Nolan.

"We'll do it Ollie's way," he said. "Catch Durant on the street, lots of witnesses, out in the open. Let everybody see what happens when we're crossed."

Nolan took a drag on his cigarette. "How bad do you want him hurt?"

"Stop just short of killing him. Use McGuire and Spadden for the job. They do good work."

"When do you want it done?"

"Tomorrow's Sunday," Quinn said, as though thinking out loud. "No need to get the preachers harping about violence on the Sabbath. Wait till Monday."

"Monday, it is," Nolan said. "Anything else?"

Quinn checked his watch and suddenly jumped to his

feet. "Dutch, will you take it from here? Jolson starts rehearsal with the band at one o'clock. I want to be there."

"Leave it to me and Jack."

A moment of silence slipped past as Quinn hurried out the door. Voight fired up a cigar in a thick wad of smoke. He laughed with satiric humor.

"What a joke. Magruder wants to play dirty, but with rules, for chrissake! By all rights, we ought to ice Durant."

"I'd second the motion, boss. Too bad we've got our hands tied."

"Just make sure you bust his big brass balls. You hear me?"

"I hear you."

A picture of McGuire and Spadden at work flashed through Nolan's mind. He thought Earl Durant would wish he was dead.

The spotlights arced through a sky bright with stars. A warm evening breeze wafted in off the Gulf, the rolling waves of high tide pounding the beach. Far out across the darkened waters a streak of lightning briefly lit the horizon.

The Hollywood Club was chaos in motion. A long line of expensive automobiles dropped off guests from as far away as Colorado and New Mexico. The ladies were clad in evening gowns, dripping with jewels, and the men wore white tie and tails. They were drawn there, in all the glitter and crush, by a once-in-a-lifetime occasion. Tonight was opening night for the man billed as "The World's Greatest Entertainer."

The club was sold out. Tickets were thirty dollars, an outrageous price for the time, and did not include dinner or drinks. Still, the clamor for admission kept the phones jangling and even the lounge by the casino was filled to capacity. The crowd, apart from those few who had been to New York, knew Jolson only by his radio show or his records. They were there to see him in person—to actually see him perform—to say they had attended opening night. The air was electric with excitement.

Quinn was in his element. He was the consummate showman, and never more alive than when he was staging an extravaganza. His vigor was contagious, infecting every employee of the club with pulsing enthusiasm. His charm, cranked up several notches, overwhelmed arriving guests and the raft of newsmen there to cover the event. He dispensed bottles of champagne to the favored few, constantly on the move, hopping from table to table, shaking men's hands and beguiling their ladies. He was everywhere at once, never still.

Dutch Voight, on the other hand, watched it all from the hallway by the lounge. He was still of the very strong opinion that Jolson had picked their pockets; but he begrudged his partner none of the glamour or the accolades from customers and press alike. He and Quinn had fought their way to the top, all too often in the literal sense, and tonight was yet another affirmation that everything on the Island, legitimate or otherwise, revolved around their enterprise. As for Al Jolson, he was pragmatic, perhaps a little philosophical. He knew the casino would have a record night.

The show was to begin at eight o'clock. A few minutes before the hour, Quinn crossed the dance floor and made his way backstage. He found Ben Pollack, the bandleader, talking with some of the musicians off to the side of the bandstand. Pollack, a dandy himself, was quick to admire Quinn's white dinner jacket, lavishly tailored from silk shantung and set off by a scarlet boutonniere. Quinn, who was usually vain to a fault about his appearance, sloughed off the compliment. His interest was fixed on the star of the show.

"Quite a crowd," he said, moving fluidly into a non sequitur. "How'd you think Jolson sounded in rehearsal?"

Pollack laughed. "Ollie, c'mon, stop worrying. You asked me that right after rehearsal."

"I did?" Quinn drew a blank. "What'd you say?"

"What everybody in the band says. He's never been in better voice."

"Yes, that's exactly what I thought. I saw him perform at the Winter Garden in June, when I was in New York. I think he sounded even better in rehearsal."

"I know."

"You do?"

Pollack patted him on the shoulder. "You told me the same thing, almost word for word, this afternoon. Calm down, Ollie. Everything's fine."

"Who's worried? I believe I'll have a word with Al. Wish him luck."

"Careful, Ollie."

"Careful of what?"

"Don't make him as nervous as you are."

"Who's nervous?"

Quinn rushed off backstage. Jolson's dressing room was along a corridor with rooms where band members and entertainers changed, and a lounge where they could relax between acts. A gold star was affixed to one of the doors, and below it, painted in gold script, the words "*Al Jolson*." Quinn rapped lightly on the door.

"C'mon in, it's open."

The dressing room was appointed with a plush couch and an easy chair, a mirrored makeup table, and a tiled bathroom. Jolson was seated before the mirror, putting the finishing touches on his makeup. He glanced at Quinn in the mirror.

"Hey there, kiddo. How's the crowd?"

"Full house," Quinn said. "You packed them in, Al."

"What the hey, I'm the greatest thing since sliced bread! I always pack 'em in."

Jolson dabbed greasepaint on his nose. He was made up in blackface, with a kinky black wig, his mouth and eyes outlined in clown white. To complete the costume, he wore a baggy black suit, a white shirt with a floppy black bow tie, and white gloves. He'd gotten his start in minstrel shows on the burlesque circuit, and later found it drew raves on Broadway. Blackface was his signature act in the world of show business.

"Everything all right?" Quinn asked anxiously. "How are you feeling?"

"Top of the world!"

"Can I get you anything?"

"Not unless you've got a blonde stashed in your pocket."

"No, sorry, Al. No blondes."

"Whatta way to treat a star!"

Jolson was at the height of his fame. He was forty years old, charismatic and full of vigor, completely taken with himself. The fact that Quinn was a mobster, and probably had people killed on the slightest whim, impressed him not in the least. He treated it all with jocular insouciance.

"Well—" Quinn hesitated, uncertain how to make his exit. "You're sure there's nothing I can do?"

"I've got my pipes tuned and I'm truckin' along to the melody. I'll lay 'em in the aisles."

"Well, then, as they say in the theater, break a leg, Al."

Jolson mugged a blackface grin. "Hang on tight, sport. We're off and runnin'!"

Quinn gave a thumbs-up sign of victory. He went out the door, rushing across the backstage area, and waved to Pollack and the orchestra as they moved onto the bandstand. In the nightclub, he table-hopped his way through the crowd, laughing and pumping hands. His jitters on opening night were linked to a superstition begun with the first act ever to play the Hollywood Club. He always stationed himself at the rear of the room.

Maxine was waiting for him. She wore a silver lamé evening gown, with sapphires at her throat, her flaxen hair piled atop her head in a French twist. She took his arm with a dazzling smile.

"Oh, it's just swell, boopsie. What a crowd!"

"I know," Quinn mumbled. "We could've sold out twice over."

She plumped her hair. "Do you like my dress? You haven't said a word all night."

"Yeah, sure, you look swell."

"A girl likes to be told once in awhile, you know. I bought this dress especially for you."

"Maxie, you look like a million dollars. I'm trying to concentrate on the show."

"Oh, stop worrying, sugar. I mean, after all, you've got Al Jolson!"

"Cross your fingers, anyway."

A murmur swept through the audience as the house-lights dimmed. The stage was faintly lit, and as a hush settled over the room, Pollack raised his baton. The orchestra broke out in a rollicking tune.

Jolson bounded onto the stage. A brilliant spotlight followed him as he opened with *Swanee*. His voice was strong, trained to fill the old vaudeville halls, and he worked without a microphone. He pranced around the stage, white eyes rolling merrily behind blackface, belting out the song. His performance was charged with vitality, energized by raw emotion.

The audience roared as the last note faded. Jolson paused at center stage, framed in the spotlight, and boomed his trademark quip. "Folks, you ain't heard nothin' yet!"

The orchestra segued into *Mammy*. Jolson's voice took on a mournful quality and his features seemed wrought with angst as he warbled the lyrics of a son lamenting for his mother. On the last stanza, he dropped to his knees on a polished ramp attached to the front of the stage. He slid down the ramp, halting in the center of the dance floor, arms spread wide, moist eyes glistening in the spotlight. His anguished voice quavered on the final line.

"My . . . my . . . mammmy!"

The crowd went mad. Women wept, men swallowed

their tears, all of them on their feet, applauding wildly. Quinn whooped and shouted, grabbed Maxine in a tight hug. His face blazed with excitement.

Jolson held them enthralled for the next two hours.

Chapter Six

The day was bright, the sky like blue muslin. A forenoon sun peeped from behind mottled clouds scudding westward on a light breeze. Galveston lay almost somnolent on a lazy Monday morning.

Clint Stoner drove down off the causeway. Janice was seated beside him in the canary-yellow Packard, her hair blowing in the wind from the open window. She pointed with little-girl wonder to the bay and tall freighters lining the portside wharves. Seagulls floated on still wings over the shimmering harbor.

The smell of jasmine and magnolia drifted through the window. Broadway was lined with stately palms, and everywhere there was the pink-and-white profusion of oleander blossoms. Janice breathed deeply, filling her lungs, and scooted closer on the seat. She gaily hugged his arm.

"Oh, Clint!" she said excitedly. "I love it. I just love it!"

"The name's Bob," Stoner corrected her. "And you're Olive and we're the Eberlings. Time to get it straight—Olive, honey."

"I will, I will, I promise. I just slipped."

"No room for slips, now. We're here, and we've got to be on our toes every minute. You remember what I told you."

"I know," she pouted prettily. "One mistake will be our last. I won't forget, sweetheart."

"I sure hope not, Olive."

The date was September 10. They had spent a day shopping, and another day rehearsing their cover story with Colonel Garrison at Ranger Headquarters. The drive from Austin had consumed the weekend, and only now, after crossing the causeway, had it become real. They were on the island where gangsters operated with impunity.

Ten minutes later they sighted the Buccaneer Hotel. To them it was palatial, four hundred rooms overlooking Seawall Boulevard and the Gulf. Intelligence reports from Ranger Headquarters indicated that Oliver Quinn, one of the two gangland kingpins, occupied the penthouse. The plan was to make themselves as obvious as possible, attract attention. They were wealthy tourists on a holiday.

Stoner braked the Packard to a halt at the entrance. A bellman rushed out, greeting them effusively, and began unloading their luggage from the trunk. The four suitcases were expensive, glossy leather tooled with their phony initials, and they were dressed for the part. Janice wore a fashionable day dress of the new artificial silk called rayon, a cloche hat, and a strand of pearls. Stoner was attired in a whipcord Western suit, pointy-toed burgundy boots, and a wide-brimmed white Stetson. They looked like money on the hoof.

The clerk at the registration desk snapped to attention. "Good day, sir. Welcome to the Buccaneer."

"I'm Robert Eberling," Stoner said. "I reserved a suite for three weeks."

"Yessir." The clerk riffled through his file cards. "Mr. and Mrs. Eberling of Johnson City. Is that correct?"

"That's me, pardner."

"You certainly picked the right place for a vacation, Mr. Eberling. The Buccaneer's the finest Galveston has to offer."

"Just make sure we've got a suite facing the Gulf. I won't settle for anything else."

"You have a wonderful view," the clerk trilled. "As a matter of fact, you're on the floor reserved for our special guests. You're just down the hall from Al Jolson."

"Al Jolson!" Janice said, round-eyed. "The New York Broadway star?"

"Yes, ma'am, Mrs. Eberling, the very one. He opened Saturday night at the Hollywood Club. That's the top nightspot on the Island."

"Oh, Bob," Janice simpered, batting her eyelashes at Stoner. "I'd so love to see Al Jolson. Wouldn't you, sweetie?"

Stoner hadn't planned to move so fast. He'd thought to establish their credentials as wealthy vacationers, and then gain entrance into the Hollywood Club casino. But any plan was governed by circumstances, and he was nothing if not flexible. He seized on opportunity.

"You heard the little lady," he said to the clerk. "Arrange us a couple tickets for tonight."

"I—" the clerk stammered, caught off guard. "I'll talk with our manager, Mr. Anderson. He handles all requests with the Hollywood Club."

"Yeah, you do that. Tell him I expect some good news pdq. Now, we'd like to see our suite."

"Yessir, Mr. Eberling."

The bellman appeared with their luggage on a cart. He led them to the elevator and escorted them to a suite on the fourth floor. The sitting room was appointed with plush furniture and tall doors leading to a balcony that offered a panoramic view of the Gulf. The bedroom was bright and airy, with broad casement windows looking out over the water. Stoner tipped the bellman twenty dollars.

"Thank you, Mr. Eberling!" the bellman said with a horsey grin. "Let me know if there's anything I can do for you. Anything at all!"

"How about you bring a bottle of bourbon and some ice? The missus and I like a nip now and then."

"Yessir, we keep bonded stock for our guests. I'll be back in a jiffy."

"Thank you kindly."

The bellman went out. Janice inspected the bedroom

clapping her hands with delight, then hurried back into the sitting room. She stepped onto the balcony.

"Oh! Oh!" she cried. "Would you look at that. Isn't it marvelous?"

Stoner joined her on the balcony. The noonday sun was at its zenith, the clouds drifting westward on a warm breeze. Light reflected off the water in sparkling colors, rolling whitecaps cresting swells to the horizon. He put his arm around her waist.

"Not bad, huh?"

"Not bad!" she exclaimed. "I think I'm going to like being rich. Can we stay forever?"

"We'll see how things play out."

Stoner inspected the shoreline. The weekend tourists were gone, and the beach was practically empty. Along the seawall, extending five miles east and west, were amusement piers, dance pavilions, restaurants, and bathhouses with indoor salt-water pools. The beachfront was advertised as the "Boardwalk of Treasure Island," and even in the daytime it was impressive. The five-mile strip was known locally as the Gold Coast.

Two blocks east of the hotel Stoner spotted the Hollywood Club. From his briefing in Austin, the pier with a T-head over the water was distinctive, and easily recognizable. He pointed it out to Janice.

"There's our target," he said. "Home base for Quinn and Voight and all their goons."

Janice shuddered. "I wish we really were here on vacation. Just the thought of them spoils the fun."

"We'll have some fun, and you won't have to act, either. People come from all over to see the sights here."

"Don't worry, sweetheart. I am Olive Eberling, housewife and tourist. I won't forget."

The phone rang. Stoner moved into the sitting room and caught it on the third ring. "Bob Eberling here."

"Mr. Eberling, this is Charles Anderson, manager of the Buccaneer. I trust your suite is satisfactory?"

"I think we'll be real comfortable, Mr. Anderson. Have you got those Al Jolson tickets for me?"

"No, sir, I'm afraid not," Anderson said apologetically. "The Jolson show has been sold out for months. I'm really very sorry."

"How long is Jolson appearing here?"

"Only this week. I understand his engagement has been extended through Saturday night."

"Your man at the front desk the same as said you've got pull with this Hollywood Club. Is that so or not?"

"Well, yes and no," Anderson said in a defensive tone. "I usually have a direct line to the club. But to be perfectly honest, I couldn't get my own mother a ticket. Not at this late date."

"I'm disappointed in you," Stoner said in a gruff voice. "We're here for three weeks and I expected better treatment. The little woman's gonna be mighty upset."

"Please extend my most sincere apologies to Mrs. Eberling. I'll make it up in some way during your stay with us."

"In Blanco County, a man's word is his bond. I'll hold you to it, pardner."

"Feel free to call on me at any time, Mr. Eberling."

Stoner hung up and turned to Janice. "Looks like we won't be seeing Al Jolson. The show's sold out."

"Oh, rats!" she said petulantly. "I was counting on it!"

"Well, in a way, it worked out to our advantage. The hotel manager owes me one."

"Owes you one what?"

Stoner grinned. "He's gonna get us into that casino."

The Hollywood Club was all but deserted. Apart from a cleaning crew, working to restore the damages from a weekend of revelry, there was hardly anyone on the premises. Monday mornings were devoted to preparing for the week ahead.

Dutch Voight was seated in his office at the rear of

the casino. Earlier, he'd emptied a safe secreted behind a painting on the wall. The desk was piled high with stacks of cash, the proceeds from the casino and the nightclub for the previous week. He methodically counted the bills.

Cuddles, the parrot, watched sleepily from his perch on the stand. He was Quinn's special bird, grudgingly tolerated by others, and no one knew it better than Cuddles himself. In the way of wild things held captive, he sensed who liked him and who didn't, and when it was best to keep his silence. He never talked when he was alone in the office with Voight.

Today, Voight wasn't in a talking mood anyway. His full concentration was on the task at hand, and he would have brooked no distractions. All of the business at the club, both the casino and the nightclub, was transacted in cash. After counting the week's take, he began skimming fifty percent off the top. Later, an accountant who subscribed to larceny, would dummy a set of books for the government. Voight's own entries were made in a ledger kept in the safe.

The books were cooked to avoid what Voight considered an onerous injustice. In 1913, with passage of the Sixteenth Amendment, Congress had legislated personal income taxes. During the World War, Congress had also enacted an excess profits tax on corporations, which had yet to be repealed. Gulf Enterprises was owned wholly by Voight and Quinn, and the double hit on taxes would have cost them dearly. They were of the opinion that the federal government was run by stick-up artists.

A few minutes after twelve, Voight finished his labors. He made a final entry in his personal ledger and returned it to the safe. From the stacks of cash on the desk, he placed thirty thousand in the safe and thirty thousand in his briefcase. He rarely carried a gun, but Mondays were the exception; he stuck a Colt .38 snub-nose in the waistband of his trousers. He closed and locked the safe, moving the painting back into position, and collected his briefcase. Cuddles, still silent, watched as he went out the door.

Elmer Spadden was waiting in the casino. He wasn't privy to what went on in the office every Monday morning; but he nonetheless knew that the briefcase was stuffed with cash. His sole purpose was to bodyguard the man who paid him liberally and treated him with the respect due someone willing to step into the path of flying bullets. Not that anyone had tried to bump off his boss, or Ollie Quinn, in almost five years. The last time it happened, he and Turk McGuire had killed three gunsels in a shootout in the bookmaking parlor at the Turf Club. The mainland gangs afterward stayed clear of Galveston island.

Outside the club, Spadden took the wheel of Voight's three-year-old Studebaker. Voight was a man of simple tastes, and he never envied Quinn his flashy Cadillac and ostentatious life-style. In many ways, Voight was a prude, and despite the ready availability of women in their business, he'd never considered taking a mistress. He admired his partner's taste in women, but always from afar. He thought one Don Juan in the organization was enough.

Business affairs were another matter entirely. Though he often grumbled about the cost, he deferred to Quinn when it came to contracting acts for the nightclub. To himself, if to no one else, he admitted that Quinn had the flair, and a certain genius, for show business. The nightclub was the engine that generated customers for the casino, and the weekend had convinced him Jolson was the greatest draw ever. He sulked about the price—calling $2,000 extortion—but he accepted Quinn's judgment. Jolson would be held over for another Saturday night.

Quinn was waiting for him at the Turf Club. Their Monday morning routine was by now standard practice, and never varied. Voight tallied the take from the Hollywood Club, and Quinn tabulated the haul from their other activities. The revenue from rumrunning, the bookmaking operation, and payoffs from speakeasies, gaming dives and whorehouses was always substantial. For tax purposes, all of the revenue was accounted as income from the Turf Club. Then fifty percent was skimmed off the top.

"We had a good week," Quinn said, indicating stacks of cash on the desk. "There's twenty-six thousand from the Turf Club. I took off another twelve from the restaurants and the amusement pier."

Voight opened his briefcase. "Some weeks are better than others. I've got thirty here."

"Goes to show you," Quinn said with a wry smile. "Didn't I tell you Jolson was worth every nickel?"

"I still say he's in the wrong business. The bastard's a born heist man."

"You're just burned he won't drop any at the tables. Count your blessings, my friend."

Voight placed the cash from the desk in his briefcase. "I'm running late. I have to get to the bank."

"Give my best to Sherm," Quinn said. "Tell him we'll have his problem solved tonight."

"Ollie, I'd lay eight to five that's the first thing he asks me."

In the hallway, Voight found Jack Nolan talking with McGuire and Spadden. He nodded to them, his expression impassive. "You boys set for tonight?"

Nolan grinned. "Got it all worked out. Nothing to worry about, boss."

"I never worry." Voight looked at Spadden. "Let's walk over to the bank."

Ten minutes later they entered the Galveston City Bank. Spadden waited in the reception area while a secretary buzzed Voight into Sherm Magruder's office. The bank was pivotal to William Magruder's myriad financial affairs, and he had appointed his son to the position of president. Sherm offered Voight a chair.

"Good afternoon, Dutch," he said pleasantly. "You're regular as clockwork. It must be Monday."

"Before you ask," Voight said, "we haven't forgotten about that Durant fellow. He'll get his tonight."

"I'll pass that along to my father. We're most appreciative of your assistance in this matter."

"Glad to lend a hand."

Voight unsnapped the clasps on his briefcase. He neatly arranged the stacks of cash on the desk. "The count's right. Sixty-eight thousand."

"You've enjoyed an excellent week. Would you like the usual?"

"Stick with a winner, that's my motto."

Sherm personally made out certificates for bearer bonds. The bonds were virtually untraceable, and redeemable at any bank. For those in the rackets, it was a foolproof method of hiding money from government tax agents. The certificates were split evenly between Edward S. Voight and Oliver J. Quinn.

There was a certain quid pro quo to the arrangement. Quinn and Voight worked closely with the Magruders and the Seagraves in controlling the political apparatus of Galveston County. Of equal import, the gambling and vice operation attracted tourists, which benefited all the city's businesses and fueled a stable economy. During 1921, when the entire country suffered an economic depression, Galveston enjoyed boom times and full employment. The mob was considered a valuable asset by the old guard of the Island.

The Magruders could have survived and thrived without the mob. The demand for cotton in Europe was such that their Galveston Cotton Exchange represented a veritable money tree. In turn, millions of dollars flowed through the Galveston City Bank from financial institutions in England, France, Germany, and other European countries. But gambling and vice were the lubricants that greased the wheels of the Island's economy, as well as the city and county governments. The Magruders were strong advocates of free enterprise, legal or otherwise.

"Service is our byword," Sherm said amiably. "And

thanks again for arranging that personal matter. We won't forget a favor."

"Consider it our treat, Sherm. What are friends for?"

Voight emerged from the bank with Spadden at his side. He wondered yet again why the Magruders were so intent on buying People's Bank & Trust. Then, just as quickly, he decided it didn't matter.

Any banker he'd ever met was a pirate at heart.

The evening was balmy. A full moon played hide-and-seek high above silvery clouds drifting on a faint breeze. The town was awash in scampering moonglow.

Durant walked along the Strand. Shops and stores were closed for the night, and the street was all but deserted. His hands were in his pockets, his expression thoughtful as he moved along at a measured stride. He occasionally glanced at the displays in store windows, but his mind was elsewhere. He felt himself at a dead end.

All day he'd been on the phone calling bankers. His list had now dwindled to the point that he had exhausted every prospective buyer between Galveston and Houston. The response, as it had been last week, was polite but firm, no interest whatever. William Magruder, even when his name wasn't mentioned, nonetheless pervaded every conversation. He was a specter from hell, all but demonized, in the world of banking.

The next step was to start trying bankers in Houston, perhaps Austin or Dallas. Ira Aldridge gave scant encouragement on that score, noting that Magruder's stranglehold on Galveston was notorious throughout all of Texas. Durant recalled Magruder saying he wouldn't find a buyer between Galveston and Chicago, and after today, he began to think it might be true. He was, for all practical purposes, stymied.

Earlier, he'd had dinner at a café on Mechanic Street. The meat loaf and vegetables, at any other time, would have rated kudos and compliments. But he had picked at his food, his appetite gone, lost in troubled thought. For a moment, he'd even considered going hat in hand to Magruder and striking the best deal possible. Then, angered by the prospect of his own humiliation, he had brushed the idea aside. He wouldn't grovel before any man.

The thing that frustrated him most was being trapped in Galveston. His original plan had been a night or two on the Island, where he would settle his uncle's estate and quickly be on his way. He had a spot waiting in Tom Mix's next moving picture, and he'd planned to return to Hollywood long before now. He wouldn't be surprised but what Mix had hired another stuntman, for Western films were shot on a tight schedule and stuntmen were plentiful. He seriously doubted a phone call to Mix would change things. Not until he was definite on leaving Galveston.

After a forgettable dinner, he decided to go for a walk. He'd been closeted in the office all day, and he thought the exercise might clear his head. He needed a new strategy, some new plan to unload the bank and put him on the road back to Los Angeles. So far no solution had presented itself, and he was surprised to find himself at the end of the Strand, across from the Santa Fe depot. He turned south on Twenty-fifth Street, thinking he would walk over to Broadway and take the long way back to his hotel. The moon was out and he had nowhere else to go, so why not? He had all night.

The intersection of Twenty-fifth and Broadway was the most historic spot in Galveston. As he approached the corner, he saw the Heroes Monument, a towering marble structure with the bronze statue of Lady Victory at the top. He recalled, from a visit before the war, that his uncle had pointed it out, explaining that it had been erected to commemorate the victory over Mexico, and the independence of Texas. He paused at the base of the monument and read the weathered plaque affixed to the marble pillar. He could almost hear the pride in his uncle's voice those many years ago.

Early in 1836, Santa Anna's army overran the Alamo

and swept unchecked across Texas. David Burnet, president of the Republic, retreated with his staff to Galveston and set up a temporary capitol. Two days later, on April 21, General Sam Houston and his volunteer army turned and attacked the Mexican forces on the San Jacinto River. The attack became a rout, lasting only eighteen minutes, with the Mexican troops in full retreat and Santa Anna captured. The battle took place some forty miles north of Galveston, and the Heroes Monument was built to honor the volunteers who brought independence to Texas. The Lady of Victory stood looking at the distant San Jacinto battlegrounds.

Tourists were drawn to the monument. Several couples, out for a stroll under a full moon, paused to stare up at the bronze Lady. The intersection was also a major artery to the Island's residential district, and heavily traveled day or night. Automobiles, as well as passersby on foot, went by in a steady stream. Durant was still thinking of his uncle as he moved through the group of sightseers gathered at the base of the memorial. He paused on the sidewalk to let another couple join the small crowd.

A car swerved to a stop at the curb. Durant turned onto Broadway as the doors slammed and he saw Jack Nolan standing beside a Buick sedan. He would later learn that the two men with Nolan were Turk McGuire and Elmer Spadden. But for now, what his mind registered was two strong-arm thugs, built for rough work. The men started toward him as Nolan lit a cigarette and leaned against the front fender of the Buick. His first instinct was to run, but he knew he'd never get away. They could easily chase him down with the car.

"Hey, tough guy," Nolan called out with a jocular smile. "You should've taken my advice."

McGuire and Spadden spread out. Durant immediately recognized the oldest trick in street fighting. They intended to flank him from either side, and force him to fight two fights at the same time. He backed away, aware that his only chance was to stay on the move and somehow keep them separated. McGuire gave him an evil grin, motioning to Spadden, and they crowded him toward the monument. Some of the men in the crowd of sightseers sensed what was happening, and pulled their women aside. The others quickly caught on, scattering into the street.

Durant saw a police car pull to the curb on Twenty-fifth Street. Two cops stepped out of the car, one of them with the chevrons of sergeant on his sleeves. For an instant, Durant thought the cavalry had arrived just in the nick of time. Then, with a sickening sensation in the pit of his stomach, he saw the sergeant flip Nolan a salute and stand back to watch the fight. He realized there would be no rescue tonight.

McGuire moved swiftly for a man of such enormous bulk. He feinted with a left jab and launched a whistling overhand right. Durant was no rookie to barroom brawls and he was fast on his feet. He slipped beneath the blow and delivered a splintering left-right combination. McGuire's lip spurted blood and a look of surprise came over his face. Before Durant could follow through, Spadden quickly stepped in from the other side and punched him in the kidney. His legs buckled as though whacked by a sledgehammer.

A woman screamed as the men jumped him in a flurry of fists. He tried to fight back, but the blows rained down in a drumming tattoo. McGuire landed a right to the jaw, followed by a crackling left hook. Spadden struck him low in the gut, then straightened him up with a sharp uppercut. The men were professionals, versed in their work, and they beat him to the ground at the base of the monument. McGuire finished it with a thudding kick to the ribs.

Jack Nolan walked forward to inspect their handiwork. He squatted down, exhaling smoke from his cigarette, and examined the wreckage of Durant's face. He smiled a lazy smile.

"Get smart and get out," he said. "You don't want there to be a next time."

Durant was barely conscious. A rivulet of blood leaked down into his eyes and he watched through a reddish mist as they walked back to the Buick. What seemed an eternity later, the car doors slammed and they drove off. The police sergeant ambled across the street. He clucked his tongue with a tsk-tsk sound.

"How you feelin', laddie?"

"Not so . . . good," Durant wheezed.

"Well, all the same, I'm placin' you under arrest."

"Me . . . what for?"

"Disturbing the peace and disorderly conduct. Shame on you."

The cops took him to the hospital to get stitched up. Then they took him to jail.

Chapter Seven

The municipal court was located on the ground floor of City Hall. A jailer brought Durant from the lockup shortly before nine the next morning. Walter Kline, his uncle's attorney, was seated at the defense table.

Durant looked like he'd been run over by a train. His bottom lip was crusted with blood, there were catgut stitches lacing his eyebrow, and his left eye was a splotchy rosette of purple and black. He was unshaven and unkempt, his suit wrinkled and dark stubble covering his jawline. His one good eye burned with anger.

The jailer removed his handcuffs and walked away. Kline rose from his chair, a look of concern on his face, and shook hands with Durant. "I tried to get you released last night," he said. "After you called, I spoke with Judge Hagan by phone. He refused to set bail."

"Doesn't surprise me," Durant said brusquely. "This whole town's as crooked as a barrel of snakes. They intended all along for me to spend the night in jail."

"Who is 'they'?"

"Magruder and his mob buddies."

"I believe you'd better give me all the details."

Until last night, when he was allowed one phone call, Durant hadn't spoken with the lawyer since he arrived in Galveston. He proceeded to brief Kline on everything that had happened, including his meeting with William Magruder and the subsequent threat by the mob. He concluded with an account of last night's beating and Jack Nolan's warning to sell the bank and leave town. He gingerly touched the stitches on his brow.

"Nolan and his hooligans made their point. I feel like I tangled with a wildcat."

"I daresay you do." Kline hesitated, considering a moment. "You've incurred some powerful enemies in a short time. I'm frankly amazed Magruder's so . . . involved . . . with racketeers."

"I'll think about that once I'm out of jail. How do I get these charges dismissed?"

"I seriously doubt you will."

"How's that?"

"Whoever is behind this—Magruder or the mob—has connections here at City Hall. Your arrest was clearly intended to underscore their message."

"To hell with that!" Durant snapped. "I didn't start that fight. It was a setup."

"Let me offer some good advice," Kline said. "Disturbing the peace is a misdemeanor. Usually a fifty-dollar fine . . ."

"I won't pay it. I'm the one that took a beating."

"Consider the alternative. If you insist on a full-blown hearing, there's no question you'll be convicted. Who's to testify you weren't the culprit? Do you have any witnesses?"

Durant's mouth set in a tight line. "You're saying I can't win, right?"

"You will most surely lose," Kline told him. "And the sentence will be thirty days on the county road gang. I strongly urge you to plead guilty."

"What a crock! The whole Goddamn thing's been rigged."

"Unfortunately, that appears to be the case."

Court convened at nine sharp, Judge Wallace Hagan presiding. Sergeant Michael O'Rielly, the beefy Irishman who had arrested Durant, was called to the stand. He told a fanciful tale of how Durant had instigated an altercation with two tourists, who subsequently fled the scene and the Island. He testified he'd witnessed the fracas from start to finish.

Durant entered a tight-lipped plea of guilty. Walter Kline then delivered an eloquent argument for leniency. He explained that his client was a visitor to Galveston, there to settle his uncle's estate, and anxious to be on his way. Judge Hagan peered down from the bench, as though weighing the sentence for an axe murderer. He finally banged his gavel and ordered Durant to pay a fine of fifty dollars. The court clerk accepted the cash with a sly smirk.

Afterward, outside City Hall, Kline assured the younger man that he'd made a wise decision. Durant thanked him for his services, shook hands, and then caught a cab back to his hotel. In his room, he discarded his soiled clothes and took a long, steamy shower. When he shaved, he hardly recognized himself in the mirror, and he swore softly under his breath. Dressed in a fresh suit, he emerged from the hotel a few minutes after ten. He walked toward the Strand.

Everyone in the bank stared at him. Catherine gasped, unable to take her eyes off his face, and Aldridge began peppering him with questions. They followed him into his office where he told the story again, including his experience in municipal court. He appeared unnaturally calm for someone who had suffered a beating and been subjected to a night in jail. The black eye and the ragged line of stitches across his brow made it all the more unusual. Aldridge studied him with a look of weary regret.

"Earl, it's time to quit," he said. "These men are dangerous, and things will only go from bad to worse. It's time for you to get out."

Durant stared at him. "Get out?"

"I never thought I'd hear myself say this. But under the circumstances, I think you should sell the bank to Magruder. You have no choice."

"Mr. Aldridge is right," Catherine said in a small voice. "You can't fight those gangsters by yourself. You're just one man."

"I had a lot of time to stew on things last night.

There's nothing to do but think when you're locked in a jail cell. I've decided to stick around."

"You're angry," Aldridge said, "and that's perfectly understandable. But you mustn't let anger cloud your judgment. These men could kill you."

"Ira, it's not debatable." Durant's gaze was steady. "How long will it take you to teach me the banking business?"

"Listen to this madness! Do you honestly believe Magruder will turn back when he's gone so far? Do you, after last night?"

"I plan to have a talk with Magruder."

"Talk?" Aldridge said incredulously. "Talk about what?"

"How to take your lumps and like it."

Some twenty minutes later Durant entered the Magruder Building. The elevator operator gave him a strange look, darting glances at his battered features as they rode to the tenth floor. In the reception room, he walked past the secretary. She hurried around her desk.

"Just a moment, sir!" she cried, rushing after him. "Do you have an appointment?"

"Mr. Magruder is expecting me."

Durant barged into the office. Magruder was seated at his ebony desk, slowly working through the morning's correspondence. He peered across the room with a startled expression. His secretary hesitated in the doorway.

"I tried to stop him, Mr. Magruder. He just—"

"Quite all right, Ellen," Magruder said with a dismissive wave. "Please close the door, and hold my calls."

Durant halted before the desk. Magruder examined him with clinical detachment. "You appear to have met with an accident, Mr. Durant. How very unfortunate."

"Magruder, I'm staying in Galveston. I'm here to tell you to call off your dogs."

"I'm sure I don't know what you're talking about."

"Don't waste my time with crapola," Durant said

bluntly. "Your gangster pals did their best and it backfired on you. I officially took over the bank this morning."

"How impressive," Magruder said in a mocking tone. "You're quite the determined young man, aren't you?"

"Determined enough to take you over the hurdles. And like it or lump it, you'd better get used to it. I'm not going away."

Magruder, despite his blasé manner, was concerned. Things weren't working the way he'd planned, and he felt a stab of anxiety about the land owned by People's Bank & Trust. Without it, he would never complete his new resort hotel. He lifted a hand in a conciliatory gesture.

"Let's both reconsider," he said in an avuncular voice. "Your life's in Hollywood, not here on Galveston Island. So I'll make it easy to overlook our little misunderstanding. I'll pay the hundred thousand you originally asked."

"Too late," Durant said. "The bank's not for sale."

"Never make rash decisions, Mr. Durant. Haste inevitably leads to regret."

"That sounds like more of your threats."

"Nothing so crass."

"Do yourself a favor," Durant said with a level stare. "Live and let live, or you're the one that'll regret it."

"Are you threatening me now?"

"Definitely."

Durant walked out of the office. Magruder's features flushed to the hairline, and he took a moment to collect himself. He'd been threatened once or twice in his life, but never before by anyone of the lower classes. Particularly a motion picture stuntman. His eyes hooded with outrage.

He put in a call to Ollie Quinn.

The meeting began at two that afternoon. George Seagrave and his son, John, arrived shortly before Quinn and Voight. Magruder, with Sherm in attendance, welcomed them to his office. The men gathered there were the movers and shakers of Galveston. Theirs was an alliance of the underworld with civic leaders, and everyone benefited equally. The businessmen never socialized with the mobsters, and that was mutually acceptable. Their single link was the future of the Island.

Politics was the glue that tightly bound their alliance. Ostensibly, the Magruders were the leaders of the Independent Party and the Seagraves were the chiefs of the City Party. In actual fact, they met behind closed doors with their underworld partners and decided the slate of candidates for every election. Quinn and Voight, apart from bribing city and county officials for their own purposes, delivered the swing vote. The sporting crowd was a major voting bloc on the Island.

Galveston was made for crooked politics. The city itself represented eighty percent of the population in Galveston County, far outweighing the towns scattered along the southern mainland. The city was governed by a five-member commission, which included the mayor, the police chief, the tax collector, the waterworks superintendent, and the head of public improvements. Like the county officials in similar posts, they were all elected by popular vote. They owed their jobs to the small coterie of men gathered in Magruder's office.

The meeting today had been set a week ago. The men were there not to discuss politics, but rather civic development. A municipal pleasure pier was being planned by the city, for construction at Twenty-fifth Street and Seawall Boulevard. The pier was to include a dance pavilion, shops and restaurants, and an outdoor amphitheater for public events. Investors were needed for the bond issue to cover construction costs, and each of the men had committed to raising funds. George Seagrave was the first to deliver an update.

"I'm pleased to report," he said in an expansive voice, "we have pledges for over a hundred thousand dollars. We'll easily double that in the weeks ahead."

Seagrave was a fleshy man, with curly gray hair and

a determined jaw. John, his son, was a Princeton graduate
and very much a chip off the old block. The family mansion was at Twenty-ninth and Broadway, not far from the
Magruder mansion, in the heart of an enclave for the
city's aristocracy. Seagrave's other son, Frank, was a
playboy who spent his time drunkenly wandering about
Europe. His name was never mentioned in polite company.

"George, my heartiest congratulations," Magruder
said. "You and John have made a splendid contribution
to this project. Absolutely splendid."

Seagrave preened. "We all have to do our share, Bill.
As President Coolidge is fond of saying, the business of
America is business." He paused, a quizzical birdlike expression on his face. "May I inquire how your efforts are
going?"

"Gentlemen, I couldn't be more pleased. Sherm has
spearheaded our campaign, and we expect to bring in a
quarter million, perhaps more. High goals inevitably lead
to high achievement."

Magruder basked in his own admiration a moment.
Then, like a rajah of financiers, he looked at Quinn. "Ollie, what have you and Dutch to report?"

"We've done pretty well, Bill."

"Any specific number as yet?"

Quinn plucked a check from inside his suit jacket.
"We're happy to present a cashier's check for two hundred and ten thousand. Courtesy of Gulf Enterprises."

Seagrave cocked his head like he had a flea in his
ear. "All of that from you and Dutch? From your company?"

"Well, not all," Quinn said with a wry smile. "We
solicited donations from our business associates. They
were generous in their support."

Quinn and Voight believed public relations was a
necessary business expense for the rackets. They were co-
founders of the Galveston Beach Association, sponsors of
a yearly Christmas party for underprivileged children, and

ready contributors to any charity's fund-raising efforts. Their generosity bought good will throughout the community.

"Ollie, Dutch," Magruder said with approval. "Allow me to commend you for your civic spirit."

Seagrave concurred. "You've set the pace for the rest of us. Very well done, indeed."

"Speaking of pace," Magruder added. "We absolutely must reach our goal by the middle of November. You know how Christmas diverts people onto personal affairs."

Construction on the Pleasure Pier was scheduled to begin in early 1927. Their objective was to have the million-dollar bond issue fully subscribed before the end of the year. They fell to discussing other avenues of raising funds, and agreed to redouble their efforts in the month ahead. The meeting broke up a few minutes before three.

Magruder asked Quinn and Voight to stay behind. He alluded in vague terms to a matter of personal business. Seagrave understood, for he occasionally did business with the mobsters himself. Just last year they had arranged a squad of goons to rout union organizers at one of his sugar mills. A round of handshakes sent the Seagraves on their way.

Magruder's demeanor changed when the door closed. His eyes narrowed and his voice took on a rasping quality. "I want the matter of Earl Durant settled. You gave me your word on this, Ollie."

Quinn nodded. "We tried persuasion and it didn't work. Our men tell us Durant's a tough cookie."

"I won't have him charging into my office and issuing threats. I want it ended."

"Let's be plain," Voight interjected. "The sure way to end it is to put him on ice. You understand what I'm saying?"

"Yes. . . ."

"No mincing words," Voight persisted. "You want him knocked off. Right?"

"I—" Magruder exchanged an uneasy look with Sherm. "I see no other way."

Voight stood. "Don't worry about a thing. We'll handle it."

"How will . . . ?"

"You don't want to know. Read about it in the papers."

"Yes, of course."

Quinn and Voight managed to suppress smiles. The situation now put Magruder even more in their debt, a chip to cash at a later time. Turk McGuire was waiting outside with the Cadillac, and drove them from the Magruder Building to the Turf Club. They called Nolan into the office.

"The ante's been upped," Voight said. "We got the go-ahead to dust off Durant."

"Huh!" Nolan looked surprised. "What happened?"

"Damn fool braced Magruder this morning. Told him to back off or he'd kill him."

"Some guys have got more balls than brains. You want to take him for a swim?"

"No," Voight said sternly. "The bastard keeps making us look bad and we've got a reputation to uphold. Do it so everybody gets the picture."

"But with caution," Quinn amended. "Catch him alone somewhere and make it look like a robbery. We don't need witnesses who could tie you to the job."

"Good idea," Voight agreed. "Wait a few days till he's forgot about the beating. Take him when his guard's down."

"Few days is better anyway," Nolan said. "That'll give me time to set it up and pick the right spot. Want me to use Elmer and Turk again?"

"Might as well," Voight said. "Let 'em finish what they started."

"I'll get rolling on it right away."

Nolan went out to talk with Spadden and McGuire. He thought it was dumb of Durant not to have taken the warning and skipped town. Some men never got the message until they were dead.

Too bad.

Stoner and Janice stepped out of the elevator. They moved through the lobby, and Stoner waved to Charles Anderson, the Buccaneer manager, who was talking with the desk clerk. Their canary-yellow Packard was waiting in front of the hotel.

Today was their day to play tourists. Janice wore a fetching little day dress, casual yet expensive. The patterned fabric clung to her svelte curves, modestly revealing her figure. But she also wore sensible walking shoes, an unadorned hat, and a muted blue scarf fluttering at her throat. She looked very much the wife of a wealthy Blanco County rancher.

"Oh, Bobby, honey!" she said with a wink as she crawled into the car. "What a wonderful day for sightseeing. Where are we going first?"

Stoner hooked the car into gear. "How about Jean Lafitte?"

"The pirate?"

"Ol' Jean flew the Jolly Roger over these very waters."

"I love it!" she squealed. "A real live pirate?"

"Not just exactly, Olive," Stoner said as he pulled away from the hotel. "Lafitte joined all his buddies in pirate heaven."

"Do pirates really go to heaven?"

"I think maybe this one did."

The hotel had provided a packet of tourist information. As they drove along Seawall Boulevard, Janice called out points of interest. The Island's original settlers were cannibals, members of the Karankawa tribe. They ate other Indians because they believed an enemy's courage was absorbed by devouring choice parts. The first white men on the Island were Spanish Conquistadors, led by Cabeza de Vaca. The expedition landed in 1528.

"All the Indians disappeared," Janice said, studying the tour booklet. "I wonder if the Spaniards ate them?"

Stoner smiled. "I think the church frowned on cannibalism."

"Well, where did they go, then?"

"Guess we'll never know."

Their first stop was where Fifteenth Street joined the coastline. Jean Lafitte's headquarters, La Mansion Rouge, was still visible in ruins maintained by the historical society. A privateer, Lafitte was nonetheless an American hero, having aided General Andrew Jackson during the War of 1812 at the Battle of New Orleans. By 1817, Lafitte ruled Galveston Island, occupying it with his band of buccaneers and claiming it as his personal kingdom. He set about building a colony.

The town was called Campeachy. There were houses and taverns, a dockyard at the edge of the bay and a major arsenal. Pirates who sailed into port were forced to abide by Lafitte's court of admiralty, which was a one-man court with no appeal. The town prospered, at its peak reaching a population of nearly two thousand, all within four years. Then, in 1821, the American and Spanish governments threatened war against Lafitte's sanctuary for privateers. The time had come to move on.

Lafitte put the torch to Campeachy. After burning it to the ground, he boarded his flagship, the *Jupiter*, and sailed off into the Gulf. History failed to record his end, though it was rumored he died at sea, off the coast of Yucatán. Jean Lafitte, ever the enigma, was mysterious even in death.

"Isn't that strange?" Janice said, staring at the ruins of the old fort. "He just sailed away and was never heard from again. What a sad ending."

"The man was a pirate," Stoner said. "Did you expect a happy ending?"

"Well, he wasn't all bad! I mean, except for him, there might not even be a Galveston."

"One thing's for sure."

"What?"

"Lafitte was better than the thugs that run this place today. They make him look like Little Orphan Annie."

"Don't remind me."

The tour guide took them north from the beach. A year after Lafitte sailed away, Texas settlers rebuilt what would become the Port of Galveston. During the Texas Revolution, the Island briefly served as the capital, and later, in the Civil War, it was captured by Union troops only to be recaptured by the Confederates. From that time until the present, Galveston was one of the major deep-water harbors in the world. Millions of dollars in tonnage went through the port every day.

Late that afternoon Stoner and Janice stopped for coffee at a café overlooking the harbor. Along Pier 20, the small boats of the Mosquito Fleet were tying up at the docks. The crews, descendants of Portuguese and Italian fishermen, began unloading their harvest of shrimp and oysters. Towering above them at the wharves were steamships, oceangoing tankers, and freighters, many flying the flags of distant nations. Seagulls kept winged sentinel over the tiny shrimp boats.

The scene was one of bustling industry, but somehow tranquil. Stoner sipped his coffee, watching with interest as the Mosquito Fleet unloaded their catch for the day. There was a strangeness to it, for during his years with the Rangers, he'd never been assigned to the coast. Yet he found it oddly peaceful, the ships, big and small, in harmony with the flat, sunlit waters of the bay. He thought it was a world apart from the nightspots on the other side of the Island.

"Penny for your thoughts," Janice said. "You look like you're a thousand miles away."

Stoner pointed to the wharves. "I was wondering what those fishermen think about the mobsters who run this town. Do they approve of the rackets, or do they just not care?"

"Aren't you the big philosopher today? I can tell you the answer."

"Go ahead."

"They don't care," Janice said with a shrug. "They're tickled pink to make a few bucks and spend the evening at their friendly speakeasy. Nobody cares, here or anywhere else."

Stoner looked at her. "You sound a little jaded."

"Listen to who's talking," she said in a teasing lilt. "You sound like a Boy Scout."

"Me?"

"Yes, precious, you. I love you to pieces, but you're treating this like a holy quest of some sort."

Stoner glanced over his shoulder. The café was almost empty, and their waitress was off somewhere in the kitchen. He lowered his voice anyway.

"I've been sent here to do a job nobody else could pull off. Lots of people are depending on me, and I mean to deliver the bacon. I thought you understood all this."

"Of course I do," she said simply. "Why else would I risk life and limb?"

"You just seemed a little lukewarm all of a sudden."

"Are you kidding? I'm so excited I still get goosebumps. I love this undercover stuff."

Stoner laughed. "All you need's a badge."

"Now that you mention it," she said, her eyes bright. "How do we get into that casino? When do we really start work?"

"We start tonight and we're gonna play it foxy. I have to establish myself as a high roller."

"What does that mean, play it foxy?"

"A loser with money to burn."

Early that evening they drove to the Garden Club, three blocks north of Seawall Boulevard. The club was an octagonal structure with flamboyant columns, stained-glass windows, and a whimsical cupola. There was dining and dancing, and at the rear of the building, a poker room with slot machines along the walls. The buy-in at the high-stakes poker table was a thousand dollars.

Janice developed an instant love affair with the nickel slots. Stoner gave her fifty dollars from the five-thousand-dollar bankroll he'd been provided by Colonel Garrison. His instructions were to use the bankroll however he saw fit to gain entry into the Hollywood Club casino. After leaving Janice with her one-armed bandit, he took a seat in the high-stakes poker game. He made a point of casually dropping his name to the house dealer.

Stoner was no novice to poker. Throughout the evening he caught several hands he knew were certain winners. Yet he was there to lose, and however much it galled him, he folded his cards. Other times, holding a poor hand, he attempted a weak bluff and donated to the pot. He looked like an amateur trying to play with the big boys.

By midnight, he'd lost five hundred and quit the game. The manager of the poker room, solicitous and smooth, lamented with him on his streak of bad luck. His here-today-gone-tomorrow attitude was that of a man who believed luck really had something to do with poker.

He was marked as a pigeon.

Chapter Eight

Arthur Scarett drove across the causeway on Friday morning. The prohibition agent was looking forward to a long relaxing weekend with his family. As head of the Houston office, he had the authority to approve leave for all agents. He'd given himself time off.

Ruby Scarett was a plain dumpling of a woman. On the drive down from Houston, she had acted as referee for their two boys, who were in the backseat. The boys were nine and ten, young hellions who enjoyed nothing quite so much as pounding the whey out of each other. She was exhausted even before her holiday began.

For his part, Scarett ignored the commotion. He was content to leave discipline to his wife, who, he was convinced, had been a drill sergeant in a previous incarnation. His mind was focused instead on sandy beaches and crystalline skies, which were a harbinger of fair weather and sunshine. He planned to spend the weekend working on his tan.

Scarett hoped to avoid running into Jack Nolan. He was on the take, turning a blind eye to the rumrunning operation, but nonetheless prudent. He could have called Nolan and been comped to hotel accommodations, top restaurants, and probably tickets to the Al Jolson show. But he saw no reason to risk exposure by openly associating with gangsters. He figured the ten thousand a month payoff was ample reward.

The Beach Hotel was located at Twentieth Street and Seawall Boulevard. A rambling five-story structure, the hotel was distinguished by its baronial rotunda, marble floors, and a grand stairway sweeping upwards from the lobby. Ruby held the boys in an iron grip while Scarett checked in at the front desk. A bellman, wary of the struggle between mother and sons, escorted them to the elevator.

Their suite was on the fifth floor. Scarett felt a man of his means could afford to splurge, and he'd reserved the best the hotel had to offer. The sitting room was bright and airy, with modernistic furnishings and broad windows that afforded a spectacular view of the Gulf. There were two bedrooms, each with its own bathroom, which ensured Ruby privacy if not security. She thought the boys would have the place wrecked before the weekend was out.

The bellman fled the suite as though escaping a war zone. Scarett, who could be a taskmaster when the occasion demanded, rapped out a command. "Let's have some *quiet!*"

The boys, Fred and Hank, snapped to attention. Their mother was tough as nails, but their father, once he got going, was hell on wheels. They waited like good little soldiers for whatever came next.

"Here's the score," Scarett said. "You break anything in this suite and I'll blister your backsides. Got it?"

"Yes, Pa," the boys mumbled in unison.

"All right, now that we have that settled, get changed into your swimsuits. We're going to the beach."

The boys scampered off to their room. In the master bedroom, Scarett avoided watching his wife change. He loved her, but Ruby in a swimsuit was like stuffing ten pounds in a five-pound bag. From the rear, he thought it looked like two porkers wriggling around in a gunnysack. He was thankful Jack Nolan wouldn't see them on the beach.

Across town, Jack Nolan walked into the Turf Club. His crew had spent the last three nights shadowing Durant, and he wasn't pleased with the results. Upstairs, he proceeded along the hallway and found Spadden, ever the faithful watchdog, posted outside the office door. Spadden greeted him with what passed for a smile.

In the office, Voight was seated behind his desk. The phone rang as Nolan came through the door. Voight caught it on the second ring. "Yeah?"

"How ya doing?" a voice said. "This is Jim Torrence, over in Texas City."

"I remember you, Jim. You run the Dixieland Club, right?"

"That's me."

"What can I do for you?"

"Well, Dutch, I think it's the other way 'round. I called to warn you about a problem you're gonna have."

"Uh-huh," Voight said, lighting the stub of a cigar. "What problem is that?"

"Joey Adonis," Torrence replied. "Him and his gunsels are headed your way."

"Adonis knows better than to set foot in Galveston."

"Not today, he don't."

Joey Adonis was an Italian mobster from Texas City. He operated nightclubs, gambling dives, and a large bootlegging network. He was Torrence's long-standing rival on the mainland.

"I'm listening," Voight said. "Why's he headed over here?"

"You've got another visitor," Torrence said. "Art Scarett, your pal, the prohibition agent? He's staying at the Beach Hotel."

"So?"

"Adonis plans to bump him off."

Voight straightened in his chair. "How'd you get wind of this?"

"I've got a pigeon in Joey's outfit. Pays to keep tabs on the competition."

"And your pigeon tells you what?"

"Adonis is one clever fucker. He'll blast Scarett in Galveston and the Feds will think it was your work. All the blame will come down on your head."

Voight munched his cigar. "You know this for a fact?"

"Think about it," Torrence said. "Suppose the Feds get pissed about Scarett and put you out of business. Who d'you think will take over Galveston and the rumrunning—your whole operation?"

"Sounds like Joey Adonis."

"Kee-recto!"

"Thanks for the tip, Jim. I owe you one and I always look after my friends."

"Hell, just take out Adonis and we'll call it even. I'll have the mainland to myself."

"I'll let you know how it works out."

Voight hung up. He stared at the phone a moment, then quickly related the gist of the conversation to Nolan. There was an instant of weighing and deliberation before Nolan spoke.

"You think Torrence is on the level?"

"One way to find out," Voight said. "Call the hotel and see if Scarett is registered. Don't let on who you are."

Nolan placed the call and spoke with the hotel operator. When he hung up, his features were solemn. "Scarett's registered, him and his family. You'd think he would've told me."

Voight grunted. "Probably didn't want to be seen with you. We've got to stop this thing in its tracks. We don't need heat from the Feds."

"How do you want it handled?"

"Take all the boys you need and put a round-the-clock tail on Scarett. We'll find Adonis by keeping a watch on his target."

"What then?" Nolan asked. "You want me to whack Adonis when I find him?"

Voight wedged the cigar into the corner of his mouth. He puffed thoughtfully, considering alternatives. "Try to take the guinea son of a bitch alive. We don't need any shooting wars." He paused, a cold smile behind the cigar. "I'd like a word with the cocksucker, anyway."

"But if I can't take him alive?"

"Why, hell, Jack, give him one with my compliments."

"Got you, boss." Nolan started out, then turned back. "What about our friend, Durant?"

"Yeah, Durant," Voight said, reminded of unfinished business. "Anything new?"

"Same old story. We've trailed him three days now, and he never goes anywhere but the bank and his hotel. You didn't want him hit anywhere too public."

"Let's put him on the back burner till you collar Adonis. Our first job's to make damn sure Art Scarett gets out of town in one piece."

"I wonder why Adonis decided to put the move on us. We haven't had any trouble in five years, maybe more."

"Who knows how a guinea thinks? You'd have to be a mind reader. Just get him before he gets Scarett."

"I'm on it."

Nolan hurried out the door. Voight leaned back in his chair, took a puff on his cigar. He blew a perfect smoke ring, watched it float lazily toward the ceiling. His mouth razored in a hard smile.

He definitely wanted Adonis taken alive.

Durant left the bank early. His head hurt from all he'd tried to absorb about the world of finance. Three days under Aldridge's tutelage only made him feel like a dullard. He thought he wasn't cut out to be a banker.

On the street, he saw the man for the second time. Over the last three days he'd had some visceral sense that he was being watched. The only one he had spotted was the short, wiry man with red hair and a pug nose. But something told him there were others.

The feeling made the hair prickle on his neck. All the more so because Aldridge was hollow-eyed with worry for his safety. Hardly a day passed that the older man didn't comment on the need for caution. He was troubled that Durant hadn't seen the last of the mob.

To himself, Durant admitted he'd been foolhardy to threaten Magruder. He had let anger override reason, and Aldridge's concern halfway had him convinced that he was in danger. Today that belief was reinforced when he again spotted the red-haired man across the street. Twice in three days seemed something more than coincidence.

Durant stepped into a drugstore. His eye was still ringed a purplish-black and the stitches on his brow had begun to itch. He bought a tube of Vaseline ointment, and while the clerk was making change, he glanced out the window. His shadow was still across the street, three stores down, pretending interest in a window display. There was no question he was being followed.

The drugstore was on a corner, with a side exit on Eighteenth Street. He wandered through the store, as if browsing, and slipped out the side door. At the corner, he peeked around the side of the building and saw the man still feigning interest in the window display. A group of pedestrians waited for a car to pass by, and he fell in beside them as they crossed the intersection. He left his shadow watching the front of the drugstore.

Two blocks down, he entered Brandt's Gun Store. On his walks around town, he had seen the shop and never given it much thought. But now, with a man tailing him and fresh memories of the beating he'd taken, he felt prudence was in order. Perhaps it was all imagined, or Aldridge's constant harping on the mob, and perhaps it wasn't. Better safe than sorry.

Durant found himself in a small ordnance depot. The walls were lined with rows of rifles and shotguns, and a double-shelved showcase was filled with pistols. At the rear of the store, he saw a portly man at a gunsmith's bench, tinkering with the extractor on a hunting rifle. The man rose from the bench, wiping his hands on a rag, and pushed his spectacles up on top of his head. He walked forward as Durant stopped in front of the showcase.

"Good day," he said. "May I help you?"

"I see you're a gunsmith."

"Yes, I'm Willie Brandt, the owner. I do all my own repairs and guarantee every gun in the shop. Are you interested in a pistol?"

Durant nodded. "Something for personal protection."

"Of course." Brandt studied his battered features, but made no comment. "Any particular pistol?"

On the showcase shelves were a wide array of revolvers and semiautomatic pistols. Durant wanted something more serious than a .38 but nothing as cumbersome as a .45. He pointed to a German Luger.

"Is the Luger in good condition?"

"Yes, quite good," Brandt said, taking it from the top shelf. "Some of these came back from France, trophies of war. Good German engineering."

Durant hefted the Luger. A semiautomatic, it was chambered for 9mm, somewhat hotter than the American .38 caliber. He pulled the toggle-bar action to the rear and locked it open. With his thumbnail in the breech, catching light reflection, he looked down the bore and checked the barrel. There was slight pitting in the lands and grooves, but nothing that would affect accuracy. He worked the action several times, then tested the trigger. He nodded to Brandt.

"I'll take it," he said. "How much?"

"Twenty dollars with a box of cartridges."

"Sold."

Durant loaded the magazine with seven rounds. He chambered a round, flipped on the safety, and stuck the Luger inside his waistband, hidden by his suit jacket. He stuffed the box of cartridges in his hip pocket, and placed a twenty-dollar bill on the counter. Willie Brandt looked at him with a curious expression.

"You seem to be a man who knows weapons."

"I was in France," Durant said evenly. "I took one of these off a German and used it most of the war. It does the job."

Brandt squinted. "I hope you don't have to use that one."

"That makes two of us."

Outside the shop, Durant turned west on the Strand. As he walked back toward the drugstore, his eyes searched both sides of the street. He saw nothing of the red-haired man, or anyone else who appeared to be watching him. But he didn't relax, for he knew he was easy to find. There was no place to hide in Galveston.

Up ahead, he saw Catherine come out of the bank. She started toward the streetcar stop at the corner, and he suddenly increased his pace. On the spur of the moment, he decided to ignore the fact that no self-respecting banker would socialize with an employee. He'd eaten too many meals alone in the last ten days, and he needed someone to talk to. Someone so attractive made it all the better.

"Hi there," he said when he stopped her at the corner. "I don't want you to think I'm forward—and I know this is awful sudden—but would you have dinner with me tonight?"

"Dinner?" She looked startled. "Oh, I don't think I could."

"Say yes to a lonely man." Durant raised his hand, palm outward. "No passes, I promise. Scout's honor."

"Oh, it's not that, really it isn't. It's just my mother's waiting dinner for me at home."

"I'll bet she'd understand if you gave her a call. Try it and see."

"Well—" Catherine hesitated with a winsome smile. "All right, I will call her. Let's find a phone."

Durant took her to Guido's Restaurant on Water Street. The place was cozy, with candlelit tables that overlooked the bay. A waiter took their orders and there was a moment of awkward silence. The Luger in his waistband reminded him there were problems he wanted to forget. At least for the night.

"Tell me about yourself," he said, trying to put her at ease. "Have you always lived in Galveston?"

"Always." She laughed softly. "I've only been off the Island twice in my life—both times to Houston."

"So your family's old-line Galveston?"

"No, not in the way you mean. My parents moved here when they were married."

"What does your father do?"

"Why . . . he was in the Coast Guard."

"Was?"

Her smile slipped. "Yes, he was killed in the Hurricane."

Durant knew all about the Hurricane. Early in September of 1900, a storm developed off the western coast of Africa. In the days that followed, it swept north of Cuba, passed by the tip of Florida, and then roared into the Gulf of Mexico. On September 7, by now a full-blown hurricane, it struck Galveston with winds in excess of 120 miles an hour. The Island's highest point was not quite nine feet above sea level, and by nightfall, the Gulf and the bay had converged. Galveston was under water.

The center of the hurricane passed over the Island late that evening. The tide off the Gulf was at least fifteen feet and breakers twenty-five feet and higher battered the shoreline. By midnight the storm had petered out, but the following morning brought a scene straight out of hell. A third of Galveston was leveled to the ground, with 4,000 houses and hundreds of buildings simply washed away. The most devastating hurricane in American history had killed 6,000 Islanders.

Everyone in Texas remembered the Hurricane of 1900. Durant was a boy at the time, but his recollection of it was still vivid. He looked at Catherine now.

"Those were hard times," he said quietly. "Losing your father like that must have been rough."

She smiled wanly. "Actually, I never knew him. I wasn't quite a year old when it happened."

"So it's been you and your mother since then?"

"Yes, she worked in a laundry to put me through high school. She's quite a lady."

"Sure sounds like it."

"Now it's your turn," Catherine said, her eyes bright with interest. "I've always been fascinated by motion pictures. How did you ever become a stuntman?"

"I was working as an extra," Durant said with an offhanded gesture. "In this one scene, the stuntman was on top of a train that was about to crash. He had to leap up and grab a rope stretched between a tree and a telegraph pole. He missed."

"Was he killed?"

"No, but he was banged up pretty good."

"And you took his place," she said excitedly. "You did, didn't you?"

"Yeah, I did," Durant admitted. "I went to the director and told him I could do the stunt. So he gave me a shot and I pulled it off. That's where it started."

"Which stars have you done stunt work for?"

"Well, I do all of Tom Mix's pictures. I doubled for Lon Chaney in *The Hunchback of Notre Dame* and *The Phantom of the Opera*. And some for Doug Fairbanks, like *The Thief of Bagdad*."

"Omigosh!" she yelped. "Do you know Mary Pickford?"

Mary Pickford was a spirited young actress known as "America's Sweetheart." Douglas Fairbanks, her husband, was a dashing hero of the silver screen. They were idolized by fans and courted by every filmmaker in the industry. Their lavish estate, Pickfair, was the focal point of Hollywood society.

Over dinner, Durant held Catherine spellbound with stories of Hollywood royalty and their escapades. He went on to tell her that his ambition was to become a movie director, and his greatest supporter was Tom Mix. But even as he talked, he was reminded that Mix's next picture started in two days. He would have to make a call tonight.

Hollywood, for now, took a back seat to Galveston.

His only other choice was to cave in and sell out. Which was no choice at all.

He refused to run.

The Funland Pier was ablaze with lights. There was a roller coaster, a Ferris wheel, a merry-go-round with painted ponies, and barkers hawking games of chance. Friday night was carnival time in Galveston.

Arthur Scarett and his wife stood in a crowd beside the merry-go-round. Their boys, astride painted wooden ponies, whooped and laughed as they rode round and round. Scarett was pink from an afternoon on the beach, stuffed with hot dogs and orange soda pop. He debated whether his stomach would tolerate the roller coaster.

Joey Adonis waited near the Ferris wheel. He was short and stout, attired in a pin-striped suit and a gray fedora. With him were two shooters, impassive cold-eyed men whose one talent was efficient, indolent murder. Their eyes flicked back and forth between the merry-go-round and Arthur Scarett. They'd had him under surveillance since he checked into the Beach Hotel.

The problem, as Adonis saw it, was how to separate the prohibition agent from his family. Everywhere Scarett went, the wife and kids went, and Adonis, being a religious man, wasn't about to pop mom and her bambinos. He had all weekend to catch Scarett alone, but he wanted to get back to Texas City and business. He was mulling the problem when he felt the snout of a pistol pressed to his backbone.

"No cute moves, Joey, or you're a dead man."

Nolan was directly behind him. Four of Nolan's boys were crowded close around the two shooters, snub-nosed revolvers tented in their suit pockets. Adonis realized he had been so intent on Scarett that he'd gotten sloppy, and now Diamond Jack himself was breathing down his neck. Nolan nudged him with the gun. "Here's the drill," he said with amiable menace. "We'll walk out of here like old pals, no fuss, no bother. Try anything sporty and you're cold meat."

Adonis snorted. "You're gonna give it to me anyway. Why should I play along?"

"No, Joey, you've got it all wrong. Mr. Voight and Mr. Quinn just want to have a talk with you, that's all. Use your beaner and you'll live to a ripe old age."

"Are you on the square with me, Jack?"

"Joey, c'mon, would I lie to you?"

Adonis thought it was highly likely. But the odds dictated that he play for time and hope the Virgin Mary was watching over him. Two cars, motors running and drivers at the wheel, were waiting outside the Funland Pier. Nolan and one of his men got into the lead car with Adonis, and the other men, after disarming the shooters, got into the second car. No one spoke as they pulled away from the curb.

Five minutes later the caravan approached the front of the Hollywood Club. The cars turned right and slowed to a stop outside the rear entrance to the kitchen. The cooks and dishwashers pretended temporary blindness as the men filed through the rear door. Nolan followed a service hallway which led to the employees' lounge at the end of the T-head pier. The croupiers and stickmen in the lounge, like the kitchen help, went momentarily blind.

The casino didn't open until eight o'clock, and it was now seven thirty-one. Nolan, with his men trailing behind, led Adonis and the shooters from the lounge to the office. Voight was seated at the desk and Quinn stood at the picture window overlooking the dark waters of the Gulf. The door closed, and Adonis, with Nolan at his side, halted before the desk. Cuddles, the parrot, cocked his head and croaked "Oh, boy! Oh, boy!"

Adonis straightened his tie. "What the hell's the idea, Dutch? Why'd you have us rousted?"

"I'll get to you," Voight said, then glanced at Nolan. "Where'd you find them?"

"Funland Pier," Nolan replied. "What with the crowd

and the noise, I figured it was time to make our move. They were on Scarett and his family like mustard plaster."

"That's bullshit!" Adonis flared. "Me and the boys was just down here seein' the sights."

"Save your breath," Voight said. "Jack and his boys were on you all day while you tailed Scarett. We're not saps, Joey."

"You don't know what the fuck you're talkin' about. I got no business with Scarett."

"No, you just planned to snuff him and put the Feds on us. After the dust settled, then you'd make your move on the Island. We know all about it."

"Like hell," Adonis snapped. "Whoever told you that's a Goddamn liar."

"Liar! Liar!" Cuddles squawked. *"Pants on fire?"*

Adonis scowled. "What's with the bird?"

"He's a psychic," Voight said with a mirthless laugh. "You're lying, Joey. Caught out by a parrot."

"Dutch, I'm tellin' you the truth. I swear it on the Holy Mother's head."

"Careful lightning doesn't strike you."

"I'm on the square here! I wasn't out to ace Scarett."

Voight snorted. "Ollie, what do you think? Is he a snarf or not?"

Quinn turned from the window. "I believe you're right, Dutch."

"Wait a minute," Adonis said, looking from one to the other. "What the hell's a snarf?"

"That's you, Joey," Voight said with open mockery. "A guy who bites the bubbles when he farts in the bathtub. Fits you to a T."

Nolan and his men chuckled out loud. Adonis glared at Voight. "You got a lotta nerve callin' me names. Come down to it, you're no better'n me, maybe worse. You've whacked a few guys in your day."

"Yeah, but my day's not over, Joey. Yours is."

"What's that supposed to mean?"

Voight nodded to Nolan. "Jack, we're through talking here. Take him for a swim."

"Bye-bye!" Cuddles piped in. "Byebyebye!"

Adonis paled. His expression was that of a man who has just heard death whisper a terrible revelation in his ear. He appealed to Quinn.

"Ollie, for Chrissake, you and me go back a long ways. You gotta stop this! I'm askin' you."

"Too late," Quinn said in a flat voice. "You should've stayed clear of the Island. Let's get it done, Jack."

Nolan and his men pulled their pistols. Whizzer Duncan, his wiry lieutenant, moved to the far corner of the room. He rolled back the carpet, then opened a trapdoor built into the floor, revealing a narrow flight of wooden steps. The sound of water slapping against timbers echoed from below.

Duncan went down first. Nolan and the others then herded Adonis and his two shooters down the steps. A wide landing was bolted between stout pylons that supported the T-head of the casino. Nolan's powerful speedboat, the *Cherokee* was lashed to the landing, bobbing gently in the surf. The prisoners were forced into the boat at gunpoint.

Twenty minutes later Nolan cut the throttles. They were ten miles or so off the coast, the *Cherokee* wallowing in swells from the southern Gulf. On the ride out, Adonis and his cohorts had been bound hand and foot, and then wrapped in heavy logging chains. At Nolan's order, the men got them on their feet, near the stern of the boat. Duncan held Adonis upright.

The two shooters were wild-eyed with terror. For all the men they'd killed, one broke into sobs, mewling pitifully for his life, and the other seemed paralyzed. One at a time, they were hoisted into the air and thrown overboard, sinking beneath the choppy surf the moment they hit the water. Adonis watched them vanish with a look of stricken dread.

"Mother of Christ," he muttered, craning his neck to

look at Nolan. "Jack, I'm begging you, shoot me first. Don't drown me like that. I'm begging you . . . have a heart."

"No can do, Joey," Nolan said with a steady gaze. "Nothing personal, I'm just following orders. Business is business."

Duncan and the other men lifted Adonis off his feet. As they tossed him overboard, his mouth opened in a shrieking curse: "You bastards, I'll see you in hell!" He hit with a splash, taken deep by the roiling waters.

Nolan engaged the throttles. He brought the *Cherokee* around and headed back to shore. Duncan stared at their wake a moment, then turned forward. He chortled sourly.

"Think Joey found his hell at the bottom?"

"No," Nolan allowed. "I'd say long before then."

"Yeah, long before then when?"

"On his way down."

Duncan thought that was rich. He got a mental picture of Adonis trying to swim in chains. Holding his breath. All the way down.

Chapter Nine

The Magruders seldom frequented the Hollywood Club. William Magruder believed entertainment was a foursome at bridge, and nightclubs seemed to him a frivolous pursuit. Gambling, in his opinion, was a pastime for the mentally deficient.

For all that, Saturday night was the exception. Magruder had asked his only daughter how she would like to celebrate her twenty-first birthday. She told him, knowing it would tilt his equilibrium, that she wanted to see Al Jolson's closing night in Galveston. He had no choice but to call Ollie Quinn.

Elizabeth, who insisted on being called Libbie, was a striking young woman. Her tawny hair and sumptuous figure was set off by bee-stung lips and an impudent nose. She was warmly attractive, by turns charming and spoiled, and she generally left men somewhat bewitched. An evening in her company, whatever her mood, was always memorable.

Libbie prided herself on being the ideal of a liberated woman, a flapper. She wore short skirts, rolled her stockings below the knee, and kept her hair bobbed in a shingle cut. She smoked cigarettes, flattened her breasts to affect a slender look, and painted her face with an exotic blend of cosmetics. Her outfit tonight was a sheer champagne slip of a dress, glistening with glass beads, and a matching silk headband. She carried a white plume fan with an air of regal disdain.

Her mother, by contrast, looked the wealthy matron. Opal Magruder, her hair piled atop her head, was pleasingly plump, her face lightly blushed by rouge. She wore an elegant black satin sheath with lace across the top and down her arms, the hem of her skirt touching the floor. Francis Magruder, Sherm's wife, was presentable, if somewhat dowdy, dressed in an evening gown of tulle silk with a scooped neckline. The men were formally attired in tuxedos.

Quinn, with Nolan at this side, greeted them at the entrance of the nightclub. He shook the men's hands, kissed the ladies' fingertips, and turned his high-wattage smile on Libbie. "Allow me to wish you a very happy birthday," he said with glib dignity. "We're honored to have you at the Hollywood Club on such a special occasion."

"Thank you so much." Libbie fluttered her fan with a delicate motion. "I'm so looking forward to seeing Al Jolson perform. Everyone says he's fabulous."

"The world's greatest," Quinn said, ever the showman. "I'm sure you won't be disappointed."

Libbie glanced past him at Nolan. He was impeccably groomed in a white dinner jacket, his piercing green eyes magnetic behind tanned features. His sleek assurance and lithe good looks reminded her of the movie idol Rudolph Valentino. She was suddenly glad she hadn't brought a date tonight.

The orchestra was playing *Japanese Sandman*. The club was packed, and on the dance floor, couples dipped and swayed to the beat of the music. Quinn led the Magruders to a large oval table centered on the stage, seating them on one side with empty chairs awaiting the rest of their party. A flurry of waiters descended on the table.

Quinn rejoined Nolan at the door as the Seagraves arrived. They were the guests of the Magruders, and like them, infrequent visitors to the Hollywood Club. With George Seagrave was his wife, Clara, locally renowned for her obsession with planting oleanders all over the Island. They were accompanied by their son, John and his wife, Mary, a woman more interested in raising children than flowers. Quinn, still playing the courtly host, escorted them to the Magruders' table.

After everyone was seated, he made his way backstage. He knocked on Jolson's dressing room door, waiting to enter until he heard a voice from inside. Jolson was in the midst of his transformation to blackface, tarlike goo smeared on his hands. He looked up in the mirror.

"Ollie, my boy," he said with a broad grin. "How's the crowd tonight?"

"Full house," Quinn said, crossing the room. "They're hanging from the rafters for your closing night."

"And Dutch was worried about an extra two grand to hold me over. I shoulda asked for five!"

"Dutch would've had a stroke. But I hope you're feeling generous tonight. I'd like to ask a favor."

"Ask away."

"I have a business associate in the audience. The whole family's here, celebrating his daughter's birthday. I was hoping you'd sing her a song—at their table."

Jolson stared at him in the mirror. "You want me to sing *Happy Birthday*?"

"No, no," Quinn said quickly. "One of your regular songs. Just sing it to her."

"Is she a looker?"

"Al, she's a knockout."

"I always was a sucker for a pretty face. What's her name?"

"Libbie," Quinn said. "There are nine of them seated at a table down front. She's the only flapper in the bunch."

"Good for her," Jolson said agreeably. "I'll give her something to remember."

"You're a sport, Al. I appreciate it."

"What the hey, why not? What's your business with her father?"

Quinn smiled. "We have mutual interests in a bank."

Their table was tiny, crammed against a wall at the rear of the room. Stoner was dressed in a double-breasted tux and Janice wore a lavender gown with a deep V in the back to her waist. They were so far away they could barely see the stage.

"I hope Jolson sings loud," she said playfully. "We'll need opera glasses from back here."

"Count your lucky stars," Stoner said. "I got the only table in the place. The *one* and only."

"Well, like they say, money talks."

"Highway robbery would be more like it."

On a hunch, Stoner had dropped by the club early that afternoon. He'd gone to the front office and talked with the business manager, asking if there had been any cancellations for tonight's show. The business manager was a slick operator, an extortionist at heart, who held back tickets for every show, for the right price. A hundred dollars a seat got Stoner a table.

Stoner thought it was worth a shot. For four nights in a row he had gambled at the Garden Club and a couple similar poker rooms. He was nursing his funds, for he needed a sizeable bankroll to pull off the last step in the plan. But he'd lost a few hundred here and a few hundred there, and his name was now known at the gaming dives. Tonight, he intended to talk his way into the only casino that mattered.

Over dinner Stoner observed how the club operated. From his briefing in Austin, he knew something of the routine as well as the personnel. He identified Oliver Quinn from the description he'd been given at Ranger Headquarters. He assumed Dutch Voight, who ran the gaming end of the business, was busy with the casino. He would verify that only if his plan worked.

Quinn held his attention throughout dinner. He watched as Quinn seated two groups of people at the same table on the edge of the dance floor. There were nine people in the party, and Quinn's manner toward the two older men was ingratiating, curiously deferential. Stoner wondered who they were, and why they rated special treatment. He made a mental note of their faces.

The other man who caught his attention was Diamond Jack Nolan. Intelligence files at Ranger Headquarters indicated that Nolan was the enforcer for the Galveston mob. His reputation, though he'd never been arrested, was that of a cold-blooded killer. Stoner saw the easy smile that never touched Nolan's eyes, and he could believe the reports were accurate. He marked Nolan as the most dangerous of the lot.

Stoner finished his steak while Janice was still savoring her shrimp Touraine. The service was faultless, and he had to admit that the Hollywood Club warranted its reputation for gourmet dining. After a glance around the room, he decided it was time to make his move. Quinn had gone backstage, and Nolan had escorted a few people to the glass doors that led to the casino. He looked across at Janice.

"I'll be right back," he said. "I want to test the waters before the show starts."

She paused, a delicate shrimp speared on the tines of her fork. "You'll be careful, won't you?"

"Careful's my middle name."

Stoner walked to the nightclub entrance. The maitre d' was slim as a greyhound, with a pencil-thin mustache, and an expression of haughty reserve. He inspected Stoner with a patronizing smile.

"Yes, sir, how may I help you?"

"I'm here with my wife," Stoner said amiably. "She's all excited to try the casino after the show. Thought you could arrange it for us."

"I'm afraid our clubroom is open only to members, Mr—?"

"Eberling. Bob Eberling. I'd be glad to pay any membership fee."

"No, I'm sorry, quite impossible, Mr. Eberling. One must be sponsored by another member."

"Well, I'm a regular at the Garden Club. Call over there and ask about Bob Eberling. They'll vouch for me."

"Our clientele doesn't frequent the Garden Club. And vice versa, if you see what I mean."

"Look here—" Stoner pulled a wad of cash from his pocket. "Suppose you get me in the casino and I'll make it worth your while. How's a hundred sound?"

The maitre d' looked down his nose. "We at the Hollywood Club do not accept bribes, Mr. Eberling. Will there be anything else?"

"The little woman's gonna be awful disappointed."

The maitre d' just stared at him. Stoner started away, and then, as if struck by an afterthought, turned back. "Say, tell me something, will you? Who're the people down by the dance floor? The ones with the good-looking girl?"

"The young lady is Miss Elizabeth Magruder. Tonight is her birthday."

"Looks like the whole family's here. Her father must have some pull to get a front-row table. Who is he?"

"William Magruder," the maitre d' said in an imperious tone. "One of Galveston's most prominent businessmen."

"Pays to have influence, huh? I'll bet you roll out the red carpet when he heads to the casino."

"You'll have to excuse me, Mr. Eberling. I have other duties."

"Yeah, sure, I understand."

Stoner filed the information away, curious that a businessman was so chummy with a gangster. He walked back to the table, seating himself, and told Janice he'd struck out on the casino. She played her role and looked properly crestfallen. He shook his head. "Guess we'll have to go back to Plan A."

"The manager at the hotel?"

"Yeah, that and more time in the poker clubs."

"Well, anyway—" She consoled him with a squeeze of his hand. "The evening's not a complete loss, sweetie. We get to see Jolson."

The houselights dimmed. A spotlight hit the stage as

the orchestra swung into a bouncy tune. Jolson exploded out of the wings.

> *The choo-choo train that takes me*
> *Away from you*
> *No words can tell how sad it makes me.*

Jolson was on bended knee. The spotlight framed him and Libbie as he knelt before her at the table. The lyrics were particularly meaningful because everyone knew he was leaving for Los Angeles in the morning. He finished the last refrain of *Toot Toot Tootsie* with outstretched arms.

The audience roared their approval. Jolson took Libbie's hand and kissed it, then skipped back up the ramp to the stage. He concluded the show with a foot-stomping rendition of *California, Here I Come*, which seemed inspired, since he was off to make the world's first talky movie. The crowd gave him a standing ovation that brought him back for four curtain calls.

When the houselights came on, Libbie was the center of attention. Quinn stopped by the table and she kissed him on the cheek for arranging a birthday song by Jolson. The conversation turned to *The Jazz Singer*, the talking motion picture Jolson would start shooting next week. Magruder and Seagrave agreed that talking pictures would prove to be a short-lived fad. Quinn reminded them that people had said motion pictures would never replace vaudeville. And now vaudeville was all but dead!

Libbie excused herself to go to the powder room. She wasn't interested in listening to her father debate the future of motion pictures. All the more pressing, she felt a buzz from too many gin rickeys and an urgent need to pee. Afterward, she paused before a vanity mirror to freshen her makeup, amused by the stares that her flapper look drew from some of the older women. When she came out of the ladies' room, she saw Quinn's green-eyed assistant standing by the doors to the casino. She thought he was devilishly handsome, temptation in a tux. And after all, it was her birthday!

She took a cigarette from her evening bag. Then, stopping directly in front of him, she looked up into his eyes. "May I have a light?"

Nolan clicked his lighter. "Having a good time, Miss Magruder?"

"Just marvelous," Libbie said, exhaling a thin streamer of smoke. "I don't believe we've met."

"I'm Jack Nolan."

"What do you do for Mr. Quinn?"

If only you knew, Nolan thought to himself. He smiled disarmingly. "I'm the club's Mr. Fixit. Whatever needs doing, I fix it."

"How very interesting," she said, vamping him with a look. "What are you fixing tonight?"

"Pardon me?"

"You could fix it quite nicely by dancing with me."

Libbie exuded sensuality. She considered herself a liberated woman, one who rejected the starchy, outdated customs of an older generation. Like many young women of the Twenties, she drank, experimented with sex, and explored everything forbidden by a moral code that seemed unbearably ancient. She had discovered the joys of burning the candle at both ends.

Nolan was tempted. He had a weakness for cute young things with no inhibitions. But rules were rules. "I'm sorry, Miss Magruder," he said with genuine regret. "Mr. Quinn doesn't allow me to dance with guests."

"Why don't you call me Libbie and I'll call you Jack?"

"All right, but that doesn't change anything."

Her voice was warm and husky, softly intimate. "We could change things."

"I don't follow you."

"Oh, I think you do. Why not give me a call at home sometime?"

"Never work," Nolan said ruefully. "Your father

wouldn't like it and Mr. Quinn definitely wouldn't like it. I'd be in hot water."

"Ummm," she murmured throatily. "I think you like hot water . . . don't you, Jack?"

Nolan watched her walk back into the club. Her short skirt revealed shapely legs and her hips wigwagged in a swishing motion that held his attention. He felt a warmth in his groin and a knot in his belly, and warned himself to forget it. Quinn would have his balls if he messed with Magruder's daughter.

The irony wasn't lost on Nolan. A little bombshell of a girl coming on to him while her father pulled the strings to have a man killed. He was amused all over again that she'd asked him what sort of work he did for Quinn. In a roundabout way, he was working for her father, and there was the real irony. She would never know.

The orchestra wailed away in an earsplitting number. He saw the girl drag her father out of his chair and pull him onto the dance floor. The crowd went wild with the music, hopping about like well-dressed acrobats in a frenzied Charleston. Magruder was hopelessly lost, merely plodding along to his daughter's flailing arms and thrashing legs. Her fluted laughter melded with the tempo of the beat.

Nolan turned into the casino. Voight gave him a quizzical look, and he nodded in the affirmative, proceeding on to the employees' lounge. He hung his tux in a wall locker and changed into a dark charcoal suit. By the time he stepped into the hallway to the kitchen, he'd forgotten the girl.

He had work to do.

The organ swelled to a crescendo. Everyone in the theater sat mesmerized by the action on the screen. The organist kept his eyes glued to a speeding motorcycle.

Manslaughter was the title of the movie. A motorcycle cop was chasing the unjustly accused heroine in her car. Catherine clutched Durant's arm as the heroine lost control and her car skidded around broadside in the road. The motorcycle struck the fender and the cop vaulted into the air, thrown over the hood. The heroine, distraught and shaken, staggered from her car.

Theaters across the country were equipped with organs. A skilled organist could provide a wide array of sound effects—thunder, gunfire, the rumble of an earthquake—and accompany the shifting moods of a film. Tonight, the organist dropped the tenor to a haunting refrain as the heroine stumbled around the car and looked down at the cop's body. A gasp went through the audience.

After the movie, Durant and Catherine walked south on Tenth Street. Last night, when he'd run into her on the corner and invited her to dinner, it had been a spur-of-the moment thing. But he had enjoyed her company, and sensed it was mutual, and tonight he'd asked her out for an early dinner and a movie. As he walked her home, she eagerly questioned him about the stunts. She was particularly intrigued by the motorcycle crash.

"I can't imagine it," she said. "A motorcycle going that fast and him flying through the air! How on earth did he live through it?"

"Well, good judgment helps," Durant said. "You have to think a stunt through, and then plan it step by step. It's all in the timing."

"Timing?"

"Let's take the split second of the crash. He had to time it perfectly to let go of the motorcycle. To let the momentum throw him over the car. Everything's timing."

Her hand was nestled in the crook of his arm. She hesitated, but curiosity got the better of her. "Have you ever misjudged the timing?"

"Oh, boy, did I," Durant said with a laugh. "I had to jump from the top of a double-decker bus to an elevated girder. I missed and hit the street like a lead brick. Broke my leg."

She winced. "How awful."

"Yeah, that's when I started thinking seriously about directing. Directors don't wind up in the hospital."

"But it's really more than that, isn't it? I think you want to create films of your own."

"Doing stunts is like a classroom. I've learned a lot from watching the way directors work. King Vidor and Tom Ince are two of the best."

Durant went on to explain that Ince had formulated a blueprint for making pictures which included a detailed shooting script and a scene-by-scene shooting schedule. King Vidor had pioneered dramatic camera techniques, where the camera moves as if it were the actor, revealing the shot from the actor's point of view. Imagination, looking at things from the camera's perspective, was the key to visual narrative.

Catherine could have listened to him all night. Everything about moving pictures captivated her, and she was engrossed by his behind-the-scenes description of Hollywood. Before she knew it, they crossed the corner of Tenth and Avenue K and turned into the walkway of her house. She didn't want the evening to end, but her mother would have gone to bed, and it was too late to invite him inside. She turned to him at the door.

"I had a wonderful time," she said, smiling happily. "I don't know when I've enjoyed myself so much."

"Same here," Durant said. "Hate to call it a night."

"Me, too."

"Maybe we could do it again."

"I'd love to."

Durant kissed her softly on the lips. Her hand went to his cheek, caressing him, and then she stepped back. She laughed nervously.

"Well . . . good night for now."

"Good night."

Durant went down the walkway as she opened the door. He looked back, waving to her, and crossed the street. His spirits were so high he felt a little drunk, and he wondered at himself. Then, thinking about it, he realized it wasn't just having a good time, or even loneliness. He was really attracted to her.

Halfway down the block he got his bearings. He decided to follow Avenue K west and cut over to his hotel. His mind was still on Catherine and he thought he would call her tomorrow. Maybe she would enjoy an outing to one of the amusement piers, or a walk along the beach. A solitary Sunday suddenly took on brighter prospects.

There was no traffic at Fifteenth Street. As he crossed to the opposite corner, he heard the muffled idle of an automobile engine. He glanced around and saw a four-door Buick sedan coasting silently toward him with the lights out. His every sense alerted as the passenger door and the right-side rear door opened, and two men stepped out with pistols. He recognized them from the beating he'd taken at the Heroes Monument.

Durant's instincts kicked in from the war. He sought cover, dodging behind a telephone pole, and pulled the Luger from his waistband. The two gunmen fired almost simultaneously, one shot nicking the telephone pole and the other whistling past his ear. He crouched, arm extended at shoulder level, and caught the sights in the reflection from the streetlight. He ripped off three quick shots.

The first shattered the car's windshield. The second plucked at the sleeve of the man by the passenger door. The man by the rear door grunted with surprise, a starburst of blood covering his shirtfront from the third slug. He lurched sideways, his legs collapsing, and slumped face down on the curb. The driver shouted a curse.

"Get the *hell* in the car!"

The other man jumped on the running board as the Buick roared away. Durant fired a departing shot, trying for the gunman and blowing out the rear window instead. He rose from behind the telephone pole, glancing at the dead hoodlum, and decided to make tracks. Houselights were coming on in the neighborhood, and he couldn't afford to be identified. The cops, given the opportunity, would charge him with murder. He hurried north on Fifteenth Street.

Four blocks away, Nolan skidded around the corner of Nineteenth. He switched on the lights, letting off the accelerator, and the Buick slowed to a moderate speed. Beside him, Turk McGuire blew out a gusty breath, still clutching his revolver. His eyes were wild with fury.

"That cocksucker killed Elmer! Where the fuck'd he get a gun?"

"I don't know," Nolan said. "But he sure as Christ knows how to shoot. Look at the windshield."

"Hell, look at the back window," McGuire snarled. "Bastard was still shootin' at us when we took off. Who the fuck is this guy?"

"Turk, that's a damn good question."

Nolan headed for the Turf Club. The car was riddled, and he wanted to get it out of sight in the garage behind the building. But as he drove, his mind returned to the shootout, and the man who took cover behind a telephone pole. The man calmly blasting away with an automatic.

He thought he wanted to know more about Earl Durant.

Chapter Ten

L ate Monday morning, Dutch Voight walked into City Hall. Nolan was acting as his bodyguard, until the right replacement was found for Elmer Spadden. The funeral was set for the next day.

The morning paper had carried a story about the shooting. According to the police, who had interviewed everyone in the neighborhood, between six and ten shots were fired. But there were no witnesses, no leads, and little to investigate. There was also no mention of who Elmer Spadden worked for.

Voight was enraged. Earlier, with Nolan at his side, he had made the weekly trip to the Galveston City Bank. Sherm Magruder, who suspected the truth, acted as though he'd never heard of Spadden. Instead, ever the friendly banker, he exchanged bearer bonds for a briefcase full of cash. The transaction was conducted in terse silence.

But now, entering City Hall, Voight put on a cheerful face. Dealing with politicians was a dirty game, and the first rule was to never let them know what you were thinking. Every Monday Voight made the rounds, and there was nothing secretive about the meetings. Vice fueled the economy of Galveston, and the public, for the most part, approved. Voters already knew their political leaders were on the pad.

The first stop was the office of the mayor. Margie Clark, the mayor's longtime secretary and occasional lover, was expecting Voight. She showed him and Nolan into the office, and gently closed the door. Edward Pryor rose from behind his desk with the smile of a man who knew how his bread got buttered. His hair was snow-white and his manner was gracious, a politician to the core. He never thought of himself as a crook.

"Good morning, Dutch," he said, waving them to chairs. "I was most distressed to hear about Elmer. Terrible thing, just terrible."

"Elmer was a good man." Voight placed his briefcase on the desk and unsnapped the latches. "Send some flowers to his funeral. He'd like that."

"I most certainly will, Dutch. Depend on it."

There was no question of Pryor or any other politician attending the funeral services. That would have been too open an association, even for the voters of Galveston. Flowers were more discreet.

Voight removed two thousand in cash from his briefcase. The mayor was his conduit to the police force and other departments of the city government. A hundred thousand a year ensured protection for all the mob's activities.

Pryor placed the cash in his desk drawer. "I'll make the usual distributions," he said. "And once again, my most sincere condolences. I know Elmer was unstintingly loyal."

"Fact is, Eddie, he wrote the book on loyal. I'll see you next week."

Nolan held the door for Voight as they went out. Their next stop was the county courthouse, where they called on Sheriff Leonard Beebe. A lanky man with a salt-and-pepper mustache, Beebe had been the sheriff of Galveston County for three terms. He was their pipeline to various judges and the county prosecutor. He greeted them with a somber look.

"Helluva note," he said. "I know Elmer was one of your top boys. Any idea who did it?"

Voight scowled. "We know exactly who did it."

"Whatever way it happened, I'd be glad to arrange murder charges. Wouldn't be any trouble at all."

"Let's just say it's a private matter. We'll take care of it ourselves."

Beebe expected nothing less. The mob operated by its own code, and transgressors were dealt with in brutal fashion. Someone would disappear, and the likelihood of his office ever learning the name was practically nil. He accepted the weekly payoff with no further reference to Elmer Spadden.

On the street again, Voight and Nolan turned toward the Turf Club. All the talk that morning about Spadden left Nolan even more puzzled than before. Saturday night, after the shooting, he'd reported back to Voight and Quinn at the Hollywood Club. They were dumbfounded that Durant had armed himself with a gun.

Voight, who was closer to Spadden, was particularly enraged. Quinn, though angry, was calmer, and assured Nolan they didn't hold him responsible. Yet, all day Sunday, he'd expected an order to snuff Durant, the faster, the better. Instead, his bosses had kept their own counsel, and kept him in the dark. He felt like it was time to ask the question.

"Tell me if I'm out of line," he said as they walked along. "Back there, you told Beebe we'd take care of business ourselves. When are we going after Durant?"

Voight frowned. "Ollie got a call from Magruder Sunday afternoon. He's meeting with him now."

"What about?"

"Magruder didn't want to talk on the phone. Just said to hold off on that 'personal matter' till him and Ollie could get together."

"I'll be damned," Nolan said in a bemused tone. "What do you think he wants?"

"We'll find out soon enough."

They walked on toward the Turf Club.

Monday mornings were always slow. The few merchants who traded with People's Bank & Trust brought their weekend receipts in for deposit. But the bank was otherwise at a standstill.

On his way in that morning, Durant had spoken

briefly with Aldridge. He'd waved to Catherine, greeting her with a smile, and thought she looked hurt that he hadn't stopped to talk. Then he retreated to his office, and stayed there all morning, with the door closed. He was still trying to piece things together.

Sunday he'd gone out of his hotel only for a late breakfast and an early supper. He hadn't called Catherine about a date, for fear of putting her in danger as well. The short time he was out of the hotel, he fully expected a car loaded with gunmen to run him down. He wondered why they were waiting.

Today, over breakfast, he'd read the newspaper story. He learned the man he had killed was named Elmer Spadden, and felt no surprise that his own name wasn't mentioned. Nor was he surprised that the police hadn't busted into his hotel room and arrested him. The mob wouldn't lower themselves to call on the cops, even crooked cops. They would settle the score on their own.

Saturday night continued to scroll through his mind like a scary movie. He was convinced Jack Nolan was the driver of the car, for Nolan had been involved from the beginning. The other man, the one built like a mastodon, he remembered from the fight at the Heroes Monument. He wasn't sure he wanted to know the man's name.

The odds dictated that he run. He had survived Saturday night only because he'd had the foresight to buy the Luger. That and the kill-or-be-killed lessons he had learned in the trenches of France. The next time, they might catch him off guard, or send thugs armed with tommy guns rather than pistols. And he had no doubt there would be a next time, for it was now a matter of payback. He had killed one of their men.

Despite the odds, he'd decided not to run. All day Sunday he had weighed the risk of staying on against the more prudent measure of fleeing Galveston. By nature he was not a quitter, and it went against the grain to be driven out by Magruder and a bunch of gangsters. No less telling, the war had taught him that a man with the guts to stand

and fight was, more often then not, a match for the bullies of the world. He was resolved to see it through.

A knock at the door interrupted his woolgathering. Aldridge stepped into the office, his features at once quizzical and concerned. He closed the door, moving across the room, and took a chair. He tried a tentative smile.

"Everything all right?" he asked. "You've hardly spoken to anyone all morning."

"Just one of those days," Durant said dismissively. "Nothing to worry about."

Aldridge studied his face. "Why don't I believe you?"

"What's not to believe?"

"You act like a man with a load too heavy to carry. Sure you don't want to talk about it?"

Durant hesitated a moment. He trusted the older man and perhaps it wouldn't hurt to confide in someone. He told himself Aldridge need to know anyway. Just in case. . . .

"You heard about the shooting Saturday night?"

"I read about it in the paper," Aldridge said carefully. "One of the hoodlums who work for Quinn and Voight was killed. Why do you ask?"

"I killed him."

"No!"

"Afraid so."

Durant quickly related the events of Saturday night. He explained his decision to buy a gun, and how he'd used it to kill Elmer Spadden. He concluded with an empty laugh.

"I didn't stick around to wait for the police. Unless I miss my guess, they'd jump at the chance to charge me with murder."

"Wise decision," Aldridge said. "But I can't say the same about staying in Galveston. You should have left town yesterday."

"Where would I go?" Durant said hollowly. "I killed one of their men and there's nowhere to run. They'd just track me down in Los Angeles."

"Yes, now that you mention it, you're right. Even selling the bank to Magruder wouldn't solve anything. Quinn and Voight are vengeful men, and you've made them look bad. You're not safe anywhere."

"Ira, I hate to say it, but it's not just me. I've been sitting here thinking about it, and these bastards make their own rules. They might try to get at me through you."

"Oh, I don't think so," Aldridge said. "What would that possibly gain them? You're the one they want."

Durant rubbed the bridge of his nose. "Do me a favor and watch your step, anyhow. Why take chances?"

"Yes, of course." Aldridge held his gaze. "I wasn't aware you were seeing Catherine. Do you think she's in any danger?"

"I doubt they'd harm a woman. Gangsters think of themselves as tough guys, and that would spoil their image. She's probably safe."

"On the other hand, you very definitely are not. How will you protect yourself?"

"Guess I'll have to grow eyes in the back of my head."

"Do you really believe that will stop them?"

Durant shrugged, let the question hang. He already knew the answer.

Quinn was waiting in the office at the Turf Club. The moment Voight and Nolan came through the door, they knew something was wrong. His features were clouded with anger.

"I've got a feeling it's bad news," Voight said. "What happened with Magruder?"

"Our friend lost his nerve." Quinn wagged his head with distaste. "He wants us to back off on Durant."

"What the hell do you mean, back off? He's the one that asked us to ice the bastard!"

"Dutch, I made that very point. I made it several times and it was a waste of breath. He wouldn't listen."

"Screw him!" Voight's dark eyes shone like nuggets

of coal. "We're burying Elmer tomorrow, and Durant killed him. Are you telling me we let the sonofabitch skate?"

"No, I'm not," Quinn said in a controlled voice. "I'm telling you Magruder's one of the big reasons we *own* the rackets in Galveston. We can't afford to offend him."

Voight stalked to the window. He stood looking out at the street, his jaws clenched. There was a moment of oppressive silence, the air thick with tension. He finally turned around.

"How about this?" he said. "We take Durant for a swim and nobody'll know the difference. He just disappears."

"Easier said than done," Quinn noted. "You'll remember he's got a gun and he's willing to fight. How do we take him without another shooting?"

"I don't know and I don't give a rat's ass. I just want him dead."

"Listen to me, Dutch. Magruder's as nervous as a whore in church. Durant knows he's behind everything that's happened, the shooting, the whole works. He's scared Durant will start broadcasting it around town."

Voight laughed bitterly. "All the more reason to clip the bastard."

"You'll get no argument from me," Quinn said. "But Magruder thinks we have to hold off, let things settle down. Let Durant think it's over. Let him think he's won."

"How about it, Jack?" Voight said, turning to Nolan. "You think Durant will think he's won?"

"Not a chance," Nolan replied with conviction. "We learned the hard way he's a sharp cookie. He knows it's not finished."

"See!" Voight said, looking at Quinn. "Magruder's talking through his hat. Nothing's solved till we nail Durant."

"And we will," Quinn told him. "Just try to be a little patient for once. Give Magruder time to get his nerve back."

"Goddamn amateurs," Voight grumped. "Never yet seen one that wasn't a pain in the ass."

A rap sounded on the door. Turk McGuire stuck his head inside, nodding to Nolan. "Jack, there's a broad on the phone for you. She won't take no for an answer."

"Always the ladies' man," Quinn said, relieved by the interruption. "How do you work them into your schedule, Jack?"

"Talking about schedules," Voight said. "You've got a ship loaded with booze coming in tonight. Don't let your love life interfere with business."

"I'll have the fleet there with time to spare. Everything's all set."

Nolan slipped out the door. He crossed the hall to a cubbyhole office, where the phone for Gulf Enterprises rang through. He picked up the receiver. "Hello."

"Hello yourself, handsome."

"Who's this?"

"Libbie Magruder. You haven't forgotten our tête-à-tête Saturday night . . . have you?"

"You'd be hard to forget."

"How very gallant. I love it!"

"What can I do for you?"

"Ummm." She laughed, a throaty growl. "I can think of several things."

Nolan wondered if she was as wild as she sounded. "I thought we settled this Saturday night."

"No, I asked you to call me and you didn't. So I've called you. Aren't you flattered?"

"Even if I am, it's not a good idea."

"Oh, I think it's a marvelous idea. And if you were truthful, so do you . . . don't you?"

"I think you're trouble."

"Yes, but you like to play with fire. I know you do."

"You don't know anything about me."

"I know enough," she purred. "Why fight kismet when it's all in the stars? Meet me for a drink this afternoon."

Nolan told himself he was nuts. But she was right about one thing. He liked to play with fire.

"There's a place in La Marque where nobody's likely to see us. The Rendezvous Roadhouse."

"Ooo, a rendezvous . . . what time?"

"How's two sound?"

"See you there, handsome."

The line went dead. Nolan replaced the receiver on the hook, certain he'd made a mistake. But then, on second thought, he shrugged it off.

Like she said, why fight kismet?

The sun stood like a blinding fireball against an azure sky. There was little traffic on the causeway, for the weekend tourists had fled the Island like lemmings. The interurban cars to Houston were running practically empty.

Nolan drove with the window down. The sparse traffic somehow reminded him of Arthur Scarett, the prohibition agent. Scarett and his family had departed yesterday, never aware that their lives had been in danger. Joey Adonis, now feeding the fishes, would become part of the lore of what happened to those who trespassed on the Island.

Today, Nolan drove his own car, a sporty Stutz Bearcat with a collapsible top. At no small cost, he'd had the latest innovation installed, a customized compact radio. The automobile, with its range and mobility, had shattered the isolation of rural America forever. Yet it was the magic of radio that had shrunk the size of the planet.

A flick of a switch brought instant access to the outside world. People clustered around their sets, already addicted to favorite programs, and sat mesmerized before the talking box. Today's news was reported today, and in a way, it was as if they were eavesdropping on the curious, and sometimes bizarre, secrets of distant places. There was a verve and excitement of immediacy about the broadcasts.

A stock market report came on as Nolan approached

La Marque. The Dow Jones was up to 102, a new benchmark, and apparently headed to dizzying heights. Listening to the report, he remembered the crash of 1921, and how get-rich-quick investors had become overnight paupers. His view was that the stock market was run by shady New York financiers who periodically bilked the public. His own road to wealth was simpler, and far more certain. He invested only in himself.

The Rendezvous Roadhouse was on the highway south of La Marque. A two-story structure, it was part speakeasy, part dance hall, and a trysting place for lovers, married or otherwise. There was a bar and gaming room on the ground floor, and cozy bedrooms for rent by the hour on the second floor. On a Monday afternoon there were few customers, and Nolan virtually had the place to himself. He took a booth on the far side of the dance floor.

Libbie arrived a fashionable ten minutes late. A cloche hat set off her bobbed hair, and she wore a slinky crepe de chine dress with pleated flounces, her stockings rolled below her knees. Nolan watched as she crossed the dance floor, and felt more amused than flattered that the performance was solely for his benefit. She was decked out as Little Miss Sexpot.

"Forgive me for being late," she said, scooting into the booth. "I had the most dreadful time deciding what to wear."

Nolan chuckled. "I'll bet you ransacked your closet."

"Well, honestly, what's a girl to wear to a *roadhouse*? I've never been to one before."

"I guess there's a first time for everything."

A waiter drifted over. Libbie ordered a gin rickey and Nolan asked for bourbon with a water chaser. They made small talk, skirting anything of a meaningful nature, until their drinks were served. She lifted her glass in a suggestive toast.

"Cheers to our very first date."

Nolan clinked glasses. "I thought we were just getting together for a drink."

"You big fibber." She fluttered her eyelashes. "You thought nothing of the kind. You know very well I have my sights set on you."

"Never try to kid an old kidder. You don't even know me."

"Oh, don't I? Diamond Jack Nolan, rumrunner, gangster, and all-around bad boy. I know *everything* about you."

Nolan thought that wasn't quite true. Only that morning her father had called off the hit on Durant, a job put on hold but not canceled. His amusement was tempered by the irony of the situation. He looked at her over the rim of his glass.

"How'd you learn all my better traits?"

"A girl's entitled to her secrets. I'll never tell."

"What makes you think I'm the guy for you?"

"Kismet, the stars," she said with a sultry laugh. "We were fated to be lovers."

Nolan stared at her. "What is it, little rich girl has a fling with a gangster? Something you can shock all your society pals with?"

She looked wounded. "Now you're being mean. I fell for you the minute I saw you. I haven't thought of anything but you since Saturday night."

"You don't pull any punches, do you? Are you always this pushy with men?"

"No, I usually let them chase me. But you would never have called me, and that would have been the end of it. So I called you."

Her honesty was strangely appealing to Nolan. He understood that liberated women of the Jazz Age were uninhibited, scornful of the old moral taboos. His own view of things was similar to hers, for he followed no rules, and few laws. Even more, she was young and vivacious, stunningly attractive. His kind of woman.

"We'd have big problems," he said seriously. "You know I can't be seen with you in Galveston. I'd get my butt kicked if anybody found out."

"No one will ever know," she said airily. "We'll meet in out-of-the-way places . . . just our secret."

"You're used to parties, and dancing, and good restaurants. Might not be much fun."

"Oh, yes, it will!" She scooted closer, shoulder to shoulder. "You must think I'm a wicked woman."

Nolan grinned. "What the hell, I'm a wicked man."

"Jeepers, I'm all tingly just thinking about it. Did you book us a room in this den of infamy?"

"Are you trying to seduce me?"

"Silly man, I already have."

They spent the afternoon entwined in fierce love.

Chapter Eleven

The red-light district was on Postoffice Street. For four blocks, between Twenty-fifth and Twenty-ninth, sin was for sale. The locals jokingly referred to it as Fat Alley.

The bordellos were conveniently wedged side by side, two-story houses with narrow porches and wooden shutters painted in garish colors. Whores tricked out in skimpy dresses posed in lighted doorways, or leaned out open windows. They offered their wares to a randy stream of seamen, dockworkers, vacationers, and college boys. The going rate for quick lust was three dollars.

There were almost sixty houses of prostitution along Fat Alley. Galveston's business leaders believed that a segregated red-light district was the only practical way to control the oldest profession. They agreed as well that ladies of the evening, like gambling dives and speakeasies, were essential to the Island's well-oiled economy. Over a thousand whores plied their trade on Postoffice Street.

The brothels operated on a time-for-hire policy. Turnover was the key to a profitable venture, and the madams kept the traffic moving. Customers were shown into a parlor where they were encouraged to buy popskull whiskey while they inspected the merchandise. Those who refused to be rushed might feed quarters into a slot machine, but they soon found themselves upstairs with one of the girls. The love-for-sale transactions rarely lasted more than a few minutes.

Fat Alley, oddly enough, was one of the safest neighborhoods on the Island. The combustible mix of whiskey, men, and whores in any other town often led to muggings, brawls, and assorted forms of mayhem. But in Galveston there was a higher law than the one enforced by the police, and it had nothing to do with courts or time in jail. Anyone who caused a disturbance would be accosted by the Night Riders, the hard-fisted thugs who worked for Quinn and Voight. The penalty was a swift and brutal beating.

On Tuesday nights business began to pick up along Postoffice Street. Mondays were a day of rest for the girls, the trade slack from the departure of weekend tourists. But by sundown on Tuesday, Fat Alley came alive with men intent on getting their wicks dipped. The girls, after lazing about for a day, thought of Tuesday as the beginning of their workweek. They greeted the johns with restored vigor.

Harry Johnson and his buddy, Fred Doolin, were out for a night on the town. They were young and single, with good jobs at the Galveston Ice Company, and regular customers on Fat Alley. Their work, loading blocks of ice from the plant onto ice wagons, kept them in top shape and ever in need of a woman. Tonight, their first stop was a speakeasy, where a few drinks would get them primed for bedroom gymnastics. They loved to hear the girls squeal.

The speakeasy was jammed with workingmen. Mae Hager, who owned the establishment, circulated through the crowd. She was the only woman in the place, for men never brought girlfriends with them to Fat Alley. Her manner was brassy, with a loud, horsey laugh, and her customers enjoyed her ribald sense of humor. Johnson and Doolin, who dropped in two or three times a week, were among her favorite customers. She was in her forties, henna-haired and overly plump, but still a flirt. She liked young men.

Mae squeezed in between Johnson and Doolin at the bar. She ordered a drink on the house, and told them a dirty joke about a virgin and a duck. As their laughter

faded, the door opened and her features suddenly turned
sober. She rolled her eyes and said, "Shit!"

"What's the matter?" Doolin asked.

"Trouble, that's what," she grouched. "Lera and his
Goddamn one-armed bandits. He's after me to put in his
slots."

Johnson, who was feeling his liquor, pushed off the
bar. "Mae, you say the word and I'll clean his clock. Nobody dumps on a friend of mine."

"Yeah," Doolin chimed in. "We'll toss his ass out."

"Boys, you don't want nothin' to do with Lera. Keep
out of it."

Lou Lera was a thickset man, who fancied himself a
gangster. He wore a dark suit and a black shirt with a
white tie, and carried himself with a cocky attitude. Quinn
and Voight, who believed competition stimulated business, had split the slots concession on the Island between
Lera and another distributor. Lera had been pressuring
Mae Hager to switch to his machines.

Mae walked forward to meet him. "Evenin', Lou,"
she said with a phony smile. "Stand you a drink?"

"Let's talk business," Lera said roughly. "I gave you
a deadline and tonight's the night. What's it gonna be?"

"I've told you a dozen times and the answer's still
the same. I'll stick with what I've got."

"You always was a stupid old cow. What say I send
my boys in here and bust this joint to splinters? Think
that'd change your mind?"

"Just you try it," Mae snapped. "You don't scare me."

"I'll do more'n scare you, you dumb cunt."

"Fuck you and the horse you rode in on!"

Lera backhanded her in the mouth. Her lip split,
smeared with blood, and she fell against the bar. Harry
Johnson took two long strides forward and slugged Lera
with a looping haymaker. Lera went down hard, sliding
on his butt across the floor. His flattened nose sprayed
blood over his face.

Johnson started toward him to finish the job. Lera

jerked a revolver from his shoulder holster and fired two shots as fast as he could pull the trigger. The first slug nipped Johnson's arm and the second struck him squarely in the chest. His shirt colored as though a rosebud had been painted on the cloth by an invisible brush. His eyes went blank and his legs buckled at the knees. He dropped dead on the floor.

"Don't nobody move!"

Lera waved the gun at the crowd. He scrambled to his feet, backing away, and disappeared through the door. Mae Hager stared down at the body, huge teardrops puddling her eyes, her mouth dripping blood. She tottered, almost fell, then recovered herself. She shook her fist at the bartender.

"Goddammit, don't just stand there! Call the *cops*!"

The murder made the front page of the *Galveston Daily Chronicle*. The newspaper account was graphic, with all the gory details related by several eyewitnesses. The police were searching for Louis R. Lera.

Early the next morning, representatives of the Galveston Ministers Association stormed into City Hall. Reverend Josiah Baldwin, speaking for the Baptists, and Reverend Tyler Adair, the Methodist pastor, demanded an audience with the mayor. They were accompanied by Herbert Cornwall, perennial reform candidate in the mayoral elections.

Mayor Edward Pryor greeted them with a conciliatory smile. Elections on the Island were decided, in large part, by the political machine and the sporting crowd's swing vote. But an astute politician nonetheless courted the clergy. No one wanted to be crosswise of God.

"Unconscionable!" thundered Reverend Baldwin. "An innocent man shot down in cold blood. We will *not* tolerate it."

Reverend Adair railed on in condemnation. "Mr. Mayor, the Christian community decries this foul and dastardly act. We demand justice!"

"Gentlemen, please," Pryor pleaded. "The police are combing the Island as we speak. I assure you an arrest will be made."

Herbert Cornwall brayed laughter. "You and your administration are corrupt. *Corrupt*!" He pointed an accusatory finger. "The good people of Galveston will unite behind a coalition to put you out of office."

"Come off it, Herbie," Pryor countered. "You'd kill somebody yourself to be mayor. Don't deny it, either."

"This isn't about politics," Reverend Baldwin pronounced. "This is about gangsters running amuck in our streets. *We—will—have—action!*"

The shouting went on for a half hour. Mayor Pryor, promising results, was finally able to usher them out the door. He immediately called Chief of Police Axel Norton to his office.

"We're in deep shit," he said, explaining the situation. "Just the excuse they needed for a reform movement. And if it goes too far, we'll be thrown out on the street."

Norton squirmed. "We're doing our damnedest, Eddie. I'm turning the Island upside down."

"Not good enough," Pryor said sternly. "I'm going to call Magruder and Seagrave, and alert them. You deliver the word to Quinn and Voight—personally."

"What do I tell them?"

"Tell them killing civilians crosses the line. Lera's their man and we're holding them responsible. We want him in custody today—*now*!"

Ten minutes later Chief Norton walked into the Turf Club. Upstairs, there was a new guard on the door, Barney Ward, who had replaced the dead-and-buried Elmer Spadden. Ward stuck his head in the door, announcing a visitor, and got the okay. He admitted Norton into the office.

Quinn and Voight were seated behind their desks. Voight was in shirtsleeves, puffing a long, black cigar. He waved Norton to a chair.

"We don't often see you around here, Chief. What's up?"

"The shit's hit the fan," Norton said, seating himself. "Your boy Lera started the reformers yapping. They jumped all over the mayor this morning."

"Who, exactly?" Quinn asked. "Which reformers?"

"Same old crowd," Norton said. "The Ministers Association, Adair and Baldwin. Herbie Cornwall was with them, too."

Quinn nodded. "And the mayor sent you to deliver a message, is that it?"

"Yeah, he did." Norton swallowed, his Adam's apple bobbing. "He says Lera's your responsibility, what with a civilian being killed. He wants you to hand him over to the police . . . today."

"Hand him over!" Voight said, puffing furiously on his cigar. "We don't even know where the son of a bitch is."

Quinn and Voight were both in a state of rage. Yesterday they had buried Elmer Spadden, and last night, Lera had violated their rule about no violence against civilians. They had a crew out searching for him, even though he'd seemingly vanished without a trace. Their orders were to shoot him on sight.

"I'm just doing what I'm told," Norton said nervously. "The mayor puts it on your head because Lera's your man."

"Screw that!" Voight exploded. "We give the orders around here, not Eddie Pryor. Tell him I said to shove it—"

The phone rang. Quinn lifted the receiver, listening and nodding, and hung up with a perplexed expression. He exchanged a quick glance with Voight, then looked at Norton. He managed a tight smile.

"Thanks for coming by," he said. "Assure the mayor we're on top of things."

Norton understood he'd been dismissed. He rose, relieved to be on his way, and moved to the door. When it closed, Voight turned to Quinn with a questioning look. He raised an eyebrow.

"Who was that on the phone?"

"Magruder," Quinn said. "We're invited to a meeting in his office at one. Seagrave will be there."

"Let me guess," Voight said. "We're gonna talk about Lera, right?"

"Dutch, I'd say it's the safest bet in town."

The bank was crowded for a Wednesday morning. Durant sat at his desk, trying to decipher balance sheets for the previous week. His mind was elsewhere.

Four days had passed since he'd killed the hoodlum named Spadden. He was still looking over his shoulder, no less convinced the mob would try to settle accounts. But he was preoccupied at the moment with an article he had read in the morning paper. There had been another killing in Galveston.

According to the newspaper, the police were scouring the Island for a thug named Lera. There was speculation that Lera had fled to the mainland, and police agencies there were on the alert. Durant toyed with the notion that the mob, with one of its own branded a murderer, would be reluctant to try another killing anytime soon. Then, on second thought, he doubted he'd gained a reprieve.

Catherine knocked, stepping inside the door. "Someone to see you. Reverend Adair and Reverend Baldwin."

"Preachers?"

"And Herbert Cornwall, who's *always* running for mayor. They say it's very important."

"Wonder what they want?"

"They didn't say."

"All right, show them in."

The men trooped into the office. They introduced themselves and Durant got them seated. There was a moment of awkward silence, as though no one had been appointed spokesman for the group. Reverend Adair finally took the lead.

"Mr. Durant, we represent the decent people of Galveston. Perhaps you've heard of the murder last night?"

"I read about it in the paper."

"Not to mention," Adair went on, "the shooting of a gangster Saturday night. Two killings in four days!"

Durant's expression was sphinxlike. "I'm not sure I follow you, Reverend. Why come to me?"

"We very much want to enlist your support in our cause."

Adair offered a quick explanation. The Galveston Ministers Association was opposed to gambling, vice, bootleg liquor, and mobsters in general. Herbert Cornwall, the Association's foremost ally, was their candidate for mayor in every election. Yet their reform movement met resistance from both the mob and many of the Island's legitimate businessmen. Money being the root of all evil, greed too often prevailed. Filthy lucre was the driving force in any election.

"We desperately need your support," Adair concluded. "You are new to town and yours will be viewed by all as an objective voice."

"I wouldn't say it's much of a voice," Durant observed. "I only got into town a couple weeks ago. Hardly anybody knows me."

"On the contrary," Reverend Baldwin announced. "Your uncle was widely respected in our community, and you have taken his place here at the bank. Your views will carry considerable weight, Mr. Durant."

"And there's William Magruder," Adair hastily added. "He actively works to defeat all reform, and he and your uncle were archenemies. You would be marching to the cause in your uncle's footsteps."

"I don't know," Durant said uncertainly. "I've never been much for politics."

Cornwall cleared his throat. "There's talk around town that the mob subjected you to a terrible beating. Diamond Jack Nolan was reported to be the ringleader." He paused, head cocked in scrutiny. "May I ask what you did to incur their anger?"

"Hard to say," Durant lied, his features deadpan. "I'd like to know myself."

"But you don't deny it's so?"

"No, I don't deny it."

Cornwall spread his hands. "Then all the more reason for you to join our cause, Mr. Durant. You will be standing foursquare against the mob *and* William Magruder."

Durant was all too aware that they were attempting to use him for their own purposes. But by joining the reform movement, there was the possibility it would deter the mob from coming after him. As he thought it through, there semed every likelihood the mob would hesitate to kill a man aligned with the clergy. There was the added bonus of hitting back at Magruder. He liked it.

"All right," he said after a prolonged silence. "I'm on the bandwagon. Count me in."

"Excellent!" Reverend Adair crowed. "We are delighted to have you with us. Absolutely delighted!"

"How do we go about it?" Durant asked. "What do you want from me?"

"Nothing just yet," Adair said. "We first have to formulate a plan to win public support. Perhaps we'll be able to get something in the newspaper."

"Our congregations are the starting point," Reverend Baldwin said, nodding sagely. "On Sunday, we'll deliver sermons condemning gangsters and murderers. We must rally the Christian brotherhood to our cause."

"Amen," Reverend Adair added. "God loves a righteous scrap."

The meeting ended on that note. Durant showed them to the door with a round of handshakes, and returned to his desk. A moment later, Aldridge stepped into the office, clearly overcome by curiosity. His expression was one of bemusement.

"Aren't you the popular fellow," he said. "What was that all about?"

Durant wagged his head. "Believe it or not, they recruited me into the reform movement."

"Yes, they've been trying to reform Galveston for years. I assume the Johnson boy's murder last night has them steaming?"

"Yeah, they're steamed, all right. They're talking about taking the fight to the mob. God against the gangsters."

"You already have a bull's-eye on your back. Doesn't joining them put you at even more risk?"

Durant smiled. "Ira, it might just save my life."

Chapter Twelve

Quinn and Voight arrived at Magruder's office shortly before one o'clock. The moment they came through the door, they knew there was trouble in the works. The air was all but frosty.

Magruder was enthroned behind his desk. George Seagrave was seated in a wingback chair, and Sherm was in his usual spot on the couch. They looked like barnyard owls, their features solemn.

"Have a chair," Magruder said without preamble. "I've called you here on a matter of the utmost urgency."

Quinn and Voight seated themselves. Seagrave gave them a perfunctory nod, then averted his gaze. There was a moment of terse silence while Magruder seemed to collect himself. His color was high.

"We have an untenable situation," he said in an orotund voice. "Last night one of your homicidal maniacs killed a man in cold blood. What do you have to say for yourselves?"

Voight glowered at him. "Who the hell are you to call us on the carpet? I don't like your Goddamn attitude."

"Nor I yours," Magruder said sullenly. "The reformers are out bleating their usual denouncements of George and myself, and the political structure of Galveston County. They threatened the mayor with everything short of crucifixion."

"Pryor scares too easy," Voight retorted. "So do you and George, if you want my opinion. These reformers are all hot air. Always have been."

"No, you're wrong," Seagrave said sharply. "The

murder of an innocent man gives them the underpinnings of a moral crusade. They could bring us all down."

Quinn shifted in his chair. "We've beaten back the reformers any number of times over the years. All this will blow over in a few days."

"You miss the point entirely," Magruder informed him. "George and I provide immunity for your activities on the Island. If they bring us down, they bring you down." He paused, staring across the desk. "We must find a solution—quickly."

"Quickly, as in today," Seagrave added. "We have to defuse these reformers before they get started. By tomorrow, they'll be pounding their drum all over town."

Voight laughed sourly. "You want 'em defused? Hell, we'll just kill Lera and dump his body outside City Hall. How's that for a solution?"

Magruder and Seagrave appeared startled. They exchanged a wary glance, weighing the repercussions of so final a solution. Magruder finally shook his head.

"However fitting, it simply won't do," he said. "We can't afford another dead man, even a murderer. More violence would add fuel to the fire."

"So what's the answer?" Quinn asked. "You don't like our solution—what's yours?"

Magruder steepled his fingers. "George and I have talked it over, and we feel there's only one prudent measure. Your man Lera must stand trial for murder."

"You're nuts!" Voight woofed. "You expect Lera to strap himself into the electric chair? That'll be the day!"

"What we expect," Seagrave said firmly, "is for you and Ollie to convince him to surrender. Only a jury trial will take the wind out of the reformers' sails. We need a public display of justice."

Quinn and Voight looked at each other. They suddenly realized that the matter had been discussed, and settled, long before they arrived. Magruder and Seagrave were playing them like violins. Cleverly, a step at a time, they were being manipulated.

"You boys are dreaming," Voight said. "You want us to convince Lera to commit suicide. Why not ask pigs to fly?"

"There is no other way," Magruder said with conviction. "The community must have its spectacle—a catharsis—see him tried and convicted in a court of law. Only then will we squelch the reformers."

Voight snorted. "How the Christ are we supposed to pull that off? Lera's on the lam and we don't have a clue where he's at. He could be in China by now."

"Yes, but you're looking for him," Seagrave said with a studious gaze. "He broke your rule—*your* law against violence—and you intend to kill him. Isn't that true?"

"So what?" Voight said gruffly. "We take care of our own in our own way. Nobody's complained so far."

"But we must have him *alive!*" Magruder trumpeted. "How can I make you understand the salient point in all this? We cannot allow the reformers to mount a crusade in the name of God and church."

"Dutch—" Quinn waited until he had Voight's attention. "I've been sitting here thinking about it, and they're right. A murder gives the reformers all they need to preach hellfire and damnation. They could bust our balloon."

"And?" Voight stared at him. "What's the rest of it? What are you saying?"

"I think we should listen to what they're saying about Lera."

"Even if we found him, so what? You think he's gonna roll over and agree to stand trial?"

"I think we could *make* him agree."

Something unspoken passed between them, and Voight finally nodded. "All right," he said, looking from Seagrave to Magruder. "No promises, but we'll give it a try. Our boys are already looking for him, anyway."

"I couldn't be more pleased," Seagrave said with a sigh of relief. "We knew we could count on you and Ollie."

The meeting concluded with a sense of harmony restored. Magruder mentioned that he would like to have a word with Quinn and Voight, on a matter of personal business. Seagrave, as usual, preferred not to know what such business entailed. He left after an exchange of handshakes.

When the door closed, Magruder sank back in his chair. "I am reminded of the line from *Macbeth*. 'Double, double, toil and trouble.' "

Voight gave him a blank look. Quinn, who had some passing knowledge of Shakespeare, suddenly became alert. "Don't tell me there are more problems?"

"I'm afraid so," Magruder said, his eyes glum. "I've learned that Earl Durant has joined forces with the reformers."

Voight frowned. "How'd you find that out?"

"Like you, Dutch, I have my sources. I received a call just before lunch."

"Talk about odd company," Quinn said speculatively. "I wouldn't think Durant has much in common with preachers. Not after the way he shot it out with our boys."

"Be that as it may," Magruder said. "So long as he is involved with the reformers, you cannot harm him. That would merely galvanize Adair and Baldwin to greater action."

"How long do we wait?" Voight said, his eyes cold. "Maybe it slipped your mind, he killed one of our men."

"You wait until I say otherwise. I must insist you follow my wishes in this matter."

"You're hurting yourself, you know," Quinn smoothly intervened. "You'll never get that bank till we get Durant."

Magruder waved him off. "We have more pressing problems at the moment. Specifically, this fellow Lera."

"And after we deliver him?" Voight persisted. "How about we tend to Durant?"

"All in good time, Dutch. All in good time."

Magruder was struck by a wayward thought. He told

himself he had much in common with Daniel Webster. So much so the irony was difficult to escape.

He too had sold his soul to the Devil.

A brilliant orange sunset shimmered off the waters of the bay. Guido's was slowly filling with the early evening dinner trade. Waiters scurried back and forth through the restaurant.

Durant and Catherine were seated at a window table. Tonight was the first time he'd asked her out since the shooting incident. He had waited, concerned for her safety, certain the mob would try to exact revenge. But his alliance with the reformers, by now public knowledge, had altered the scheme of things. He thought he'd bought himself some insurance.

Catherine was confused. She was immensely attracted to him, and after their date Saturday night, she believed it was mutual. Then four days had passed with hardly a word or a smile, his manner somehow distant, strangely impersonal. She had accepted his invitation tonight, hoping she'd imagined his odd behavior. She tried to put a bright face on things.

"You're the talk of the office," she said, after the waiter had taken their orders. "Two pastors and Herbert Cornwall calling on you! Everyone's dying of curiosity."

Durant chuckled. "Believe it or not, I've been enlisted into the reform movement. Just about the last thing I ever expected."

"What are they reforming against?"

"You heard about the shooting last night?"

"Yes, it was dreadful," she said with a little shudder. "No one's safe from these gangsters."

"That's the whole idea," Durant said. "The preachers and Cornwall intend to use the murder as a political springboard. They want to run the mob out of town."

"Oh, they've been trying to do that for years. I'm not surprised a murder has set them off again. But why would they come to you?"

"Couple reasons, the first being Magruder. They know I'm at odds with him because of the bank, and they say he's involved in dirty politics. They figured I'd be a natural to hop on the bandwagon."

"Magruder's certainly dirty," she agreed. "You said there was another reason?"

"The mob," Durant replied. "They knew I'd gotten beat up by Nolan and his thugs. Cornwall was especially interested about why I'm on the outs with the mob."

"What did you tell him?"

"Nothing even close to the truth. Fact is, I pretty much lied."

Durant thought he was lying to her as well. A lie of omission, however justified, was nonetheless a lie. Yet he couldn't bring himself to tell her he'd killed one of Nolan's men in the shootout Saturday night. He didn't want her to see him in that light, to think of him in that way. A killer.

"Listening to you—" she hesitated, her features set in a musing expression. "Well, I was wondering if this wouldn't anger those gangsters even more. You joining with the reformers, I mean."

"Ira asked me the same thing. I'm betting they'll think twice now. Wouldn't look good to jump a man associated with preachers."

"I hope you're right."

"That makes two of us."

The waiter brought their plates. He served Catherine veal cutlets with carrots and peas, and Durant a T-bone steak with a baked potato. As Durant cut into his steak, he told himself he'd let the conversation drift off course. A pretty girl deserved to be entertained, not frightened. He tried for a lighter note.

"You remember you told me how crazy you are about motion pictures?"

"Yes, I did, didn't I? What made you think of that?"

"I got to wondering—" Durant paused, a hunk of

beefsteak speared on his fork. "What's your favorite movie of all time?"

"Oh, there's no question!" her eyes shone with excitement. "It would definitely have to be *Don't Change Your Husband*."

"What was it you liked about it?"

"The laughs and humor—you'll think I'm terrible . . . and the marvelous naughtiness."

Cecil B. DeMille, the director, was ever aware of the box office. Cynicism was an outgrowth of the World War, and he sensed that audiences were bored with traditional heroes and histrionic villains. The Victorian Age was falling before the Jazz Age, rapidly being replaced by a new morality. Sex and sex appeal were in.

DeMille introduced avarice and lust, human frailty and fallibility in *Don't Change Your Husband*. In the end, virtue triumphed over infidelity, but not until the audience had a full serving of vice. DeMille's star in the movie, and a sequel, *Why Change Your Wife?*, was Gloria Swanson. She projected the glamour of a Roaring Twenties emancipated woman.

"I just adore Gloria Swanson," Catherine said gaily. "She's so beautiful, and all those furs and jewels. Have you ever met her?"

"Only in passing," Durant said with a crooked smile. "She's a real card, though. Regular prima donna."

"Oh, I love Hollywood gossip. Tell me!"

"Well, they play music on some of the sets. Directors like to put their actors in the mood."

Catherine forgot her veal cutlets as he went on to explain. The cranking grind of cameras often intruded on the concentration of actors. The noise of nearby sets being constructed or dismantled unsettled the mood as well. The sets were built next to one another, and sometimes, three or four films might be shooting at once. Every studio kept several small orchestras on hand to work different sets.

"So this one day," Durant elaborated, "Pola Negri was shooting on one set and Gloria Swanson was on the set beside her. Keep in mind, they hate each other. Couple of real cutthroats."

"I can't stand it!" Her eyes sparkled with merriment. "Don't stop, go on!"

"You have to remember movie actors take themselves pretty seriously. Especially when they're into emoting hearts and flowers."

Pola Negri, he went on, was faced with a particularly difficult emotional scene. She insisted on the soft, woeful strains of a single violin to establish the mood. She insisted as well that musicians on other sets stand down until her scene was completed. Gloria Swanson, who was piqued by the demands, quickly recruited a brass band and played a rousing military march at the critical moment. Pola Negri threw a fit, and a Hollywood feud was born.

"I love it!" Catherine said with a mischievous laugh. "I can just see it now. Gloria Swanson at the head of a brass band!"

Durant grinned. "Yeah, it blew the lid off things. Turned into a real catfight."

Her expression was still animated with laughter. "You're better than a movie magazine," she said, picking at her veal. "Do you know Greta Garbo, too?"

"I've seen her around the studios."

"Is it true what they say about her and John Gilbert?"

John Gilbert was a handsome matinee idol of the day. Greta Garbo was an exotic Swedish actress, recently imported to Hollywood. Their torrid love affair was the talk of fans everywhere.

"You haven't heard the half of it," Durant said. "Movie magazines leave out all the good stuff."

"Nooo," she breathed. "You mean there's more?"

"Lots more."

"Oh, I can't wait. Tell me!"

Durant told her all the racy details.

Bubba's Roadhouse was located on the outskirts of Texas City. The ramshackle structure was a dive that catered to the rougher crowd. Gambling, prostitution, and bootleg hooch were housed under one roof.

The dimly lighted parking lot was full. A black four-door Buick was positioned with a view of the main entrance to the roadhouse. Nolan was in the passenger seat, with Whizzer Duncan at the steering wheel, and Turk McGuire in the backseat. They waited in stony silence.

Two days had passed in their search for Lou Lera. Since Tuesday night, when he'd killed the man in Galveston, they had put out feelers to all their contacts on the mainland. Tonight, not an hour before, Nolan had received a call from a bootlegger in Texas City. Lera was bedded down with a whore at Bubba's.

Not long after ten o'clock, Lera emerged from the roadhouse. He was still dressed in the dark suit, black shirt, and white tie he'd worn the night of the shooting. As though he hadn't a care in the world, he walked toward his car, shoulders squared in a cocky manner. Nolan and his men stepped out of the Buick.

"Hello there, Lou," Nolan said in a breezy voice. "Don't try to run or I'll have Turk break your legs."

Lera's face went chalky. McGuire boxed him in from one side and Duncan the other. His mouth ticced in a weak smile, his teeth as yellow as old dice. "How'd you find me?"

Nolan shrugged. "Got a tip you were here."

"Not a smart move," Duncan said, relieving him of his pistol. "Pussy's put more'n one man in his grave. You shoulda stayed hid out."

Lera flinched. "You boys gonna kill me?"

"Depends," Nolan said cryptically. "Let's go for a ride."

"Where you takin' me?"

"Lou, the pleasure of your company has been requested. Leave it at that."

The ride back to Galveston passed in terse silence. A half hour later the Buick rolled to a stop at the side of the Hollywood Club. Nolan led the way through the kitchen entrance, with Lera sandwiched between Duncan and McGuire. The foursome followed the hall to the employees' lounge, where Duncan and McGuire stayed behind. Nolan escorted Lera next door into the office.

Quinn was seated at the desk. Voight stood by the window, a cigar jutting from his mouth. There was a cold stagnancy in his eyes as he turned, waiting for Nolan to close the door. He crossed the room, puffing his cigar, and slugged Lera with a straight shot to the jaw. Cuddles, the parrot, screeched, hiding his eyes behind a wing. Lera hit the floor on the seat of his pants.

"You stupid sonovbitch," Voight raged. "Why'd you kill that guy?"

Lera got to his knees. "Dutch, he coldcocked me, just like you done. What was I supposed to do?"

"You weren't supposed to kill him. Why didn't you stand up and fight him like a man?"

"Honest to Christ, you should've seen the fucker. He was built like a barn."

Voight walked away in a cloud of smoke. Lera slowly levered himself off the floor and got to his feet. Quinn stared at him across the desk.

"You know the rule, Lou. We never harm civilians and we never *ever* kill them. Where was your brain?"

"Ollie, it happened too fast." Lera massaged his jaw, blood leaking from the corner of his mouth. "The cocksucker popped me, all because of that bitch Mae Hager. I just reacted, that's all."

"You just *reacted*," Voight mocked him. "That's the lamest excuse I ever heard. You went dumb in the clutch, admit it."

"Look, I'm sorry," Lera said. "I know I didn't handle it right. I got hot and lost my head."

"Too late for hindsight," Quinn said sternly. "You've put the organization in a bad light, and brought the reformers out of their holes. There's hell to pay."

"I'll do anything you say, Ollie. I swear to God I will. How do I make it right?"

"I'm glad you asked," Quinn said. "We want you to stand trial for murder."

Lera blanched. "How's that again?"

Voight's laugh was thick with anger. "Get the wax out of your ears and pay attention. You're going to stand trial and no two ways about it. Understand?"

"Gimme a break, Dutch." Lera's mouth tightened in a ghastly grimace. "They'll jam my ass in the electric chair. I'm not gonna ride Old Sparky."

"Well, you've got a choice," Voight said. "Go to trial and take your chances with a jury. Or we'll let Jack take you for a swim—right Goddamn now."

"Ohboyohboy!" Cuddles squawked. "Take him for a swim!"

Everyone looked at the parrot. Cuddles held their gazes a moment, then cocked his head and pretended interest in the ceiling. Quinn shifted in his chair.

"Lou, it's not as bad as it sounds," he said. "We'll hire the top defense attorney in Texas, whatever it costs. You'll probably walk out of court a free man."

Lera broke out in a frosty sweat. "Ollie, there's witnesses. Mae Hager'll put me in the hot seat! They'll fry my ass."

"Not to worry," Quinn assured him. "We'll send Jack around to have a talk with Mae. Depend on it, she'll have a loss of memory. Won't she, Jack?"

Nolan nodded. "She won't remember her own name. Guaranteed."

"I dunno," Lera said hesitantly. "There must've been ten or twelve people in the joint that night. How you gonna shut 'em all up?"

"Leave it to me," Nolan said confidently. "The whole bunch will turn dummy. Nothing to it."

"Yeah, but they already identified me to the cops. How you gonna get around that?"

"Quit weaseling!" Voight roared. "You've only got one choice here. Stand trial or go for a swim. Take your pick."

Lera ducked his head. "I'll stand trial."

"Good thinking," Quinn counseled. "Just make sure you keep your mouth shut about the organization. Anybody asks, you just stopped off in Mae's for a drink."

"I got it, Ollie."

"Damn sure better," Voight warned him. "You rat us out and you're a dead man. We'll get to you in jail or anywhere else."

"Hey, I'm no squealer," Lera protested. "I never met you guys in my life. Don't even know your names. How's that?"

"Keep it that way," Voight said. "You walk over to the police station and turn yourself in. Tell 'em you're surrendering voluntarily."

"I won't let you down."

"Jack will be right behind you. Change your mind between here and there, and guess what?"

Lera swallowed hard. "I'm dead."

"You finally got smart," Voight said with a mirthless laugh. "Trot on over to the cops and keep your lip buttoned. We'll have a lawyer there first thing in the morning."

Lera obediently bobbed his head. Nolan ushered him out of the office, and Quinn waited until the door closed. He looked at Voight.

"Think he'll stay mum?"

"Sure he will," Voight said with cold conviction. "Dumb as he is, he knows we mean business."

Quinn took the receiver off the phone. He jiggled the hook. "Operator, get me 8414."

There was a tinny ring on the line and William Magruder answered. "Hello."

"Bill, Ollie Quinn here."

"Why are you calling me at home? Don't you know what time it is?"

"I thought you'd want to hear the latest. Louis Lera is on his way to the police station. He's turning himself in."

"Well now, that is good news. Excellent work, Ollie. Excellent."

"All's well that ends well, Bill. We'll talk tomorrow."

Quinn replaced the receiver on the hook. He smiled humorously at Voight. "Dutch, we've saved Galveston again. We deserve a medal."

"Forget the medal," Voight said gruffly. "I want Durant."

"And you'll have him. Once the reformers lose steam, he's all yours."

"We'll see if the bastard can walk on water."

"Waterwater!" Cuddles echoed. "Take him for a swim!"

Voight grunted. "Goddamn bird's too smart for his own good."

Cuddles wisely said no more.

Chapter Thirteen

The sun burnished the Gulf waters with coppery flame. The sky was opalescent and there was the smell of salt spray on the wind. Wispy clouds sped westward like ghosts fleeing an exorcism.

Clint Stoner was seated on the balcony overlooking the Gulf. The remnants of breakfast, delivered by room service, lay scattered across the table beside his chair. His attention was focused on the Friday morning edition of the *Galveston Daily Chronicle*.

The article dealt with events of late last night. He got the impression that the paper had held the presses in order to make the morning edition. The gist of the story was that Louis Lera, accused of murder, had surrendered himself to the authorities. County Prosecutor Sherwood Butler was quoted as saying he would press for a speedy trial and the death penalty. A preliminary hearing was scheduled that morning in Superior Court.

Stoner was intrigued by the case. He'd followed developments in the *Chronicle* which reported the killing as taking place Tuesday evening. Several identified Lera, and there was little question he was guilty of cold-blooded murder. There seemed no question as well that Lera was in the rackets, operating the slot machine concession. A henchman of Oliver Quinn and Dutch Voight.

The manhunt that followed was heavily reported in the paper. Every lawman from Houston to the Gulf was on the lookout, and Lera had clearly gone into hiding to avoid arrest. Yet, out of the blue and with no explanation, he had surfaced last night and voluntarily surrendered to the police. All of which raised the question of why a man facing the electric chair would suddenly turn himself in. Why indeed?

Janice came out of the suite onto the balcony. She was dressed for the day, wearing a navy skirt and a pastel blue blouse, with a scarf at the throat. Stoner gave her an appreciative look remembering last night in bed, when she wore nothing at all. Their eleven days on the Island seemed to have passed in a blur, except for the nights. She made the nights memorable.

"Look at you," she said, kissing him on the cheek. "A man of leisure sunning himself with his newspaper."

"I need my rest," Stoner said with a sly smile. "You keep me all wore out."

"I recall I had a little help, pumpkin. I think I'll rename you Randy Andy."

"Things come over me when the lights go out."

"You're telling me!"

She poured coffee and nibbled on toast, ever conscious of her figure. Stoner laid the paper on the table, tapping the article, and gave her a nutshell version of Lera's surrender. She glanced at him over the rim of her cup.

"That's one for the funny farm," she said, puzzling on it a moment. "Why would someone who's sure to get electrified just up and surrender? It doesn't make sense."

"Maybe it does," Stoner said. "What if there was something worse than the electric chair?"

"Cripes, what could be worse than that?"

"I've been sitting here thinking about it. Only one thing comes to me."

"Aha! Sherlock at work again. Go ahead, enlighten me, Mr. Holmes."

"Glad to, Dr. Watson." Stoner leaned forward, elbows on the table. "Suppose Quinn and Voight somehow got their hands on this guy Lera. Suppose they put it to him in a way he couldn't refuse."

"Ummm," she said, munching toast. "Why couldn't he refuse?"

"Suppose there were only two options. One, you turn yourself into the cops. Or two, you get killed right now, something tough and dirty. Which would you choose?"

"You think they would really do something horrendous?"

"Jan, they're gangsters," Stoner said grimly. "Forget the Hollywood Club and all the glitz. They've got ways to kill people that would spoil your breakfast."

"Now you tell me!" she yelped. "What happens if they catch us?"

"I warned you before we came here. Don't get nervous on me now."

"Who, me? For your information, I have nerves of steel. Nothing fazes me."

"I'll hold you to it," Stoner said with a smile. "You're my number-one undercover operative."

"I'm your *only* undercover operative," she informed him. "Something bothers me about this Lera, though."

"What's that?"

"Why would Quinn and Voight want him to stand trial? What do they gain?"

Stoner thought it was a key question. Over the last week or so he'd eavesdropped on conversations in bars and gaming dives, and studiously read everything printed in the paper. Slowly, like an intricate mosaic, he had pieced together who was who in the Galveston power structure. Quinn and Voight, with their army of hoodlums, controlled the rackets. Yet the real power brokers, from all he could determine, were William Magruder and George Seagrave.

Magruder and Seagrave, by all accounts, controlled the political apparatus of Galveston County. Quinn and Voight, by virtue of bribes and payoffs, operated under immunity from law enforcement and the courts. So it followed, as he fitted the pieces together, that some link existed between the mob and the two most prominent men on the Island. Corrupt politicians wedded to racketeers required the blessing of those who ruled the ballot box.

Magruder and Seagrave were the names that came to mind.

Stoner recalled as well the evening he'd tried to bluff his way into the Hollywood Club casino. He remembered that Oliver Quinn had shown special treatment to a large party celebrating a girl's birthday. The maitre d' had told him the girl's father was William Magruder, and, in retrospect, it made sense that the other older man at the table was George Seagrave. Thinking about it now, Stoner wasn't surprised that Quinn was playing footsy with the Island's royal families. Even racketeers sometimes went on bended knee.

How all that played on his investigation was, for the moment, a matter of conjecture. His assignment was to bring down Quinn and Voight, and he warned himself not to muddy the waters with dirty politics. He suddenly realized he'd drifted off into woolgathering about things beyond the scope of his investigation. Janice was watching him with a pixilated expression.

"Knock, knock, anybody there? Aren't you going to answer my question?"

"I don't know the answer," Stoner said with a shrug. "Why Quinn and Voight put Lera in jail is anybody's guess. We've got other things on our plate anyhow."

"Let me consult my crystal ball." She wrinkled her brow in mock concentration. "Yes, I believe I see it now—the Hollywood Club."

"Give the little lady a cigar. I think it's time we made our move."

"Dare I ask why, Mr. Holmes?"

"Elementary, Dr. Watson." Stoner wagged a hand back and forth. "We've built our cover story with me the rich sucker and money to burn. Today's our day."

"So how do we work this magic act?"

"I'd say it's more of a tap dance. Let's go see our buddy Charlie Anderson."

Downstairs, they walked through the lobby to the office of the manager. By now, with their lavish suite and generous tips, they were familiar to every employee in the hotel. Charles Anderson, the manager, welcomed them into his office with the courtesy reserved for wealthy guests. He offered them chairs before his desk.

"Mr. Eberling. Mrs. Eberling," he said unctuously. "Hope you're enjoying your stay with us. How may I help you today?"

"Need you to use your influence," Stoner said, adopting his rancher persona. "You'll recollect you told me to call on you for a favor? Anything at all?"

"Why, yes, of course, I certainly do. How may I be of assistance?"

"The missus and me would like to have a whirl at the casino over in the Hollywood Club. I figured you're just the man to open the door."

"Easier said than done," Anderson remarked. "The Hollywood Club requires membership for the casino. They're very selective about their patrons."

"Hell's bells and little fishes!" Stoner grumped. "I've been losin' money hand over fist at the Garden Club and all these other crooked joints. I hear the Hollywood Club's got square games. I want you to fix it for me, Charlie."

"Well—" Anderson appeared uncomfortable. "As I said, they are very, *very* selective."

Stoner slapped a hundred-dollar bill on the desk. "Lookit here now, Charlie, I'm plumb serious. Olive'll tell you so herself."

"Oh my, yes," Janice said, jumping into her role of the good little wife. "Bob just has his heart set on this, Mr. Anderson. Couldn't you help us . . . *pleeeze*?"

"Perhaps I could." Anderson deftly palmed the hundred-dollar bill. "I'll make a call and see what might be arranged. No promises, you understand. I can only try."

"Good enough for me," Stoner said with a broad grin. "I knew you'd pull it off, Charlie. Let me know, you hear?"

"I'll definitely be in touch, Mr. Eberling."

Outside the office, Janice laughed gaily. "What a ham

you are, *Mr. Eberling.* I think you tap-danced us into the Hollywood Club."

"Olive, darlin', I think you're right. Damned if I don't!"

They went off for a day of sight-seeing.

"Your friends are here again."

"What friends?"

"Reverend Adair and Reverend Baldwin. And of course, our mayor in waiting, Herbie Cornwall."

Durant's brow furrowed. "Wonder what they want?"

"I don't know," Catherine said with an ingenuous smile. "Should I ask them?"

"No, send them in."

Durant was immediately on guard. In the morning paper, he'd read that Louis Lera had surrendered to the police last night. His first reaction was one of surprise, for men who faced the death penalty rarely surrendered themselves voluntarily. His second was that Lera's surrender would largely defuse the reform movement. The preachers would have little to preach about on Sunday, for the accused was now in jail. Justice was taking its course.

The clergymen, followed by Cornwall, filed into the office. Their manner was that of Crusaders who had been thwarted in their quest for the Holy Grail. Durant got them seated as Catherine gave him a waggish look and closed the door. Reverend Baldwin went straight to the point.

"I assume you've read the paper?"

Durant nodded. "Most men wouldn't turn themselves in, not with the evidence that's been reported. Curious thing."

"Curious indeed," Baldwin said. "We've talked it over, and we're of the opinion there was nothing voluntary about his surrender. He was forced into it."

"That's even curiouser," Durant commented. "How do you force a man to risk the electric chair?"

Adair grunted. "Oliver Quinn and Dutch Voight are in league with the Devil. I'm sure they found a way."

"All part of a greater conspiracy," Baldwin added. "The objective being to derail the impetus of our reform movement. Which they have accomplished with infuriating ease."

Cornwall arched an eyebrow. "Does the idea of a conspiracy surprise you, Mr. Durant?"

"I'm not sure I follow you," Durant said. "Are you talking about Quinn and Voight?"

"Think back to our last visit," Cornwall said. "Do you recall I asked about the beating you took at the hands of Nolan and his thugs?"

Durant held his gaze. "What's that got to do with anything?"

"Your answer was quite evasive," Cornwall said. "Something to the effect you weren't sure of the reason yourself."

"So?"

"So we think you were less than candid."

"Are you calling me a liar?"

"Nothing of the kind!" Baldwin interrupted. "Let us raise a hypothetical. Is that agreeable?"

Durant shrugged. "Fire away."

"Everyone accepts without question that William Magruder and George Seagrave are the political kingpins of Galveston County."

"And it's hardly a secret," Adair chimed in, "that Magruder and Seagrave tacitly condone the mob's illegal enterprises. All for the sake of a booming economy."

"Which leads to the conclusion," Baldwin carried on, "that Magruder and Seagrave have a working relationship—perhaps mutual interests—with the underworld element. From that, we might naturally assume there is a reciprocal arrangement of some nature."

"So we could hypothesize," Adair said, "that if—*if!*—Magruder had designs on your bank, and you refused to sell. . . ."

"Presto!" Baldwin took his cue. "Magruder might well request assistance from his underworld cronies. . . ."

"And have you beat to a pulp," Cornwall concluded. "All to intimidate you into selling your bank. How does that sound for a hypothetical?"

Durant stared at them. "How long did you boys rehearse this act?"

"We beg your candor," Adair said. "Is it true or not?"

"Sticking to the hypothetical," Durant replied, "what if it was? What's your point?"

"We have a common foe," Adair said earnestly. "Our community is under siege by a criminal conspiracy. Your bank is in jeopardy."

"Not to mention you, personally," Baldwin observed. "The next time these hooligans attack you they may not stop with a simple beating. And I believe you'll agree, Magruder will ensure there is a next time."

Durant's expression betrayed nothing. He wasn't about to tell them that there had already been a next time, men with guns intent on killing him. Nor was he willing to entrust them with the knowledge that he'd killed one of the mob's men. His gut warned him that no secret was safe with holier-than-thou reformers.

"Why the big sales pitch?" he said at length. "What is it you want from me?"

"We want proof," Baldwin said simply. "Proof that links William Magruder to these mobsters."

"And everyone benefits," Adair hurried on. "We obtain substantial grounds for reform, and you save your bank as well as eliminating the risk of further violence. Nothing could be more perfect."

"You just lost me," Durant said. "How am I supposed to get proof on Magruder?"

"Trick him," Cornwall said slyly. "By outwitting Magruder this long, you've shown yourself to be a clever man. Trick him into an admission of his dealings with Quinn and Voight."

"What if I did?" Durant said skeptically. "It's his

word against mine, and he's top dog in Galveston. Who'd believe me?"

Baldwin laughed softly. "We're not talking a court of law, Mr. Durant. We're talking a court of public opinion, as preached from our pulpits. That is where the next election will be won."

"And your private fight as well," Cornwall rushed to add. "Your bank will be saved, and your personal safety will be assured. Neither Magruder nor the mob will defy public opinion."

Durant looked from one to the other. Their argument was persuasive, for public opinion was not a force to be ignored. Yet he saw even greater risk if he tried to trick Magruder into something incriminating and failed. He warned himself not to jump too fast.

"I'll think about it," he said finally. "No promises, but I'll think it over."

"Time is of the essence," Baldwin persisted. "How long will you need?"

"I'll give you an answer tomorrow."

"Splendid!" Adair grinned like a horse eating briars. "We know you won't let us down. Nor yourself, for that matter. All in a good cause!"

The three men left after wringing his hand in fellowship. Durant leaned back in his chair, his eyes fixed on the middle distance. Nothing was ever as simple as it seemed to the schemers of the world.

He wondered how the hell he could trap Magruder.

The men began trooping into the Turf Club shortly before eleven o'clock. They took the elevator to the third floor, where they were frisked by Jack Nolan and Turk McGuire. Firearms, knives and brass knuckles were consigned to a box in the athletic club.

The meeting was held across the hall in the billiards room. The men gathered there were the vice chiefs of the Island, operating under the largesse of their overlords. Quinn and Voight had summoned them, though the purpose of the meeting was not announced. None of the men felt bold enough to ask.

Dan Lampis ran part of the slot machine concession. His counterpart, Lou Lera, was in jail for murder, and he hoped to take over the entire business. Sam Amelio owned seven whorehouses, and Gus Allen operated two of the larger gaming joints, the Garden Club and the Grotto Club. The other men, five in all, had various concessions for juke-boxes, pinball machines, and bootlegging. They were the underbosses of Galveston's underworld.

The men seated themselves in chairs arranged along the back wall of the billiards room. Nolan and McGuire took positions on either side of the door, there to ensure that the meeting was conducted in a businesslike manner. Quinn and Voight walked through the door at the stroke of eleven, and halted behind the snooker table, facing their underbosses. The room fell quiet as the men ranged along the wall waited to hear the purpose of the meeting.

Voight nodded around the room. "You boys are here because of what's happened over the past week. Anybody that's not deaf, dumb and blind knows we damn near handed the reformers our operation on a silver platter."

The men murmured their assent. Quinn silenced them with an upraised palm. "We got off the hook with some fast moves and a little luck. Lou Lera's surrender to the cops was the only thing that saved us. Otherwise the reformers would have started a crusade to clean us out."

"Holy roller cocksuckers," Sam Amelio grated. "Why don't we bump off a couple and teach 'em a lesson? They'd learn to keep their traps shut."

"You always were a stupe," Voight said, fixing him with a hard glare. "Lera killin' that civilian was what got us into hot water. Wise up, for chrissake."

Amelio looked stung. "I didn't mean no harm, Dutch."

"That's the trouble with you lunkheads," Voight said hotly. "Your mouth gets ahead of your brain, and before you know it, you've done something stupid. All that's gonna end today."

"Lera's a case in point," Quinn said. "He pulled a gun when he should've walked away, or at worst, fought the guy even-steven. Everybody has to put the good of the organization first. Forget the rough stuff."

The men swapped glances. They thought it was an odd statement, considering the fate of Joey Adonis. A week ago today Adonis and a couple of his goons were spotted at the Funland Amusement Pier. They seemingly vanished that evening, and while no one had the moxie to ask what happened, everyone in the room knew. Adonis and his boys were at the bottom of the Gulf.

"Talkin' about Lera," Dan Lampis said, his expression one of guileless curiosity. "How'd you and Dutch get him to face charges . . . if you don't mind my askin'?"

"Lou's a stand-up guy," Quinn said with genuine duplicity. "He understood what was best for the organization and he did it. Our hats are off to him."

No one believed a word of it. There was talk that Quinn and Voight had brought in a top defense attorney from Houston, and Lera intended to enter a plea of not guilty. The consensus was that he would nonetheless ride Old Sparky into the next life.

"The reason I asked about Lou," Lampis said, pressing his case. "Somebody's got to take over his end of the slots, and it ought to be somebody that knows the territory. I was thinkin' it might be me."

"Hold that for another time," Quinn said. "We're here to talk about other things."

"Get the wax out of your ears and pay attention!"

Voight's tone was like the rasp of sandpaper. He leaned forward, his hands gripping the edge of the snooker table, and his cold stare ranged over the men along the wall. His attitude was one of open menace.

"The *Rule*," he said coarsely. "The Rule says you don't touch a civilian, don't rough him up, and you Goddamn sure don't kill him. That's the way we've operated from day one."

"And for good reason," Quinn added. "We need good public relations to keep things perking along. Harm a civilian and you put the organization at risk."

"Lou Lera's the exception," Voight told them. "We needed him to stand trial to get the reformers off our back. But starting today, there's not gonna be any more exceptions. No way, no how."

The men returned his gaze as though under the spell of a hypnotist. A leaden stillness settled over the room as he glowered at them, his icy stare touching one, then another. His eyes were hooded.

"Here's the story," he said. "From now on, you break the Rule and there's no excuses, no second chances. Jack will take it from there."

Every eye in the room shifted to Diamond Jack Nolan. He looked back at them with an ironic smile, and they understood exactly what the smile meant. He would kill any man who broke the Rule.

"Everybody got it?" Voight demanded. "You screw up, we're not gonna go through this again. Now's the time to speak up if you've got any questions."

There were no questions. Quinn, never one for loose ends, decided to tie it off. "One last thing," he said. "Spread the word to everybody who works for you, anybody you're associated with, anybody who could get you in hot water. No matter what, no matter why—" he paused for emphasis—"live by the Rule."

The alternative, they all understood, would be unpleasant, and final. The men filed out of the room, bobbing their heads with nervous smiles as they turned toward the elevator. Quinn and Voight walked down the hall to their office. The phone rang as they came through the door. Voight lifted the receiver.

"Yeah."

"Mr. Voight?"

"How'd you get my private number?"

"You gave it to me, Mr. Voight. This is Charles Anderson, manager at the Buccaneer."

"How're things, Chuck? What can I do for you?"

"I have a guest in the hotel," Anderson said. "A wealthy rancher with more money than sense. He's set on trying his luck at your casino."

"Where's he from?" Voight said. "You know anything about him?"

"His ranch is in Blanco County. I know he's lost considerable money at the Garden Club and other spots. He's heard you have the only honest games in town."

"How long's he been at the hotel?"

"Almost two weeks."

"Would you vouch for him?"

"Well, yes, I suppose," Anderson said hesitantly. "He and his wife are big spenders. Very generous."

Voight laughed. "Gave you a tip to call me, did he?"

"Only a hundred, Mr. Voight. I didn't see any harm."

"What's his name?"

"Robert Eberling."

"I'll get back to you."

Voight disconnected. He waited a moment, then jiggled the hook. "Operator? Get me 3684 in Austin."

"Yessir, connecting your call."

There was a metallic buzz on the line, three rings, and a man answered. "Burnett Detective Agency."

"John, this is Dutch Voight. I want you to check somebody out for me."

"Glad to, Mr. Voight," Burnett said. "Who's the party?"

"Robert Eberling," Voight told him. "Supposed to have a big ranch in Blanco County. Find out if he's legit."

"I'll call you with the rundown, Mr. Voight. Probably later today."

Voight replaced the receiver on the hook. One gambler more or less was of no great concern, and he dismissed the matter from mind. He looked around at Quinn.

"So how'd we do, Ollie? Think the boys will toe the line?"

Quinn smiled. "Dutch, I just suspect our troubles are over. No more grist for the reformers."

Voight thought brute force and sudden death were the most persuasive of arguments. He told himself the message would spread through town by noon. Live by the Rule. . . .

Or say hello and good-bye to Diamond Jack Nolan.

Chapter Fourteen

The Rice Hotel was located in downtown Houston. One of the city's older hotels, it was home away from home for visiting salesmen and businessmen. The lobby was appointed with heroic murals of the Texas Revolution.

Nolan, right on time, arrived at two o'clock. He went into the coffee shop and took a table with a view of the door. Earlier, after the meeting with the underbosses, he'd told Quinn he needed the afternoon off. The hours he worked entitled him to free time whenever he could fit it into the schedule. He wasn't expected at the Hollywood Club until that evening.

Libbie entered the coffee shop a few minutes after two. She had taken the interurban railway from Galveston, rather than be seen driving her sporty Chevrolet coupe. Her simple day dress was conservative compared to her flapper outfits, worn so she wouldn't attract undue attention. She crossed to the table and took a seat, her cheeks flushed with excitement. She breathed a nervous little laugh.

"God, I feel like Mata Hari. Do I look like I'm spying for the Germans?"

"You look beautiful," Nolan said, trying to calm her nerves. "Sorry for all the sneaking around, but it couldn't be helped. I'd be up the creek if my bosses found out."

Four days had passed since their afternoon of love-making at the Rendezvous Roadhouse. They had talked on the phone in the interim and decided the roadhouse was too close to Galveston. Nolan had suggested Houston, and the Rice Hotel, for their liaison today. Neither of them questioned that their affair was worth any risk.

A waitress drifted by and took their orders for coffee. Libbie waited until she was out of earshot. "I hate to sound naïve, but I've never done this before. How do we arrange a room?"

"Already done," Nolan said in a low voice. "I registered before you got here. We're in Room three-o-four."

"Do we just take the elevator up there—in broad daylight?"

"No, I'll leave and you finish your coffee. Give it five minutes and then come on up."

"Now I do feel like Mata Hari."

"Just act natural and nobody's the wiser. See you upstairs."

Nolan dropped a dollar on the table and left the coffee shop. A few minutes later he opened the door of Room 304 and Libbie quickly stepped inside from the hallway. Her cheeks were even rosier.

"The elevator operator ogled me all the way up. I don't think we fooled him."

"Elevator operators don't bother me."

Nolan enfolded her in his arms. She pressed herself against him, her arms around his neck, and their mouths met in a feverish kiss. They'd both spent four days thinking about the last time, and there was an urgency in their need. He lifted her in his arms and carried her to the bed.

Their haste left clothes strewn across the floor. Her passion was wild and atavistic, and he marveled again at her total lack of inhibition. Their lovemaking was filled with the zest of discovery, playful yet lustily fierce, unbounded by convention. When at last they parted, exquisitely sated, he was still amazed by the depth of her hunger. A welter of claw marks on his back bore testament to her fiery nature.

She snuggled close, her head against his shoulder. A warm breath, soft and velvety, eddied through the hair on his chest. He glanced around and found her watching him with an impish smile. She hugged him in a tight embrace.

"Do you believe in love at first sight?"

Nolan looked away. "I'm not the kind of guy you want to love."

"Because you're a gangster?" She plucked a hair from his chest, laughing when he winced. "I'll choose my own man, thank you very much."

"We're from worlds about as far apart as you can get. I don't think you'd much like mine."

"Oh, so it's just a quick roll in the hay. Wham, bam and thank you, ma'am?"

"You know better than that."

"'Fess up, tough guy." She wrapped a knot of his hair around her finger and threatened to pull. "Did you fall for me or not? Am I your girl?"

Nolan was forced to grin. "You're my girl if that's what you want. You're asking for trouble, though."

"I'm perfectly content to worry about that when it happens."

Libbie was less certain than she sounded. She was a spoiled rich girl, her father's favorite, even though Sherm was the heir to the throne. She had attended Bryn Mawr, a college for rich girls in Pennsylvania, where she became a convert in the struggle for women's emancipation. Her heroine was Susan B. Anthony, who had founded the suffrage movement almost seventy-five years ago. She often thought Susan B. would have approved of flappers.

Women got the vote when the Nineteenth Amendment cleared Congress in 1920. Four years ago, Libbie had cast her ballot for Warren G. Harding, who disappointed her by being branded the most corrupt president in history. But she had studied Lenin and the Bolshevist movement in school, and later waded through the uneasy marriage of democracy, free enterprise, and capitalism. Whatever the form of government, corruption seemed an integral part of the system, and if America could survive a crooked president, she saw nothing wrong with a gangster for a boyfriend. She wasn't so sure about her father.

Nolan, for his part, was crystal clear about their situation. Before the war, like his father and his father's father, he had worked on fishing boats operating out of Texas City. He had known poverty and hardship, scrimping to pay the rent and put food on the table, and it shaded his outlook on life. During the war, his father had died aboard a boat caught in a Gulf storm, and a few months later, his mother passed away of a broken heart. His background, a workingman who won some medals in France and then turned gangster, was not the stuff of high society. He thought Libbie was fooling herself if she believed it didn't matter.

Then, as she snuggled closer in his arms, he realized he was just as foolish. Quinn and Voight, if they ever learned he was sleeping with Magruder's daughter, would probably take *him* for a swim. Their political ties to Magruder, and the continued prosperity of their criminal enterprises, would cast him as the sacrificial goat. Yet, even as he considered the possibility, he knew he wouldn't stop seeing her. He'd survived the Krauts and the trenches of France, and working for the mob, he lived with danger every day of his life. A little more danger, in the form of the girl cuddled next to him, added spice to the game.

She darted his ear with her tongue. She laughed, her mouth moist and inviting, and he kissed her. His hand covered one of her high, jutting breasts, and the nipple swelled instantly. For several moments they caressed and fondled, until finally, aroused and aching, she drew him on top of her. A shudder racked her, and her legs spidered around him, pulling faster and faster with the rhythm of his stroke. Her nails pierced his back like talons as they joined in an explosive spasm.

Afterward, breathing heavily, time lost all meaning. She clung to his hard-muscled frame, carried far beyond her most vivid fantasies. A while later, drifting on a quenched flame, they kissed again, their bodies warm and their legs intertwined. She pressed her mouth to his ear in a throaty whisper.

"Any doubts now?"

"About what?"

"Love at first sight."

Nolan chuckled softly. "You want the truth?"

"Nothing but."

"I think we're stuck with one another."

"Oh, God, isn't it great!"

She kissed him so hard his ears rang.

Durant sat staring at the wall. All morning, and during a solitary lunch at a nearby café, he'd mulled over his meeting with the reform committee. He still hadn't made a decision.

The problem was twofold. First, he kept asking himself if an attempt to trap Magruder would provoke further action by the mob. And second, he stewed on how he might gull Magruder into what amounted to a confession. Hard questions with no ready answers.

Around three o'clock he came to the conclusion he was getting nowhere. He generally kept his own counsel, but today he realized the road walked by an individualist was a lonely one. If nothing else, he needed a sounding board, or maybe a devil's advocate, to put things in perspective. He buzzed Aldridge and Catherine, and asked them to come in.

They already knew something was up. He'd hardly spoken to anyone since the meeting that morning with the reformers. Even more telling, he had put Aldridge off on pending bank affairs, and done it in a rather abrupt manner. Neither of them doubted that it somehow involved the clergymen and Herbert Cornwall. But they couldn't have imagined what he was about to tell them.

Durant waited until they'd taken chairs before his desk. He then explained that he faced a difficult decision, and asked for their opinion. As they listened, he summarized the salient points, stressing the fact that the surrender of Louis Lera, the accused murderer, had undercut the chances of a reform movement. He went on to relate the plan that had been proposed, and how the reformers believed it would ignite their crusade. He admitted he was stumped.

"I'm damned if I do and damned if I don't," he concluded. "Whichever way I turn it, I don't see a smart choice."

"Good Lord," Aldridge said with a troubled frown. "Confronting Magruder would most certainly trigger another assault by his mobster friends. How can you even consider it?"

"Question is, would it?" Durant said. "It's been almost a week since they jumped me. Maybe siding with the reformers bought me a pass."

"A week?" Catherine sounded confused. "It was almost two weeks ago they beat you up. Has something happened I don't know about?"

Durant realized he'd made a slip of the lip. He involuntarily glanced at Aldridge, who kept a straight face. His lie of omission—not telling Catherine he had shot and killed a gangster—seemed in retrospect a mistake. Yet he saw nothing for it but to carry on with the deception. He gestured in an idle motion.

"You're right," he said dismissively. "Too many things on my mind. It's closer to two weeks."

Catherine searched his eyes. "Well, anyway," she said after a moment, "I'm not sure I agree with Mr. Aldridge. I hope you won't be offended. . . ."

"No, no," Aldridge said hurriedly. "Say whatever's on your mind."

"I think Earl—Mr. Durant—was right. Working with the reformers might protect him rather than harm him. Even gangsters have to be concerned with public opinion."

"Yes, that's true," Aldridge conceded. "Earl and I talked it over and came to the same conclusion. The thing that bothers me most is the idea of confronting Magruder."

"What's the option?" Durant said, probing for a reaction. "Without a strong reform movement, we're back to status quo. Magruder could sic his pals on me and nothing to stop him. He still wants to get his hands on this bank."

"No question of it," Aldridge agreed. "Nothing has changed with respect to his designs on the bank."

"So the only solution is to bring him down. Him *and* his mob buddies."

"Yes, that's what I meant a moment ago," Catherine said. "To protect yourself and the bank, you have to put them on the defensive. You really have no choice."

"You know—" Durant rubbed the bridge of his nose, thoughtful. "I think you just helped me to make up my mind. It's time to take the fight to them."

"And then what?" Aldridge asked. "Even if Magruder admits his complicity, it's your word against his. What would you have accomplished?"

"Ira, I raised the same point with Adair and Baldwin. They plan to expose Magruder in their sermons, take the whole thing public. They all but guaranteed me it'll work."

"Nonsense!" Aldridge grumped. "William Magruder owns half this town and the people in it. Whose word do you think they'll accept?"

"I know the problem," Durant countered. "What's the solution?"

"You need corroboration. A witness to whatever Magruder says."

"And where would I find a witness?"

"I volunteer," Aldridge said dryly. "However reluctantly, I enlist in the cause."

"I don't know." Durant hesitated, scratching his jaw. "Magruder might not open up with just me. Why would he talk with two of us there?"

"We'll think of something," Aldridge said. "Perhaps something to do with the bank that involves me. The point is, you have nothing unless you have corroboration."

Durant looked at him. "You'd be putting yourself at risk, Ira. You ought to think about it."

"I already have," Aldridge told him. "More than the bank—or for that matter, you or me—we're talking about the community, what's best for Galveston. I believe it's time to take a stand."

"Don't turn noble on me. That's no reason to go in harm's way."

"Noble has nothing to do with it. I'm just tired of being kicked around by Magruder and his crowd. I realized it here today."

"You're sure?"

"Yes, I am."

Durant called Magruder's office. He spoke to a secretary, who connected him with Magruder. He kept the conversation vague, piquing Magruder's interest with the thought that a discussion about People's Bank & Trust might be beneficial to all concerned. He hung up with a tight smile.

"We're on," he said. "Tomorrow morning at nine."

Catherine was silent, her eyes suddenly filled with concern. Aldridge steepled his fingers, nodding wisely. "So there we are," he said. "I believe we need to talk strategy."

They began discussing ways to snare William Magruder.

The Santa Fe depot was like an overturned beehive. On Friday the railroad put on extra trains to handle the weekend tourists bound for Galveston. A thousand people or more were looking for a taxi.

Quinn waited outside the station house. The four-thirty train, having disgorged its load, finally pulled away toward the switching yard. He checked his watch, wondering if the five o'clock train would be on time. He had to be at the club by six.

Today, a figure of sartorial splendor, he wore a dove-gray tropical worsted suit, with a striped shirt and a blue tie, and a light-gray fedora. Rags Martin, the comedian, was closing tonight, and Quinn was there to meet the Hollywood Club's latest attraction. Sophie Tucker, direct from Broadway, would open tomorrow night.

All in all, Quinn thought things were going his way. The surrender of Lou Lera, engineered with perfect timing, had put the quietus on the reformers. The meeting that morning with the underbosses had put everyone on notice about further violence. He liked an orderliness to things, and he felt the situation on the Island had returned to normal. His mind was now free to concentrate on his newest sensation, a stage spectacular. Yet another coup for Galveston's Mr. Showbiz!

The five o'clock train chuffed to a halt, belching steam, at five-o-one. The weekenders swarmed off the coaches like revelers late for a party. There was a mad dash for taxis and the jitney buses that trundled back and forth between hotels. The weather was balmy for late September, and the tourists had visions of sandy beaches and warm surf. The amusement piers and nightspots would be packed over the weekend.

Sophie Tucker stepped off the private compartment car. She was a small, plumpish woman with a saucy disposition and a kind of bustling vitality. She wore a floral dress with a fur stole and a hat bedecked with bright feathers. Her oval features were framed by hair red as a sunset, and something puckish lurked behind eyes as wide and dark as buttons. Quinn hurried forward to meet her.

"Miss Tucker!" he called affably. "Welcome to Galveston. I'm Oliver Quinn."

"A pleasure," she said with a dimpled smile. "I began to wonder if the train ride would ever end. Is this still the United States?"

"Only for a couple miles, Miss Tucker. The next stop from here is Mexico."

"I can't sing a note in Spanish. And enough already with that Miss Tucker stuff. All my friends call me Sophie. What do I call you?"

"Ollie," Quinn said, doffing his fedora in a gallant gesture. "Your most ardent admirer."

"Well, now," she said, a pudgy fist on her hip. "I do like my men ardent, Ollie. Galveston's looking better all the time."

Sophie Tucker was a show-business icon. A star of burlesque, vaudeville and nightclubs, her career had spanned twenty years. On Broadway, she had captured national fame in the *Ziegfeld Follies* and Earl Carroll's *Vanities*. At forty-two, with a zoftig figure, her brassy, flamboyant style was perfectly suited to risqué ballads. Her show was so bawdy, sometimes raw and ribald, that she'd been arrested three times in New York for indecent performances. She was billed as "The Last of the Red Hot Mamas."

"Tell me, Ollie," she said with amused eyes. "I'm an inquisitive broad and no apologies for it. You mind a couple questions?"

"No, not at all . . . Sophie."

The depot platform was pandemonium in motion, tourists rushing off in every direction. She flung out an arm. "Who the hell are all these people?"

"Your fans," Quinn said with sly eloquence. "Come all this way for your opening night."

"Sold out, are you?"

"Full house, every night."

"I knew I shoulda charged you more."

Quinn was paying her six thousand for a week's appearance. She was not a star on the order of Al Jolson, but he'd casually dismissed Voight's objections about her pricey fee. A Red Hot Mama, he'd argued, would be a sellout. And she was.

"A deal's a deal," he said to her now. "Besides, you'll like it so much here, you'll never want to leave. We had to shanghai Jolson onto the train out of town."

"You're a card, Ollie." She swatted him with the tip of her fur stole. "Anyway, I started to ask you something else. Where's a gal get a drink around here? My pipes are parched."

"We have a suite for you at the Buccaneer. Overlooks

the Gulf with the best view on the Island. And the bar's fully stocked."

Sophie wasn't surprised. Some of her oldest friends in New York were gangsters, and she'd heard all about Oliver Quinn and Dutch Voight. Their control of the Island, the Hollywood Club and the rumrunning operation, made them the envy of every hood east of the Mississippi. She thought she was going to enjoy her stay in Galveston.

Quinn got a porter busy collecting her luggage. He offered her his arm and led her around the depot to the parking lot. Turk McGuire was waiting with the Cadillac Phaeton, the teardrop fenders and gold body polished to a gloss. He knuckled the brim of his hat, nodding with his gravedigger's smile, and held open the rear door. Sophie gave him a slow, appreciative once-over.

"Ummm," she murmured, glancing sideways at Quinn. "You grow them big in Texas. Just my style."

"Hear that, Turk?" Quinn said with a chuckle. "What do you say when a lady pays you a compliment?"

McGuire blushed like a schoolboy. "Guess I'd tell her it's mutual."

Sophie batted her lashes. "Your boss says I'm in a suite stocked with booze. Why don't you come up and see me sometime?"

On the way to the hotel, though she was talking to Quinn, she kept dropping suggestive remarks directed at McGuire. Quinn realized she wasn't merely flirting, that she was indeed a Red Hot Mama. McGuire, staring straight ahead over the steering wheel, was beet red from his neckline to his ears. He seemed relieved when they pulled into the circular drive outside the Buccaneer.

Quinn escorted her to her suite. She marveled at the view, the westerly sun splashing the waters of the Gulf with splotches of orange and vermilion. Then she checked out the bar, clucking approvingly, while a bellboy carried her bags into the bedroom. Quinn waited until she'd inspected the accommodations before mentioning he had scheduled a rehearsal with the band the next morning. She laughed.

"Honey, I could sing if you tap your foot. I've been known to drown out the band."

"We'll let you rehearse the band," Quinn said jokingly. "I'll have Turk pick you up in the morning."

"Um-hmm." She stared him boldly in the eye. "I have a free night and nobody but little ol' me in this great big suite. How about you give Turk the night off?"

Quinn, for one of the few times in his life, was nonplussed. "Sophie, I'll be happy to let him have the night off. Whether he drops by to see you—well . . . that's up to him."

"Tell him he'll never know what he missed if he doesn't. I'm a lotta woman, Ollie."

"I'll relay the message."

Quinn escaped before the conversation went any further. On the short drive to the club, he gave McGuire the gist of her invitation. McGuire was silent a moment, his ears as red as oxblood. He finally found his voice.

"What d'ya think, boss?" he said. "Was she jokin' or what?"

"Turk, I think it might be the experience of your life."

McGuire lapsed into a prolonged silence. "Well—" he said as they pulled into the club. "Okay with you if I take the night off?"

"I'd be disappointed if you didn't. See you in the morning."

Quinn walked from the car to the office at the rear of the casino. He found Voight seated behind the desk, in the midst of lighting a cigar. Before he could speak, the phone rang. Voight lifted the receiver.

"Yeah?"

"Mr. Voight," a voice said at the other end of the line. "This is John Burnett, in Austin. You asked me to run a check for you on Robert Eberling."

"Yeah, sure, the rancher. What's the story?"

"Well, it turns out he's on the square. Owns a big

cattle spread in Blanco County and folks say he's worth a million, maybe more. Solid citizen."

"Anything else?"

"I called a friend at the Motor Vehicles Department and got the plate numbers on Eberling's car. Maybe you want to check 'em out against what he's driving."

"No, from what you say, he's legit. Thanks for hopping on it, John. Send me a bill."

Voight disconnected and called the manager's office at the Buccaneer. A moment later Charles Anderson came on the line.

"Yessir, Mr. Voight."

"Chuck, you know that fellow you asked about, the rancher? Tell him he's been approved for the casino. Have him ask for me when he comes in."

"Yessir, I certainly will. I know Mr. Eberling will be pleased."

"Always happy to take a man's money. See you around, Chuck."

Voight rang off. Quinn gave him a curious look and he shrugged. "Another sucker with money to burn. I had him checked out."

"We can always use another high roller. I just came back from picking up Sophie Tucker."

"Yeah, what's new with 'The Last of the Red Hot Mamas'?"

Quinn laughed. "Dutch, you're not gonna believe it."

Chapter Fifteen

The Strand got busy early on Saturday morning. Stores and businesses opened at eight, and soon thereafter the sidewalks were crowded with weekend shoppers. Intersections were clogged as more tourists in cars spilled over the causeway.

A warm sun rose higher against banks of cottony clouds. Durant and Aldridge left the bank a few minutes before nine and turned west along the Strand. Earlier, in Durant's office, they had reviewed their strategy one last time. Aldridge, though nervous, felt it would work.

"Just remember," Durant said as they walked along. "Let me do the talking and try to stay out of it. I want his attention on me."

"You needn't worry," Aldridge said, a light sheen of perspiration covering his face. "I have no intention of speaking unless spoken to. I'm along strictly as an observer."

"Whatever happens, don't cross swords with him. Getting him mad won't turn the trick. We have to finesse him."

"Earl, we've gone over it a dozen times. You needn't concern yourself with me. I'm fine."

"All right, Ira, let's do it."

They crossed Twenty-second Street and entered the Magruder Building. Dappled streamers of sunshine filtered through the skylight as the birdcage elevator took them to the tenth floor. In the anteroom of Magruder & Company, the secretary greeted Durant by name, darting a curious glance at Aldridge. She ushered them into the inner office.

Magruder was seated behind his ebony desk. His eyes touched on Aldridge, then shifted back to Durant. He motioned them to chairs.

"You asked to meet alone," he said. "Not that it isn't a pleasure to see Mr. Aldridge. But curiosity forces me to ask why?"

"Saves time," Durant replied. "If we make a deal, Ira's included in the package. I wanted him involved in our discussion."

Magruder pursed his mouth. "You said on the phone you might consider selling the bank. How does that involve Mr. Aldridge?"

"Ira comes with the bank," Durant said flatly. "It's not a negotiable point. Without him, there's no deal."

"In what capacity would he remain with the bank?"

"You'd agree to keep him on as vice president. And you'd guarantee it with an airtight, ironclad contract for five years."

"Indeed?" Magruder said slowly. "You drive a hard bargain on behalf of Mr. Aldridge."

Durant shrugged. "Like I said, it's not negotiable."

The strategy was to provide a credible reason for Aldridge's presence at the meeting. Until that was established, there was nothing to be gained in probing more sensitive matters. Durant waited for a response.

"Very well," Magruder said at length. "I assume all of that is acceptable to you, Mr. Aldridge?"

Aldrige held his gaze. "Yes, it is."

"You don't like me much, do you?"

"Business is business, Mr. Magruder. Personal likes or dislikes have no place in the scheme of things."

Magruder's jowls shook with silent laughter. "So long as everyone benefits, who cares about a son of a bitch? Is that the idea?"

"Your words, not mine."

"You always were the tactful one."

Magruder looked back at Durant. "Your uncle and Mr. Aldridge here never approved of my business tactics.

Of course, your uncle was always outspoken about it. No diplomacy."

"No hypocrite either," Durant said. "Was that what you held against him?"

"On the contrary," Magruder said magnanimously. "I respect a man who speaks his mind."

"So where are we with Ira? Do you agree or not?"

"I will provide him with—what was your term?—an airtight, ironclad contract. Which brings us to the matter at hand. How much to buy you out?"

"A hundred thousand," Durant said evenly. "And that's not negotiable, either."

"You surprise me," Magruder said, his eyes narrowed. "You once refused my offer in the same amount. Why accept it now?"

"I've had a bellyful of Galveston. On top of that, I'm bored stiff trying to act the part of a banker. Time to head back to California."

"And your motion pictures."

"That's about the size of it."

"A wise decision," Magruder announced. "Of course, I will require an agreement in writing that you sever all connections with these so-called reformers. Adair and Baldwin, and that jackass, Cornwall. No statements from you, public or otherwise . . . even from California."

"Now that you mention it—" Durant hesitated, set the trap. "I have a condition of my own."

"Condition of what sort?"

"I want an apology."

"Do you indeed?" Magruder appeared amused. "Apology for what?"

"For putting the mob on me."

"I haven't the faintest idea what you're talking about."

"Sure you do," Durant said equably. "You sicced those hoods on me, and had me beat up and almost shot. I want to hear you say you're sorry."

"You've been misinformed," Magruder said, shaking

his head. "Whatever happened to you was not of my doing. You have my word on it."

"Do you want the bank or not?"

"One has nothing to do with the other."

"Don't play me for a fool," Durant said shortly. "You made a call to Quinn or Voight, and they sent their boys looking for me. You know it and I know it."

"You are mistaken," Magruder said. "I resent the implication."

"No apology, no deal," Durant told him. "Phrase it any way you choose, but that's the only way you get the bank. I want your apology."

Magruder leaned back in his chair. He stared across the desk, and then, abruptly, some inner revelation lighted his features. His eyes went cold.

"You're a clever one, bub. Damn me if you're not."

"Nothing clever about it," Durant said. "All I'm asking is to hear you say you're sorry."

"Yes, indeed, very clever." Magruder's gaze flicked to Aldridge. "You brought along a witness and threw out the hook. I almost fell for it."

"Fell for what?" Durant tried for a note of confusion. "I offered you a pretty sweet deal. Do you want it or not?"

"No, I do not," Magruder said in a dismissive tone. "I believe that concludes our meeting. Good morning, gentlemen."

"You went from hot to cold mighty fast. What's the problem?"

"I have nothing further to say to you, Mr. Durant. Get out of my office."

Magruder began shuffling papers on his desk. Durant nodded to Aldridge and they walked to the door. On the elevator ride to the lobby they were silent, wondering where it had gone wrong. Outside the building, they turned back toward the bank.

"Don't feel too bad," Aldridge said. "In a way, I'm not surprised he caught on. He always was a shrewd one."

Durant grunted unpleasantly. "Ira, I'm sorry I got you involved in this. There'll be hell to pay."

"How do you mean?"

"Guess who Magruder's calling right now."

"Quinn and Voight?"

"Nobody else."

There were always large crowds for the opening night of a new act. Everyone wanted to say they were the first to see an entertainer imported from the Great White Way in New York. Tonight was no different at the Hollywood Club.

Clint Stoner looked dapper in his tuxedo. Janice, who had gone to the beauty shop at the hotel, was a vision of loveliness. Her hair was upswept, coifed in the latest Parisian style, and she wore an elegant satin sheath trimmed with lace to accentuate her décolletage. She turned heads.

The maitre d', who had snubbed them on their last visit, practically fawned over them tonight. Charles Anderson, the manager of the Buccaneer, had assured them of special treatment, and guest membership to the casino. Their table in the nightclub was beside the dance floor, near the stage. The maitre d', with only slight exaggeration, called them the best seats in the house.

"How about this!" Janice said as a waiter appeared with menus. "Last time we were at the back of the room."

"Well, Olive, honey," Stoner said, opening his menu, "it pays to know people in high places. All this and the casino, too."

"I can't wait to see Sophie Tucker. Everything I've read says she's absolutely shocking!"

"Hope she doesn't offend your sensitive nature."

"Every little housewife lives to be shocked. Didn't you know that, sweetheart?"

Stoner ordered a bottle of champagne. They dined on foie gras, terrapin soup, and braised pheasant. Between the main course and dessert, the orchestra swung into a medley of lively tunes, and they joined other couples on the dance floor. Janice, her spirits soaring on champagne, dragged him into a fast-stepping fox-trot. He clumped around in his cowboy boots like a rancher stomping crickets.

A while later the houselights dimmed. Sophie Tucker shimmied onstage, centered in a rosy spotlight, as the orchestra segued into show numbers. Her scarlet gown hugged her ample figure and she carried a glittery fan of peacock feathers. Her first song, playing off her trademark billing, was *There'll Be a Hot Time in the Old Town Tonight.* Her voice, a booming alto trained for vaudeville halls, rang throughout the club.

The show became steadily more risqué. Sophie strutted around the stage, belting out songs laced with sexual innuendo and naughty words. She paused for a bawdy wink here and a roll of her eyes there, and punctuated suggestive bedroom lyrics with a flip of her peacock fan. On her last number, she blink-blinked her hips like a hootchy-cootchy dancer and ended on a warbling high note. The audience roared their approval.

By the time she did an encore, and pranced offstage with a bump and grind, it was approaching ten o'clock. Janice applauded until the houselights came up, her eyes merry with excitement. "Did you ever!" she said, giddy with laughter. "No wonder they call her the Red Hot Mama!"

"Time to go to work," Stoner said, lowering his voice. "Let's drift on back to the casino."

"Spoilsport, just when I was enjoying myself."

"No more champagne for you, Olive. Keep your mind on who we are and why we're here."

"Do you think Sophie Tucker will come to the casino? I'd love to get her autograph!"

"Maybe tonight's your lucky night."

They walked to the far side of the room. Stoner gave his alias to the bruisers guarding the glass doors, and they were admitted with courteous smiles. As they moved through the lounge, the oak doors to the casino opened, and a stocky man in a double-breasted tux waited at the entrance. Stoner pegged him immediately as Dutch Voight.

"Mr. and Mrs. Eberling," he said with an amiable nod. "Welcome to our casino."

"Thank you kindly." Stoner made a mental note that there was a hidden intercom between the doors to the lounge and the casino. Otherwise Voight would not have known their names, or appeared so quickly. "Are you the manager, Mr.—"

"Voight," Voight supplied. "You might say I look after things. What is your game, Mr. Eberling?"

"Dice, roulette," Stoner said with a touch of bravado. "Anything that's got numbers on it. I play 'em all."

"We'll do our best to accommodate you. I've arranged an opening line of credit for five thousand. Will that be satisfactory?"

"Well now, that's mighty neighborly of you, Mr. Voight. You make a fella feel right at home."

"We do our best, Mr. Eberling. Enjoy yourselves—and good luck."

"Take all the luck I can get. I'm obliged, Mr. Voight."

"Not at all."

The casino was rapidly filling with patrons. Stoner collected a thousand dollars in chips from the cashier's cage, signing a chit with his alias. Janice, who smiled shyly, playing the part of the little woman, turned with him to survey the action. There were roulette tables, craps tables, and blackjack layouts aligned in orderly precision around the room. Banks of slot machines lined the walls.

"Olive, honey," Stoner said, "how'd you like to try them one-armed bandits? Think I'll have a crack at the roulette wheel."

"Anything you say, sweetie. I believe I might just break the bank!"

"That's the spirit."

Stoner signed another chit with the cashier for a hundred dollars. The cashier gave him a silver bucket, adorned with mother-of-pearl handle, filled with a hundred silver dollars. Janice, cradling the bucket in her arms, made a beeline for the nearest bank of slots. Stoner wandered over to a roulette table.

The game of roulette was one in which true aficionados played complicated betting systems. Stoner preferred to appear the wealthy high roller who relied on luck rather than skill. He randomly scattered chips around the numbered layout, alternately placing a larger wager on red or black, which was the safest bet. The wheel spun and the ivory ball clattered while Stoner and the other players waited in hushed expectation. He regularly lost more than he won.

The game was played at dizzying speed. The croupiers and pit bosses were cordial yet alert, raking in losing bets and paying winners with quick professionalism. All the while Stoner was casually inspecting the tables, the room, and the office at the rear of the casino. At one point, he clumsily dropped a few chips and knelt down, examining the understructure of the table and the floor. He saw nothing suspicious or unusual.

The mystery of it left him baffled. On previous raids by the Rangers, he'd been told the gaming tables and slot machines vanished in a matter of minutes. The Rangers found instead a well-appointed game room, filled with billiards tables, backgammon boards, and bridge tables. What mystified him was not just how the switch was made, but where all the heavy gambling paraphernalia disappeared to, and so rapidly. He was thoroughly stumped.

Across the room, he saw Voight approach Janice. She stopped playing the slot machine, and Voight, acting the convivial host, engaged her in conversation. Stoner pretended he'd lost interest in roulette and moved to one of the craps tables, where he whooped loudly, coaxing Lady Luck every time he tossed the dice. By the time he dropped a couple hundred, Voight had walked away from

Janice with an encouraging smile. He meandered over to the slot machines.

"Act happy," he said to Janice, motioning back at the tables, "while I act like the big-time gambler. What did Voight want?"

"Sweetie, I just got interrogated." Janice fed a dollar into the machine and jiggled with excitement as cherries and lemons and numbers spun. "He was smooth as silk, just making friendly conversation."

"About what?"

"Oh, he asked about the ranch, and the house, and how long we've lived in Blanco County. Things like that."

"And?"

"And I gave him all the right answers." She pouted prettily when the wheels stopped spinning without a winner. "No wonder they call these things one-armed bandits. Would you look at that!"

"Honey, you'll beat it yet. Just keep pumpin' in them dollars. Think I'll try my hand at blackjack."

Stoner took a seat at one of the blackjack tables. He wasn't particularly surprised by Voight's questions, and he was pleased by Janice's artful talent for guile. But he was at a loss as to how the casino was converted into a social club, and irritated with himself that he hadn't readily solved the problem. He mulled it over as the dealer dealt him a blackjack on his first hand.

For the night, Stoner lost seven hundred and Janice dropped two hundred more at the slots. As they were departing, Voight walked them to the door, properly conciliatory over their losses. He wished them better luck next time.

Stoner laughingly assured him they would be back.

Saturday night was the busiest night of the week on Post-office Street. The bordellos and speakeasies were mobbed with weekend tourists as well as Islanders. The four-block stretch that encompassed the red-light district was like a seedy carnival that separated workingmen from their wages.

Late that night, Sam Amelio emerged from a brothel near the intersection of Postoffice and Twenty-sixth Streets. He owned seven whorehouses, and on Saturday nights, he made it a practice to visit them at regular intervals. His madams were terrified of him, but he trusted no one, and he periodically dropped by to collect the proceeds. He was carrying almost two thousand in cash.

Amelio turned toward the corner. He never worried about carrying so much cash, and he saw no need for a bodyguard. Everyone in the district knew him on sight, and they knew as well his reputation for violence. He owned seven houses by virtue of having intimidated his rivals, and, in two instances, beating pimps so badly they left town. He prided himself on being known as the "Prince of Pussy."

One of Amelio's houses was located between Twenty-sixth and Twenty-seventh. As he approached the corner, mentally calculating the take for the night, he heard someone call his name. He stopped, looking south on Twenty-sixth, and saw Jack Nolan leaning against the fender of a Buick. Amelio considered himself a tough nut, but Nolan was one of the few men he genuinely feared. He turned down the block with a sense of something not quite right.

"Hey, Jack," he said, trying to sound jocular. "What brings you to nookieville?"

Nolan flicked an ash off his cigarette. His diamond pinky ring caught the light from the corner lamppost, glinting fire. He smiled a lazy smile.

"Just call me an errand boy, Sam. The boss wants to see you."

"Which boss is that?"

"Mr. Voight."

Amelio felt a tingle along his backbone. He wasn't fooled by Nolan's relaxed manner, the easy smile. He was even more concerned that Voight had sent the mob's chief enforcer out on a Saturday night. Something was definitely wrong.

"C'mon, Jack," Amelio said, suddenly wary. "You know Saturday's my big night. What's Mr. Voight want?"

"Search me," Nolan said, exhaling a thin streamer of smoke. "Probably won't take long, whatever it is. Your girls won't even miss you."

"Look, tell him I'll come by later tonight. Quick as things slow down, I'll be right there."

"No, he wants to see you now."

Turk McGuire stepped out the rear door of the Buick. The driver's door opened and Whizzer Duncan leaned out, his ferret eyes bright with malice. Nolan took a final drag, then crushed his cigarette underfoot. He pushed off the fender.

"Don't make it hard on yourself, Sam. Get in the car."

Amelio looked on the verge of running. His features went taut, the skin tight over his cheekbones, and he took a step back. McGuire, moving quickly for a man of his bulk, strode forward and gripped Amelio's arm in a vise-lock. Duncan, almost as quick, grabbed the other arm. They shoved him into the backseat.

Nolan moved around the car. Duncan slipped behind the steering wheel, and McGuire got in beside Amelio. No one spoke as Duncan started the engine and drove off in the direction of Seawall Boulevard. Five minutes later, the Buick slowed to a stop outside the Hollywood Club, near the kitchen door. The club, even on Saturday nights, closed at two, and the lights out front were already extinguished. The kitchen workers were busy scrubbing down for the night.

"Listen to me, Sam," Nolan said, twisting around in the passenger seat. "You make any trouble and I'll turn you over to Turk. You understand?"

"Who, me?" Amelio's mouth jerked in a rictus of a smile. "Why would I cause you any trouble? I haven't done nothin' wrong."

"Well, it's late and the kitchen help's got enough to

do without you raising a stink. Just mind your manners. Got it?"

"Yeah, sure, I got it."

Nolan led the way through the kitchen. They followed the hallway to the employees' lounge, and then into the casino, which was closed. The croupiers and dealers were sorting chips, waiting for the pit bosses to make a count, and paid them no attention. Nolan rapped lightly on the office door and stepped inside, McGuire and Duncan on either side of Amelio. Duncan shut the door.

Voight was seated behind the desk. Quinn was slumped in an easy chair, his bow tie undone, a drink in his hand. Amelio looked from one to the other, still uncertain as to why he was there, but nonetheless petrified. Voight wagged his head with disgust.

"You dumb guinea bastard. What the hell was that meeting we had yesterday? Tell me, what?"

"Up at the Turf Club?" Amelio said, rattled. "Me and Gus and Dan?"

"What the hell else would I be talking about? What'd I tell you? Ollie and me both?"

"You told us no more rough stuff. Lay off the civilians."

"So you were listening?" Voight said sarcastically. "You got the message?"

Amelio seemed confused. "I'm not following you here, boss. I haven't done nothin' out of line."

"Then how come I got a call from the police chief tonight?"

"I don't know what you're talkin' about. On my mother's head, honest."

"Forget your mother," Voight said. "Sally Urschel runs one of your houses, right? The one off Twenty-fifth and Postoffice?"

"Yeah," Amelio said blankly. "What about her?"

"One of her girls rolled a john tonight. You with me now?"

"No—"

"And when the john started yelling, Sally's bouncer whipped his ass and tossed him out the door. Get the picture?"

Amelio paled. "Boss, you gotta—"

"And the john went to the cops, bleeding like a God-damn stuck pig. And that's why the police chief called me. What do you think of that?"

"Oh, boy!" Cuddles nervously flapped his feathers. "Deeep shit!"

Everyone looked at the parrot. Cuddles hopped to the end of his perch and pretended to ignore them. Quinn stirred from his easy chair, finishing off his drink. His gaze fixed on Amelio.

"Did you tell your people? Spread the word about laying off civilians?"

"You betcha, I did," Amelio said in a shaky voice. "Yesterday, right after the meeting, told 'em all. No more rough stuff."

Quinn stared at him. "The john pressed charges. Sally and the bouncer and the girl that fingered the wallet are being arrested right about now. You've made a big prob-lem for us, Sam."

"*I told 'em!*" Amelio protested. "Honest to Christ, I told 'em!"

"You're lying," Voight said. "It's written all over your face."

"Think you're right, Dutch," Quinn agreed. "Sam's the one who broke the Rule. Not his people."

Voight slapped the desk with the flat of his hand. The sound was like a gunshot in the office, and his eyes went hard. "We told you in plain English. Nobody—*nobody*—breaks the Rule."

"Take him for a swim!" Cuddles squawked. "Swim-swimswim!"

"You heard the bird," Voight said, nodding to Nolan. "Take him out and don't bring him back."

"*No!*" Amelio lunged toward the desk, his features wild. "You cocksuckers can't—"

McGuire slugged him in the back of the head. He went down as though struck by lightning, and lay still. Nolan moved the carpet aside in the far corner and opened the trapdoor. Duncan took Amelio's feet and McGuire his shoulders, and they carried him down the steps. Nolan followed them to the landing below, then closed the door.

A few moments later the engines of the *Cherokee* rumbled to life. The speedboat pulled away from the landing, gaining headway, throttles opened to full pitch. The sound of the engines faded as the *Cherokee* headed south into the Gulf. A stillness settled over the office.

"Too bad," Quinn said, slouching in his easy chair. "Sam ran a good operation. He'll be hard to replace."

Voight snorted derisively. "One thing's for damn sure, Ollie. Nobody'll break the Rule now."

Cuddles, ever the shrewd mimic, merely nodded. There was nothing more to say.

Chapter Sixteen

Galveston's aristocracy lived on Broadway. The street was lined with palatial homes on a wide esplanade bordered by oleanders and palms. Streetcars festooned with electric lights clanged along the esplanade.

Broadway was one of the first streets platted by the original settlers. The name was chosen because it was a broad thoroughfare, and the Island's oldest and wealthiest families built their mansions overlooking the esplanade. One block, between Twenty-eighth and Twenty-ninth, was preeminent among the town's elite. There, on opposite sides of the street, were the homes of William Magruder and George Seagrave.

The Magruder mansion was an imposing structure, with large windows surrounded by heavy stone and Corinthian columns, and covered with a patterned slate mansard roof. In front, the entrance pavilion formed a tower with a series of grotesque superposed orders, ending at the top in a crown of garlands and cornices and iron spikes. Tourists came on weekends just to stand and stare at it.

Late Monday morning Libbie turned off Broadway in her sporty Chevrolet coupe. She pulled into the pavilion, braked to a stop, and hopped out with an armload of parcels. Her morning had been spent in some of Galveston's tonier shops, where she had purchased a cerulean silk dress, high-heeled pumps, and a pert little hat. She hurried up the steps, delighted with her new outfit, certain it would please Nolan. She planned to meet him in Houston that afternoon.

The mansion was on three floors, with twenty-two

rooms, and a lush floral garden in the rear. She came through the foyer, moving quickly toward a sweeping stairway off the main hall. Her bedroom was on the second floor, and she was in a rush to bathe, slip into her new outfit, and catch the one o'clock interurban to Houston. Last Friday, upon leaving the hotel, she and Nolan had made a date for this afternoon. Two days apart seemed an eternity, and she felt like a schoolgirl with a frantic crush. She couldn't wait to see him.

Opal Magruder came in from the back hallway. Her dress was baggy, her hands soiled, and she was carrying a long-stemmed red rose. She had a household staff of eight, including maids and cooks, a chauffeur and a gardener. Yet, while she let the house run itself, she was forever grubbing around in the garden. Her roses were her passion.

"Look, dear," she said, holding the rose out to Libbie. "Have you ever seen anything so beautiful?"

Libbie halted at the bottom of the stairway. "Oh, that is gorgeous, Mother. What a lovely shade of magenta."

"Yes, it's one of the best of the year. I do so dread the season nearly over. How will I survive without my roses?"

"You'll have to start planning early for Christmas."

Her mother prided herself on having not just the largest, but the most elaborately decorated Christmas tree on the Island. Libbie often thought her father was wedded to his business empire, and her mother was the bride of horticulture and holidays. She wondered that they had ever gotten together to produce children.

"Been shopping, dear?" her mother said, eyeing her packages. "I do hope you bought yourself something nice."

"Nothing really special," Libbie said evasively. "I'm meeting some of the girls this afternoon."

"Well, enjoy yourself, dear. A girl can't have too many friends."

The front door opened. William Magruder moved

into the foyer and hooked his homburg on a hat rack. He saw them standing by the stairway and walked forward into the hall. His features appeared flushed.

"Goodness gracious," Opal said, genuinely surprised. "Why aren't you at the office?"

"Because I'm here," Magruder said brusquely. "I have to talk with Elizabeth."

Libbie sensed there was something terribly wrong. Her father never addressed her in a formal manner unless he meant to find fault, or show displeasure. Nor had she ever known him to leave the office in the morning except on business. She was no less amazed than her mother.

"I don't understand," Opal said. "What on earth do you want with Libbie?"

"Nothing that concerns you, my dear. I prefer to speak with her alone."

"Honestly, how can you say that? Anything that brings you home in the middle—"

"Opal." Magruder silenced her with a frown. "I intend to speak with our daughter in private. Go tend to your roses, or whatever it is you do."

Opal was shocked by his tone of voice. She gave him a wounded look, and then, glancing at Libbie in bewilderment, she marched off toward the kitchen. Magruder turned off the hall into his study.

"I'll have a word with you, young lady."

Libbie followed him through the door. The study was a male sanctuary, all dark hardwood and furnished in leather. Magruder seated himself behind his desk and motioned her to a chair. She placed her packages on the floor.

"I had a call not an hour ago," he said. "A call about a man named Jack Nolan."

Libbie was stunned. Her nerves almost betrayed her, but she managed to hold her composure. "Who is Jack Nolan?"

"Don't act the innocent with me," Magruder growled. "You were seen with him at the Rice Hotel in Houston last Friday. I have it from a reliable source."

"Your *source* must be mistaken, Daddy."

"The call was from a business associate. Someone who knows you and someone who knows Nolan from the Hollywood Club. He was not mistaken."

"Oh, really?" Libbie said, trying for a flippant attitude. "Today is Monday and your business associate is talking about Friday. Why did he wait so long to call you?"

"Charity," Magruder said shortly. "He spent the weekend deliberating whether or not to tell me. He finally decided a father should know his daughter is—involved . . . with a gangster."

"Well, what if I am? I don't need your permission anymore, Daddy. I'll choose my own friends."

"Do you realize what you're saying? The man is a criminal, part of the underworld mob. Haven't you any decency?"

"Haven't you?" Libbie fired back. "You're very palsy-walsy with his boss, that Oliver Quinn. Don't you dare lecture me on disgracing the family name."

Magruder inwardly winced. She was too close to the truth, for his involvement with the mob went far beyond what anyone suspected. He decided the situation called for a harder line.

"I forbid it," he said with authority. "You will not see this man again, and there's an end to it. Do you understand?"

Libbie laughed at him. "Please spare me your ultimatums. I'm of age and I'll see whomever I choose." Her chin tilted defiantly. "That includes Jack Nolan."

"I daresay Mr. Nolan can be persuaded otherwise. You leave me no choice."

"What does that mean?"

"One way or another, young lady, it's ended. Mark my word."

Magruder stormed out of the study. A moment later the front door slammed, and she suddenly knew what he intended. She moved to the phone at her father's desk and placed a hurried call to the Turf Club. She waited impatiently until Nolan came on the line and then quickly explained what had happened. His reaction was much as she'd expected.

"Forget meeting me today," he said. "Once your dad tells Quinn, I'm in big trouble. I'll have to do some fast talking."

Her mouth went dry. "He won't do anything to you, will he? You'll be all right, won't you?"

"Don't worry, I'll think of something. I've been in tighter fixes before."

"When will I see you? You won't let them come between us . . . will you?"

"Never happen," Nolan said with certainty. "I'll find a way, trust me on that. You're my girl."

"No matter what?"

"No matter what."

Nolan promised he would call her later that afternoon. When they rang off, Libbie sat for a moment wondering if he meant it. Then, his voice still fresh in her memory, she heard him say it again. She was his girl . . . no matter what.

She desperately wanted it to be true.

Durant found it hard to believe. He read the article again, shaking his head, still dumbfounded. It just didn't seem possible.

On Saturday, only two days ago, Jack Dempsey had lost the heavyweight championship. The fight was held in a pouring rain at the Sesquicentennial Stadium in Philadelphia. Over 120,000 spectators saw the underdog, Gene Tunney, outbox the Manassa Mauler and take the heavyweight crown. Bookmakers across America had lost their shirts.

Durant could hardly credit it. Dempsey had held the championship for seven years, defending his title against such great fighters as Tommy Gibbons, Luis Firpo, and Georges Carpenter. A savage puncher, inevitably winning by a knockout, no one in the fight game thought he could ever be beat. The one consolation, as Durant saw it, was that the new champion was a former serviceman. Gene Tunney had served in the Marines.

A light rap sounded at the door. Durant hastily folded the newspaper and dropped it beneath his desk. All morning he'd been absorbed in his own problems, and then, after glancing at the sports page, the astounding defeat of the Manassa Mauler. He hadn't yet so much as looked at the bank's financial summary for last week. Catherine stuck her head into the office.

"Your friends are back again."

"Friends?"

"You know," she said, rolling her eyes. "Your partners in reform."

Durant wondered what they wanted now. Late Saturday morning, following his and Aldridge's meeting with Magruder, they had come by the office. He had related the details of the fiasco with Magruder, and went on to explain that there was no hope of establishing a mob connection. None of them seemed willing to accept the facts.

A heated exchange ensued. Herbert Cornwall took the lead, urging him to issue a public statement regarding Magruder's ties to the underworld. Durant argued that it was speculation on his part, his word against Magruder's; nothing to substantiate the connection. Cornwall pushed, backed by Adair and Baldwin, and he flatly refused. They left the office in a doleful mood.

Saturday night, he and Catherine had attended a movie. On Sunday afternoon, they had toured the amusement piers and finished the day with dinner at one of the seafood places on the beach. While he was with her, he was able to set his troubles aside and simply enjoy her quick laughter and vivacious spirit. But the thought that Magruder had once again unleashed the mob was never far from mind. The reformers seemed to him yet another fly in the ointment.

"Go ahead, send them in," he said in a gruff voice. "I'm ripe for an argument, anyway."

Catherine frowned prettily. "Don't let them get under your skin."

"I'll try."

The clergymen, followed by Cornwall, stepped into the office. Durant gave them a neutral look and waved them to chairs. After they were seated, there was a moment of strained silence. Reverend Baldwin finally cleared his throat.

"We wish to apologize," he said with an offhand gesture. "We've talked it over and come to the conclusion we pressed you too hard on Saturday. Magruder would indeed prevail in a war of words."

The tone was too tactful by half, almost obsequious. Durant was immediately on guard. "Glad to hear we agree," he said. "So what brings you around today?"

Baldwin smiled slyly. "We spent the weekend exploring new avenues, new strategies. We believe we've found one that is—dare I say . . . Machiavellian."

Durant shrugged. "A three-dollar word for deceit and chicanery. I'm surprised at you, Parson."

"All in a good cause," Adair chimed in. "God wages His battle against evil with every weapon at hand. We are but His servants."

"Which is to say," Baldwin went on, "we have evolved a plan with considerable merit. One we believe will bear fruit."

"Why come to me?" Durant asked. "I've burned my bridges in Galveston."

"Hardly, hardly," Adair assured him. "In fact, you are the very man for our crafty little plan. The only man!"

"How so?"

"Shall we say you are on personal acquaintance with one Diamond Jack Nolan."

"Nolan?"

"Permit me to explain," Baldwin said unctuously. "Jack Nolan is foremost among the mob's henchmen.

Every dirty secret there is to know, he knows intimately. Wouldn't you agree?"

"Yeah, I suppose," Durant allowed. "What's your point?"

"Imagine—" Baldwin thrust a finger in the air for emphasis. "Imagine that Mr. Nolan could be persuaded to betray his associates. And in particular, give evidence against William Magruder."

"Nolan?" Durant said incredulously. "A turncoat?"

"Precisely!"

"You're nuts."

"Perhaps not," Baldwin countered. "Particularly if Mr. Nolan was permitted to walk away a free man. A clean slate, let us say."

"That'd be a nifty trick," Durant conceded. "How do you propose to pull it off?"

"Praise the Lord, Herbert has shown us the way."

Cornwall took his cue. "Mr. Durant, I am a longtime friend and supporter of Attorney General Robert Richardson. I spoke with him by phone this morning."

"And?" Durant said skeptically. "What's the good news?"

"The attorney general has agreed to offer Jack Nolan complete immunity. Not only that, he will receive a ten-thousand-dollar reward, courtesy of the state of Texas. He will, in a word, be redeemed."

"Congratulations," Durant said. "Sounds like a sweet deal. He might even accept."

"Indeed so," Cornwall said with conviction. "And we believe you are the man to offer him such a deal. As Reverend Adair so astutely observed, the only man."

"Why me?" Durant said. "You could just as easily offer him the deal yourself. You're the one with the pipeline to the attorney general."

"Nolan has no reason to trust me," Cornwall replied. "On the other hand, he knows you have a vested interest in your own health. He would believe you are sincere . . . trustworthy."

"Would he?" Durant said. "You assume a lot."

"How else will you save your bank, Mr. Durant? Isn't it worth it to bring down William Magruder?"

Durant thought it was a fanciful scheme. Yet, even if it was one in a million, it was better than nothing at all. He hadn't come up with any bright ideas himself, and he was tired of waiting for the mob to make another attempt on his life. The mere notion of Jack Nolan as a turncoat made for intriguing speculation. It might not only save his bank; it might save his neck.

"You're in the wrong business," he said, looking from one to the other. "You fellows ought to be selling used cars."

"I knew it!" Adair crowed. "I knew you wouldn't let us down!"

"Question is, how do I get in touch with Nolan? Any meeting would have to be held in secret."

"Call the Turf Club," Cornwall suggested. "That's the mob headquarters, their hangout. Just be very careful what you say."

Durant got the operator on the line. She rang the Turf Club and a man with a gravelly voice answered. The man asked who was calling and he said to tell Nolan it was an old friend. A moment later Nolan came on the line.

"Yeah, this is Nolan."

"Earl Durant here."

"Old friend, huh?" Nolan laughed. "You've got a sense of humor, slick. What can I do for you?"

"I'd like to meet with you—in private."

"What about?"

"Let's just say it would be to your advantage."

There was a long pause. Durant could almost hear him calculating, suspicious but nonetheless intrigued. "All right," Nolan finally said. "The Rendezvous Roadhouse in La Marque. Tomorrow morning, ten o'clock."

"I'll be there," Durant said. "Do us both a favor and keep it to yourself."

"Don't worry about it, slick."

The line went dead. Durant looked at the three re-formers and nodded. "It's on," he said. "Tomorrow at ten."

"Hallelujah!" Adair exclaimed.

"Indeed so," Baldwin intoned. "God helps those who help themselves."

Durant considered it a long shot, even for God.

The Beach Hotel was vaguely reminiscent of Byzantine architecture. The two-hundred-room hostelry was painted mauve and an octagonal dome centered on the roof was adorned with flashy orange-and-white stripes. A fountain bubbled tall jets of water in the middle of a circular drive-way.

Frank Nitti emerged from the hotel late that morning. He was accompanied by Sal "Knuckles" Drago, his per-sonal attendant and bodyguard. Drago was built like a block of granite, and his nickname stemmed from his abil-ity with his fists. Nitti, by contrast, was a dapper man with an air of authority. He was accustomed to being obeyed.

A valet waited with their car. "Good morning, Mr. Murphy, Mr. Reilly. You have a fine day for sight-seeing."

"Always this bright?" Nitti asked, squinting into the sun. "You'd think we were in the tropics."

"Blue skies and sunshine!" the valet boasted pleas-antly. "Galveston Island's own brand of paradise, Mr. Murphy."

Nitti was amused by the alias. He was registered at the hotel as Thomas Murphy, and Drago was listed as George Reilly. He thought a couple of wops posing as Irishmen was a fine joke on everyone. None more so than Ollie Quinn and Dutch Voight.

The car was a loan from Johnny Renzullo, a gangster who controlled many of the rackets in Houston. Nitti and Drago had arrived by train last night, and after meeting with Renzullo, they had driven on to Galveston. Renzullo,

a friend of the late Joey Adonis, was an associate and
their chief source of intelligence. He was interested in
avenging Adonis, now assumed to be at the bottom of the
Gulf. He meant to share in the spoils of the Island as well.

Drago climbed behind the wheel of the car. "Where
to, boss?"

"Where else?" Nitti said. "Let's have a look at the
Hollywood Club. We'll go on from there."

"Whatcha think, boss, wouldn't Mr. Capone like this
place? He's big on all this sunny stuff."

"Knuckles, that's one reason he sent us. All that snow
up north gets to him in the winter."

"Yeah, I wouldn't mind havin' a place to go myself.
When it snows, I mean."

"I've got a feeling Galveston's our spot."

Frank Nitti was the right-hand man of Al Capone.
The most notorious gangster in America, Capone was
ruthless and wily, the overlord of nearly all criminal enterprises in Chicago. Nitti was known as "The Enforcer,"
and he savagely defended Capone's empire from rival
mobs. Almost four hundred men had been gunned down
in Chicago within the last year.

Today, Nitti was on a reconnaissance mission. Capone was a man whose reach exceeded his grasp, and he
was forever searching for ways to expand his empire. Galveston Island was all but fabled in the underworld, a
sunny paradise where tourists were fleeced of millions of
dollars a year. To Capone, it seemed a peach worth pluck-
ing.

Nitti's assignment was to scout out the possibility of
a takeover. As the car rolled past the Hollywood Club, he
wasn't particularly impressed with the look of the place
from the outside. But he knew the interior was lavishly
appointed, and he felt a grudging admiration for the crafty
move of positioning the casino over the Gulf. He thought
a club that could afford Al Jolson was a joint worth stealing.

In fact, all of Seawall Boulevard was a revelation.

The amusement piers and nightspots reminded Nitti of Coney Island in New York. His intelligence sources told him that Quinn and Voight extorted a king's ransom in protection payoffs from gaming dives and speakeasies throughout town. The rumrunning operation, which represented a monopoly on illegal booze, was even sweeter. He figured a couple million a year, easy.

"So what d'ya think, boss?" Drago asked as they neared the eastern tip of the Island. "Like what you seen so far?"

"Not bad," Nitti admitted. "Quinn and Voight have done a good job. Built themselves a regular money tree."

"Johnny Renzullo says they got a big organization, too. Lots of heavy artillery."

"I'm not planning a war, Knuckles. Way I see it, what works in Chicago won't work in Galveston. Too many dead men in the streets might turn the law against us."

"Yeah, right." Drago muddled on it a moment, suddenly grinned with comprehension. "You're gonna knock 'em off, aren't you, boss? Just Quinn and Voight."

"Simplest plan is the best plan," Nitti said, as though thinking out loud. "We'll import some shooters from Renzullo's outfit and let them do the job. Renzullo wants payback for Adonis, anyway."

"You know, boss, that's a funny thing. Johnny don't seem the kinda guy to go all hearts and flowers. Why's he so pissed about Adonis?"

"Adonis was his brother-in-law. Married his little sister and left her with three or four kids."

"No shit!" Drago's jaw hung open. "How come you never told me that?"

"Just drive the car," Nitti ordered. "I never told you because I don't want you cryin' in your beer for Renzullo and his sister. We might have to ice him before it's over."

"Why's that?"

"Once we take over Galveston, we don't want any partners. Renzullo will likely figure he deserves a piece of the action."

"Oh." Drago's bulldog features appeared melancholy. "Too bad it's gotta be that way. Johnny's a stand-up guy."

Nitti sighed. "Take a right at the corner. I want to have a look at the red-light district."

On the way across town they saw the Garden Club and several other nightspots. Nitti was impressed by the fact that every time he turned his head he saw yet another dive dangling off the money tree. A few minutes later Drago parked the car on Postoffice Street, between Twenty-sixth and Twenty-seventh. They got out for a walking tour of the district.

A strong mix of avarice and admiration came over Nitti. Within a block he stopped counting speakeasies, and after a couple blocks he gave up counting whorehouses. He was impressed all over again by the orderly arrangement of things in Galveston, something they had never been able to accomplish in the far-flung environs of Chicago. Everything seemed engineered for the sole purpose of taking down the loot.

Quinn and Voight, of course, would have to go. Yet Nitti was hopeful it wouldn't be necessary to kill Jack Nolan. His sources told him Nolan was a master rumrunner, tough but brainy, and an inside player with the Feds. Keeping Nolan on was the smart move, for there were always unforeseen twists and turns in any takeover. A smooth transition of power required someone familiar with the local ground rules.

Nitti could visualize it in his head, see it all coming together. Sun and surf, a place to escape the wintry winds of Chicago. A pleasant little island all but floating on money.

He thought Capone was going to like Galveston.

Chapter Seventeen

Sherm Magruder knew something was definitely wrong. Every Monday morning at ten o'clock he and his father got together for their weekly planning session. Today, just before ten, the old man had canceled the meeting.

What bothered Sherm the most was that his father was a man of habit. The meeting was part of their weekly ritual, immutable as stone, and it had never before been called off. William Magruder always devoted Monday morning to their diverse business affairs.

Even more, Sherm was troubled by the way it had happened. Ellen Morse, his father's secretary, had called and canceled the meeting without offering an explanation. When he'd asked to speak with his father, she had told him Mr. Magruder was not taking any calls. She seemed perplexed herself by the situation.

Later, around eleven o'clock, he had called her back. She informed him that his father had rushed out of the office, with no word as to where he could be reached. Sherm started to call the house, then thought better of worrying his mother until he knew something more. Never in memory could he recall the old man leaving the office on a Monday morning.

Then, shortly before noon, he'd been summoned to the office. Ellen Morse still had no explanation, but she said his father wanted him to come right away. All the way over from the bank, he tried to fathom the events of the morning, but none of it made any sense. Ellen merely gave him a shrug and a look of concern when he hurried through the waiting room. He found his father staring out the window at the harbor.

Sherm knew it was bad. Magruder turned from the window with cloudy features and something strange in his bearing. He walked to his desk, seating himself, and motioned Sherm to a chair. His eyes were leaden.

"We have some serious problems," he said. "One with Earl Durant and the other with your sister."

"Libbie?"

"Yes, I just came from the house and a very unpleasant conversation with your sister. I sometimes wonder she's a Magruder."

Sherm suddenly knew why the morning meeting had been canceled. He was curious as to the reason. "What's she done now?"

"I'll get to that," Magruder said. "Oddly enough, both of our problems involve Quinn and Voight." He paused, slowly shook his head. "I never thought I'd hear myself mention your sister's name in context with those two."

"I'm a little lost here, Pop. How's Libbie involved with Quinn and Voight?"

"For the life of me, I'm not sure I can discuss it in a rational manner. Let's deal with Durant first."

"All right," Sherm replied, now thoroughly confused. "What's he done?"

"Young Mr. Durant came to see me Saturday morning, on the pretext of selling People's Bank & Trust. He brought Ira Aldridge with him."

"Why didn't you tell me?"

"I wanted the weekend to think it over. Time to decide."

"Decide what?"

Magruder briefly recounted the meeting with Durant and Aldridge. He explained that it was all a trap, an attempt to trick him into admitting illicit dealings with the mob. With Aldridge as a witness.

"I don't get it," Sherm said dubiously. "Even if you admitted it, what good would it do Durant?"

"The very question I asked myself," Magruder acknowledged. "We know Durant is involved with those damnable reformers. What does that tell you?"

"I'm not sure it tells me anything."

"Suppose they meant to start a smear campaign? Tie me to the mob—with Aldridge the unimpeachable witness—and blacken my name. Think about it."

Sherm considered a moment. "For one thing, public opinion would swing to Durant and we wouldn't be able to touch him. Not to mention the damage it would do you politically."

"Exactly my thought," Magruder agreed. "Durant clearly believes the way to save himself *and* his bank is to vilify me in public. So what should we do?"

"Pop, I think you've already made up your mind. Why ask me?"

"I value your judgment, my boy. After all, you will one day assume the helm of Magruder & Company. What would you do in my position?"

"Call Quinn and Voight," Sherm said without hesitation. "Have them remove Durant before it goes any further. He's turned it into a vendetta."

"What about the reformers?"

"I'm sure they'll make the most of it. But when you come down to it, Durant's the problem. He has to be stopped before he can do *real* harm."

Magruder nodded. "Today seems to be our day for Quinn and Voight. I have to call them about Libbie as well."

"I'm still in the dark," Sherm said. "What's all this about Libbie?"

"Your sister. . . ."

"Yes, go on, Pop."

"How can I say this?" Magruder's voice was dull with anger. "Libbie has become romantically involved with a gangster. One of Quinn and Voight's men. His name is Jack Nolan."

Sherm was appalled. "Are you saying she's . . . you know?"

"Yes, I regret to say I am. She was seen with Nolan last Friday in Houston—at the Rice Hotel."

"Who saw her?"

"Oscar Whitney. We both know Oscar wouldn't lie about such a thing. He wrestled with it over the weekend and finally called me this morning. He felt friendship demanded it, one father to another."

Sherm went from shock to anger. He loved his sister, but he thought she was a spoiled brat. All her flapper nonsense, and the women's liberation, and now she was bedding a gangster. He looked at his father.

"Do you think Oscar will keep it quiet?"

"Yes, I do," Magruder said firmly. "Oscar does a good bit of business with us. He knows better than to gossip."

"Let's hope so," Sherm said. "Jack Nolan isn't just any gangster. He does the dirty work for Quinn and Voight."

"I'm all too aware of his reputation. We have to put a stop to it before it becomes public knowledge. I won't have the family name disgraced."

"What did Libbie say? Surely she'll stop seeing him."

"No, I'm afraid not," Magruder said harshly. "Your sister is headstrong and stubborn as a post. She told me to mind my own business."

"Sounds like her," Sherm admitted. "So what's the solution?"

"I plan to have a talk with Quinn. In no uncertain terms, he can lay down the law to this Jack Nolan. We will not tolerate it one day longer."

"I'm not sure that's a good idea, Pop."

"Why not?"

"Quinn might be insulted. By association, you're implying he's no better than Nolan. He has a high opinion of himself."

"I see your point," Magruder said with a thoughtful frown. "We're asking him to take care of Durant, and it wouldn't do to offend him. What do you suggest?"

"An intermediary."

"Isn't that somewhat risky? Who could we trust with . . . this?"

"Monsignor O'Donnell," Sherm said without hesitation. "Quinn donates quite heavily to the Catholic Church. And the monsignor would understand the need for discretion."

Magruder thought there was something to be said for an education at Yale. His son understood the nuances of diplomacy, circuitous rather than direct, exactly what the situation demanded. Still, in the scheme of things, the more immediate threat came first. He placed a call to Quinn at the Turf Club.

"Good morning, Bill," Quinn said when he came on the line. "What can I do for you today?"

"Old business, Ollie," Magruder replied. "That worrisome fellow we've ignored for too long? Find a way to resolve the matter . . . quickly."

"A wise decision, Bill. I know just who you mean. Consider it done."

Magruder hung up, nodding to Sherm. Then he jiggled the hook and asked the operator for another number. A courteous young man answered.

"St. Mary's Rectory."

"Monsignor O'Donnell, please."

"May I tell the Monsignor who's calling?"

"William Magruder."

"And the purpose of your call, Mr. Magruder?"

"A personal matter."

"High time!"

"Dutch, I told you he'd come around."

"Yeah, you did," Voight said. "Wonder what took him so long?"

Quinn smiled. "Magruder works at his own speed. You wanted Durant and you've got him. Don't ask questions."

"Who's asking?"

The phone rang. Voight lifted the receiver, still grinning. "Yeah."

"Dutch, this is Dan Lampis."

"What's up?"

"I was out checking the slots this morning. Guess who I saw on Postoffice Street?"

"Who?"

"Frank Nitti."

Voight's grin slipped. "You're sure?"

"Dead certain," Lampis said. "How could I forget his ugly mug?"

Voight was formerly from Chicago. Four years ago, he had imported Lampis from the Windy City to handle part of the slots concession. They both knew Frank Nitti on sight.

"Keep it to yourself for now, Dan. I'll get back to you."

Voight replaced the receiver on the hook. "Frank Nitti's in town," he said to Quinn in a cold voice. "Dan Lampis saw him on Postoffice Street."

"Nitti?" Quinn repeated hollowly. "You're talking about Nitti from Chicago?"

"One and the same. He's Al Capone's right-hand boy. And I don't need a crystal ball to tell me why he's here."

"You think Capone means to put a move on us?"

"Nothing but," Voight said tightly. "Capone knows there's only one way to get his hands on Galveston. He sent Nitti here to plan our funeral."

Quinn's jaws clenched. "We'll scotch that in a hurry. Capone doesn't know who he's dealing with."

They called Nolan into the office. He listened without expression as Voight told him about Nitti. His eyes narrowed.

"I'll get on it right away. You want him aced?"

"Not just yet," Voight said. "Find him and bring him here. I've got some questions I want answered."

"Whatever you say." Nolan started toward the door,

then stopped. "What with Nitti in town, I almost forgot to tell you. Earl Durant called me a little while ago."

"Durant?" Quinn echoed. "Why would he call you?"

"I haven't got a clue. He said he wanted to meet, something about it would be to my advantage. Sounded pretty mysterious."

"What did you say?"

"I agreed to meet him tomorrow morning. Figured I'd see what's what."

Quinn and Voight exchanged a puzzled glance. After a moment, Quinn looked back at Nolan. "Something screwy's going on here. Magruder just called and gave us the green light on Durant. Said to take him out."

"Why so sudden?" Nolan asked quizzically. "I mean, him and Durant calling at the same time? Doesn't make sense."

"No, it doesn't," Quinn remarked uneasily. "You're sure that's all Durant said?"

"Yeah, he kept it short and sweet."

"I don't like it," Voight interjected. "Somebody knows something we don't. Too much coincidence for my money."

"Dutch, I couldn't agree more." Quinn walked to the window, gazed down at the street. "I think we'd better go slow here. See how it plays out."

"Damn right," Voight said sternly. "Could be somebody's playing us for a patsy. Question is, who?"

"How about Durant?" Nolan said, looking from one to the other. "Do I meet him or not?"

Quinn turned from the window. "String him along and see what he wants. We might learn what we're missing in all this."

"Good idea," Voight said. "We can settle his hash anytime. Nitti's our first order of business."

Nolan nodded. "I'll take some of the boys and hit the streets. He shouldn't be hard to find."

Voight grunted. "Look for a wop with a hooked nose. Fancy dresser, about my size. Always wears spats."

"I'm on it."

Nolan went out. When the door closed, Voight bit off the end of a cigar and lit up in a dinge of smoke. Quinn again turned his gaze out the window.

"What do you make of it, Dutch?"

"I think something's fishy. Stinks to high heaven."

"Yes," Quinn said quietly. "I can smell it from here."

Catherine invited Durant to dinner that evening. She expressed the opinion that he was in desperate need of a home-cooked meal, and she also wanted him to meet her mother. Durant readily accepted.

The Ludlow home was pleasantly comfortable. The living room was filled with overstuffed furniture, bric-a-brac scattered here and there in playful groupings. A sideboard with hand-carved garlands dominated the dining room, and the table was piled high with steaming dishes. Durant's invitation was clearly an occasion.

Alma Ludlow was a slim woman in her early fifties. She was animated and cheery, with bright blue eyes and wisps of gray in her hair. Durant thought it was apparent where Catherine got her good looks and spirited disposition. Her mother would have been a beauty in her day.

Alma stifled her curiosity until they were seated at the dinner table. Then, much like her daughter, she proved to be a devotee of motion pictures, and more particularly, movie stars. She began peppering Durant with questions once his plate was loaded with food.

"Catherine tells me you're a stuntman in motion pictures?"

"Yes ma'am," Durant said, ladling gravy onto his mashed potatoes. "I've been working at it pretty regular the last few years."

"Well, then, you must know everyone's juicy secrets. Is it true, what the papers say? Did Fatty Arbuckle really kill that girl?"

Scandals gave Hollywood the unsavory image of a modern Babylon. Fatty Arbuckle, a popular comedian, allegedly raped an actress, adding a sadistic twist by using a Coke bottle. The actress died and he was charged with murder, facing trial three times. Twice he got a hung jury, and in the third trial he was acquitted. The scandal nonetheless resulted in him being blackballed from movies forever.

Durant wasn't surprised by Mrs. Ludlow's interest. The story had been covered extensively in the press, and movie fans everywhere were fascinated by the sordid headlines. He tried to answer the question without getting drawn into details.

"Everyone in Hollywood thought Arbuckle was guilty. The general feeling was that he got away with murder."

"How terrible," Alma said with a little shudder. "And is it true what they say about John Barrymore? Is he a drunk?"

"Yes, ma'am, it's a fact." Durant paused, a chunk of pot roast speared on his fork. "Barrymore's half stiff all the time and sloshed most of the time. He's still a good actor, though."

"Oh, I think so, too. You must think it's silly of me, but I just love all these handsome leading men. Did you know Rudolph Valentino?"

"Well, I wouldn't say we were buddies. I doubled for him in stunts on *The Four Horsemen of the Apocalypse*. He seemed like a pretty nice guy."

Rudolph Valentino was the matinee idol of the day. He had died little more than a month before from a peritonitis infection following an appendicitis operation. Thousands attended the funeral of the man who would forever be known for his role in *The Sheik*. Women across America were still in a state of mourning.

"How tragic," Alma said weepily. "To die so young, at the height of his fame. I read he was only thirty-one."

"Mother!" Catherine scolded. "Let Earl eat his dinner. You haven't stopped to catch a breath."

"Well, honestly, dear, how often do you meet some-one from Hollywood? I'm just making conversation."

"I don't mind," Durant said with a smile. "For a meal like this, I'd talk all night. You're a mighty fine cook, Mrs. Ludlow."

"Aren't you the flatterer," Alma simpered. "All right, I'll ask only one more question and then I'm through. Does Mary Pickford really earn a million dollars a year?"

Durant verified it was true. He went on to explain that Mary Pickford's husband, Douglas Fairbanks, as well as Charlie Chaplin, made a million a year. Not long ago, he noted, the threesome had pooled their resources to form United Artists Studio and produce their own pictures. They were now millionaires many times over.

Alma clapped her hands with delight, and then true to her promise, let him finish his dinner. Later, while she was clearing the table, Catherine led Durant into the living room and took a seat beside him on the sofa. She shook her head with a rueful smile.

"I apologize for Mama," she said, clearly embar-rassed. "She's even more star-struck than I am. Do you forgive me?"

"Nothing to forgive," Durant assured her. "Tell you the truth, it was good to talk about something else. Took my mind off my problems."

"Things were so hectic today I didn't have a chance to ask. Are the reformers still pestering you to make a public statement about Magruder?"

"No, we're into a whole new game. I'm meeting with Jack Nolan tomorrow."

"My God!" she blurted. "What on earth for?"

Durant shrugged it off. "Let's just say he might be able to help out. I'll know more after I've talked with him."

"You've said any number of times how dangerous he is. Aren't you taking an awful chance?"

"Sometimes you've got no choice but to take a chance. Don't worry, I'll keep both eyes open."

She felt clotted with emotion, and fear. She took his hand in hers, squeezed tightly. "Promise you'll be careful."

Durant smiled. "Cross my heart."

Alma bustled in from the kitchen. "Now!" she said eagerly, seating herself in an overstuffed chair. Her eyes sparkled with excitement.

"Tell me everything unprintable about Greta Garbo."

The car pulled into the Beach Hotel early that evening. Knuckles Drago was at the wheel, and Nitti, stuffed with seafood, was in the passenger seat. He was pleased with himself, satisfied he'd learned all he needed to know about Galveston. He planned to call Capone when he got to his room.

There was no valet attendant out front. Drago honked the horn, peering past Nitti through the doors into the lobby. The back doors of the car suddenly popped open, and Drago automatically reached for his gun. Turk McGuire jammed the snout of a pistol into his neck with a rumbled warning. Nolan scooted in behind Nitti.

"Easy does it, Nitti," he said in an amiable voice. "Mr. Voight just wants to talk. Let's keep it simple."

Nitti craned around. "I'd lay odds you're Jack Nolan."

"You win your bet."

"How'd you get on to me?"

"Wasn't all that hard, Mr. *Murphy*. We have friends here at the hotel."

"I'll make it worth your while to forget you found me."

"Save your breath and enjoy the ride."

Ten minutes later the car pulled into the garage behind the Turf Club. McGuire relieved Drago of his gun, and after Nolan unlocked the back door, they were marched inside. A narrow stairway, closed to the public, led them to the third floor. Barney Ward waited at the end of the hall, posted outside the office. He knocked three light raps, then opened the door.

Voight was seated behind his desk. His eyes were coldly impersonal, touching an instant on Drago, then shifting to Nitti. Nolan shoved them forward as Barney Ward closed the door. A moment of strained silence slipped past.

"Well, Frank," Voight said without a trace of warmth. "Long time, no see."

"Too long, Dutch," Nitti replied evenly. "What's the idea of rousting us?"

"I've got a better one for you. What's the idea of sneaking into Galveston on the q.t.?"

"We're here for a couple days' vacation. Little surf and sand."

"You're a fucking liar."

Nitti was a man of carefully calibrated composure, mandarin inscrutability. He stared back across the desk with a level gaze. "It's a free country, Dutch. I don't owe you any explanation."

"Let me guess," Voight said, as though contemplating some arcane riddle. "Capone sent you here to scout out the territory. Arrange a nice funeral for Ollie Quinn and me. How's that sound?"

"Sounds like something out of left field. I told you why we're here."

"Don't try to play dumb on me. How many shooters was Johnny Renzullo gonna supply? What'd he promise you?"

Nitti smiled a frosty little grin. "Who's Renzullo?"

"What do you take me for?" Voight said coarsely. "You think I don't know Joey Adonis was married to Renzullo's sister? I had it figured the minute I heard you were in town."

"Nobody ever gave you much credit for smarts. Good thing you left Chicago when you did."

"You guinea son of a bitch! I ought to send you back to Capone in a box."

"Dutch, you don't have the guts for it. You never did."

Voight opened the desk drawer. He took out a .38 snub-nose and moved around the desk. He pressed the muzzle between Nitti's eyes.

"Say that again, hotshot. Let's see who's got the guts!"

Everyone in the room went stock-still. Nitti stared into the bore of the pistol, and his eyes blinked once, then twice. He drew a deep breath.

"You don't want to kill me, Dutch. All that would get you is a war with Capone."

"Looks like I've already got a war. What's the difference?"

"Let me go and that'll be the end of it. You know I never break my word."

Voight cocked the hammer on his pistol. "Say 'please.'"

A doomsday silence settled over the room. Nitti swallowed against a rush of bile in his throat. His voice, when he spoke, was almost inaudible.

"Please."

"You just bought your life." Voight eased the hammer down, lowered the pistol. "Get out of Galveston tonight. Don't go back to the hotel. Don't even stop to take a piss. Got it?"

Nitti slowly nodded. "Got it."

"Tell Capone to stick to Chicago. The climate down here's not good for his health—or yours."

"I'll give him the message."

Voight dismissed him with a curt gesture. McGuire opened the door, where Barney Ward waited in the hall, and motioned Nitti and Drago out of the office. Nolan started after them.

"Jack," Voight said. "Wait up a minute."

"Yeah, boss?"

"Follow them over the causeway. Let Nitti know he's being tailed."

"Good as done."

"One other thing," Voight said with quiet malice. "I want the score settled with Johnny Renzullo. Figure out a way to pop him in Houston. The sooner, the better."

"I'll take care of it."

Nolan went out. Voight returned to his desk and lit a cigar. He chuckled to himself, puffing smoke. Sometimes things worked out just right.

Al Capone would never set foot on Galveston Island.

Chapter Eighteen

On Tuesday morning, Stoner and Janice came down in the elevator a little before ten. As they moved through the lobby, Charles Anderson stepped out of his office. He greeted them with an effusive smile.

"Good morning," he said, nodding politely to Janice. "Off for more sight-seeing?"

"You bet," Stoner said with a chipper manner. "The missus never gets enough of the Island. Do you, Olive, honey?"

"Oh, dear me, no!" Janice trilled. "You are so very fortunate to live here, Mr. Anderson. I envy you greatly."

"Yes, ma'am, I sometimes envy myself." Anderson laughed at his own wit, glancing at Stoner. "I trust they're treating you well at the Hollywood Club, Mr. Eberling?"

"Well, I'll tell you, pardner, it's the old case of win some and lose some. I've got a ways to go to get even."

"I am sorry to hear that. Of course, I've heard gambling men say that luck does require patience."

"Yessir, the worm always turns. I'll get mine back and then some."

"I'm sure you will," Anderson said, stepping aside with a little bow. "You folks enjoy your day."

"We plan to, Charlie. We surely do."

Stoner led Janice toward the entrance. He thought the likelihood of getting even was practically nil. They were now welcome guests at the casino, having played there Saturday night, Sunday night, and last night. So far, even though he believed the games were honest, he was down almost two thousand dollars. He felt he was playing against time with a dwindling bankroll.

Their canary-yellow Packard waited outside the hotel. The valet attendant kept the car washed and polished, and it gleamed beneath golden sunlight and a cloudless sky. Stoner marked the date as September 26, slightly more than two weeks since they had arrived in Galveston. Yet, despite his slimmer bankroll, he was still obliged to play the part of the wealthy rancher. He tipped the attendant ten dollars.

A short while later they drove onto the causeway. Seagulls wheeled and circled above the harbor as a freighter slowly maneuvered into the docks. Janice watched the tranquil scene while Stoner concentrated on the road and the rearview mirror. Over the past two weeks, he had called Colonel Garrison twice, always from phone booths in La Marque. He was wary of calling from the hotel, for fear a curious operator might eavesdrop. He was wary as well of being followed.

The Packard was so distinctive that it attracted attention. By now, tooling around Galveston for two weeks, practically everyone in town recognized the car. All the more troublesome, three nights at the Hollywood Club made it known to parking attendants and others who worked at the casino. Stoner was not apprehensive by nature, but he thought it better to err on the side of caution. Someone with a sharp eye might wonder why they drove over to La Marque so frequently. Or even worse, why a wealthy rancher used phone booths.

Stoner was focused as well on what he planned to say to Garrison. In their last talk, almost a week ago, he hadn't yet gained entrance into the casino. Garrison had expressed displeasure with his lack of progress, and urged him to redouble his efforts. Still, after three nights at the gaming tables, he'd learned nothing about how the casino was mysteriously made to disappear. Yet he had formulated a plan—subterfuge mixed with deception—that he was confident would work. He hoped Garrison would agree.

Stoner never used the same phone booth twice. Today, not long after ten o'clock, he turned off the highway onto the main street of La Marque. On previous trips, playing the tourist with Janice, he had scouted about and found that there were three enclosed phone booths. One was in the town's only hotel, which he had used the first week, and another, where he had placed a call last week, was in the pharmacy. The third was in a tobacco shop and newsstand, a couple of blocks off the highway. He parked the Packard at the curb.

Janice came in with him. The phone booth was at the back of the store, with racks of magazines and newspapers on one side, and an array of cigars and packaged cigarettes behind the front counter. He nodded pleasantly to the shop owner, exchanging three dollars for a handful of quarters, while Janice wandered over to the racks and began browsing through magazines. The phone booth had a low seat, and after he'd closed the door, he gave the operator the number in Austin. He began feeding quarters into the coin slot.

A receptionist answered after a couple of tinny rings. "Colonel Garrison's office."

Stoner kept his voice low. "Tell the Colonel it's Clint Stoner. He'll take my call."

Garrison came on the line within moments. "Well, Sergeant, I'd about given you up for lost. I trust you have good news to report."

"Yes and no, Colonel," Stoner said. "I finally managed to con my way into the casino. Matter of fact, I gambled there the last three nights."

"I'd say you've made excellent progress. Why do I detect a note of reservation in your voice?"

"Well, sir, you might say I'm only half there. I haven't found out how they make the casino disappear. I'm just plain stumped."

"Nothing?" Garrison demanded. "Surely you've seen something that raised your suspicion."

"Colonel, there's nothing suspicious," Stoner said. "I've done everything but crawl under the tables, and I still don't have the least notion of how they pull it off. I'll blow my cover if I try anything more."

"Then you'll just have to keep at it. I have confidence you'll get to the bottom of it, Sergeant. Something will turn up."

"No, sir, I don't think so. They're a tricky bunch, and I doubt we'll get anywhere unless we force their hand. We have to smoke 'em out in the open."

"How would we accomplish that?"

Stoner outlined the details of his plan. Garrison listened without interruption, and then considered it a moment in silence. He finally chuckled with approval.

"I like it," he said. "Hoodwink them into revealing their most prized secret. You're a clever tactician, Sergeant."

"The timing's the thing," Stoner said. "I'll have to work it out with Captain Purvis, and that ought to be done in person. How do we handle that, Colonel?"

"Purvis still doesn't know you're working undercover. I'll have to call him and arrange a meeting. Could you drive to Houston today?"

"Yes, sir, I could be there by early afternoon."

"Excellent." Garrison hesitated, as though thinking something through, then went on. "I received a call from the attorney general yesterday afternoon. You're familiar with a man named Jack Nolan?"

"Yes, sir," Stoner said. "He's the enforcer for the Galveston mob. You briefed me on him before I left Austin."

"Now that you mention it, I believe I did. In any event, the attorney general may offer him immunity if he turns state's evidence against Quinn and Voight. I thought you should know."

"Colonel, I'd be floored if it happened. Nolan's not the sort to turn stool pigeon. Who's behind it?"

"A reform committee," Garrison told him. "Apparently they're talking to Nolan through a man named Earl Durant. I gather he's a banker there in Galveston. Have you heard of him?"

"No, sir, that's a new one on me."

"Well, as you say, it may come to nothing. Even if it did, these things take time. No reason to let it delay our plans."

"I'm with you there, Colonel. So far as I'm concerned, a bird in the hand's the way to go. We could wrap this up by Saturday night."

"Nothing would please me more," Garrison said. "I'll call Captain Purvis now and call you back. Give me your number."

Stoner read off the number on the pay phone. When they hung up, he opened the door of the booth and joined Janice at the magazine racks. She glanced up from a copy of *Vogue* and gave him a questioning look. He nodded at the phone booth with a wry smile.

"Mom has to call me back."

Durant pulled off the highway. The only cars in the parking lot were a Stutz Bearcat and a shiny new Ford. He braked to a halt, hooking the gearshift into reverse, and cut the engine. He sat for a moment surveying the Rendezvous Roadhouse.

Ira Aldridge had loaned him the car, a four-door Chevrolet. As part of the loan, Aldridge had again attempted to dissuade him from meeting with Nolan. Aldridge had argued that Nolan was a killer, untrustworthy, and might very well be setting a trap. The Rendezvous Roadhouse was a known hangout for gangsters.

Durant wondered now if he should have taken the advice. Apart from the cars in the parking lot, the roadhouse look deserted, the perfect place for a quiet murder. Still, he was armed, the Luger stuffed in his waistband, and some visceral instinct told him that Nolan's curiosity was a safety net of sorts. He decided there was one way to find out.

The front hall of the roadhouse was empty. Durant heard distant voices from the rear, what was probably the kitchen. Off to the right, he saw a room filled with card tables, all vacant and no one in sight. To his left was a dim bar with tables and booths, and a small dance floor. He thought it was empty as well until he spotted a tendril of smoke drifting toward the ceiling. He saw Jack Nolan seated in one of the booths.

Durant crossed the dance floor. Nolan watched him with the look of a fox eyeing a lone partridge. "Hey, slick," he said with a breezy smile. "I see you found the place."

"Easy enough to find," Durant said, settling into the booth. "First person I asked gave me directions."

"Well, I like a man that's on time. Just so we get off on the right foot—you packin' heat?"

"Yeah, I'm carrying a gun."

"Thought so," Nolan said. "Automatic, is it?"

Durant nodded. "A Luger."

"I prefer a revolver myself. Automatics tend to jam when you need 'em most."

"Depends on how you treat them. I clean mine every night."

"Do you?" Nolan seemed amused. "I guess Elmer Spadden's a testament to that. You stopped his ticker p.d.q."

"I didn't have much choice."

"Elmer was always better with his dukes than a gun. Where'd you learn to shoot so good?"

Durant shrugged. "Mostly in France."

"No kiddin'!" Nolan said, exhaling smoke. "You were in the war?"

"Wasn't everybody?"

"What part of France?"

"Chateau-Thierry. Belleau Wood. Other places I've forgot."

"I'll be damned." Nolan took a drag on his cigarette, oddly pleased. "I was a Leatherneck, Fifth Marines. How about you?"

"Infantry," Durant said. "Just another doughboy."

"No, slick, not the way you shoot. I'll bet you came home with a chestful of medals."

"I'd bet the same about you."

"Something, isn't it?" Nolan's voice was almost nostalgic, tinged with camaraderie. "Funny the way wars turn out. You a movie stuntman and me a . . . what can I say— a jack-of-all-trades."

"Anything's better than war," Durant said, surprised by the tone of the conversation. "How'd you make it back home in one piece?"

"I'd have to put it down to pure luck. And you?"

"Well, like they say, there weren't any atheists in the trenches. God or luck, take your choice."

"A good eye helped, too."

"How do you mean?"

"Knocking off Krauts." Nolan studied him with a crooked smile. "The way you took down Spadden—in the dark."

Durant returned the smile. "You'll recall there was a streetlight. Luck was on my side, too."

"Not God?"

"Who had time to pray?"

Nolan grinned. "Too bad we're on opposite sides of the fence. I might've liked you."

"Not too late," Durant said, spreading his hands. "You might like me more than you thought."

"Time to get down to business, huh? You said on the phone something could work to my advantage. What was that all about?"

"How'd you like to walk away from Galveston with a fresh start? Wipe the slate clean?"

"That'd be some wipe," Nolan said with an ironic smile. "Go ahead, I'm all ears."

Durant leaned forward. "I've got a direct line to the attorney general of Texas. I can arrange immunity for any crime you've ever done." He paused for emphasis. "And ten thousand in cash to seal the bargain."

"Judas only got thirty pieces of silver. Who do I have to betray?"

"Tie William Magruder to Quinn and Voight. That gets the mob off my back and it saves my bank. And you're off scot-free."

Nolan held his gaze. "I suppose you'd expect me to testify in court?"

"It won't come to that," Durant said earnestly. "Magruder will be ruined in politics and your bosses won't be able to help him. A sworn affidavit with all the details should turn the trick."

"Which you and your reformer buddies would publish in the newspaper. Do I hear this right?"

"That's the general idea."

Nolan laughed. "I always said you had brass balls. You really thought I'd rat out Quinn and Voight?"

"They're not important," Durant said. "I'm after Magruder."

"They're important to me, slick. Forget loyalty and talk about staying alive. I couldn't run far enough fast enough. You'd be reading my obituary."

"Something tells me that wouldn't happen. Who'd have the guts to go up against Diamond Jack Nolan?"

"Save the sales pitch," Nolan said firmly. "Tell the attorney general I decline the offer. No deal."

"Why not sleep on it?" Durant said. "A deal like this comes along once in a lifetime. You might feel different tomorrow."

"Yessir, I do admire a man with balls. Too bad we didn't meet someplace besides Galveston."

"That's your final word on it?"

"Yeah, that's final."

"Sorry to hear it, Jack."

"Life's a bitch, ain't it?"

They parted with a handshake in the parking lot. Durant drove off in his Chevy wondering where the deal had gone sour. Nolan followed a short distance behind in his Stutz Bearcat, stewing on just how much he'd tell Quinn and Voight. He hadn't been kidding when he said he admired a man with balls. He hoped he wouldn't have to kill Durant.

Nolan reached for his cigarettes. He discovered the pack had only one left just as he approached the intersection for La Marque. He turned onto Main Street, remembering there was a tobacco shop a couple blocks down. His attention was drawn to a snazzy canary-yellow Packard that looked vaguely familiar. He pulled into the curb.

A bell jingled over the door as he entered the tobacco shop. Off to the side, at the magazine racks, a man and a woman were standing with their backs to him. The phone in the phone booth blasted a strident ring, and the man hurried toward the rear of the store. As he turned into the phone booth, his features were visible for the first time, his profile caught in a moment of hard intensity. He closed the door.

Nolan recognized him immediately. For the last three nights he'd watched Robert Eberling at the tables in the casino. He recalled Voight mentioning that Eberling was a well-to-do rancher and a high roller, and by his play at the tables, a born loser. The woman still had her face buried in a magazine, but Nolan recognized her as well. She was Eberling's wife.

"Morning," the shop owner said. "What can I do for you?"

"Lucky Strikes," Nolan said, turning away from the woman. "Make it a couple packs."

After paying for the cigarettes, Nolan stepped outside and climbed into his car. He pulled away with one eye on the road and the other on the tobacco shop. Some snatch of conversation he'd overheard reminded him that Eberling had a suite at the Buccaneer. He asked himself why a high roller would be waiting for calls at a phone booth. A phone booth in La Marque.

He thought Dutch Voight would definitely be interested. Something about it didn't rhyme.

• • •

"Thirty-one thousand apiece."

"Another good week."

"Yeah, not bad," Voight said, removing the bearer bonds from his briefcase. "Sophie Tucker damn sure doesn't draw as good as Jolson."

Quinn chortled. "Nobody draws as good as Jolson."

They were in the office at the Turf Club. Yesterday, under pressure to deal with Frank Nitti, Voight had completely forgotten about the bonds. Their split was thirty-one thousand each from money skimmed off last week's operations. He placed the bonds in the massive safe which occupied one corner of the office.

"That's that," he said, closing the safe door. "Wonder what's keeping Jack?"

Quinn checked his watch. "You're right, going on eleven-thirty. I expected him back by now."

"Tell you one thing, Ollie. Nothing good will come of him meeting with Durant. We should've stopped it."

"We had our hands full with your old pal Nitti. Besides, I don't see any harm in their getting together. We'll find out what clever new scheme Durant has up his sleeve."

"To hell with his scheme!" Voight grunted, "High time the bastard was dead and gone."

"We'll get to it, Dutch. Let's wait to hear what Jack has to say."

The phone rang. Quinn answered and a quick smile came over his features. "Good morning, Father Rourke. Always a pleasure to hear your voice." He listened, nodding, his expression suddenly quizzical. "Yes, of course, Father. I'll be right over."

"That's odd," he said when he hung up. "Monsignor O'Donnell wants to see me and it sounded a little urgent. Wonder what's up?"

"Probably another contribution," Voight said. "You're the softest touch in town."

"All in a good cause, Dutch. You know how I feel about public relations."

Quinn and Voight donated to every church on the Island. Their purpose was to garner the goodwill of the people, and thus undermine the periodic outcries by reformist clergymen. But the population of Galveston was predominately Catholic, and their largest contributions were to the Catholic church. Quinn, who was Catholic himself, also considered it an investment in the Hereafter. He hoped to be forgiven, if not redeemed, of his sins.

"I'll be back shortly," he said, moving toward the door. "Keep Jack around till I hear what he has to say."

Voight pulled a frown. "Just remember half of these donations come out of my pocket. Don't let the monsignor soft-soap you."

"Think of your immortal soul, Dutch. You might still have a chance at the Pearly Gates."

"That'll be the day!"

Quinn found Turk McGuire waiting in the hall. Downstairs, the Cadillac Phaeton was parked at the curb in front of the club. McGuire held the door while Quinn climbed into the backseat, then got behind the wheel and started the engine. He swung the car around in a U-turn and headed south.

Quinn's thoughts jumped from the monsignor to things that needed doing at the Hollywood Club. Voight's remark about Sophie Tucker popped into his mind, and from there it was but a short hop to the ox behind the wheel. Everyone at the club knew McGuire was spending his nights in Sophie Tucker's hotel suite. Only Quinn dared mention it.

"Tell me, Turk," he said with a straight face. "How are things with you and Miss Tucker? Keeping her happy, are you?"

McGuire glanced at him in the rearview mirror. "Well, tell you the truth, it's the other way round. She's a lotta woman, boss."

"I suppose that accounts for the dark circles under your eyes. Not getting much sleep these nights?"

"Not a whole lot."

"Business before pleasure," Quinn said, forcing himself not to smile. "Don't overdo things in the romance department. We need her fresh for the show."

McGuire flushed with embarrassment. He managed a dopey grin. "Nothing to worry about there, boss. She's a regular firecracker."

"Turk, I'd say you're a lucky dog. Keep up the good work."

"I'll do my best, boss."

A few minutes later, they turned into the seashell driveway beside St. Mary's Cathedral. Tall towers framed the front of the basilica, with a central tower from which a statue of the Virgin Mary gazed out over the Island. The compound, which included the monsignor's quarters, was located on Twenty-first Street near Broadway. A few blocks to the west was the Ursuline Convent for nuns.

Father Rourke met Quinn at the door of the rectory. He escorted him down a long hallway to the monsignor's study. The room was appointed with furniture of dark teak and polished leather, the waxed hardwood floor glistening from a spill of sunlight through broad windows. A marble statue of the Blessed Virgin stood beneath a large, ornate crucifix.

Monsignor O'Donnell rose from behind his desk. He was a bear of a man, with a square, determined jaw, a broad forehead, and dark, bushy brows sprinkled with gray. His robes were plain, though finely tailored, and a silver crucifix hung suspended over the expanse of his chest. He gave the impression of rocklike strength, and authority.

"Oliver," he said, extending a meaty handshake. "How nice of you to come on such short notice."

"A pleasure, Monsignor." Quinn let himself be directed to a leather armchair. "We see each other too seldom."

"Yes, indeed, particularly for old friends."

Their relationship was one of cordial distance. They never appeared in public together, for a prince of the church could not be seen to socialize with the Island's most visible gangster. Yet Quinn, with steamship tickets delivered anonymously every summer, enabled the monsignor to visit his mother in Ireland. They were comfortable with discreet arrangements.

"Yesterday I received a call," O'Donnell said without further ceremony. "I've been asked to intercede in a delicate matter, and I prayed on it overnight. The caller was William Magruder."

"Magruder?" Quinn looked astonished. "Why would he call you about me?"

"There's the rub, isn't it? Mr. Magruder is concerned about his daughter, Elizabeth. A fine girl, I'm told."

"Yes, I know her personally. We hosted her birthday party at the club a week or so ago."

"Twenty-one, I believe she is," O'Donnell said, the trace of a brogue in his voice. "A young lass, so impressionable, and like many, so naïve. I'm sad to say she's become involved with one of your men, Oliver." He arched an eyebrow. "Romantically involved."

Quinn's jaw dropped. "Who?"

"A lad by the name of Jack Nolan."

"Why didn't Magruder come to me? Why drag you into it?"

"Think on it a moment," O'Donnell said with a sage nod. "A direct approach, or so Mr. Magruder believed, might offend you. As you can imagine, he's an outraged father, and properly so. He asked me to speak on his behalf."

"I understand," Quinn said, sitting stiff in his chair. "Monsignor, you have my word that Miss Magruder has seen the last of Jack Nolan. I'll put an end to it today."

"Nothing too drastic, Oliver. A word to the wise should be sufficient. Don't you agree?"

"A word or three, or four or more. You won't be bothered again, Monsignor."

"I knew we'd find a way between us. God bless you, Oliver."

Quinn departed with unusual haste. When he was gone, Monsignor O'Donnell leaned back in his chair and idly fingered the crucifix suspended from his neck. In many ways, he admired Quinn, and privately, he thought of him as a friend. A relationship not all that unusual within the church.

The idea, as he toyed with it, somehow brought to mind the Borgias. A noble Italian family, central figures in the Renaissance, with two popes and a saint to their credit. Then there was Cesare Borgia, son of a pope, ruthless and murderous, once a cardinal of the church. A man who strangled his enemies to death.

O'Donnell told himself there was ample precedent, established centuries ago by those who ruled the Vatican. A prince of the church and a gangster were entitled to be friends.

He thought Jack Nolan might soon appreciate the irony.

Chapter Nineteen

Nolan parked in front of the Turf Club. He knew he was running late, and strangely enough, he didn't care. He'd stopped at a hamburger joint for lunch, and tried to get his mind straight before reporting to Quinn and Voight. He still wasn't sure how it would play out.

The bookmaking parlor was slow for a Tuesday afternoon. There were a couple of horse races later on the West Coast, and die-hard bettors were already gathering to pore over the scratch sheets. Football games, both pro and college, weren't scheduled until the weekend, and there was little action. He glanced at the tote board as he walked through the club room.

Joe Reed, the elevator operator, greeted him with a sly grin. "Late night, was it, Jack? You rumrunners have all the fun."

"No, wasn't that, Joe." Nolan stepped onto the elevator. "We're bringing in a load tonight. I'll save you a bottle."

"Never turn down bonded whiskey. Nosiree, not me."

Reed was closer to the truth than he suspected. Tonight, rather than last night, would be the late night. Early that morning he'd called the Magruder home and spoken with Libbie. She was frantic to see him, and he'd agreed to meet her on a beach west of the amusement piers before tonight's rumrunning operation. He wasn't yet sure how they would get around the problem of her father. Or for that matter, the bigger problem of Quinn and Voight. He wondered that Magruder hadn't already contacted them.

Upstairs, Barney Ward was stationed at his usual post outside the office. Nolan didn't see McGuire in the bil-

liards room or the athletic club and that gave him pause.
He had somehow assumed Quinn would be there, waiting
with Voight, for his report on the meeting with Durant.
There was sure to be fireworks, and he silently wished
they were both present. Quinn always had a tempering
effect on Voight.

Ward nodded. "How's things, Jack?"

"Good as gold, Barney. Where's Mr. Quinn?"

"Dunno and didn't ask. Him and Turk went out a
while back."

Ward held the door and Nolan stepped into the office.
Voight was seated at his desk, a cigar clamped in his
mouth, scanning entries in a ledger. He looked up with a
sour expression.

"Where you been?" he said. "I expected you back an
hour ago."

"Stopped off for lunch," Nolan said, dropping into a
chair. "Figured it might be a long afternoon."

"Next time don't keep me coolin' my heels. What
happened with Durant?"

"I'd have to say he surprised me. Him and his reformer pals cooked up a deal with the attorney general.
They offered me immunity."

"Immunity from what?"

"Anything crooked I've ever done."

Voight stared at him. "I think you'd better spell that
out."

Nolan recounted the gist of the meeting. He explained
that Durant's chief goal was to establish a link between
Magruder and the mob. In exchange for turning stool pigeon, Nolan would receive a grant of immunity from the
attorney general, plus ten thousand dollars. A neat little
package to entice him to turn Judas.

"Dirty bastards!" Voight fumed when he finished.
"They really thought you'd go for that?"

"Well, it was worth a try," Nolan said. "Durant's
dead set on nailing Magruder's hide to the wall. He
doesn't care one way or the other about you and Ollie."

"I don't give a rat's ass whether he does or doesn't. Time to wash our hands of this whole mess. I want you—"

The door opened. Quinn walked into the office like a dragon breathing fire. His teeth were clenched, a knot pulsing at his jawline, and his eyes burned with anger. Voight looked at him with a dumbfounded expression.

"What the hell happened to you?"

"I just had a talk with Monsignor O'Donnell. Bill Magruder asked him to call me in and oh-so-politely slap my wrists. Care to guess why?"

"Why don't you just tell me?"

Quinn paced across to the window, then turned back and stopped. His eyes drilled into Nolan. "So I'm informed, one of our men has been screwing Magruder's daughter. Anything to it, Jack?"

"Not the way you mean," Nolan said, taken aback by the suddenness of the assault. "Sometimes you meet a girl and things just click. I'm stuck on her and it's mutual."

"Who gives a damn!" Quinn exploded. "You put us at risk with Magruder. Get your head on straight!"

"I'll take you off the hook," Nolan said in a reasonable tone. "I'll have a talk with Magruder and explain it to him. He'll see I'm serious."

"Jesus Christ! Do you think he wants a gangster in the family? Where's your brain?"

"What's the harm in trying? Who knows, I might win him over."

"Listen to me, Jack." Quinn's voice was glacial, his eyes suddenly cold. "Dutch and I won't let you jeopardize our business, everything we've taken years to build. Do you understand what I'm saying?"

Nolan understood exactly what he was saying. All it required was for them to open the door and call in McGuire and Ward. There was no loyalty, no friendship, certainly no brotherhood in the rackets. By nightfall, he would be swimming with the fishes at the bottom of the

Gulf. He decided the only way out was to lie. Convincingly.

"I hear you," he said with a lame shrug. "I just wasn't thinking straight."

"Then we're agreed," Quinn persisted. "You'll ditch the girl?"

"Yeah, sure, it's over and done with. I won't see her anymore."

"No pulling my chain here, Jack. You're on the level?"

"Yeah, boss, on the level."

Quinn studied him. "I've got your word?"

Nolan lied with the aplomb of a Chinese bandit. "I give you my word."

"Now you're talking sense."

"Are we through with the hearts and flowers?" Voight said, clearly disgusted with the whole conversation. "We've got business here that needs tending."

"Oh?" Quinn looked around. "What business is that?"

"Tell him, Jack."

Nolan again related the details of his meeting with Durant. Voight, puffing furiously on his cigar, was quick to add his own opinion. Quinn heard them out, then slowly nodded his head.

"Dutch is right," he said. "Time to get rid of Durant."

"Won't be all that easy," Nolan amended. "You mind a suggestion?"

"Let's hear it," Voight prompted with a wave of his cigar. "You're our boy when it comes to rough stuff."

Nolan steeled himself to lie earnestly. After all that had happened, he'd decided he didn't want to kill Durant. Maybe it was the way Durant had stood and fought that night, the night he'd killed Elmer Spadden. Maybe it was the fact that Durant had survived the trenches of France, and understood there were worse things than dying. Or maybe it had to do with Libbie, and Nolan's abrupt realization that he might get himself killed. He wasn't sure in his own mind as to the real reason. He only knew he had to play for time.

"Durant's dangerous," he said, wording it to get their attention. "After this morning, he knows we'll come at him again. He killed Elmer, and if we try him head-on, he could kill me, or Turk, or anybody else. We have to outsmart him to take him out."

"So?" Quinn said impatiently. "How do we outsmart him?"

"We move on him from a different direction. Maybe through the old guy at his bank, Aldridge. Or maybe the Ludlow girl, the one he's been dating. I'll figure out a way, don't worry about it. Something that'll force him to play into our hands."

"Like what?" Voight said. "Kidnap the girl, force him to come to you? Play him for a slip-up?"

Nolan smiled. "Something tricky, boss. Real tricky."

Voight and Quinn exchanged a glance. Something unspoken passed between them, and Voight finally nodded, "All right, Jack," he said. "Do it your way, but get it done by this weekend. I want him dead."

"I'll take care of it, neat and quick."

Nolan got out before they could ask more questions. Only later, after he'd left the Turf Club, did he remember he'd forgotten to mention the rancher, Robert Eberling. The one who hung around pay phones waiting for a call. He decided to keep it to himself.

One problem more might be one problem too many.

Durant drove around the Island for almost an hour. He needed time to think, to weigh what he would do next. All his options seemed foreclosed.

Shortly after one o'clock, he parked on the Strand. He knew he should eat something, but his stomach resisted the idea of food. Instead, he walked into the bank, offering Catherine a forced smile, and returned the car keys to Aldridge. He asked the older man into his office.

Aldridge closed the door, then took a seat. His eyes narrowed in assessment. "I take it things didn't go well?"

Durant laughed without humor. "Am I that obvious?"

"You look a little green around the gills. What happened?"

"Nolan turned me down cold. I think he was amused by the whole thing."

"Amused?"

"You know, like I was a numbskull to even think he'd go for it. He all but laughed."

Durant gave him a nutshell version of the meeting. He left out a good deal, but he covered what seemed to him the relevant points. He finished with a lame shrug.

"For the most part, it was a waste of breath. Nolan said if he took the deal, there'd be no place to hide. Quinn and Voight would have him killed."

"No question of it," Aldridge said. "I told you as much this morning. He would have been signing his own death warrant."

Durant nodded, his expression abstract. "The really strange thing was that I liked him. Once you get past that tough guy attitude, he's a regular joe."

"A regular joe who just happens to murder people for a living. Have you forgotten he tried to kill you?"

"No, I haven't forgotten, Ira. I'm just saying. . . ."

"Yes?" Aldridge prodded. "Saying what?"

"Nothing important," Durant said. "The only thing that counts is that he turned me down. I'm right back where I started."

"Earl, if anything, you're worse off. I tried to warn you of that before you met with him. You've gone from the skillet to the fire."

"How could it be worse than it was?"

Aldridge shifted in his chair. "Nolan will report everything you said to Quinn and Voight. Their view—and, unfortunately, it's correct—will be that you tried to bribe him to betray them. How do you suppose they will react?"

"Don't have to be a mind reader," Durant replied. "They'll order Nolan to plant me six feet under. What's new?"

"What's new is that you've attacked them personally. Before, they were doing Magruder a favor, or perhaps looking for revenge because you killed one of their men. Now you've made it personal, very personal. You've threatened *them*."

"Yeah, you're probably right."

"I know I'm right," Aldridge said soberly. "And to compound matters, Magruder's applying pressure of his own. Do you remember what you said when we left his office Saturday?"

"What?" Durant searched his memory. "That he was already on the horn to Quinn and Voight?"

"Exactly. So now, in addition to Magruder, Quinn and Voight have a personal stake. They want you dead as much as Magruder—perhaps more."

"Got myself in a helluva fix, didn't I, Ira?"

"I'm afraid so." Aldridge sat forward, his concern genuine. "You really need to leave town, the quicker, the better. You're in great danger, Earl."

Durant waved him off. "I told you once before, that's not an option. There's no place to hide, anyway. They could find me."

"You're more resourceful than that. If you really wanted to, I'm sure you could disappear and not be found. And you needn't worry yourself about the bank. I'll protect your interests."

"Hell, Ira, you're the banker around here anyhow. I guess I'm just too stubborn to run. Or maybe too dumb. Take your pick."

Aldridge sighed heavily. "You know you don't have a chance. They'll kill you."

"Maybe, maybe not," Durant said, his features stoic. "But that doesn't change anything. I won't run."

Catherine stuck her head in the door. "The Holy Trinity is here to see you. Should I tell them to wait?"

"No need to wait," Durant said. "Might as well get it over with."

Aldridge rose. "I'll step outside."

"No, stick around, Ira. I could use the moral support."

Baldwin and Adair, followed by Herbert Cornwall, filed into the office. Aldridge leaned against the wall, arms folded across his chest, while they arranged themselves in chairs before the desk. Their faces were expectant, eager for good news.

"We couldn't stand it any longer," Baldwin said. "How did things go with Jack Nolan?"

"Not good," Durant told them. "He refused the offer. Wouldn't even discuss it."

Their features registered first surprise, then shock. Adair fidgeted nervously. "How could he not discuss it? What did he say?"

"What he said was 'Thanks, but no thanks.' A flat turndown."

"I'm sure there was more to it than that, Mr. Durant. Could you be a little more specific?"

Durant once again related the tone of the meeting. He left out anything about the war, and the discovery that he and Nolan had served in France at the same time. When he finished, the men sat for a moment in bewildered silence. Cornwall finally found his voice.

"I don't understand," he said. "Why would anyone refuse immunity? It doesn't make sense."

"Look at it from his standpoint," Durant said. "He figured he wouldn't live long enough to enjoy his new freedom. Why get yourself killed for nothing?"

Baldwin stiffened. "Do I detect a note of sympathy, Mr. Durant? Why would you care what happens to Jack Nolan?"

"Don't put words in my mouth," Durant said bluntly. "I told you why he refused, and what I think doesn't matter. His reasons were good enough for him."

"All's not lost," Cornwall broke in. "You could still issue a public statement."

"A statement about what?"

"Something to the effect that you met with Nolan and offered him immunity. But while he refused the offer, he nonetheless confirmed the link between Magruder and the mob. How does that sound?"

"Sounds like a lie," Durant informed him. "Nolan didn't say that."

"Who's to know?" Cornwall said with a conspiratorial smile. "It's your word against that of a notorious gangster. I think public opinion would be on our side."

Aldridge, silent until now, could no longer contain himself. "Herbie, how bad do you want to be mayor? Enough to make a liar of Earl, not to mention yourself? I don't think I'd vote for you."

"This isn't your affair," Cornwall said testily. "We're discussing what's best for the community. The people!"

Durant stood. "Gentlemen, I think that concludes our business. Today or any other day."

"Wait now!" Baldwin sputtered. "We can still—"

"No, we can't," Durant cut him short. "Ira, would you show these gentlemen the door?"

Aldridge moved across the room and opened the door. Baldwin looked as though he was on the verge of saying something, but he was silenced by Durant's dark scowl. The men trooped out of the office and Aldridge closed the door behind them. He turned back to Durant.

"To paraphrase Lord Bolingbroke—the art of a politician is to disguise vice in a way that serves virtue."

"Who's Lord Bolingbroke?"

"An English nobleman," Aldridge said. "He made that remark about two hundred years ago."

"You a student of history, Ira?"

"Only where it concerns rascals and liars—like Herbie Cornwall."

Durant thought it went further. The Englishman's remark, though he'd never heard it before, seemed to hit the mark for all of Galveston. Politicians, unscrupulous businessmen, and the mob.

Vice disguised as virtue.

· · ·

Stoner kept one eye on the rearview mirror. He and Janice were approaching Houston, and he was still wary of being followed. His appointment with Captain Purvis was set for two o'clock.

Earlier, on the telephone, Colonel Garrison had given him directions. The headquarters for the Ranger Company was located on the outskirts of the city, not far from Rice University. The single-story frame building was set back off the road, identified by a sign hung between stout posts. They pulled into the parking lot with time to spare.

The reception room inside was manned by a sergeant and two orderlies. Stoner identified himself by name only, reluctant to say anything more until he'd spoken with Captain Purvis. The sergeant inspected Janice with a quick, appreciative glance, then disappeared into the back of the building. He returned shortly and led them down a hallway to a door without markings. He motioned them into an office.

Captain Hardy Purvis rose from behind his desk. A tall man, he was in his early forties, with angular features and sparse ginger hair. He had served with distinction in the Ranger Batallion posted along the Rio Grande during the war in Europe. His promotion to captain was the result of breaking a German spy ring operating out of Mexico and infiltrating agents across the border. He was known in the Rangers as an officer who went by the book.

"Come in, Stoner," he said, waiting for the sergeant to close the door. "I've been expecting you."

"Captain," Stoner said by way of acknowledgment. "I'd like you to meet Janice Overton. She's working with me on the Galveston case."

"Miss Overton." Purvis gestured them to chairs before his desk. "Colonel Garrison gave you quite a recommendation. He said you volunteered for the job."

"Actually, I got drafted," Janice said with a coy

smile. "I think I was the only girl Clint knew who was crazy enough to go undercover."

"I see." Purvis seemed uncertain how to take her flippant manner. He turned to Stoner. "The colonel tells me you insisted that I not be informed of this operation. Why was that?"

"Mostly for security, Cap'n," Stoner said frankly. "I was told the mobsters in Galveston don't take prisoners. Seemed like the fewer who knew, the better."

"In other words, you were concerned there might be leaks out of my office. Do I hear you right?"

"No, sir, not just exactly. I figured it was safer—for Janice and me—if everything was kept on the q.t."

"You're giving me the runaround, Sergeant. I'd like a straight answer."

Stoner cocked his head. "How long have you been trying to shut down Galveston?"

"Over a year," Purvis snapped. "What's that got to do with anything?"

"Well, Cap'n, we've been there a little over two weeks. So far, one gangster's been killed, and another one killed a civilian in a speakeasy. Galveston's a dangerous place."

"Get to the point."

"I guess the point's pretty simple. Janice and me are at risk every day we're working undercover. I like the odds better if nobody knows we're there."

Purvis knotted his brow in irritation. "Sergeant, I don't like anyone working my district without my knowledge. Just to be frank about it, I don't give a damn what your reason is."

"I understand, sir," Stoner said in a level voice. "Maybe you ought to talk with Colonel Garrison."

A dark look came over Purvis. He had spoken with Garrison at length on the telephone that morning. Garrison told him in no uncertain terms that he endorsed Stoner's plan for the raid on the Hollywood Club. Purvis was to be in nominal command, Garrison said, but Stoner would call the shots on the raid. The order, though tactfully phrased, was nonetheless an order.

Janice watched the byplay with a secret smile. She knew the score, and she knew that Sergeant Stoner was politely reminding Captain Purvis of who was in charge. On the phone that morning, Stoner had presented his case in the strongest possible terms, pointedly noting that it was his and Janice's lives at stake. His arguments were short of insubordination, but he'd insisted that he control the operation. Garrison, impressed by his plan, had finally agreed.

"Let's move on," Purvis said in an attempt to save face. "Colonel Garrison said you've worked out a plan for a raid. Tell me about it."

"Yessir," Stoner said with just the proper note of respect. "You've seen the inside of the club, right?"

"Several times."

"Then you know how they control those doors. The one into the lounge and the one beyond that into the casino."

"Of course," Purvis said impatiently. "They slow us down until, by the time we get there, the gaming devices have disappeared. I'm waiting for you to tell me how they do it."

"I don't have any idea," Stoner said. "That's the whole point of setting up the raid."

"Wait a minute, I'm missing something here. Are you telling me you haven't figured out how they get rid of the gaming equipment?"

"Yessir, that's exactly what I'm saying."

"Judas Priest!" Purvis barked. "You don't know any more about the casino than I do. Garrison led me to believe you have a plan. A foolproof plan."

Stoner wagged his head. "Captain, I don't know that anything's foolproof. But I'd have to say this comes pretty close."

A moment elapsed in turgid silence. Purvis abruptly realized that Garrison had purposely withheld critical information. He'd been painted into a corner and subtly placed at the command of a sergeant. He took a slow, deep breath.

"All right, Sergeant," he said in a resigned tone. "Let's hear your plan."

"Works like this, Cap'n," Stoner said, watching him closely. "Janice and I will be in the casino Friday night. You and your men pull a raid at nine sharp. Any problem with the timing?"

"No problem at all. Go ahead."

"Your raid's the key to the whole thing. They'll slow you down and do whatever they do to make the casino disappear. But this time, Janice and I will be there to see how it happens."

"Won't work," Purvis said. "We have to catch the gaming devices in actual operation. Otherwise we can't make an arrest."

"That's the second step," Stoner informed him. "You and your men will pull another raid Saturday night."

"Saturday night?"

"Yessir, at ten o'clock on the button. Voight and Quinn will never expect you to hit the place two nights in a row. We'll catch them with their pants down."

"No, I'm sure they won't," Purvis said. "But what does that accomplish? We still have to catch them in the act of operating gaming tables."

"You will, Cap'n."

"What makes you so certain?"

"I'm going to hold the casino till you and your men get there."

"Are you?" Purvis scoffed. "How do you propose to do that?"

Stoner grinned like a jack-o'-lantern, and told him.

Chapter Twenty

A crescent moon hung like a crooked lantern in a velvet sky. The Gulf was calm under a light breeze, the tide lapping gently against the shoreline. Silvery beams of starlight skipped and skittered across the dark waters.

Libbie waited in her Chevy coupe. The car was parked at a sheltered cove five miles west of the amusement piers. The spot was a short distance off the road and overlooked the white sand of a moonlit beach. Hers was the only car at the cove.

The call that morning from Nolan had been a godsend. She was still infuriated with her father, and hadn't spoken to him since their argument yesterday morning. Yet her concern was for Jack, and the deeper fear that her father had reported him to Quinn and Voight. She was worried for his safety.

A car pulled in behind her, quickly cut the headlights. She looked around and saw Nolan step out of his Stutz Bearcat, his features visible in the faint cast of the moon. He glanced back at the road, as though assuring himself they wouldn't be seen, and then walked around the side of her car. He slipped into the passenger seat.

"Hi there, gorgeous," he said lightly, cupping a hand behind her neck. "Been waiting long?"

"All my life."

His touch was like fire against her skin. She scooted across the seat, into his open arms, and he enfolded her in an embrace. She kissed him fiercely, wriggling to get closer, her breasts pressed against the holstered gun beneath his suit jacket. She didn't care about the gun, or who he was, or what he might have done. She never wanted to let go.

They finally parted, slightly breathless, his mouth smeared with lipstick. "Damn," he said with a jester's smile. "I think maybe you missed me."

"Don't you dare kid," she said, nuzzling into his shoulder. "I've been worried sick about you."

"Tell you the truth, I felt the same way. How's things with you and your dad?"

"After yesterday, we aren't speaking. Has he said anything to your bosses?"

"No, not directly." Nolan hesitated, suddenly somber. "He sent the message through Monsignor O'Donnell. Quinn got called on the carpet this morning."

"What!" She sat up, rigid with shock. "He told Monsignor O'Donnell about us? About our—?"

"The whole kit and caboodle. Quinn even heard about the hotel in Houston."

"The son of a bitch! I can't believe he's my father. Why didn't he just take an ad in the newspaper?"

"Didn't need to," Nolan allowed. "Monsignor O'Donnell evidently read the riot act to Quinn. I got the story first hand, loud and clear."

"What happened?" she said, a little hitch in her voice. "Are you in trouble?"

A wayward thought flashed through Nolan's mind. Her father was yet another reason why he wouldn't kill Durant, perhaps the best reason. There was revenge of sorts in letting Durant continue to frustrate the old bastard. He liked the idea, a lot.

"Jack, didn't you hear me? Are you in trouble?"

"I was," Nolan said, wishing he could tell her the truth about her father. "Quinn and Voight raked me over the coals pretty good. We finally came to an agreement."

"I don't understand," she said, looking at him. "What kind of agreement?"

"I took a blood oath I'd never see you again. Told them we were finished."

"You're not serious!"

"On my honor."

"But you're here."

Nolan smiled. "I lied like a dog."

"Tell me it's true," she said, staring into his eyes. "Tell me you'll never leave me."

"I'll never leave you, and that is the honest-to-God's truth. What was it you said once, kismet? We're stuck with one another."

"Oh, Jack!" She hugged him desperately. "I love you so much. You just don't know."

"Yeah, I do," Nolan said softly. "It's the same for me."

"Is it, you mean it? You'll never take it back?"

"Never in a month of Sundays. You've got me hooked."

"Good Lord!" Her features went taut. "I just happened to think. What will Quinn and Voight do if they find out?"

"That's not an option," Nolan said seriously. "We have to be damn careful from now on. Double damn careful."

"But we can't sneak around like this all the time. The Island's too small, and there are too many busybodies. We're bound to be seen."

"I'm already working on it. I'll think of something."

"Jack."

"Yeah?"

"Make love to me."

"In a car?"

"Yes, dammit!" she said in a husky voice. "I need you."

Nolan hadn't done it in a car since he was in high school. Though the seat made it awkward, they managed to stretch out just enough by opening the door. She loosened her garter belt and slipped off her panties, and he fumbled his pants down. She took him in a rush of emotion, pulling him deep inside, and they both peaked within moments. When they finished, spent and breathing hard, she clung to him, unwilling to let go. She whispered in his ear.

"Jack."

"Yeah?"

"Next time bring a blanket."

"What for?"

"Silly," she said, kissing him tenderly. "We'll do it on the beach."

"The beach?" he said doubtfully. "Won't that be a little sandy?"

"Well, good-lookin', we're definitely going to make love. So it's the beach or the car. Which would you prefer?"

"I'll bring the blanket."

They decided to leave ten minutes apart. After they were dressed, she walked him to his car. He took her in his arms, holding her a moment in a snug embrace, then stepped back. He looked down at her in the moonlight.

"One last thing, and it's important."

"Okay."

"You've got to convince your dad we're finished. You can't let on we're playing for time."

She laughed wickedly. "Oh, don't worry, I'll convince him."

"You're sure?"

"Yes, sweetheart mine, I'm very sure."

"Good, give me a kiss for luck."

She kissed him soundly on the mouth. "When will I see you again?"

"I'll call you tomorrow."

Delmonte's was one of the finer restaurants in Galveston. A family-owned establishment, it was off the beaten path, and seldom frequented by tourists. The clientele was composed primarily of Islanders who appreciated fine food.

Durant had a reservation. Earlier, at the bank, he'd asked Aldridge to recommend a restaurant for a special

occasion. He declined to elaborate even when the older
man gave him a questioning look, but Aldridge nonetheless told him of Delmonte's. All that afternoon he had
avoided talking with Catherine, and just before closing
time, he'd invited her to dinner. She readily accepted.

The special occasion Durant had in mind was an ending. Alone, sequestered in his office, he'd spent the afternoon deliberating his future. He knew the mob would
attempt to kill him, and for every attempt that failed, there
would be others. His refusal to run was a mixture of pride
and anger, and the knowledge that he couldn't live with
himself if he turned tail. All that said, he now viewed his
prospects with a degree of fatalism. Yet he would not
allow fear to make him a coward.

Which left the matter of Catherine. He felt he had at
last found a woman who interested him and kindled a
depth of affection he'd never known with other women.
Those feelings led inevitably to the realization that every
time they were together, he placed her life in jeopardy.
There was no absolute that the mob wouldn't try to kill
him when he was with her, and however inadvertently,
catch her in the crossfire. That was a risk he was unwilling
to take, one he would never ask her to share. He planned
to end their relationship tonight.

The service at Delmonte's was impeccable. They
were shown to a cozy booth, where the table was appointed with linen and fine crystal. A waiter materialized
to fill their water glasses and present a basket of freshly
baked bread. He nodded approvingly when Catherine selected the braised squab, and all but shrugged when Durant ordered a rib-eye steak. Dinner began with a delicate
squash soup, followed by salad.

Durant played on Catherine's fascination with motion
pictures. He subtly led her into a conversation about some
of the more bizarre stunts he'd been involved with, dwell-
ing on humorous mishaps that went with the job. From
there, he easily prompted her questions about movie stars,
particularly glamorous women, and their madcap eccen-

tricities. He kept it light and entertaining, a last dinner she would remember with fondness. He intended to end it when he took her home.

A story about Gloria Swanson, just as Catherine finished her squab, brought tears of laughter to her eyes. She dabbed away the tears with her napkin, her cheeks flushed with happiness, and calmed herself with a sip of water. She looked at him across the table, still smiling, and shook her head with amusement. He thought he'd never seen her more radiant.

"All right, now," she said, composing herself. "You've kept me in stitches long enough for one night. I want to hear what happened with Jack Nolan."

Durant tried to shrug it off. "Another harebrained idea that went nowhere. There's nothing much to tell."

"No?" Her gaiety of a moment ago suddenly vanished. "Then why is Mr. Aldridge so desperate for you to leave town?"

"How'd you know that?"

"Earl, he's worried to death about you. He said he argued himself hoarse and you wouldn't listen. He asked me to talk with you."

"Nothing to talk about," Durant said, sloughing it off. "Ira's jumping at shadows."

She studied him intently. "You're not telling me the truth, are you? There's something more."

"Why would you say that?"

"Because of the way Mr. Aldridge is acting. I think Nolan threatened you this morning. Threatened you with more than another beating. Didn't he?"

"Yes and no," Durant said slowly. "There's more to it than you know."

"Things you haven't told me."

"Yes."

"Earl—" She touched his hand. "Do you know what I feel for you? Do you?"

"We're probably feeling the same thing."

"Then don't you think I deserve to know?"

Durant saw his good intentions slipping away. Despite himself, he ended up telling her everything, including how he'd killed Elmer Spadden. She was shocked, but at the same time, she felt an incredible sense of relief. She finally understood what he'd been facing alone for so long.

"I'm glad you told me," she said when he finished. "You never again have to hide anything from me."

"Catherine, there's even more to it. These men don't give a damn who they hurt. They're the sort—"

"You believe I'm in danger, don't you?"

"Yeah, I do." Durant was startled by her intuition. "Look, I think it'd be better—"

"You want to stop seeing me, don't you? So I won't get hurt?"

"Only till things shake out. Another week or so and we'll know what's what."

"No."

"No what?"

"I won't stop seeing you," she said in a no-nonsense voice. "And let's not discuss it any further. I've made up my mind."

"Well, I think I've got something to say about that. I'm the one who has to be the judge of what's best."

"Earl."

"What?"

"My mind's made up. Okay?"

Durant knew better than to argue it further. When they left the restaurant, he walked her home, alert and watchful, expecting Nolan and his goons to appear at any moment. He fully intended to end it once they reached the house. A quick kiss and a firm good-bye. Discussion closed.

She surprised him again. The house was dark, even though it was only a few minutes past nine. At the door, when he started to kiss her, she took his hand and pulled him inside. She shushed him with a finger to her lips.

"Mother's already asleep," she whispered. "Just follow me and don't bump into anything."

"Don't you think—"

"Will you please *hush*!"

She led him to her bedroom. A faint blush of moonlight filtered through the window, and she tugged him inside, then gently closed the door. She put her arms around his neck and gave him a smoldering kiss, darting his mouth with her tongue. She pressed herself to his groin, felt him grow hard, and laughed a minxish little laugh.

He knew then they would never argue about it again.

Libbie arrived home shortly before ten o'clock. She sat in the car a moment, composing herself for the charade she was about to play. Her one imperative was that her father be convinced she was the jilted woman.

On the drive back to town, she had come to grips with the reality of the situation. The most vivid part of the evening was Jack's entreaty that she persuade her father their affair was over. She realized what he was saying between the lines, trying not to frighten her too much. Quinn and Voight would have him killed unless they believed it was finished.

The key was her father. She somehow had to dupe him to the point that he believed she'd seen the last of Jack Nolan. Only then would he express a genuine thanks to Quinn and Voight for having ended the affair. Only then would Quinn and Voight feel confident their intervention had brought the affair to an abrupt, and final, halt. Her father was the key to Jack's survival.

She would have to trust Jack to find a way from there. She knew in her heart of hearts that he loved her, and she believed him when he said he would never leave her. Though he hadn't said as much, she knew he would never be content with furtive meetings on the beach, so shabby it was almost gauche. She was certain he had some scheme in mind he hadn't told her about, something he was working on. Something clever and secure, something lasting.

Which meant she had to be equally clever. Her father was quick and perceptive, nobody's fool. On the way into town, she had stopped at a bootlegger's and bought a pint of Old Crow. She'd taken a slug to fortify her nerves, and then dabbed drops here and there on her dress. The whiskey overpowered not only the scent of her perfume, but also the musk of love. She reeked when she walked into the house.

A light was on in her father's study. She was thankful the scene wouldn't be played out in front of her mother. Opal Magruder, unfailingly, retired to the master bedroom suite around nine o'clock. Her father was generally not far behind, for he arose at sunup and was in the office precisely at seven every morning. The light in the study indicated he was waiting for her to come home. She braced herself for a convincing performance.

Magruder was seated in a leather wingback chair. He was reading the *Southwest Cotton Journal*, and he lowered it to his lap when she stepped through the door. He wrinkled his nose in distaste. "You smell like a brewery."

"Wrong again, Daddy." She crossed the room and flopped into a chair, legs spraddled. "Your little angel wouldn't drink beer on a bet. I'm oh-too-much the sophisticate."

"Where have you been?"

"At Mary Lou Henley's."

"I could check on that, you know?"

"Why, please do. Give her a call."

Libbie wasn't worried. Mary Lou Henley was her best friend, and they had a pact to cover for each other in case their parents inquired. She took a cigarette from her purse and lit it with a gold lighter. Magruder folded his trade journal.

"What were you doing at Mary Lou's?"

"Drowning my sorrows." She exhaled a streamer of

smoke. "Girls love to exchange sob stories. Didn't you know that, Daddy?"

"Not particularly," Magruder said. "What sorrow are you drowning?"

"Oh, I have so many to choose from. How about my father's a cheesy, unfeeling bastard?"

"How dare you!"

"How *dare* you!" she fired back. "How dare you involve other people in my personal life. How *dare* you go to Monsignor O'Donnell!"

Magruder blinked with surprise. "I intended that to be a private matter. How did you find out?"

"Jack told me."

"Jack who?"

"Innocence doesn't become you. What other Jack are we talking about? Jack Nolan, my lover."

"You've seen him?" Magruder demanded.

"No, I regret to say." Libbie deliberately tapped ash from her cigarette on the Persian carpet. "He called me this afternoon and told me about Monsignor O'Donnell. How could you reveal my innermost secrets to a stranger? We're not even Catholic!"

"Monsignor O'Donnell is a man of discretion. He and Oliver Quinn are friends, and I needed a suitable intermediary. I could hardly go to Quinn myself."

"Why go to him at all?"

"You left me no choice," Magruder said churlishly. "I will not have this family dragged into a scandal and held up to public ridicule. Your *lover,* as you shamelessly portray him, is a gangster. A common hoodlum."

"Ex-lover," she said softly, concentrating on forcing a tear to her eye. "He broke it off on the phone this afternoon. I've lost him."

"Good riddance," Magruder pronounced. "You're far better off for it, my dear. The man would have ruined your life."

"You are so callous it scares me. Do you have any idea why he called it off? Do you, Daddy?"

"I presume Quinn spoke to him."

"Spoke to him!" she said sharply. "Oh, yes, Quinn and the other one, Voight, spoke to him all right. They threatened his life unless he jilted me. They all but put a gun to his head!"

"You make my point," Magruder admonished. "These men are thugs, very lower-class indeed. And Jack Nolan is one of them."

"You don't know anything about him! Nothing at all."

"I know who he works for, and that is more than sufficient. Quinn and Voight are not accepted in polite society."

"Aren't we sanctimonious?" she said cattily. "Everyone in town knows you have political arrangements with them. Doesn't that scandalize the family name?"

"Not in the least," Magruder huffed. "Politics oftentimes requires alliances of an expedient nature. That doesn't mean I would invite them into my home."

"Or into your daughter's bed."

"I'll thank you to keep a civil tongue in your head, young lady."

"You drove Jack off and you expect me to be civil? You don't understand at all, do you?"

"Understand what?"

"You broke my heart, Daddy. You broke it into little pieces, and I'll never forgive you. Not ever."

Libbie crushed her cigarette in an ashtray. She focused all her willpower into a single moment, and brought tears brimming into her eyes. She stood, walking to the door, then turned back. She looked at him with a little-girl-hurt expression.

"I feel all dead inside, Daddy. I only wish you knew."

The front door opened as she moved into the hallway. Sherm stepped into the foyer, closing the door, and walked toward her. He saw the tears glistening on her cheeks.

"Libbie." He stopped, taking her arm. "What's the matter?"

She swiped at her nose. "I'm surprised Francis lets you stay out so late. You're such the devoted husband."

"I was at a beauty pageant meeting. I saw the lights still on and thought I'd stop by."

Sherm was co-chairman of the International Pageant of Pulchritude. Young, shapely contestants came from all over the world to participate in a swimsuit revue, which was held every year in late spring. The pageant drew crowds of fifty thousand or more, pumping revenue into the town's economy, both legal and illicit. Oliver Quinn was the other co-chairman.

"How very timely," Libbie said in a wounded voice. "Did you and Mr. Quinn discuss my scandalous little romance?"

Sherm squinted at her. "What the devil are you talking about?"

"Ask Daddy."

She walked to the stairway. She bowed her head, sniffling loudly, and mounted the stairs as though sapped of energy. A small, hidden smile touched the corners of her mouth.

She thought Jack would have been proud of her.

The moon stood high at midnight. Nolan was alert for a signal as he steered the *Cherokee* south into the Gulf. Whizzer Duncan, armed with a Thompson submachine gun, was beside him in the cockpit. The fleet of lugger boats manned by his rumrunning crew plowed along in his wake. The dim glow of a lantern suddenly appeared off the starboard bow.

Nolan turned the wheel over to his pilot. Some minutes later, the motors throttled down, they swung in under the lee of the *Shark*. The schooner, painted black and almost invisible in the pale moonlight, swayed at anchor against gentle swells. The lugger boats stood off from the *Shark* as Nolan clambered up a rope ladder.

Captain Rob McBride waited amidships. "Jack, my boy!" he called out with a jaunty laugh. "I've missed the sight of you, and there's a truth."

"Goes both ways, Rob." Nolan handed him a manila envelope stuffed with cash. "Sixty thousand and not a penny less. I know you'll count it."

"Why of course I will, laddie. What's a count between friends?"

A short while afterward they stood watching crates of liquor being off-loaded onto the lugger boats. McBride, one eye on a net slowly clearing the hold, glanced at Nolan. He grinned his pirate's grin.

"Tell me, Jacko," he said. "Have you ever given any thought to smugglin'? There's far more money in it, and pleasurable work it is."

Nolan looked at him. "You offering me a job?"

"Aye, indeed I am! I've just bought another schooner and I'm lookin' for a captain with a head on his shoulders. We'd go partners."

"A speedboat and a schooner are just kissing cousins. I'm no sailor, Rob."

"Nothin' to it," McBride assured him. "A couple runs with me and you're ready for the high seas. You'll be lazin' about in Jamaica with rum punch in one hand and a lass in the other. Never a better place to hang your hat."

"Well, it's a twist," Nolan said with a humorous smile. "I never pictured myself as Blackbeard."

"I've been watchin' you, laddie. You're tough and you're smart, and you've got what it takes to make a smuggler. Put on your thinkin' cap."

"I might just do that, Rob. No harm in thinking, is there?"

"None a'tall!"

The lugger boats loaded, Nolan went down the ladder to the *Cherokee*. As they pulled away from the schooner, he looked back and saw McBride in the spill of light from the lantern. The old pirate waved, and Nolan tried to picture himself flying the Jolly Roger. Then, almost unbidden, he took it a step further.

He wondered how Libbie would like Jamaica.

Chapter Twenty-One

Stoner enjoyed watching her dress or undress. Either way, he thought of it as his own personal floor show, naughty but nice. He couldn't imagine that anyone on a burlesque stage had ever done it better.

Janice artfully played to her audience of one. They were in the bedroom of the suite, with Stoner seated in a chair by the windows. She knew there was no serious risk of hanky-panky when she was dressing; he seemed fascinated by what went into the creation. Undressing was an altogether different matter, somehow more provocative. Day or night, she was almost assured they would end up in bed.

The sun dipped below the horizon like a cauldron of smothered coals. Stoner was already attired in his tux, apart from his jacket, which was hanging in the closet. Outside the hotel, Seawall Boulevard was jammed with weekend tourists, a typical Friday night. Later, he and Janice would pretend shock when Captain Purvis and his Rangers raided the Hollywood Club. But that was later, and he saw no reason to let it intrude on the moment. He was watching the floor show.

Janice was naked. She felt his eyes on her as she stepped into her panties, then slipped into a bandeau brassiere designed for gowns cut low in the back. She next adjusted the straps on an elasticized garter belt, carefully rolled on sheer silk hose, and snapped the tops into fasteners. Her slip was crepe de chine, snug around the hips and trimmed in delicate lace. The slip was short, hugging her knees, and displayed the shapely curve of her legs. She moved to the vanity table.

The ritual of a woman dressing seemed to Stoner a work in progress. Her eyebrows were plucked, made fashionable by the French designer Erte, and she penciled a fine, thin arc in black. Kohl was applied around the eyes to give them an almond shape, then highlighted with blue eye shadow, and dark mascara was used to enhance the curl of the eyelashes. Her rouge was worn in the manner currently in vogue, concentric patches which accentuated her cheekbones. Her lipstick, a cherry red, was painted on like a bright rosebud.

The last touch was dabs of Shalimar on her neck, wrists, and behind her knees. A miracle of modern marketing, Shalimar meant "abode of love" and signified the passion of Shah Jahan, who built the Taj Mahal for the woman of his life. The fragrance was warm and sensual, exotically oriental, and widely believed to have a seductive effect on men of all ages. Janice knew it certainly worked on Stoner, and secretly thought of it as catnip for the boudoir. She smiled at him as she posed in a sleek evening gown that emphasized what it concealed.

"There!" she said with a coquettish little wink. "Olive Eberling never looked so good."

Stoner grinned. "You'll make the ladies jealous tonight."

"Flattery will get you *anything*, precious."

"I'll hold you to it after the raid. We'll have reason enough to celebrate."

"Darn," she moped, the sparkle suddenly gone from her eyes. "I hate to think it's going to end so soon. I've gotten to like being rich."

"Don't let down now," Stoner cautioned. "We've come too far to drop the ball. We're almost there."

"Oh, you needn't worry about me, Sherlock. I'm still up for the game."

"I like your spirit, Dr. Watson. Like your cute outfit, too."

"I think you like it better off than on."

"Yeah, maybe so, but you're dressed now. Time to go to work."

"Once more into the breaches, boys and girls. We'll fight the good fight tonight."

"Let's go get 'em, tiger."

The Hollywood Club was packed. Tonight was Sophie Tucker's closing night, and she'd again drawn a full house. Stoner and Janice were by now regular patrons, and the maitre d' greeted them with an obsequious bow. Their usual table was reserved by the dance floor, and waiters descended on them hardly before they were seated. Stoner, whose mood was already celebratory, ordered champagne.

The orchestra wailed away at the *St. Louis Blues*. The music of the Roaring Twenties was conspicuously lacking in nostalgia, the traditional ballad replaced by blues and jazz. Songs were abbreviated, a series of vocal ejaculations evoking a sense of primitive rivalry, or spiritual misery. Jazz in particular was brazenly defiant, music in the nude, rapid and feverish and exciting. A jazz musician's triumph was erratic syncopation, a bizarre and outré rhythm.

Janice, all but jiggling in her seat, thought it was the cat's meow. Blues and jazz had come upriver from New Orleans, spreading across the land so quickly it seemed an overnight sensation. In an era desperate with the need for escape, and cynical of anything conventional, the stuttered wailing of a saxophone became the salvation of white America. The big thing that year was the music of Jelly Roll Morton, and with it, a frenzied new dance. The orchestra segued into the Black Bottom.

Oliver Quinn stopped by the table. "Good evening," he said with the charm reserved for wealthy patrons. "Enjoying the music?"

"I just love it!" Janice cried. "Bob's such a stick-in-the-mud about anything new. I can't get him on the dance floor."

The floor was crowded, men flailing their arms and

women waggling their pert little bottoms with abandon. Stoner was not surprised by Quinn's cordial manner, for he'd lost something over three thousand in six nights at the casino. He saw nothing of Jack Nolan, who usually assisted Quinn in greeting the club's steady clientele, particularly high rollers. He wondered if Nolan was off on another rumrunning operation.

"I wish I could help, Mrs. Eberling," Quinn said, smiling at Janice. "Unfortunately, I'm not too much on these new dances myself. I seem to miss the beat somewhere."

"Know exactly what you mean," Stoner said with a haughty gesture toward the dance floor. "Give me a foxtrot any old day. That's my speed."

Quinn nodded affably. "We try to provide something for everyone here at the Hollywood Club. I'd say the casino is more your speed, Mr. Eberling."

"Well, that's yet to be proved," Stoner said ruefully. "You boys are into my pocket pretty deep. I'm lookin' to make a comeback."

"I'm sure you will, and then some. Your luck's bound to change."

"We're sure enough gonna find out tonight. I aim to hit the craps table like a bulldog on a bone."

"Mr. Quinn," Janice said, dismissing the subject with wifely disdain. "I understand the Ritz Brothers are opening tomorrow night. Are they as good as everyone says?"

"Even better," Quinn assured her. "They're born clowns, the jesters of Broadway. The best comedy act you'll ever see."

"Oh, I just can't wait!" Janice exclaimed. "You be sure to reserve our table, you hear? I adore comedy."

"You always have a table with us, Mrs. Eberling. We appreciate your patronage."

Quinn wandered off to greet other customers. Stoner watched him with an amused look. "Tomorrow night he'll wish he'd never seen us. Talk about a rude awakening."

"Careful, Mr. Eberling," Janice said sweetly. "Don't

count your chickens before they hatch. Isn't that what ranchers always say?"

"You're thinking of chicken farmers, Olive. Ranchers raise cows."

"Six of one and half a dozen of another, Roberto. You know what I mean."

"Honey, we're gonna take this place like Grant took Richmond. You wait and see."

The houselights dimmed as they finished their dinner. Trumpets blared and drums rattled as Sophie Tucker strutted onto the stage, framed in a rosy spotlight. "The Last of the Red Hot Mamas" wore a spangled gown that left little of her zoftig figure to the imagination. She carried a large feathered fan that swished with sexual innuendo.

She opened her closing show with what audiences now thought of as her signature song. The orchestra led her into *There'll Be a Hot Time in the Old Town Tonight.*

"I should be back by ten."

"You need your sleep, Ira. You're not getting any younger."

"Yes, dear."

"You're not listening to a word I say. You never do."

Naomi Aldridge was seated in an overstuffed chair. Her crocheting needle moved with steady precision as she worked on an elaborate lace doily. She was short and plump, and believed that men were overgrown boys who required constant bossing. She darted Aldridge a sharp look.

"No later than ten, you hear me?"

"Yes, dear, I hear you."

Aldridge gave her a peck on the cheek. He went out the front door and walked to his Chevy, which was parked in the driveway. The house, a modest two-story Victorian, was on a quiet, tree-lined street west of the business district. He backed out of the driveway and drove toward the Strand.

The problem, as Aldridge saw it, was that they'd

never had children. Whether Naomi was barren or he was sterile seemed to him a moot point. All her friends had children, and with age, she'd grown increasingly bitter with her empty nest. He felt her frustration, but at times she could be a handful. She treated him more like a mother than a wife.

On the way downtown it occurred to him that he had no room to talk. In private moments, he sometimes wished Earl Durant was the son he'd never had. He liked to think that his son would have been just as intelligent and resourceful, though perhaps not so foolhardy. He still couldn't understand Durant's obstinate refusal to leave Galveston. Discretion, given the situation, was absolutely the better part of valor.

Downtown, Aldridge turned north on Fourteenth Street. The Knights of Pythias building was located on the Strand at Fourteenth, and tonight was the night for the weekly board meeting. The Knights of Pythias was a fraternal and benevolent organization that devoted its resources to a range of charitable causes. He'd been a member for twenty-three years, and was quite honored to serve on the board of directors. His particular interest was the plight of needy children.

Aldridge parked the car around the corner on Fourteenth. He got out, dropping the keys in his suit pocket, and walked toward the Strand. A dark four-door Buick coasted to a halt beside him, and two men jumped out, crossing to the sidewalk. One was lean and wiry, the other was stout as a bull, and in light from the street lamp, he recognized them as hoodlums. Underlings, but nonetheless men known to virtually everyone in town. Turk McGuire and Whizzer Duncan.

"Don't give us no trouble," Duncan said in a clipped voice. "Come along nice and peaceful."

"What's the meaning of this?" Aldridge searched the street for any sign of help and saw no one about. "Take your hands off me!"

"Get in the Goddamn car."

McGuire grabbed him by the scruff of the neck and bodily lifted him into the backseat of the Buick. Duncan hopped into the passenger seat and McGuire crawled in beside Aldridge, slamming the door. The car pulled away, braking at the corner, then crossed the intersection headed south on Fourteenth. Aldridge, still trying to collect his wits, realized there were four men in the car. He looked at the man seated on his left.

"Evening, Mr. Aldridge," Nolan said with a roguish smile. "Hope the boys weren't too rough. We had to move right along."

"I resent being manhandled," Aldridge said indignantly. "What is it you want with me?"

"Just business, Mr. Aldridge. Nothing personal."

"I demand an explanation."

"Well, you might say you're our hostage. We're holding you for ransom."

"I don't believe you," Aldridge said. "This has to do with Earl Durant and the bank, doesn't it?"

"You'll find out soon enough." Nolan lit a cigarette, exhaled smoke. "Just play along and don't worry about it. We're not going to hurt you."

Aldridge didn't buy it. They had abducted him by force, which under Texas law was punishable by life in prison. Even worse, he could identify them, and they weren't the sort of men to chance a live witness. He thought it very unlikely he would ever see his wife again.

The Buick turned a corner, moving west on Stewart Road. Nolan stared out the window, smoking his cigarette in silence. His crew had tailed Aldridge for the last three days, looking for the right moment to make the snatch. He had decided on Aldridge, rather than the Ludlow girl, for what seemed to him the most practical of reasons. Aldridge, who handled the day-by-day operations of People's Bank & Trust, was the better bargaining chip. Durant could never run the bank by himself.

Nolan was nonetheless troubled. Until he found a way out for himself and Libbie, he had to stall for time with Quinn and Voight. Grabbing Aldridge would make them think he was on the job, and perhaps string them along a few days more. Yet he was under orders to dust Durant by the weekend, and he'd already decided it would never happen. Somehow, between tonight and Sunday, he had to come up with a ploy that worked for him and Libbie, *and* Durant. He didn't have the least idea how he would pull it off.

Some six miles west of the downtown area, the car turned north onto a dirt road. Aldridge saw Sweetwater Lake on their right, a part of the Island that was largely uninhabited except for scattered farms. A short distance down the road, the driver turned onto a dirt track that meandered through a stand of trees and ended at a clearing overlooking the lake. Closer to the water, visible in the pale moonlight, was a ramshackle cabin. The windows were dark.

The men climbed out of the Buick. McGuire took a firm grip on Aldridge's arm, and with Nolan leading the way, they walked to the cabin. Inside, Nolan struck a match, lighting a coal oil lamp, and the sudden flare revealed what looked to be a backwoods camp for fishermen and hunters. There was a main room with a woodburning stove, rickety table and chairs, and a window looking out onto the lake. Through a door was a small bedroom, with two iron-framed single beds and a window at the side of the cabin. The smell of the place was musty, ripe with odors.

"All the comforts of home," Nolan said with a casual wave of his hand. "Think of it as your hideaway, Mr. Aldridge. You get your choice of beds."

Aldridge felt dizzy with fear. "I take it I'm being held prisoner."

"Let's say you're our guest. We stocked the place with groceries and Whizzer's not a bad cook. You could do worse."

"How long do you intend to hold me?"

"I'll let you know when I know."

Duncan and the driver, Lem Brewster, were assigned to stay behind and guard Aldridge. Nolan motioned to Duncan as he went out the door with McGuire. They stopped in the shadow of the cabin.

"No rough stuff," Nolan said pointedly, staring at Duncan. "Anything happens to that old man, I'll have your balls. Got it?"

"Hey, Jack," Duncan said with a wiseacre grin. "No need to throw your weight around. I'll treat him like he was my own father."

"Just make sure there's no slip-ups."

"What if he tries to escape?"

"You better hope you can outrun him. Otherwise you'll have to outrun me."

Duncan frowned. "I don't get you, Jack. What's the old fart to you?"

"We're not playing twenty questions here. Do like you're told, understand?"

"Yeah, sure, whatever you say."

They left Duncan standing in front of the cabin. McGuire got behind the wheel of the Buick, starting the engine, and Nolan took the passenger seat. A short while later they turned on to Stewart Road and headed back to town. McGuire glanced across at Nolan.

"What was that with Duncan? You think he'd croak the old guy?"

"Whizzer's got a mean streak that pops out now and then. Better safe than sorry."

"Why you so worried one way or the other?"

"Without Aldridge we don't have the bait for Durant. You follow me, Turk?"

"You're sayin' we need him alive to set the trap, right?"

"You just won the nickel cigar."

McGuire was Quinn's man, loyal to the last. Nolan knew that everything he'd said tonight would be reported to Quinn, and not long afterward, to Voight. The problem he'd now set in motion was running a con with no end in sight. No clear way out.

He thought he might yet get himself killed.

Traffic was heavy on the causeway. The crush was particularly bad on Friday nights as weekenders rushed to join the revelry. The Island was a carnival in motion.

There were three cars in the Ranger convoy. Captain Hardy Purvis and four men rode in a Buick, the doors emblazoned with the Ranger emblem. Directly behind were two Chevrolets, standard departmental patrol cars, each carrying five men. One man in every car was armed with a Winchester pump shotgun.

The traffic inched off the causeway at a sluggish crawl. Taillights blinked along the esplanade of Broadway, where cars were jammed bumper-to-bumper, barely moving. The towering electric sign at roadside—GALVESTON, THE TREASURE ISLAND OF AMERICA— seemed to mock those stranded in traffic. Their weekend was off to a slow start.

Hardy Purvis checked his watch. The raid on the Hollywood Club was scheduled for nine o'clock and it was now eight-fifty. He cursed, surveying the traffic jam, all too aware his raiding party would never make it across the Island in ten minutes. His anger was compounded by the thought of Stoner waiting in the casino, tonight's plan stymied by their late arrival. He opened the door and stood on the running board, scanning the street ahead. He saw no break in the traffic.

A part of his anger was born of resentment. For three days he had stewed on what he considered an affront to his rank and his years of service. Colonel Garrison had effectively placed him under the command of a sergeant, and there was nothing for it but to swallow his pride. But now, the damnable Friday night traffic was about to make it appear he couldn't execute the simplest part of the plan. Garrison was sure to rate his performance tonight with the deadliest threat to a Ranger's career, the ominous Four Ps: Piss Poor Prior Planning.

Purvis made a spur-of-the-moment decision. Far better to announce your arrival, he told himself, than to be thirty minutes late. He turned, looking at the Ranger cars directly behind, and rapidly pumped his arm up and down in the air. Then he stepped off the running board and slid back in the passenger seat. He motioned to the driver.

"Let's have the siren and the chase lights."

"You sure, Cap'n?" the Ranger said blankly. "They'll hear us a mile away."

"Goddammit!" Purvis thundered. "Don't argue with me. Do it!"

The driver hit the switches. The siren blasted a shrill wail and the bubble-gum lights on top of the Buick began flashing. The cars to their front were stuck in traffic, nowhere to go and unable to move out of the way. For a moment, with Purvis glowering like a singed rooster, they sat locked in place. He abruptly flung an arm off to the side.

"Take to the curb," he ordered. "Get around 'em, Goddammit!"

The Buick bounced over the curb. Two wheels on the street and two wheels on the lawn of a house, they lurched east along Broadway. The patrol cars followed, sirens blaring and lights flashing, plowing ruts in one lawn after another as they bumped down the street. Purvis ordered a right turn at the corner of Broadway and Fiftieth. They headed south toward Seawall Boulevard.

Twelve minutes later the cars skidded to a halt in front of the Hollywood Club. The sirens wound down with a mournful screech and the bubble-gum lights winked off as the Rangers piled out and rushed the door. The doorman, resplendent in top hat and tails, quickly moved aside. He waved them on with a pearly grin.

"Good evening, Cap'n," he said in a piping voice. "Mighty fine to see you again."

Purvis slammed through the door. The Rangers,

formed in a tight phalanx, followed him down a hall lined with exotic plants. As they disappeared into the club, the doorman moved to a small button secreted behind one of the plants, mounted on the wall. He pressed it three times.

"Yessir, Cap'n," he said merrily. "Welcome to the Hollywood Club!"

Stoner was standing at the craps table. Another customer was rolling the dice and he was betting the numbers on the felt layout. Out of the corner of his eye, he saw Janice playing the slots along the far wall. He sneaked a peek at his watch.

Seven minutes past nine. He wondered what was keeping Purvis and his Rangers. Early that morning, he'd driven into La Marque, using the phone booth in the pharmacy, and called Houston. Purvis, irked at being questioned, had assured him the raid would come off as planned. Nine o'clock sharp.

So where the hell were they?

Three sharp blasts sounded on a gong. Stoner turned and saw the hammer pounding on a fire alarm at the rear of the room. For a moment, everyone in the casino froze, and then Dutch Voight appeared in the doorway of the office. He raised his arms as the fire alarm went silent.

"Ladies and gentlemen," he called out. "We are about to be raided by the Texas Rangers. Please follow the directions of the housemen and don't worry about a thing. Just stay calm."

The dealers and croupiers instructed the customers to pocket their chips and move back from the tables. Voight waited until everyone was clear of the equipment and then stepped into the office. Through the open door, Stoner saw him walk to his desk, stoop down, and pull a lever mounted in the floor. A low hum of machinery vibrated through the casino.

The slot machines folded like Murphy beds, rolling into the walls. The reverse sides of the slots, now facing outward, were framed posters of popular motion pictures.

The floor separated beside the craps tables and the roulette tables as housemen hurriedly slipped elasticized covers over the equipment. In the next instant, the gaming tables rotated 180°, turning top to bottom as the floors cranked back into place. The bottoms of the tables, when they appeared, were baize-covered billiards tables. The cue sticks and balls were quickly removed from compartments along the edges.

Stoner was no engineer, but he immediately grasped the fundamental concept. Beneath the floor, and in the walls, was a massive hydraulic system, powered by electricity. He suddenly understood why the casino had been built at the end of the T-head pier, suspended over water. Below the casino, probably housed in steel and hidden from view, was a custom-designed marvel of hydraulic engineering. His respect for Quinn and Voight went up a couple of notches.

Even as he watched, the blackjack tables revolved into the floor, replaced by backgammon and bridge tables. Housemen produced cards and chairs, got the guests seated at the tables, and then mingled with the crowd. Gamblers who only moments ago were tossing dice and playing roulette now took up cue sticks and began banging balls around on billiards tables. The swiftness of the transformation was startling, hard to comprehend unless seen firsthand. A casino had been converted into a social club in less than three minutes.

Janice paused at Stoner's side. "Have you ever!" she said in a breathless voice. "Houdini has nothing on these people."

"Maybe he designed it for them," Stoner said with a bemused look. "I wouldn't have believed it if I hadn't seen it for myself."

"Sweetie, we're talking serious magic here."

"Yeah, and all without smoke or mirrors. A nifty operation. Damn nifty."

Voight walked to the front and unlocked the heavy oak doors. Hardy Purvis and his Rangers burst into the room as though storming fortified battlements. From the nightclub, announcing their arrival, came the strains of the orchestra playing *The Eyes of Texas*. Everyone looked up as if sharing a private joke.

"Come right in, Captain Purvis," Voight said with a wry smile. "What can we do for you tonight?"

"None of your wisecracks, Voight." Purvis glowered around at the billiards tables and backgammon players. "We're here to shut you down for good."

"Well, in that case, be my guest."

The Rangers conducted their usually thorough search. As with previous raids, they tapped the walls, stomped on the floor, and inspected the billiards tables. Stoner was impressed, and relieved, that Purvis never once looked in his direction. He thought the Ranger captain was a surprisingly good actor.

The search lasted almost thirty minutes. Finally, with a parting shot at Voight, Purvis led his Rangers back through the nightclub. The orchestra playfully announced their departure, and the audience joined in the spirit of things. Their voices carried through the lounge to the casino.

"The eyes of Texas are upon you
All the livelong day!"

"Well, Sherlock?" Janice whispered, her eyes bright with excitement. "What do you think?"

Stoner grinned. "I think Saturday night's our night. Our last night."

Chapter Twenty-Two

Durant got to the bank about eight-thirty on Saturday morning. The doors opened at eight but he was rarely ever there on time. The bank functioned just as well with or without him.

Nothing about People's Bank & Trust interested Durant. At first, when he'd decided to stay on, he had attempted to assume the duties of president. But he soon realized that the thing holding him in Galveston was his determination to thwart William Magruder. The bank itself was like a yoke around his neck.

There was never a moment he didn't resent how the bank had changed his life. He'd been in Galveston almost four weeks, and not a day passed without some bitter reflection about Hollywood. Though he kept in contact by phone, his friends in motion pictures were beginning to doubt he would ever return. He wasn't all that certain himself.

The phone conversations with Tom Mix and others in the film industry were frustrating. He found it impossible to unburden himself and tell them the truth. How could he explain that the mob had tried to kill him and would try again? How could he explain refusing to run and not come off sounding like some dime-store hero in a low-budget film?

The upshot was that he fudged the truth. He told them that selling a bank was far more difficult than he'd ever envisioned. Yet that explanation wore thin, particularly over a period of weeks. His friends listened, sometimes with sympathy, but they really had no interest in his problems. People in motion pictures were single-minded about their work, and they were quick to point out that Hollywood had a short memory. Your reputation was pegged to what you did today. Everything else was history.

The mere thought of it put Durant in a bleak mood. He wasn't sure he would get out of Galveston alive, much less return to the life he'd known in Hollywood. Entering the bank, he dreaded yet another day of twiddling his thumbs while pretending he understood balance sheets and financial summaries. Catherine intercepted him outside his office.

"Good morning." Her usual cheeriness seemed off a note. "Have you seen Mr. Aldridge?"

"No," Durant said. "He's not here?"

"Not yet. Fortunately, Mr. Jenks knows the combination to the safe. Otherwise we wouldn't be open for business."

Jenks was the head teller, Aldridge's principal assistant. Durant was at a loss. "Have you tried Ira at home?"

"Mrs. Aldridge called here." Catherine looked perplexed. "She said he went out last night and hasn't come home. She's so upset she started crying."

"Did she say where he went last night?"

"Some sort of meeting at the Knights of Pythias."

"Did she try calling any of the other members?"

"Early this morning she talked to two of them. They both said Mr. Aldridge didn't attend the meeting. Don't you think that's awfully strange?"

Durant felt a sudden chill. For four days, since his meeting with Jack Nolan, he'd expected another attack by the mob. He'd taken Catherine out twice in that time, always armed with his Luger, and always on guard against another assault. Yet nothing had happened, and with every passing day, he'd grown increasingly wary. He wondered now if they had decided on a different tack.

"I'm very worried," Catherine said, interrupting his ruminations. "Shouldn't we call the police?"

"Let me talk with Mrs. Aldridge first. Maybe there's something we. . . ."

Jack Nolan walked through the front door. Whatever doubt Durant might have had abruptly turned to certainty. Catherine saw the change in his expression and looked around, watching as Nolan moved toward them. Her mouth ovaled.

"Oh, God," she said on an indrawn breath. "I'm going to call the police."

"No," Durant said crisply. "Let me handle this."

Durant reassured Catherine with a touch on her arm. He entered the office, closing the door, and seated himself behind his desk. Nolan took a chair, tapping a cigarette from a pack of Luckies, and clicked a lighter. He lit up in a haze of smoke.

"We've got Aldridge," he said, pocketing his lighter. "Or maybe you hadn't noticed he's missing."

"I noticed," Durant said without inflection. "What do you want?"

"Same thing we wanted all along. Sell your bank to Magruder and you get Aldridge back in one piece. Otherwise. . . ."

"You'll kill him."

"Your words, not mine."

Durant stared at him. "Do you enjoy hurting old men?"

"Not my style." Nolan exhaled a cloud of smoke. "Look, chum, it's just business. Nobody has to get hurt."

"Why the turnaround? I thought you were after me, not the bank. Magruder refused my last offer."

"So he's in the market again."

Nolan was playing a new angle. Late last night, in an effort to stall for time, he'd talked to Quinn at the club. He suggested that Magruder would be even more in their debt if they convinced Durant to sell the bank before killing him. Quinn, after only a moment's thought, agreed.

Whether it was the late hour, or simply that he was pleased with himself, Quinn was in an expansive mood. He mentioned having met with Magruder on charity matters Friday afternoon, and then bragged about finally discovering the importance of People's Bank & Trust. Magruder, in a rare moment of candor, let slip that the bank controlled property he needed to complete his new resort project. His on-again, off-again ambivalence was now understandable. He might not get the bank, and the property, if Durant were dead.

Quinn then convinced Voight to follow Nolan's suggestion. By arranging for Magruder to acquire the bank, they positioned themselves to take a piece of the action on the resort project. Magruder had always insisted that they stay out of the hotel business; but with the debt so large in their favor, he could be persuaded to accept them as partners. Voight liked the idea so much he agreed to let Durant live a little longer. Still, he insisted that the bank deal be closed by Monday. He wanted Durant dead by Monday night.

Nolan had bought less time than he'd hoped. Yet he knew that running a con required not just craft but flexibility. By Monday he might think of a new angle that would spare him from killing Durant. Somehow, though he couldn't have explained it, he saw a link between sparing Durant and finding a way out for himself and Libbie. He thought perhaps it was Irish superstition, the ancient Gaelic belief that God granted favors for favors done. Whatever the reason, he'd already decided he would never kill Durant.

"Your move, slick," he said now. "The bank or Aldridge?"

"How do I know you'll let him go?"

"Hey, what more do you want? You've got my word."

Durant placed a call to Magruder's office. He went straight to the point when Magruder came on the phone. "Your mob buddies are holding Ira Aldridge hostage. How would you like to buy a bank?"

Magruder hesitated, as though digesting the news. "How much do you want?"

"One hundred thousand, and it's not negotiable. I get my price or your pals can keep Aldridge."

"Quite frankly, I am tired of haggling with you, Mr. Durant. Your terms are acceptable."

"How soon can your lawyer draw up the papers?"

"I'll have him work on it over the weekend."

"Tell him to work fast. I get Aldridge back by Monday or it's no deal."

Durant hung up. He nodded curtly to Nolan. "Satisfied?"

"You're a tough cookie," Nolan said, stubbing his cigarette in an ashtray. "What if he hadn't met your price? Would you've walked away from Aldridge?"

"Like you said before, it's just business."

"Well, whatever the case, looks like we're on hold till Monday. I'll see you around, slick."

Nolan rose with an unreadable smile and went out. When the door closed, Durant told himself it was all hot air and soap bubbles. Even if he sold the bank, they would never run the risk of a live witness who could charge them with felony abduction. Aldridge would be killed.

So all he'd done today, Durant realized, was to buy some time. He had to find another way to bring Aldridge home alive. And the clock was ticking.

He had to get it done before Monday.

The spotlights cast flashing beams a thousand feet into a moonlit sky. Tonight was opening night for the Ritz Brothers, and a line of cars crept forward outside the Hollywood Club. Parking attendants rushed to keep them from blocking the entrance.

Stoner and Janice arrived in their canary-yellow Packard. She wore a gold lamé gown with a matching stole, and he was attired in a tuxedo and cummerbund. Earlier, when they were dressing, he had wedged a Colt .45 automatic into the cummerbund, at the back of his trousers. In his hip pocket, he carried a leather badge holder with the shield of a Texas Ranger. He felt confident that tonight's raid would close the place down.

The nightclub was packed. Quinn, ever the genial host, greeted guests as they came through the doors. He looked the debonair showman in a white dinner jacket, a scarlet boutonniere blazing from his lapel. His manner was lighthearted, almost ebullient, the impresario staging yet another extravaganza. Jack Nolan, in a double-breasted tux, was at his side.

"Mr. Eberling! Mrs. Eberling!" Quinn offered them a warm handshake as they entered the club. "Your table's reserved, just as you requested. The best seats in the house."

"We're much obliged," Stoner said, noting that Nolan was back on duty tonight. "You folks sure know how to treat your customers right. Wasn't I just sayin' that, Olive?"

"Yes, you were, sweetheart." Janice dimpled her cheeks in a bubbly smile. "We just love your club, Mr. Quinn. You're sooo gracious."

Quinn preened. "Nothing's too good for our guests. We even bring in the Texas Rangers for added entertainment. How'd you like our little improvisation last night?"

"Oh, an absolute riot!" Janice squealed. "Honestly, those Ranger boys were fit to be tied. I could hardly keep a straight face."

"Same for me," Stoner added, bobbing his head in admiration. "We were sayin' Houdini must've rigged them topsy-turvy tables. Regular magic show."

"We're proud of it ourselves," Quinn said with a beaming grin. "The Rangers are always good for a few laughs. I get a kick out of it."

"Bet you do," Stoner said, forcing himself to smile. "Speakin' of laughs, we're lookin' forward to the Ritz Brothers. Hope they're as funny as the Rangers."

"Funnier by far," Quinn assured him. "I know you'll like the show. Enjoy yourselves."

The maitre d' led Stoner and Janice to their table.

Nolan watched them as Quinn turned to greet other guests.
All through the conversation he'd been reminded of Tuesday morning, at the tobacco shop in La Marque. He still
thought it strange that a wealthy high roller would be
standing around a phone booth, waiting for calls. But he
decided once again to say nothing to Quinn or Voight. He
had all the problems he could handle for the moment.

Stoner, after being seated at the table, was having
second thoughts himself, He was glad to see Nolan in the
club, for the mob's enforcer, more so than dealers or pit
bosses, deserved to be arrested. But he filed a mental note
to keep an eye on Nolan when he made his move on the
casino. No need to get careless and risk getting himself
shot. He'd staked everything on pulling it off tonight.

"I'm so proud of you," Janice said, after the waiter
had taken their orders. "The way Quinn was talking, I
thought for sure you'd belt him in the puss. He has nothing but contempt for . . . well, you know who."

Stoner's mouth curled in a cagey smile. "Before the
night's over he'll have nothing but respect for you know
who. We'll wipe that grin off his face."

"I still think you're a model of restraint."

"Well now, Olive, you were pretty good yourself.
Nobody could've done it any better."

"You're so nice to say so, Robert, honey lamb. I just
love working with you . . . among other things."

Stoner laughed. "Don't go practicing your wiles on
me."

"Why not?" She gave him a lewd wink. "Don't you
like it?"

"What do you think?"

"Oh, I think you do."

"I think you're right, Mrs. Eberling."

"I'm always right, Mr. Eberling."

The houselights dimmed shortly after they finshed
their dinner. A buzz of excitement went through the audience, for everyone eagerly anticipated the show. The
Ritz Brothers were an antic trio—Al, Jimmy, and Harry—

celebrated for their slapstick humor. The oldest was twenty-five and the youngest nineteen, and they were already stars of vaudeville and the Broadway stage. Their act featured dizzy comedy routines and raunchy songs.

The orchestra brought them skipping onstage in baggy pants and floppy jackets. Their first number was a bawdy tune about a one-eyed nymph and her energetic lover, a peg-legged sailor. The audience followed the lyrics with gasps and giggles from the women and guffaws of laughter from the men. The end of the song prompted the crowd to a wild round of applause.

The orchestra stilled, and without missing a beat, the brothers went into a comedy routine. Al, the oldest, began talking about the dumbest man he'd ever known. "So dumb," he said with a straight face, "that he only took a bath when it rained."

"Hey, that ain't so bad," Jimmy said, rolling his eyes. "I knew a guy one time, when they said brains, he thought they said trains. He got on the wrong one."

"You wanna hear dumb?" Harry jumped in with a goofy smile. "Fella in the neighborhood, you gave him a penny for his thoughts—you got change!"

The crowd responded with a wave of laughter. Quinn, ever constant to his superstition about opening nights, was standing at the back of the room. His girlfriend, Maxine, looked like she'd been poured into a silk dress that revealed every curve. Her hair was piled atop her head in a French twist and her breasts threatened to spill out of her low-cut gown. She hugged his arm.

"Oh, Ollie, I just love opening nights. It's all so swell!"

"There's no business like show business, Maxie. Nothing even comes close."

"And you're the best showman there ever was. I mean, golly, you're an artiste!"

Quinn chuckled. "Don't tell Dutch."

Durant stepped out of a taxicab. The doorman was busy with people waiting for their cars to be brought around, and didn't pay him any attention. He walked into the Hollywood Club.

The layout was generally familiar. From what he'd heard around town, there was a nightclub, and then, at the end of the T-head pier, the casino. He moved through the entry hall, opening a set of glass doors, and heard the sound of an orchestra. He was alert to any sign of Jack Nolan.

All day, Durant had deliberated on a course of action. The police would be of no help, and if he waited until Monday, he knew Aldridge would be killed. Even if he sold the bank, he was convinced the mob would eliminate the only witness. Then, at the first opportunity, they would kill him.

There was nothing for it but to take the fight to them. He wouldn't allow Aldridge to be killed, and the only way to stop it was to force their hand. Whether it was Quinn or Voight, or maybe both, he meant to offer them their lives in exchange for Aldridge. The only place he knew to find them was the Hollywood Club, and he'd waited until they were busy with a Saturday night crowd. Surprise was his one advantage.

The orchestra was playing dance tunes. On the way in, Durant had noticed a billboard advertising the Ritz Brothers, and he assumed the show was over. The nightclub was nonetheless still crowded, and several couples were dipping and swaying on the dance floor. The maitre d' stopped him at the door.

"May I help you, sir?"

"You sure can." Durant had already concocted his story. "I represent Al Jolson and Mr. Quinn asked me to stop by when I was in town. Trouble is, we've never met, except on the phone. Could you point him out?"

"Certainly." The maitre d' nodded to a man talking with several guests at a table. "The gentleman in the white dinner jacket."

"Appreciate your help."

"Not at all."

Durant intercepted Quinn as he turned away from the table. "Hello, Quinn," he said, blocking the club owner's path. "We need to talk."

Quinn smiled amiably. "I don't believe we've met."

"I'm Earl Durant."

"Well—" Quinn seemed momentarily at a loss. "What can I do for you, Mr. Durant?"

"Act like we're old pals." Durant brushed his suit jacket aside, tapping the butt of the Luger in his waistband. "Don't sic anybody on me or I'll kill you. Got it?"

"You'll never get out of here alive."

"How would you know? You'd already be dead."

Quinn thought about it. "What do you want?"

"Ira Aldridge."

"Sorry, never heard the name."

"Yeah, you have," Durant said. "Where's your office?"

"At the back of the casino."

"Let's go."

The two bruisers at the rear of the nightclub opened the door into the lounge. Quinn nodded to them without expression. "This gentleman's with me."

Durant followed him through the lounge. There were people sitting around drinking and talking, and a waiter bustled past with a tray of cocktails. At the heavy oak doors to the casino, Quinn took a ring of keys from his pocket. He unlocked the door and they moved inside.

There were two hundred or more people crowded around the gaming tables. As Durant nudged Quinn forward, the hammering clang of a fire-bell went off with an ear-splitting din. For an instant everything in the casino seemed arrested in motion, then the fire bell stopped. A man suddenly vaulted on top of one of the craps tables.

"Texas Rangers!" Stoner shouted, the Colt automatic in one hand and his badge in the other. "This is a raid and you're all under arrest. Don't anybody move!"

Durant and Nolan saw each other at the same moment. Nolan was on the far side of the room, his hand edging inside his jacket, when he spotted Durant standing behind Quinn. A look of astonishment came over his face, and as Durant slowly wagged his head, he removed his hand from his jacket. A man in a double-breasted tux rushed toward the office.

"Hold it, Voight!" the Ranger commanded. "Take another step and I'll drill you!"

Voight abruptly stopped, then spun around, his face a mask of rage. "Eberling, you're a dead man."

"Sergeant Clint Stoner," Stoner informed him. "Stand right where you are."

"You're still dead," Voight growled. "Nobody makes a monkey out of me."

"Just stay put." Stoner swung the pistol around, the sights trained on Quinn. "Glad you could join us, Quinn. Get that door open—now!"

Quinn hesitated only an instant. The gun at his front was more threatening than the one at his back, and he hardly glanced at Durant as he opened the door. Captain Hardy Purvis and his squad of Rangers were just entering the lounge. They rushed through the door of the casino and spread out, some armed with revolvers and others with shotguns. Purvis snorted a barking laugh when he saw the gaming paraphernalia still intact. He looked at Stoner on top of the craps table.

"Well done, Sergeant," he said in a loud, authoritative voice. "We'll take it from here."

"Cap'n, it's all yours."

Stoner swapped a glance with Janice. She was standing by a slot machine, and she smiled proudly as he hopped off the craps table. The Rangers, with Purvis directing the operation, began separating club patrons from the casino staff. The guests were herded out the door and released, while the housemen were held under guard along the far wall. Durant, who appeared to be with Quinn, allowed himself to be forced in with the staff members. He was thinking fast, searching for an angle.

Hardy Purvis shouted a command. The five Rangers

with shotguns moved about the room and systematically blasted holes in the tops of the gaming tables. Purvis turned with a spiteful grin and looked at Voight and Quinn, who were standing at the front of the loosely bunched housemen. The roar of the shotguns reverberated through the casino like rolling claps of thunder.

Voight and Quinn watched the carnage with hollow stares. Durant seized on the diversion, backing away to stand by Nolan. His voice was muted by the steady barrage of gunfire. "Let's make a trade."

Nolan gave him a sideways glance. "Trade for what?"

"Tell me where you're holding Aldridge. I'll never let the Rangers know you were involved."

"Two of my boys are guarding him. No way you'll get him out by yourself."

"I'll take my chances."

Nolan quickly assessed his situation. The casino would be shut down, and along with the others, he would be arrested. The last thing he needed was a felony charge for abduction, and if he worked it right, tonight's raid might provide an out for himself and Libbie. He thought it was worth a shot.

"Do we have a deal?" Durant goaded him. "Or do I talk to the Rangers?"

"Are you on the square? You won't turn me in?"

"You've got my word. Give me Aldridge and you're in the clear."

Nolan told him about the cabin on Sweetwater Lake. The men around them were distracted as one table after another was blown apart, and his voice was muffled by the drumming roar of the shotguns. He quickly gave Durant directions to the lake and the turnoff to the cabin. He ended with a warning.

"Watch yourself," he said soberly. "The boys I left out there are both shooters. They play dirty."

"I'll keep it in mind. Thanks, Jack."

Durant brushed past the men in front of them. He made a snap decision to say nothing to the Rangers. The story would require too much explanation, and he couldn't risk being slowed down. Once the shooters heard about the raid, they might very well panic and kill Aldridge. He had to move quickly and find the cabin. Tonight.

"Sergeant Stoner," he said to the man who had taken the casino. "I shouldn't be held here. Your Rangers made a mistake."

Stoner looked him over. "Who are you?"

"I'm Earl Durant," Durant said, moving forward. "I own the People's Bank & Trust."

"Durant?" Stoner paused, the name somehow familiar, and suddenly it came to him. "Aren't you the banker working with the reformers?"

"How'd you know about that?"

"Doesn't matter how I know. I saw you come in with Quinn just before the raid. Why were you with him?"

"Quinn and Voight threatened me," Durant said honestly, motioning to the club owners. "I came here to have it out with them."

"All by yourself?"

"I'm all I've got."

Stoner glanced around at Quinn and Voight. The shotguns abruptly stopped firing, and they were now staring at Durant with murderous scowls. Stoner thought their expressions spoke to the truth of Durant's story.

Hardy Purvis, with the look of Caesar triumphant, drifted over. "What's going on here, Sergeant?"

"Just a mix-up, Cap'n," Stoner said. "This man's not part of the casino crew."

"Then get him out of here," Purvis said, jerking a thumb at the housemen. "I want the whole bunch handcuffed."

Stoner nodded. "You're free to go, Mr. Durant."

"Thanks for your help, Sergeant."

Durant walked to the door. As he went out, Stoner borrowed handcuffs from a couple Rangers and moved across to Quinn and Voight. He clamped the cuffs around their wrists with a little chuckle.

"I have to tell you it's a real pleasure. Never had so much fun in my life."

"You and me aren't finished," Voight said, his eyes dark with menace. "I'll see you around one of these days."

Stoner smiled. "Not if I see you first."

By midnight, Voight and Quinn and their men had been transported to the county jail. All the nightclub guests, as well as the orchestra, the Ritz Brothers, and the kitchen staff, were ordered off the premises. A stout chain was snapped in place across the front doors with a padlock.

The lights went out at the Hollywood Club.

Chapter Twenty-Three

Durant held the speed to a sedate twenty miles an hour. He was on Stewart Road, west of town, looking for the turnoff to Sweetwater Lake. He knew it was somewhere off to the right, but he was wary of missing the turn. A half-moon, directly overhead, was almost as bright as the headlights.

Earlier, when he'd left the club, he realized he needed a car. The problem stumped him for a few seconds, and then the solution came in a moment of what he considered poetic justice. All the parking attendants were gathered by the front door, talking excitedly about the Rangers' second raid in as many nights. He walked off into the parking lot.

Nolan's cherry-red Stutz Bearcat was three rows down. Durant had driven practically every car ever manufactured in his years as a stuntman. Even more important, he'd worked with mechanics whose knowledge of the internal combustion engine was essential to any stunt involving a car. A minute or so under the hood and he had the Sutuz hot-wired and the engine purring. He drove out of the parking lot headed west.

Durant thought Nolan would appreciate the irony. But as he passed the amusement piers, which were ablaze with lights and crowded with tourists, he experienced a moment of uncertainty. For the job ahead, the odds would have improved greatly if he had enlisted the aid of the Rangers. Still, even in hindsight, he knew it would have taken half the night to persuade them that a man held captive was more important than closing down a casino. And in the process, simply mentioning the cabin on the lake, he would have betrayed Nolan to Quinn and Voight. He felt he'd had no choice but to play a lone hand.

Nolan had told him the turnoff was five or six miles west of town. Off to the right, glistening in the moonlight, he saw the glassy surface of Sweetwater Lake. The highway made a sharp curve and then, less than a mile farther on, he spotted a dirt road angling off to the north. He turned onto the road, working the clutch and shifting down into second gear, cutting his speed to a crawl. He doused the headlights.

The moon cast a spectral glow across a land flat as a dime. Up ahead, perhaps a quarter mile past the turnoff, he saw the dirt track that Nolan had described. There was a slight shoulder on the road, and he coasted to a halt, letting the hot-wired engine die as he released the clutch. After hooking the gearshift into reverse, he stepped out of the car and gently closed the door. A faint breeze drifted down from the northeast.

The dirt track was bumpy and rutted, barely wide enough for a car. Trees bordered either side of the lane, and Durant caught a whiff of wood smoke on the breeze. He pulled the Luger from his waistband, clicked off the safety, and walked forward through dappled moonlight. A hundred yards or so ahead, he came to a clearing, where a small cabin was perched on the shore of the lake. Off to the right, he saw a one-holer privy, which meant the cabin didn't have indoor plumbing. He paused at the edge of the treeline.

The cider glow of a lamp lighted a window at the front of the cabin. Durant heard the muted sound of voices from inside, and he waited a moment, slowly reconnoitering the open terrain for any sign of movement. He stepped from the shadow of the trees, carefully avoiding the shaft of light from the window, and circled around from the south. He eased forward, a step at a time, along the front wall.

The voices were now more distinct. He stopped beside the window, listening a moment, then gradually moved his head past the casement. There were two men seated at a table, playing cards, their faces bathed in the glow of a coal oil lamp. One was wiry and beady-eyed, and the other was thickset with a thatch of bushy black hair. A wood stove was positioned against the wall nearest the lake, and opposite the men was a door that apparently led to another room. There was no sign of Aldridge.

Durant ducked below the window. On the other side, he passed by the door and turned the corner on the north side of the cabin. A window was set into the wall, and again, gingerly, he eased his head around the casement. The spill of light from the front room revealed a crude bedroom, devoid of furniture except for two single beds. Aldridge was asleep on one of the beds, lying on his back, his features visible in the dim lampglow. The men kept an eye on him through the door.

Nolan's warning came back to Durant. The men were shooters—mob parlance for killers—and unlikely to be taken without a fight. A moment ago, watching them play cards, he'd observed they were in shirtsleeves, their coats off, each of them carrying a revolver in a shoulder holster. The idea of busting through the door, particularly if it was locked, would alert them before he ever got inside. The alternative was to break the front window and shoot them where they sat, without warning. The notion was fleeting, quickly discarded as unworkable. He couldn't picture himself an assassin.

Which left only the door. He went back around the corner of the cabin and moved along the wall. His one hope was that the door was unlocked and he could burst inside before they had time to react. There was a slim chance that if he got the drop on them, they would surrender without a fight. The odds were long but the situation left him short on options. His throat dry, he dropped to one knee beside the door, the Luger gripped tightly in his right hand. He reached with his left hand to test the doorknob.

"I gotta take a piss."

"Lem, you oughta get your kidneys checked."

"Hey, you gotta go, you gotta go."

The men's voices carried clearly from inside. A chair scraped against the floor and heavy footsteps crossed toward the door. Durant quickly pulled back, rising to his feet, and flattened himself against the wall. The door opened in a sudden flood of light and the thickset man with bushy hair stepped outside. He walked to the treeline, unbuttoned his pants, and pulled out his pud. A stream arced outward and splashed on the ground.

Durant ghosted across the clearing. He jammed the muzzle of the Luger into the man's spine. "Don't say a word."

The man sucked in a breath. He stood stock-still, and his steamy stream abruptly went dry. Durant nudged him with the pistol. "Put it in your pants."

Hastily, the man tucked himself away. Durant spoke into his ear. "I'll be right behind you. Walk back in there like you've finished your business. One peep, one wrong move, and you're dead. Let's go."

Durant marched him to the cabin. As they came through the door, Whizzer Duncan looked up from shuffling the cards. He saw something odd on his friend's face, and then, in the silty lamplight, he saw Durant. The cards fluttered from his hands and he kicked back his chair. He clawed at his revolver.

"Move, Lem!" he shouted. "Goddammit, move!"

Brewster struggled to break free. He heaved one way, then the other, but Durant had a tight grip on his shirt collar. As he was jerked back into place, Duncan whipped the revolver from his shoulder holster and fired. The slug hit Brewster in the sternum and he grunted, then slumped forward. He dropped heavily to the floor.

Durant leveled the Luger in a fluid motion. He stitched three red dots on Duncan's shirtfront, the shots not a handspan apart. Duncan stumbled backward in a nerveless dance, tripping over his chair, and fell to the floor. He groaned, splattered with blood, and by some inhuman effort of will raised his gun in a shaky hand. Durant shot him in the head.

The room was pungent with the acrid smell of gun smoke. Durant stood there a moment, staring at the body, then slowly lowered the Luger. He knelt down, pressing a finger to Brewster's neck, and found no pulse. Then, still dazed by the swift brutality of death, he remembered why he was there. He walked to the bedroom door.

Aldridge was cowering behind the bed. He looked at the figure silhouetted by lamplight in the doorway and pushed to his knees. His voice was a strangled rasp: "Earl?"

"It's over," Durant said with quiet resignation. "They're dead."

"How in God's name did you find me?"

"I'll tell you later. It's a long story."

"Yes, of course . . . later."

"Let's go home, Ira."

On Monday morning a crowd began gathering in Superior Court. The newspaper had reported the Rangers' raid on the Hollywood Club, and there was widespread interest in the case. Many thought a conviction would mean the beginning of the end for Galveston.

Captain Hardy Purvis, with Stoner and Janice, was seated directly behind the prosecution table. Stoner was in uniform, the sleeves of his shirt adorned with sergeant's stripes, a holstered pistol at his side. He and Janice were prepared to testify about their undercover assignment and their roundabout infiltration of the casino. Purvis believed they had an airtight case.

Quinn and Voight arrived shortly before nine o'clock. They were accompanied by Nolan and twenty-two housemen who had been arrested during the raid. Early yesterday morning, in a hastily convened court session, all of them had been released on bail. Quinn and Voight joined their attorney, Lester Maddox, at the defense table. The others took seats on benches at the left side of the court-room.

County Prosecutor Sherwood Butler arrived as the benches filled with spectators. He had spent a good part of Sunday with Purvis and Stoner, reviewing the facts of the case. His manner was that of a man pressed to take on an unsavory task, and he had been less than forthcoming in his discussions with Purvis and Stoner. He nodded to them now, quickly averting his eyes, and seated himself at the prosecution table. He opened his briefcase and removed a single sheet of paper.

A door opened at the rear of the courtroom. The bailiff jumped to his feet. "This court is now in session, the Honorable Thomas Woodruff presiding. All rise!"

Judge Woodruff mounted the steps to the bench. A large man with florid features and graying hair, he wore a voluminous black robe and a benign expression. After lowering himself into a high-backed leather chair, he opened a file folder as the bailiff ordered everyone to be seated. He peered down from the bench.

"This is a preliminary hearing," he said in a deep voice. "The accused are Oliver J. Quinn and Edward S. Voight and twenty-three of their employees, charged with operating an illegal gambling enterprise. We are here to determine whether or not the accused should be bound over for trial."

A murmur of anticipation swept through the spectators. Judge Woodruff waited until they fell slent, then looked from the prosecution table to the defense table. "Mr. Butler, Mr. Maddox," he said in acknowledgment. "Are you ready to proceed?"

"Yes, Your Honor," Butler said.

Maddox half rose from his seat. "The defense is prepared, Your Honor."

"Very well," Woodruff said. "For the record, the accused pleaded not guilty in a bail hearing yesterday morning. Mr. Butler, what say you for the state?"

Butler got to his feet. "Your Honor, I have here a

copy of the state statute governing such matters." He
walked forward and placed the single sheet of paper before the judge. "Under the statute, the state feels there is
insufficient evidence to warrant a felony indictment. We
move that the charge be reduced to a misdemeanor."

"Wait a minute—!"

Hardy Purvis bounced out of his seat and pushed
through the balustrade separating the spectators from the
court well. His features were wreathed in anger.

"Judge, just hold on," he fumed, striding toward the
bench. "You can't allow this travesty to go on. There's
been a fix put in here."

"Stop right there," Woodruff commanded. "I will not
have disruption in my courtroom."

"Your Honor, I'm a captain in the Texas Rangers!"

"I don't care if you're John the Baptist. You will not
upset these proceedings."

"I raided the place," Purvis said hotly, shaking his
fist in the general direction of Quinn and Voight. "Saturday night me and my Rangers caught 'em red-handed.
I know a felony arrest when I make one."

"You are out of order." Woodruff squinted down at
him from the bench. "Mr. Butler represents the state and
has every right to put forth any motion he sees fit. Return
to your seat."

"Butler's been bought! Don't you see what I'm telling you, Judge? It's been fixed!"

"Bailiff, escort this man from my courtroom."

"You can't throw me out of here. I'm a Texas
Ranger!"

"You will be a Texas Ranger in the county jail unless
you obey the orders of this court. Bailiff, show him out."

The bailiff was a stout man with rubbery jowls. When
he started forward, Purvis turned about and stalked back
through the balustrade. Stoner gave him a weary shrug as
he went past, as if to say they'd played into a rigged game.
Purvis marched out of the courtroom.

"Mr. Butler," Woodruff said in the sudden silence. "Do you have anything to add?"

"No, Your Honor," Butler said in a low voice. "The motion stands."

"So ruled." Woodruff nodded to the defense counsel. "Mr. Maddox, the charge has been reduced to a misdemeanor offense. How do your clients plead?"

"Guilty, Your Honor," Maddox replied, as though reading lines from a script. "My clients beg the court's leniency in view of the fact that they have never before been arrested. This is their first offense."

Judge Thomas Woodruff fined them each one hundred dollars. The crowd broke out in applause, and Woodruff, unable to suppress a slight smile, quickly retired to his chambers. Voight peeled off hundred-dollar bills from a wad of cash and settled the fines with the court clerk. Nolan led the band of grinning housemen up the aisle.

Stoner watched with a bitter expression. His mind played back over the last month, and he thought justice bent like a reed before the wind when county officials were on the pad. He got to his feet, Janice at his side, as Quinn and Voight came through the balustrade. Quinn was in a chipper mood, and he put out a hand, stopping Voight in the aisle. He smiled at Stoner.

"You missed your calling, Sergeant. You should have gone into show business. You're quite an actor."

"I'm strictly an amateur," Stoner said. "You boys wrote and directed your own little drama here today. Shows you what bums with money can do."

"Hey!" Voight pushed forward with a rough look. "You remember what I told you, hotshot. You'll get yours."

Quinn warded him off. "Dutch, let's call it water under the bridge. Sergeant Stoner was just doing his job."

"I still am," Stoner said sharply. "You want threats, I'll give you one. Let's talk about Earl Durant."

Voight bridled. "What about him?"

"I don't know the whole story. All he said Saturday

night was that you're after him. I'm telling you to lay off."

Quinn and Voight exchanged a glance. Two of their men had been killed Saturday night at the cabin on Sweetwater Lake. They were stymied as to how Durant had found the cabin; but they were certain he'd killed the men. Quinn looked back at Stoner. "What's Durant to you?"

"Just another innocent party," Stoner said. "Anything happens to him, you boys won't know what hit you. I'll take it real personal."

Quinn laughed. "Sergeant, I don't think you care one way or another about Durant. I think you're ticked off about the casino."

"If you're saying I hold a grudge, you're absolutely right. I'll get you bozos any way I can."

Later, in the car crossing the causeway, Stoner was still steaming. He thought he'd wasted nearly a month of his life, and all for nothing. His threat about Earl Durant had been made in earnest. He would welcome the opportunity to come after Quinn and Voight.

"I almost hate to leave." Janice was staring out the window as seagulls floated lazily over the harbor. "Even if things went wrong, we still had some good times here. Didn't we, pumpkin?"

Stoner was forced to smile. "You're easy to take on a regular basis. Never thought I'd hear myself say that."

"Oh?" she said, looking at him with surprise. "So, what are you saying?"

"Maybe we ought to play house more often."

"I don't believe it! Are you serious?"

Stoner thought perhaps he was . . . maybe.

Late Friday morning Durant came through the door of the bank. He was carrying a legal portfolio, and he glanced at a calendar on the wall behind the tellers' cages. The date was October 5.

Catherine was typing a letter. She paused, looking up with a humorous smile, as he stopped at her desk. "Almost lunchtime," she said. "Some people would say you're keeping banker's hours."

"Not much longer." Durant grinned and patted the legal portfolio. "I've just come from Walter Kline's office."

"Everything's set, then? You're really going to sell the bank?"

"Lock, stock and barrel. By this afternoon I'll be an ex-banker."

She pouted. "It won't be the same without you."

"You never know," Durant said, his grin wider. "How about dinner tonight?"

"I thought you'd never ask."

"It's a date."

Durant motioned to Aldridge, who followed him into his office. The older man appeared recovered from his ordeal, and they had agreed never to speak of it to anyone. The police hadn't yet uncovered a suspect in the killings at Sweetwater Lake, and Durant intended to keep it that way. He meant to leave Galveston a free man.

In the office, Durant seated himself behind his desk. He opened the portfolio and placed a document in front of Aldridge. "Kline covered everything from A-to-Z. Look it over and see what you think."

"You're sure about this?" Aldridge said, pulling his chair closer to the desk. "Anything could happen in five years."

"Ira, I've never been more sure of anything in my life."

Durant was in a buoyant mood. On Monday morning he had received a call from Clint Stoner, the Texas Ranger. Stoner was on his way back to Austin and had stopped at a phone booth in La Marque. The purpose of his call had little to do with Quinn and Voight getting off on a misdemeanor charge. Everyone in town had already heard about the political shenanigans in the courtroom that morning. And hardly anyone was surprised.

Stoner's call was more of a personal nature. He ex-

plained that he had confronted Quinn and Voight in the
courtroom and put them on warning. Should anything
happen to Durant, he would bring the full force of the
Rangers to bear, and at the very least, send them to prison.
Durant gathered that the Ranger, though concerned for his
welfare, was more interested in keeping the heat on Quinn
and Voight. Stoner ended the call by saying he thought
Durant's troubles were over. Mobsters, perhaps more than
anyone else, understood a threat.

The call restored Durant's resolve that he would escape Galveston alive. Then, early Monday afternoon, he
had received a call from Jack Nolan. Dumbfounded, he
listened as Nolan explained William Magruder's true interest in People's Bank & Trust. Magruder was in the
midst of planning a resort hotel, and the bank owned property essential to the project. The land alone, Nolan went
on, was why Magruder had gotten the mob involved. Durant was floored by Nolan's sudden revelation.

"I don't get it," he'd said. "Why are you telling me
all this?"

Nolan had laughed. "Let's just say I'm wiping the
slate clean."

"What slate?"

"Galveston."

The call ended on that cryptic note. In the space of
a few hours, Durant felt he'd been handed a new lease on
life. Sergeant Clint Stoner had bought him immunity of
sorts from the mob, and Diamond Jack Nolan had revealed the source of all his problems. By late Monday
afternoon, working with Aldridge, he had identified the
piece of property so vital to Magruder's hotel project. A
few minutes later, he'd offered Aldridge a deal no one
could refuse. He saw it as his ticket out of Galveston.

Early Tuesday, Durant went to see his late uncle's
attorney, Walter Kline. He instructed Kline to draw up
two contracts, one for the sale of the bank, and one for
the land contiguous to Magruder's property on Seawall
Boulevard. The bank contract transferred ownership of

People's Bank & Trust to Aldridge for ten thousand dollars down, paid out of bank funds, and ten thousand a year for five years. The contract for the land was drawn between Durant and William Magruder.

"Looks fine to me," Aldridge said now, placing the contract on the desk. "Those are the most generous terms a man could hope for."

Durant, as president of the bank, had loaned Aldridge the down payment on a personal note. He dismissed his generosity with a casual wave. "Ira, I think Uncle Joe would rest easy knowing the bank's in safe hands. Let's get it done before you change your mind."

Catherine was called into the office. She was a notary public, and after they signed the contract, she witnessed their signatures. Durant, grinning broadly, clasped Aldridge's hand with genuine warmth.

"Congratulations, Ira, you've just bought yourself a bank."

Ten minutes later Durant walked into the waiting room of Magruder & Company. Ellen Morse, Magruder's secretary, remembered his previous visits all too well. She rushed around her desk and blocked the door to the inner office.

"No farther, Mr. Durant," she said acidly. "Leave now or I'll call the police. I mean it!"

"Don't worry, your boss will want to see me. Tell him Santa Claus is here."

"I beg your pardon?"

"Just tell him Christmas came early this year. Mention a piece of land on Seawall Boulevard."

"You wait right where you are."

She disappeared into the office. A moment elapsed, then she opened the door, motioning him inside with a suspicious little frown. Magruder was seated behind his ebony desk, fingers laced over his expansive belly. His eyes were hooded, and alert.

"Well, Mr. Durant," he said without expression. "I

must say you bear scant resemblance to Santa Claus. What's this about a piece of land?"

"Merry Christmas." Durant took the contract from his jacket pocket and dropped it on the desk. "Read it for yourself."

The contract was two pages long, double-spaced. Magruder scanned through it quickly, then turned back and read it line for line. He grunted something unintelligible, his mouth pursed in thought. He finally looked up.

"You're a surprise a minute, bub. How'd you find out about the hotel?"

"What's the difference?" Durant said, taking a chair. "Do you want the land or not?"

"Not for fifty thousand."

"The price isn't negotiable. I'm sure I could find other buyers."

Magruder studied the contract. "I see nothing in here about the bank."

"That's true," Durant said with a tight smile. "You'll be happy to know that I'm leaving Galveston. I've just sold the bank to Ira Aldridge."

"Aldridge won't last six months."

"You're wrong there. He'll last the same way my uncle lasted all those years. Lots of people in town don't like you or your bank."

"Nonetheless, the bank made the deal more attractive. I dislike competition."

"You're wasting my time. You wanted the land and it's right there in front of you. Take it or I'll put it on the open market."

"You always were a hard one, weren't you, bub?"

Durant stood. "Is that a yes or a no?"

"Keep your pants on," Magruder said gruffly. "I'll call my secretary in and have her witness our signatures. How do you want your money?"

"A cashier's check."

"You don't trust my company check?"

"I don't trust you."

Ellen Morse, also a notary public, witnessed the signing of the contract. She was then dispatched to Magruder's bank and returned a short while later with a cashier's check. Magruder waited until she was out of the room.

"Fifty thousand," he said, passing across the check. "I believe that concludes our business."

"One last thing," Durant remarked. "You know Walter Kline, the attorney?"

"Yes, I know him."

"I've left a long, detailed letter in his safe. Guess what it says about you and your mob buddies?"

Magruder scowled. "Have you lowered yourself to blackmail?"

"Let's call it insurance. Anything happens to me—anywhere, anyhow, anytime—Kline will deliver it to the attorney general and every newspaper in Texas. Think about it."

"I'll be glad to see the last of you, Mr. Durant."

"The sentiment's mutual."

Durant walked out of the office. He thought the warning delivered by Sergeant Stoner offered a degree of protection. Yet he felt even more certain about the letter in his lawyer's safe.

William Magruder knew when to call it quits.

Chapter Twenty-Four

The Hollywood Club was back in operation. By Saturday evening, the casino had been restored to its former elegance, with new gaming tables delivered by truck from the manufacturer. The raid of a week ago might never have happened.

Quinn thought of it as a cloud with a silver lining. The raid had brought the club even more notoriety, and reams of free publicity. Newspapers in Houston and other cities carried tongue-in-cheek articles comparing the Texas Rangers to the bumbling Keystone Cops of movie comedies. The Associated Press put the story on the national wire in what amounted to journalistic satire.

The publicity provided promotion as well for the club's latest headliners. Saturday night was opening night for the acclaimed dance team of Fred and Adele Astaire. A brother-and-sister act, the Astaires were two of the most popular figures in show business. Their singing and dancing career began as children in vaudeville, and now, in their twenties, they were the darlings of Broadway. Their most recent stage hit was the musical comedy *Lady, Be Good!*

The house was sold out. Quinn, with Nolan at his side, was stationed by the door to greet arriving guests. Those who were regular club patrons inevitably stopped to chat a moment about the raid, and congratulate Quinn on outwitting the Rangers in court. The cynicism of a generation was never more apparent than in their amusement at law enforcement officers being ridiculed in the press. Quinn treated it with witty nonchalance.

The Magruders arrived shortly before seven o'clock.

The party included Magruder with Opal on one arm and
Libbie on the other, followed by Sherm and his wife,
Francis. The women wore expensive gowns and diamonds, except for Libbie, whose beaded flapper dress revealed a good bit of leg. Magruder's expression was that
of a man who had been shanghaied away from his pipe
and slippers. His eyes flashed with anger when he saw
Nolan at the door.

"Good evening," Quinn said smoothly, the hand behind his back motioning Nolan to stand aside. "Always a
pleasure to have the Magruders as our guests."

"Speak for yourself," Magruder grumped. "My
daughter insisted on dragging us down here to see the
Astaires. She says they're the most sophisticated thing on
Broadway."

"Class with a capital C," Quinn assured him. "Adele
and Fred have taken dance to the pinnacle of the art. I'm
sure you'll enjoy the show."

"I think I'd need rose-colored glasses. I'm here under
protest."

Libbie carried a white plume fan. She raised it in an
airy movement, shielding her face from Quinn and her
father, and lowered one eyelid in a slow, suggestive wink.
Nolan caught the wink and looked off into the club,
amused by her audacity but forcing himself to hold a
sphinxlike expression. Then the maitre d' stepped forward, cued by Quinn, and led them to a table near the
dance floor. The orchestra was playing the *Sugartime Rag*.

Magruder, at Libbie's insistence, ordered champagne.
After glasses were poured, and the waiter had taken their
dinner orders, he excused himself. He threaded his way
back through the tables, stopping here and there to greet
friends, and approached the door. Quinn spotted him coming and saw the stinging look of anger he shot at Nolan.
Magruder stopped a short distance away.

"What is it, Bill?" Quinn said, moving forward.
"Something not right with your table?"

"No, no." Magruder leaned closer, lowering his voice.

"I trust the personal matter we discussed is no longer an issue."

Quinn appeared confused. "I thought Monsignor O'Donnell would have passed along my message. Jack Nolan will never see your daughter again. You have my word on it."

"I wasn't referring to Nolan. Although I do appreciate your discretion in that regard. I'm talking about Earl Durant."

Magruder had called Quinn yesterday afternoon. He'd briefly explained the land deal, and then elaborated on the fact that he was no longer at odds with Durant. He hadn't mentioned the letter in Walter Kline's safe, or that it would cause him irreparable harm if Durant met with foul play. He had simply expressed his concern for Durant's continued good health.

"All taken care of, Bill," Quinn said with a raffish smile. "I talked it over with Dutch and we'll respect your wishes in the matter. Nothing will happen to Durant."

"Splendid," Magruder said, visibly relieved. "I'm once again in your debt, Ollie. Thank you so much."

"Hey, that's what friends are for."

Quinn watched him walk back to his table. Yesterday, after the phone call, Quinn had indeed talked to Voight. The upshot was an argument, with Voight still strongly determined to put Durant on ice. But Quinn had eventually persuaded him that Durant was worth more to them alive than dead. At the right time, they would call in the chit on Magruder—a debt that had gotten three of their men killed—and make themselves silent partners in the resort hotel. Voight, however grudgingly, finally conceded that business was business. He agreed to let Durant skate.

Later that evening, when the show began, Quinn joined Maxine at the back of the room. Fred Astaire, who was widely regarded as the greatest tap dancer of the era, always opened the show with a solo routine. Quinn watched the nimble little man skip around the dance floor, feet tapping with swift grace to the beat of the music. He smiled at the sheer delight of it all.

"Maxie, there's something mystical about it, isn't there?"

"Of course there is, sugar," she purred, molding herself tight against his arm. "I get dizzy sometimes just thinking about you."

"Yes," Quinn said absently, watching Astaire. "That, too."

The sky was clear and black as velvet, bursting with stars. Tiny streaks of lightning, distant on the southern horizon, flickered over the Gulf. High tide brought an indigo surf pounding against the shore.

Durant and Catherine walked along a pathway above the beach. They were beyond the amusement piers, still loud with weekend tourists and incandescent with a swirl of colored lights. A woman shrieked in the distance as a roller coaster plunged into the depths of clattering tracks.

Earlier, over dinner at Delmonte's, Durant had been unusually quiet. Catherine was subdued as well, for she sensed there was something of farewell in the evening. The bank was sold, the land deal was closed, and he'd engineered an armistice, if not peace, with the mob. She knew he was thinking now of Hollywood.

Durant was actually thinking of her. Scarcely a month had passed since they'd met, and oddly, he found himself unable to say good-bye. His life was restored to some degree of normalcy, though he was still watchful, and for the moment, still carried the Luger. Yet he had more money than he'd ever imagined, and he could have easily booked passage on the noon train. There was nothing holding him in Galveston . . . except Catherine.

They stopped where a stretch of opalescent beach glittered beneath starlight. He put his arm around her waist, and they watched a moment as whitecaps rippled landward across the Gulf. She was overcome by the certainty that he was about to say something she didn't want to hear. Something kind and gently endearing, and final. She willed herself not to cry.

"I'm going back to Hollywood," he said, staring off at the distant waters. "Talked to Tom Mix on the phone this morning. Told him I was through with stunt work."

"Oh?" She struggled to control her voice. "What will you do?"

"Well, I asked him to give me a shot at directing one of his pictures. I think it's time I took the leap."

"And will he . . . let you direct?"

"We shook hands on the phone. I'm all set for his next picture. We start filming in two weeks."

"That's wonderful!" she said, forcing herself to sound thrilled. "I just know you'll be a great success. I'm so happy for you."

"Yeah, it's a big break," Durant said thoughtfully. "Tom always said I should be a director, and he's got the clout to choose who's behind the camera. I'm lucky to have him in my corner."

"Why, I'd bet anything it's only the beginning. Douglas Fairbanks and who knows who else will want you on their pictures."

"You're right, it could lead anywhere. I've got money to invest, and in Hollywood, nothing talks louder than hard cash. A good picture with Tom Mix could open all sorts of doors."

"Of course it will," she said vividly. "You'll be a mogul in no time. I just know you will."

"I'll settle for director." Durant hesitated, as though searching for the right words. "The thing is, I need you in my corner, too. I want you to come with me."

She caught her breath. "How do you mean . . . come with you?"

"Well, you know . . ."

"No, tell me."

"I'm trying to say we'll be married in Los Angeles. I want you to be my wife."

Her heart hammered wildly. She suddenly seemed

unable to breathe, and her voice failed her. She leaned into him, her head against his shoulder. He pressed his face to hers.

"What's wrong?" he asked. "Are you worried about your mother?"

"No, not at all." She wrapped herself in his arms. "Mama's life revolves around her friends and everything here on the Island. She'll do just fine."

"So we're off to Hollywood—if you'll marry me."

"Yes," she whispered tenderly. "I'd love to marry you."

Durant kissed her full on the mouth. She hugged him fiercely, and then, unable to restrain herself, she began laughing. He looked down at her with a bemused smile.

"What's so funny?"

"You're the one who should be worried about Mama."

"Me?"

"You know how she is about motion pictures. She'll insist on visiting us."

"And—?"

"She'll want to meet every movie star in Hollywood."

"Well, why not?" Durant said with a chuckle. "Nothing's too good for the grandmother of my children."

"Children?" Catherine said. "What happened to the honeymoon?"

"We'll get an early start."

"How early?"

Durant grinned. "On the train to California."

Libbie came down the staircase one step at a time. A few of the stairs creaked with age and she paused, fearful of awakening her father. She was carrying a small valise, with a change of clothing, her cosmetics, and her jewelry. The lights were off throughout the house.

The grandfather clock in the hallway chimed four times as she tiptoed across the foyer. She unlocked the front door and stepped outside, gingerly closing the door until the latch clicked. As she started away, it occurred to her that she would never return to the house, and she placed her key on the doorstep. She hurried off into the night.

Nolan was parked around the corner, on Twenty-ninth Street. His Stutz Bearcat, stolen from the club parking lot last Saturday night, had been found by the police the following morning outside City Hall. Nothing had been damaged, though he discovered the car had been hot-wired, and he suspected he knew the name of the thief. The gas gauge was down just enough for a round-trip to the cabin on Sweetwater Lake.

Libbie opened the passenger door. She tossed her valise in the back and scooted across the seat into his arms. "Hi there, handsome," she said, kissing him with nervous excitement. "Been waiting long?"

"You're right on time." Nolan felt energized himself, somewhat like the first night he'd led a rumrunning operation. "Any trouble getting out of the house?"

"You'd be surprised the things a girl learns in college. I used to sneak out of the sorority house the same way."

"You're sure about this? It's not some college prank where tomorrow's just like usual. We're burning our bridges."

"Of course I'm sure!" She took his face in her hands and kissed him hard on the mouth. "You'll never, ever get rid of me. I hope you know that."

"I wouldn't have it any other way."

Nolan started the car. The streets were deserted, and five minutes later, they rumbled over the causeway. Libbie glanced out the window at the darkened harbor, and then turned in her seat, looking back at the galaxy of street-lights on the Island. Her family, all of her friends, the people she'd known all her life passed through her mind in fleeting images. She silently said good-bye to Galveston, a small lump in her throat. She knew she would never return.

"Any regrets?" Nolan asked quietly.

"No, just memories," she said, moving closer, her hand tucked into his arm. "I'm leaving nothing behind that really matters. What about you?"

"Not even memories. Quinn and Voight weren't exactly family. I've forgotten them already."

"Yes, but will they forget you?"

"I told them I was taking Sunday off. We'll be long gone before they know the difference."

"You didn't answer the question," she said, poking him in the ribs. "Or maybe I didn't ask it right. Will they *forgive* you for walking out on them?"

"Doesn't matter," Nolan said with a rakish smile. "I've got too much on them and their whole operation. They'll let bygones be bygones."

"You sound awfully sure of yourself."

"Well, that's how the rackets work. You never cause trouble for a guy who's got the goods on you."

Nolan disliked starting out with secrets. Still, given what Quinn and Voight would learn on Monday, the truth might frighten her even more. He reassured her with a light-hearted chuckle. "Don't worry your pretty head about it. Nobody's gonna be looking for me."

"But if they were," she said, unable to shake the thought, "you could always find another job of some sort. You could succeed at anything. Anything at all!"

"Go straight?" Nolan scoffed. "Too late for that in this lifetime. I'm a gangster."

"Yes, I know," she said with a little laugh. "I think that's why I fell for you. I never could resist a rogue."

"Yeah, that's me all right. A rascal through and through."

"So tell me, my darling rogue—where are you taking me?"

Nolan grinned. "I thought our first stop would be Louisiana."

"Really?" she said, her expression puzzled. "Why Louisiana?"

"Couple reasons. One, they don't have a waiting period for a marriage license. So we'll find ourselves a justice of the peace and make it Mr. and Mrs."

"Oh, jeepers, Mrs. Jack Nolan! I love the sound of it."

"Only right that I make an honest woman of you."

"I couldn't agree more," she said happily. "Where will we go on our honeymoon?"

"That's the second reason," Nolan told her. "I thought we'd spend a week in New Orleans. Lots to see in the Old French Quarter. The natives call it the *Vieux Carre*."

"Who cares what they call it? You'll be lucky to get a peek at it, Mr. Nolan."

"Why's that?"

"Because Mrs. Nolan intends to keep you in bed the entire week."

"Do you?" Nolan said with mock irony. "Guess I'm marrying the right woman, after all."

"You certainly are," she purred, nuzzling his shoulder. "And after I've worn you out in New Orleans? What are your plans for the rest of our lives?"

"How do you feel about the tropics?"

"Something like Hawaii, or Tahiti?"

"No, I was thinking more of Jamaica."

"Oh, I adore the Caribbean. Who do you know in Jamaica?"

Nolan told her about Captain Rob McBride. He finished with a wry shake of his head. "The old pirate offered me a ship of my own. You'd be Mrs. Captain Nolan."

"I love it!" she cried gaily. "And smugglers must make tons and tons of money. Don't they?"

"We'd be living in the lap of luxury. I'll get you one of those villas overlooking the sea."

"And you really aren't changing occupations so much, are you? You'll still be my rogue."

"A seafaring rogue," Nolan amended. "I'll fly the Jolly Roger in your honor."

"I can't wait!" She hugged his arm. "When do we leave?"

"A week from Monday. I booked passage on a ship out of New Orleans."

"Oh God, Jack, we'll have a marvelous life, won't we?"

"Yeah, I think the world's gonna be our lollipop."

The lights of Galveston Island faded as they drove off the causeway. Neither of them thought to look back.

Opal Magruder came downstairs about nine Sunday morning. She was refreshed from a good night's sleep, humming a tune she'd heard at the Hollywood Club last night. She moved along the hallway to the dining room.

Magruder was seated at the head of the table. His plate was piled high with waffles, scrambled eggs, and thick slices of ham. He looked up with a nod. "Good morning, my dear."

"Good morning, William."

Opal helped herself from warmer trays on a sideboard. She took her place at the opposite end of the table and unfolded her napkin. The maid came out of the kitchen, filled her cup with coffee, then returned through the swinging door. She picked at her eggs, nibbled on a piece of toast.

"Weren't the Astaires wonderful?" she said, trying to make conversation. "So graceful, like two young swans."

"Yes, I suppose." Magruder pretended no great interest in the arts. "For my money, dinner was the best part of their show."

"We really should go out more often. All you ever think about is business and more business. You should take the time to stop and smell the roses."

"I'll leave the roses to you, my dear."

Jason, the chauffeur and sometimes butler, came through the door. He walked to the head of the table and placed the Sunday *Galveston Daily Chronicle* at Magruder's elbow. He waited for Magruder to look up.

"Something else?"

"Yessir." Jason placed a house key on the table. "I

found this on the doorstep when I went to collect the paper."

"Did you try it?" Magruder asked. "Does it fit our door?"

"Yessir, it does."

Magruder studied the key with a perplexed expression. His gaze shifted to the opposite end of the table. "Where's Libbie?" he said. "Have you seen her this morning?"

"Why, no, I haven't," Opal replied. "Girls do need their beauty rest. She's probably sleeping late."

Magruder grunted. "Go upstairs," he said to Jason. "Tell Miss Libbie I want to see her down here."

"Yessir."

Jason went out the door. Magruder unfolded the newspaper and began pursuing the front page. "Now that's progress," he said, tapping the paper. "Wall Street can now talk by radiophone with the London stock exchange. Quite a boon for world trade."

Opal nodded. "How nice."

"One day we'll have that for the cotton exchange."

"I'm sure you will."

Their conversation lapsed into silence. A few minutes later Jason returned with a lavender-scented envelope and placed it beside Magruder. "Miss Libbie was not in her room," he said. "Her bed appears not to have been slept in. I found this on the dresser. Will there be anything else, sir?"

"No, that's all."

Magruder opened the envelope as the butler walked to the door. There was a single sheet of stationery, with Libbie's initials printed at the top. He scanned the contents and his features flushed with rage. He angrily shook the letter.

"We're ruined," he said, his jowls quivering. "She's eloped with a gangster. Do you hear me, a gangster!"

"Yes, I know," Opal said calmly. "We had a long

talk last night after you went to bed. She told me all about her young man."

"And you didn't say anything to me? You didn't try to stop her?"

"Libbie is a grown woman and she knows her own mind. Why would I stop her?"

"Why?" Magruder exploded. "Because we'll be disgraced, that's why! Have you suddenly gone senile?"

Opal pushed back her chair. "You really are an old fud, William. I often wonder I've stayed with you all these years."

"What in God's name are you talking about?"

"Our daughter's happiness. Or have you forgotten what it was like to be in love?"

"Her happiness," Magruder said with heavy sarcasm. "For your information, her happiness will be our scandal. What does love have to do with it?"

"Everything."

Opal turned with great dignity and walked from the room. Magruder was taken aback, thoroughly baffled by her cool, inimical manner. After a moment, he snatched the letter off the table and hurried along the hall to his study. He placed a call to Sherm's home.

"I have to talk with you," he shouted into the phone. "Get over here right now!"

Some ten minutes later Sherm came through the door of the study. Magruder, who was seated at his desk, silently handed him the letter. Sherm read it once, then twice, and slowly shook his head with disbelief. He dropped the letter on the desk.

"I thought it was over," he said dully. "I thought Monsignor O'Donnell put a stop to it."

"Don't fault him," Magruder grouched. "All the blame goes to our friends Quinn and Voight. Quinn gave me his word on it."

"When was this?"

"Last night, at the club. He said Nolan would never see Libbie again. And this morning, she's gone!"

Sherm lowered himself into a chair. "From the sound of it, Nolan pulled the wool over their eyes. He and Libbie had this planned all along."

"I don't care," Magruder raged. "Quinn gave me his word, *his word!* I'm going to destroy both of them— Quinn and Voight."

"You're forgetting something."

"What's that?"

"They could destroy us," Sherm said. "Anything we use against them, they could turn it around on us. We'd go down in flames with them."

"I—" Magruder's features were ashen. "How did it come to this?"

"In for a penny, in for a pound. We have to think of the business before anything else. We have too much to lose."

Magruder slumped in his chair. "My God, my daughter a gangster's moll. I'll be the laughingstock of Galveston."

"What the hell, Pop," Sherm said with grim humor. "We've been sleeping with the mob for years. Why not Libbie?"

Later, when Sherm was gone, Magruder sat staring at the letter. The lines blurred, and he wondered where she was, how he'd lost her. He damned Quinn and Voight and Nolan.

And most of all, he damned himself.

Chapter Twenty-Five

The dome of the state capitol glittered beneath golden sunlight. The day was bright and crisp, and cumulus clouds drifted high in an azure sky. Congress Avenue was clogged with traffic.

Early Monday morning Stoner parked his car at the side of the capitol. He had been granted a week's furlough, and after leaving Galveston, he'd leisurely toured the coastline with Janice. They had arrived in Austin yesterday evening and he'd dropped her off at her apartment. Their parting had been bittersweet.

For almost five weeks, they had been inseparable. Their undercover assignment had cast them as man and wife, and they had shared not only a brief marriage, but the constant hazard of duping the mob. The experience had brought them closer together, and kindled a sense of mutual trust that few married couples ever achieved. They were, more so than most couples, a team.

Yet something had changed within the last week. As they drove the coast, stopping at Padre Island and Corpus Christi, any further talk of marriage had been put on hold. Their last night on the road, spent at the fabled Menger Hotel in San Antonio, had led to a frank discussion about the future. Janice, no less than Stoner, wanted some time to think. Neither of them felt compelled to rush things.

Their lovemaking that night had been tender, fervid but poignant. Whether they were in love, or simply great together in bed, seemed to them a moot point. They enjoyed one another, there was humor and laughter mixed with their passion, and they would forever be linked by the excitement and danger of what they had shared in

Galveston. Hardly needing words, they knew they wouldn't date anyone else once they returned to Austin. They just wouldn't get married—for now.

Stoner mounted the broad, stone steps to the capitol building. He was still assigned to Ranger Headquarters, and he'd been ordered to report to Colonel Garrison upon returning from furlough. Even though he and Captain Hardy Purvis had submitted written reports, he thought Garrison probably wanted a firsthand account. On the second floor, he tugged his uniform jacket tight and entered the reception room. The secretary, still wearing her hair in a chignon, greeted him with a pleasant smile. She ushered him into the office.

Homer Garrison rose from behind his desk. He extended a firm handshake and motioned Stoner to a chair. "Welcome back, Sergeant," he said. "How was your furlough?"

"Good, thank you, sir." Stoner seated himself, his Stetson hooked over a knee. "Spent some time on the coast not doing much of anything."

"Well, you certainly deserved the time off. How is Miss Overton?"

"She's just fine, sir. She asked me to pass along her regards."

"From your report, I gather she performed admirably in Galveston. Quite brave of her, working undercover."

"Yessir, she's a regular little soldier. And a real good actress, too. She had them all fooled."

"Commendable." Garrison slid an envelope across the desk. "There's a check in there for a thousand dollars. Please ask her to accept it with my compliments."

"That's very generous, Colonel." Stoner slipped the envelope inside his jacket. "I know she'll appreciate it."

"Not at all. She did a crackerjack job. Tell her I said so."

"Yessir, I will."

"And now to you." Garrison tapped a file folder on

his desk. "Captain Purvis gave you high marks in his report. I endorse the commendation."

"Thank you, sir," Stoner said, his features sober. "Captain Purvis did a mighty fine job himself. Too bad it was all for nothing."

"I wouldn't agree, Sergeant. You and Miss Overton accomplished something thought to be impossible. We finally know how that damnable casino disappears."

"Colonel, that turned out to be the easy part. What good's it do if we can't get a conviction?"

"You're talking about the prosecutor and the court being fixed?"

"Yessir, I am," Stoner said shortly. "Crooked judges just let the mob thumb their nose at the law. The almighty dollar calls the tune in Galveston."

"Unfortunately so," Garrison acknowledged. "We nonetheless learned a valuable lesson. Our efforts must be directed at attacking the mob in other ways."

"I don't follow you, Colonel."

"Suppose there was a method that couldn't be overturned in the courts. Would that get your attention?"

Stoner sat straighter. "Yessir, it sure would."

"I suspected as much."

Garrison went on to explain. For the past week, he had been huddled in meetings with the attorney general. Their purpose was to find a legal mechanism that would negate the mob's influence with prosecutors and courts. After several days of reviewing the Texas statutes, a junior staff member came up with a technicality in the laws directed at illegal gaming. The simplicity of it made it virtually foolproof.

The attorney general, under Texas law, had no prosecutorial powers. Yet the lawmakers, with an eye toward unscrupulous business practices, had given the attorney general the power of civil injunction. Once a law officer presented evidence of illegal gambling, the technicality applied as it would in any business enterprise. A court was required by law to issue a restraining order that halted gambling operations for ten days. And a judge was allowed no discretion in the matter. The restraining order must be issued.

There were further complexities on the theme. After ten days, if the evidence warranted, a civil injunction was mandated by the law. In the event the injunction was violated, the gaming club owner was automatically sentenced to three days in jail. By law, the attorney general was permitted to attach several injunctions together, each of which added to the jail sentence. There was no jury trial involved, and the process could be repeated endlessly. A judge who tried to tamper with the civil code faced the very certain risk of impeachment.

"Water on stone," Garrison concluded. "Not as quick as criminal charges, but the end result is the same. The mob will ultimately be worn down and worn out."

Stoner nodded hesitantly. "Colonel, you're talking a long time. Months, maybe even years."

"Exactly right," Garrison agreed. "Which demands that we have the right man for the job. I believe you're our man."

"Well, sir, if you'll pardon the expression, I'd give my left nut for another crack at Quinn and Voight. I consider those two unfinished business."

"I expected nothing less. How would you feel about working under Captain Purvis?"

"I'd like that just fine," Stoner replied. "Captain Purvis and me look at things the same way. We're both sore losers."

"Excellent," Garrison said. "As of today, you are transferred to the Houston office. You will head up a new division, the Rackets Squad. How does that sound?"

"Colonel, I couldn't ask for anything better. Any limits on how hard I push Quinn and Voight?"

"Your sole purpose will be to break the back of the mob in Galveston. You'll have a free hand."

"I'll leave for Houston tomorrow."

"One other thing."

"Yessir."

Garrison removed a leather badge holder from his desk drawer. He opened it, placing it on the desk, points of light reflecting off a gold shield. "Sergeant, I suggest you take those stripes off your sleeve. Effective today, you're Lieutenant Stoner."

Stoner accepted the badge holder. He stared down at the gold shield a moment, then looked up with a wide grin. "Well, sir—" he faltered, groping for words. "You sort of took me by surprise. I don't know what to say."

"Don't say anything," Garrison said with gruff good humor. "Just bring me Quinn and Voight."

"You can count on it, Colonel. One way or another, they're done."

Later, as he was leaving the capitol, Stoner wondered how Janice would feel about moving to Houston. Then, in the next instant, his mind turned to Galveston, and the mob. Quinn and Voight thought they'd seen the last of him, and he laughed, imagining their reaction when they got the news. Life was sweet.

Justice, with a dab of retribution, was sweeter still.

Voight made his usual Monday morning trip to the bank. Sherm Magruder, all the while he was exchanging bearer bonds for cash, expected some remark about Libbie and Nolan. When nothing was said, he decided to follow the advice he'd given his father. He acted as though it was business as normal.

Barney Ward was waiting in the reception area. Like everyone else, he knew a transaction had taken place, even though he wasn't aware of the details. His job was to act as bodyguard, ensuring that Voight and the briefcase made the appointed rounds in safety. He followed Voight out of the bank.

Five minutes later they entered the Turf Club. There was little action on a Monday and the bookmaking parlor was practically empty. As they crossed the room, Joe Reed came out of the manager's office with a bundle of mail. He saw Voight and hurried ahead to hold the elevator door.

"Just in time, boss," he said with a beaming grin. "I was on my way up with the mail."

"I'll take it." Voight stuck the bundle under his arm. "Seems like all the bills show up on Monday. Never fails."

"Same with me." Reed waited for Voight and Ward to step aboard the elevator, then closed the door. " 'Course, I let the little woman handle it. I hate payin' bills."

"Good idea," Voight said as the elevator shuddered upward. "How's Leann doing these days?"

Reed was always impressed by Voight's memory for family. "She's just fine, boss," he said, bobbing his head. "She'll be tickled you asked."

"Give her my best, Joe."

"I surely will, boss. Surely will."

The elevator bumped to a stop at the third floor. Reed opened the door, and Voight and Ward stepped off. There were several men in the athletic club, working out with weights and punching the heavy bag. At the end of the hall, Turk McGuire was posted outside the office. Voight nodded to him.

"I don't see Jack anywhere. Has he been around this morning?"

"Haven't seen him, boss," McGuire said. "Maybe he had a late date."

"His love life's his problem. Call him and tell him to trot it on over here."

"Sure thing, boss."

Voight went through the door to the office. Quinn was seated at his desk, poring over the legalese in an entertainment contract. He looked up as Voight dumped the mail in front of him, then moved to the safe and began working the combination. Quinn set the contract aside and began sorting through the mail.

"Helluva note," Voight said over his shoulder. "Going on noontime and Jack hasn't shown up."

"You're right," Quinn said. "Especially since we gave him yesterday off. Any of the boys know anything?"

"I told Turk to call him and tell him to get a move on. We're running a business here."

Voight placed the bearer bonds in the safe. He closed the door, spun the combination knob, and set the briefcase on the floor beside his desk. After taking a seat, he nipped the end off a cigar and lit up in a cloud of smoke. He glanced across at Quinn.

"Anything important in the mail?"

"Nothing—" Quinn hesitated, staring at a plain white envelope. He opened it, quickly read the note inside, and his jaw dropped. "Jesus Christ!"

"What?"

"Jack won't be answering his telephone. Here, read it for yourself."

Voight took the note. He recognized Nolan's loopy scrawl even before he began reading. The message was short and to the point.

> *Dear Dutch & Ollie,*
> *Sorry I wasn't able to give you more notice. Figured a letter was the best way to let you know I've quit. Libbie Magruder and I will be married and long gone by the time you get this. Your secrets are my secrets unless you send somebody looking for me. Let's just live and let live, and nobody gets hurt.*
>
> *Your pal,*
> *Jack*

"Sonovabitch!" Voight grated, his eyes rimmed with anger. "He quit us and ran off with that little broad. Goddamn him!"

"Postmarked Saturday," Quinn said, holding up the envelope. "That means he had everything planned out and probably took off Saturday night after the club closed. He played us along like we've got strings."

"Nobody quits me and gets away with it. Dirty bastard knows our operation inside out."

"Read the note again," Quinn said. "That part about 'live and let live.' "

"Yeah?" Voight flung the note on his desk. "So what?"

"Jack's telling us to leave well enough alone. He won't turn on us, because if he did, we'd turn on him. We all know who's at the bottom of the Gulf."

"You're saying we just grin and bear it. Pretend like he didn't crap on the guys that treated him like family. That's it?"

"That's it," Quinn said evenly. "There's nothing to be gained in trying to square accounts. We'd just hurt ourselves."

Voight seemed reluctant to let it go. "What about Magruder?" he said. "He'll be plenty pissed that our boy Jack went bye-bye with his daughter. How's that gonna affect business?"

"In a way, Jack did us a favor. I think this gives us some added leverage."

"How so?"

Quinn smiled. "Magruder wouldn't want it known he has a gangster for a son-in-law. I think we can make him jump through hoops—to keep his secret."

"You've got a point," Voight conceded with a grumpy smile. "He wouldn't want us leaking that to his society swells, would he? We've got his fat ass over a barrel."

"Dutch, I believe we've come out of this smelling like a rose."

"Yeah, maybe so, but I'm still burned. Jack was the best damn rumrunner anybody ever saw. Who the hell we gonna get to replace him?"

"We'll find someone," Quinn said without concern.

"After all, that's why we built an organization. No one man is indispensable."

"Ollie, when you're right, you're right." Voight blew a perfect smoke ring and watched it float toward the ceiling. "We practically own this Island, and five'll get you ten we've seen the last of the Rangers. We're sitting pretty, top of the world."

"Never rest on your laurels."

"What's that supposed to mean?"

Quinn signed the entertainment contract with a flourish. He held it up like a trophy. "I've just booked Mae West for a two-week engagement."

Mae West was one of the hottest stars on Broadway. She was infamous for risqué songs and racy comedy, and only recently, she'd been arrested for appearing in a scandalous play titled *Sex*. Her name alone conjured visions of raw sensuality.

"God," Voight moaned. "What's she gonna cost?"

"Sixteen thousand."

"Are you nuts? *Sixteen* thousand!"

"For two weeks," Quinn reminded him. "It's a steal, Dutch."

"I still say you're nuts," Voight grouched. "No broad's worth that much."

"Has Mr. Showbiz ever led you wrong?"

"Ollie, you'll be the death of me yet. Honest to Christ."

Voight furiously puffed his cigar. Quinn chuckled softly, leaning back in his chair, and visualized Mae West strutting about on the stage. Her brassy voice came to him amidst thunderous applause from the crowd.

His chuckle became deeper, and with it, the certainty that Galveston Island was the playground of America. He told himself the Hollywood Club would last forever.

For he was, with no jest whatever intended, Mr. Showbiz.

Alma Ludlow stood on the platform outside the Santa Fe depot. She waved to Catherine as the train chuffed smoke and slowly pulled away from the station house. Her hanky was sodden with tears.

Catherine turned from the window as the train gathered speed. She dabbed at her eyes and smiled sadly at Durant. "Mama doesn't believe we'll really get married. She thinks I'm running off to live in sin."

Durant laughed. "We'll send her a photostat of the marriage license. She'll know it's official, then."

"Yes, of course, that's a marvelous idea! She'll have something to show her friends."

"I don't get it. Why would she give us her blessing if she thought we wouldn't be married? She acted happy enough."

"Oh, she's very happy," Catherine said with conviction. "She couldn't imagine anything grander than living in Hollywood. So that makes it perfect for me."

"She never said a word," Durant remarked in a puzzled voice. "Yesterday, she fussed over me like I was a member of the family. She asked me to call her 'Mom.'"

"She thinks it's a fairy tale come true. Her daughter off to Hollywood with the big movie director. She's dying for an invitation to come visit."

All day Sunday had been spent at the Ludlow house. Catherine was busy preparing for the trip, packing bags to take on the train and boxing odds and ends to be shipped later. Her mother was back and forth, helping her pack in between peppering Durant with endless questions about movie stars. Dinner that evening had been something of a farewell supper, a quiet but happy celebration. Alma Ludlow had cooked all her daughter's favorite dishes.

Durant had booked a private compartment for the trip to California. The compartment was spacious, with double bunk beds that converted into a couch, a sitting area by the window, and a lavatory with a small shower stall. Catherine had been surprised and pleased, and her mother was thrilled that she was traveling in such luxury. But now, as the train trundled north over the causeway, she stared out the window at the sunlit harbor. Her features were pensive.

"Feeling sad?" Durant asked, noting her expression. "Sorry to be leaving your mother?"

"No, not at all," she said with a quick smile. "I'm sure Mama will invite herself to California for Christmas. She hinted at it last night."

"Why the sad look then?"

"Oh, I was just thinking about those gangsters. Quinn and Voight and all the others."

"What about them?"

"Well, in a way, I suppose it is sad." She glanced out the window and caught a last glimpse of the Island beneath a midday sun. "After everything you went through, almost getting yourself killed, and nothing's changed. They still run Galveston like it was their own little kingdom."

"Maybe not for long," Durant said. "You remember the Ranger I told you about? Sergeant Stoner?"

"Yes, the one who helped you that night at the casino."

"I got a call from him this morning, just before I checked out of the hotel. Caught me by surprise."

"Why would he call you?"

"Well, he didn't know I was leaving Galveston, and he thought I'd want to hear the news. He was flying high."

"You make it sound like good news."

"Good as it gets," Durant said with a grin. "Stoner's been promoted and put in charge of a Rackets Squad. His only job will be to nail Quinn and Voight."

"Omigosh!" Her eyes were round as buttons. "Do you think he can do it? Does he really have a chance?"

"I think Quinn and Voight are in for rough times. Stoner's determined to close them down."

Durant was glad to see the last of Galveston. There were no fond memories left behind, and his most fervent wish was that Stoner would rout the mob and drive them off the Island. Yet, odd as it seemed, he hoped Jack Nolan would somehow escape the law. Another time, another place, and they might have been friends.

All things considered, though, he felt himself the luckiest of men. He'd fought the mob and Magruder to a stalemate and he had cashier's checks for sixty thousand in his wallet. Even more, he would soon direct his first motion picture, and something deep inside, visceral in its certainty, told him it was only the beginning. And best of all, he was returning to Hollywood with Catherine.

"Let's forget Galveston," he said, taking her in his arms. "From here on, it's just you and me. Nothing but good times ahead."

"Ummm, I like the sound of that." She snuggled closer, her head against his shoulder. "Tell me stories about making movies, something outlandish. Anything at all."

"Anything at all covers a lot of ground. What would you like to hear?"

"Tell me how you first met Douglas Fairbanks."

"The first time was when we were shooting *The Mark of Zorro*. I did most of the stunts."

"And Mary Pickford?"

"Oh." Durant smiled, laughter in his voice. "Mary's another story entirely."

"Are you saying—" Catherine suddenly gasped, her eyes luminous with wonder. "You don't mean it . . . do you?"

"Well, you have to understand, that was before she met Doug. She'd just come to Hollywood."

"Yes?" Her curiosity overcame her. "And?"

"You really want to hear this?"

"I'm dying to hear it."

"You're sure?"

"I'm sure!"

Durant told her everything. Almost.

Epilogue

Galveston Island remained the mecca of gambling and vice for more than three decades. Civil injunctions filed by the attorney general were a nuisance, but the Hollywood Club always reopened and stayed open. The mob came to look on it as just another cost of doing business.

Oliver Quinn and Dutch Voight ultimately wearied of the battle. Age, and a fortune stashed away in bearer bonds, influenced them to sell their interests to a new generation of mobsters. These new overlords of crime were smart and sophisticated, but they were caught in the tidal undertow of a changing morality. The Texas Rangers finally turned out the lights on Galveston in 1957.

Diamond Jack Nolan became a smuggler, operating out of Jamaica. In 1928, during a run of bootleg liquor to Miami, his schooner was caught in a storm off the Florida Keys. The *Libbie*, named in honor of his wife, went down with all hands aboard. Elizabeth Magruder Nolan, the mother of two strapping boys, lived out her life in Jamaica, in her villa by the sea. She never remarried, and she never returned to Galveston.

Clint Stoner rose to the rank of captain in the Texas Rangers. For twenty years he stormed Galveston, raiding casinos and gambling dives, plastering the town with civil injunctions. His obsession with the mob left little time for a private life, and he and Janice Overton gradually drifted apart. He retired in 1946 and watched his successors close down Galveston eleven years later. Yet he remained a legend to all of Texas, the Ranger who never quit.

Earl Durant and Catherine Ludlow were married in October 1926. His first film, a Tom Mix western, revealed a remarkable talent as a director. He was in the vanguard of those who made the transition from silent movies to sound, and he worked with stars of the era in comedies as well as drama. He went on to make thirty-four films, and he won the Oscar for *Northern Lights* in 1932. He and Catherine had three children, and were among the first to build a mansion in Beverly Hills.

Cuddles the parrot lived to be sixteen. In 1927, when Oliver Quinn married Maxine Baxter, Cuddles was moved from the club to the penthouse suite in the Buccaneer. Quinn, whose many business affairs occupied his time, felt a talking parrot would be the perfect companion for Maxine. The first time Cuddles saw her in a negligee, he let loose a loud wolf whistle and squawked: "Ohboy! Ohboy! Lookathetits! Lookathetits!" Maxine, always receptive to a compliment, thought he was adorable.

The Wild Ones

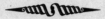

ACTING THE PART ...

Lillian finally joined the fight. After a struggle to cock both hammers on the shotgun, she found it required all her strength to raise the heavy weapon. She brought it to shoulder level, trying to steady the long barrels, and accidentally tripped both triggers. The shotgun boomed, the double hammers dropping almost simultaneously, and a hail of buckshot sizzled into the charging Indians. The brutal kick of the recoil knocked Lillian off her feet.

A warrior flung out his arms and toppled dead from his pony. The others swerved aside as buckshot simmered through their ranks like angry hornets. Their charge was broken not ten feet from the overhang, and Fontaine and Chester continued to blast away with their Henry repeaters ...

The Wild Ones

————◦◦◦◦◦————

MATT BRAUN

St. Martin's Paperbacks

THE OVERLORDS / THE WILD ONES

The Overlords copyright © 2003 by Matt Braun.
The Wild Ones copyright © 2002 by Winchester Productions, Ltd.

All rights reserved.

For information address St. Martin's Press, 175 Fifth Avenue, New York, NY 10010.

ISBN: 978-1-250-19628-6

Our books may be purchased in bulk for promotional, educational, or business use. Please contact your local bookseller or the Macmillan Corporate and Premium Sales Department at 1-800-221-7945, ext. 5442, or by e-mail at MacmillanSpecialMarkets@macmillan.com.

Printed in the United States of America

The Overlords St. Martin's Paperbacks edition / January 2003
The Wild Ones St. Martin's Paperbacks edition / January 2002

St. Martin's Paperbacks are published by St. Martin's Press, 175 Fifth Avenue, New York, NY 10010.

10 9 8 7 6 5 4 3 2 1

IN MEMORY OF ALL THOSE LOST AT
THE WORLD TRADE CENTER
AND THE PENTAGON
SEPTEMBER 11, 2001

The Wild Ones

CHAPTER 1

THE TRAIN was some miles west of Boonville. Lillian sat by the window, staring out at the verdant countryside. She thought Missouri looked little different from Indiana or Ohio, though perhaps not so flat. Her expression was pensive.

September lay across the land. Fields tall with corn, bordered by stands of trees, fleeted past the coach window under a waning sun. There was a monotonous sameness to the landscape, and the clickety-clack of steel wheels on rails made it all but hypnotic. She wondered if she would ever again see New York.

Chester, her brother, was seated beside her. Three years older, recently turned twenty-two, he was a solid six-footer, with chiseled features and a shock of wavy dark hair. His head bobbed to the sway of the coach and his eyes were closed in a light slumber. He seemed intent on sleeping his way through Missouri.

Alistair Fontaine, their father, was seated across from them. A slender man, his angular features and leonine head of gray hair gave him a distinguished appearance. He was forty-four, an impeccable dresser, his customary attire a three-piece suit with a gold watch chain draped over the expanse of his vest. He looked at Lillian.

"A penny for your thoughts, my dear." Lillian loved the sound of her father's voice. Even as a young child, she had been entranced by his sonorous baritone, cultured and uniquely rich in timbre. She smiled at him.

"Oh, just daydreaming, Papa," she said with a small shrug. "I miss New York so much. Don't you?"

"Never look back," Fontaine said cheerfully. "Westward the sun and westward our fortune. Our brightest days are yet ahead."

"Do you really think so?"

"Why, child, I have no doubt of it whatever. We are but stars following our destiny."

She sensed the lie beneath his words. He always put the best face on things, no matter how dismal. His wonderfully aristocratic bearing gave his pronouncements the ring of an oracle. But then, she reminded herself, he was an actor. He made reality of illusion.

"Yes, of course, you're right," she said. "Abilene just seems like the end of the earth. I feel as though we've been . . . banished."

"Nonsense," Fontaine gently admonished her. "We will take Abilene by storm, and our notices will have New York clamoring for our return. You mark my words!"

Chester was roused by his father's voice. He yawned, rubbing sleep from his eyes. "What's that about New York?"

"I was telling Lillian," Fontaine informed him. "Our trip West is but a way station on the road of life. We've not seen the last of Broadway."

"Dad, I hope to God you're right."

"Never doubt it for a moment, my boy. I have utter faith."

Lillian wasn't so sure. On the variety circuit, *The Fontaines*, as they were billed, was a headline act. Her earliest memories were of traveling the circuit of variety theaters throughout the Northeast and the Eastern Seaboard. Originated in England and imported across the Atlantic, variety theaters were the most popular form of entertainment in America.

A child of the theater, Lillian had been raised among performers. Her playmates were the offspring of chorus girls, song-and-dance men, comics, contortionists, and acrobats. At an early age, she and Chester became a part of the family troupe, acting in melodramas with their parents and sometimes accompanying their mother in song. The family ensemble presented entertainment for the masses, something for everyone.

Alistair Fontaine played to popular tastes by appearing in the sometimes-histrionic melodramas. At heart, he considered himself a tragedian, and his greatest joy was in emoting Shakespearean soliloquies in full costume. Yet it was his wife, Estell Fontaine, who was the true star of the show. Her extraordinary voice rendered audiences spellbound, and she might have had a career in opera. She chose instead her family. And the variety stage.

The magnitude of her stardom became apparent just three months ago, in the early summer of 1871. A bout of influenza quickly turned to pneumonia, and two days later she died in a New York hospital. Her loss devastated Alistair, who stayed drunk for a week, and left Lillian and Chester undone by grief. Estell was the bulwark of the family, wife, mother, and matriarch. They were lost without her, emotionally adrift. Yet, strangely, made somehow closer by her death.

Their personal tragedy was compounded in their professional lives. With Estell gone, the Fontaines soon discovered they were no longer a headline act. Her voice was the stardust of the show, and without her, they were suddenly unemployable anywhere on the variety circuit. Theater owners were sympathetic, but in the months following Estell's death there were no offers for an engagement, even on the undercard. Their booking agent suggested they try the budding variety circuit in the West.

Alistair Fontaine was at first opposed and not a little offended. But then, after three months without work and facing poverty, he reluctantly agreed. Their agent finally obtained a booking in Abilene, Kansas, the major railhead for shipping Texas cattle. Whatever was to be learned of their destination was to be found in the pages of the *Police Gazette.* Abilene was reported to be the wildest town in the Wild West.

Today, watching her father, Lillian wasn't at all convinced that he had reconciled himself with their situation. In off moments, she caught him staring dully into space and sensed his uncertainty about their trip West. Even more, she knew his posturing and his confident manner were meant to reassure herself and Chester. His oft-repeated assertion that they would return to New York and Broadway was fanciful, a dream at best.

She longed for the counsel of her mother.

"When's our next stop?" Chester abruptly asked. "I wouldn't mind a hot meal for a change."

There was no dining car on the train. A vendor periodically prowled the aisles, selling stale sandwiches and assorted sundries. Their last decent meal had been in St. Louis.

Fontaine chuckled amiably. "I fear you'll have a wait, my boy. We're scheduled to arrive in Kansas City about midnight."

"Wish it was New York instead."

"Be of stout heart, Chet. Think of us as thespians off on a grand adventure."

Lillian turned her gaze out the window. Abilene, for all her father's cheery bluster, hardly seemed to her a grand adventure. The middle of nowhere sounded a bit more like it.

She, too, wished for New York.

The train hurtled through the hamlet of Sweet Springs. Coupled to the rear of the engine and the tender were an express car and five passenger coaches. As the locomotive sped past the small depot, the engineer tooted his whistle. On the horizon, the sun dropped toward the rim of the earth.

A mile west of town, a tree had been felled across the tracks on the approach to a bridge. The engineer set the brakes, wheels grinding on the rails, and the train jarred to a screeching halt. The sudden jolt caught the passengers unawares, and there was a moment of pandemonium in the coaches. Luggage went flying from the overhead racks as women screamed and men cursed.

Then, suddenly, a collective hush fell over the coaches. From under the bridge where trees bordered a swift stream, a gang of riders burst out of the woods. Five men rode directly to the express car, pouring a volley of shots through the door. Another man, pistol drawn, jumped from his horse to the steps of the locomotive. The engineer and the fireman dutifully raised their hands.

Four remaining gang members, spurring their horses hard, charged up and down the track bed. Their pistols were cocked and pointed at the passengers, who stared openmouthed through the coach windows. No shots were fired, but the men's menacing attitude and tough appearance made the message all too clear. Anyone who resisted or attempted to flee the train would be killed.

"My God!" Alistair Fontaine said in an awed tone. "The train is being robbed."

Lillian shrank back into her seat. Her eyes were fastened on the riders waving their pistols. "Are we in danger, Papa?"

"Stay calm, my dear," Fontaine cautioned. "I daresay the rascals are more interested in the express car."

The threat posed by the armed horsemen made eminent good sense to the passengers. Like most railroads, the Kansas Pacific was not revered by the public. For years, eastern robber barons had plundered the West on land grants and freight rates. A holdup, according to common wisdom, was a matter between the railroad and the bandits. Only a fool would risk his life to thwart a robbery. There were no fools aboard today.

From the coaches, the passengers had a ringside seat. They watched as the five men outside the express car demonstrated a no-nonsense approach to train robbery. One of the riders produced a stick of dynamite and held the fuse only inches away from the tip of a lighted cigar. Another rider, whose commanding presence pegged him as the gang leader, gigged his horse onto the roadbed. His voice raised in a shout, he informed the express guards that their options were limited.

"Open the door or get blown to hell!"

The guards, much like the passengers, were unwilling to die for the Kansas Pacific. The door quickly slid open and they tossed their pistols onto the ground. Three of the robbers dismounted and scrambled inside the express car. The leader, positioned outside the car, directed the operation from aboard his horse. His tone had the ring of authority, brusque and demanding. His attitude was that of a man accustomed to being obeyed.

"Holy Hannah!" one of the passengers exclaimed. "That there's the James boys. There's Jesse himself!"

Jesse and Frank James were the most famous outlaws in America. Their legend began in 1866, when they rode into Liberty, Missouri, and robbed the Clay County Savings Association of $70,000. It was the first daylight bank robbery in American history and created a furor in the nation's press. It also served as a template by which the gang would operate over the years ahead, robbing trains and looting banks. Their raids were conducted with military precision.

A master of propaganda, Jesse James frequently wrote articulate letters to editors of influential midwestern newspapers. The letters were duly reprinted and accounted, in large measure, for the myth that "he robbed from the rich and gave to the poor." Comparisons were drawn between Jesse and Robin Hood, the legendary outlaw of Sherwood Forest. Not entirely in jest, newspaper editorials made reference to "Jesse and his merry band of robbers."

Tales were widely circulated with regard to Jesse's charitable nature toward the poor. The loot taken in the robberies, so he contended in his letters, was simply liberated from the coffers of greedy bankers and corrupt railroads. In time, with such tales multiplying, Jesse became known as a champion of the oppressed and the downtrodden. To backwoods Missourians and gullible Easterners alike he came to represent a larger-than-life figure. A Robin Hood reborn—who wore a six-gun and puckishly thumbed his nose at the law.

The holdup took less than five minutes. The robbers inside the express car emerged with a mail sack that appeared painfully empty of cash. There was a hurried conference with their leader, and his harsh curses indicated his displeasure. He dismounted, ordering one man to guard the train crew, and waved the others toward the passenger coaches. They split into pairs, two men to a coach, and clambered up the steps at the end of each car. The leader and another man burst through the door of the lead coach.

A murmur swept through the passengers. The two men were instantly recognizable, their faces plastered on wanted dodgers from Iowa to Texas. Jesse and Frank James stood at the front of the car, brandishing cocked pistols.

"Sorry to trouble you folks," Jesse said with cold levity. "That express safe was mighty poor pickin's. We'll have to ask you for a donation."

Frank lifted a derby off the head of a notions drummer. He started down the aisle, the upturned hat in one hand and a pistol in the other. His mouth creased in a sanguine smile as passengers obediently filled the hat with cash and gold coins. He paused where the Fontaines were seated.

Lillian blushed under his appreciative inspection. She was rather tall, with enormous china blue eyes and exquisite features. Vibrant even in the face of a robber, she wore her tawny hair upswept, with fluffs of curls spilling over her forehead. Her demure dimity cotton dress did nothing to hide her tiny waist and sumptuous figure. She quickly averted her eyes.

"Beauty's ensign"—Frank James nodded, still staring at her—"is crimson in thy lips and in thy cheeks."

Alistair Fontaine was an avid reader of periodicals. He recalled a curious item from the *Police Gazette,* noting the anomaly that robber and mankiller Frank James was a student of Shakespeare. He rose as though taking center stage.

"M'lord," he said in a mellifluous voice. "You see me here before you a poor man, as full of grief as age, wretched in both."

"King Lear," Frank said, grinning. "I take it you fancy the Bard."

"A mere actor," Fontaine replied modestly. "Known to some as a Shakespearean."

"Well, friend, never let it be said I'd rob a man that carries the word. Keep your money."

"Frank!" Jesse snapped. "Quite jawin' and tend to business. We ain't got all night."

Frank winked slyly at Fontaine. He went down the aisle and returned with the derby stuffed to overflowing. Jesse covered his retreat through the door and followed him out. Some moments later the gang mounted their horses and rode north from the railroad tracks. A smothered sun cloaked them in silty twilight.

The passengers watched them in stunned silence. Then, as though a floodgate was released, they began babbling to one another about being robbed by the James Boys. Chester shook his head in mild wonder.

"Some introduction to the Wild West," he muttered. "I hope Abilene's nothing like that."

Lillian turned to her father. "Oh, Papa, you were wonderful!"

"Yes," Fontaine agreed. "I surprised myself."

Twilight slowly faded to dusk. Fontaine stared off at the shelterbelt of woods where the riders had disappeared. Abruptly, his legs gone shaky with a delayed reaction, he sank down into his seat. Yet he thought he would remember Frank James with fondness.

It had been the finest performance of his life.

CHAPTER 2

ABILENE WAS situated along a dogleg of the Smoky Hill River. The town was a crude collection of buildings, surrounded by milling herds of longhorn cattle. The Kansas plains, flat as a billiard table, stretched endlessly to the points of the compass.

The Fontaines stepped off the train early the next afternoon. They stood for a moment on the depot platform, staring aghast at the squalid, ramshackle structures. Eastern newspapers, overly charitable in their accounts, labeled Abilene as the first of its kind. One of a kind. A cowtown.

"Good heavens," Fontaine said in a bemused tone. "I confess I expected something more . . . civilized."

Lillian wrinkled her nose. "What a horrid smell."

There was an enervating odor of cow dung in the air. The prairie encircling Abilene was a vast bawling sea of longhorns awaiting shipment to eastern slaughterhouses, and a barnyard scent assailed their nostrils. The pungency of it hung like a fetid mist over the town.

"Perhaps there's more than meets the eye," Fontaine said, ever the optimist. "Let's not jump to hasty conclusions."

Chester grunted. "I can't wait to see the theater."

A porter claimed their steamer trunks from the baggage car. He muscled the trunks onto a handcart and led the way around the depot. The Kansas Pacific railroad tracks bisected the town east to west, cleaving it in half. Texas Street, the main thoroughfare, ran north to south.

Lillian was appalled. Her first impression was that every storefront in Abilene was dedicated to separating the Texan cattlemen from their money. With the exception of two hotels, three mercantile emporiums, and one bank, the entire business community was devoted to either avarice or lust. The street was lined with saloons, gambling dives, and dancehalls.

The boardwalks were jammed with throngs of cowhands. Every saloon and dancehall shook with the strident chords of brass bands and rinky-dink pianos. Smiling brightly, hard-eyed girls in gaudy dresses enticed the trailhands through the doors, where a quarter bought a slug of whiskey or a trip around the dance floor. The music blared amidst a swirl of jangling spurs and painted women.

"Regular circus, ain't it?" the porter said, leading them past hitch racks lined with horses. "You folks from back East, are you?"

"New York," Fontaine advised him. "We have reservations at the Drover's Cottage."

"Well, you won't go wrong there. Best digs this side of Kansas City."

"Are the streets always so crowded?"

"Night or day, don't make no nevermind. There's mebbe a thousand Texans in town most of the trailin' season."

The porter went on to enlighten them about Abilene. Joseph McCoy, a land speculator and promoter, was the founder of America's first cowtown. Texans were beef-rich and money-poor, and he proposed to exchange Northern currency for longhorn cows. The fact that a railhead didn't exist deterred him not in the least. He proceeded with an enterprise that would alter the character of the West.

McCoy found his spot along the Smoky Hill River. There was water, and a boundless stretch of grassland, all situated near the Chisholm Trail. After a whirlwind courtship of the Kansas Pacific, he convinced the railroad to lay track across the western plains. In 1867, he bought 250 acres on the river, built a town and stockyards, and lured the Texas cattlemen north. Four years later, upward of 100,000 cows would be shipped from Abilene in a single season.

"Don't that beat all!" the porter concluded. "Dangblasted pot o'gold, that's what it is."

"Yes indeed," Fontaine said dryly. "A veritable metropolis."

The Drover's Cottage was a two-story structure hammered together with ripsawed lumber. A favorite of Texas cowmen, the exterior was whitewashed and the interior was sparsely decorated. The Fontaines were shown to their rooms, and the porter lugged their steamer trunks to the second floor. They agreed to meet in the lobby in an hour.

Lillian closed the door with a sigh. Her room was appointed with a single bed, a washstand and a rickety dresser, and one straight-backed chair. There were wall pegs for hanging clothes and a grimy window with tattered curtains that overlooked Texas Street. The mirror over the washbasin was cracked, and there was a sense of a monk's cell about the whole affair. She thought she'd never seen anything so dreary.

After undressing, she poured water from a pitcher into the basin and took a birdbath. The water was tepid and thick with silt, but she felt refreshed after so many days on a train. Then, peering into the faded mirror above the washstand, she rearranged her hair, fluffing the curls over her forehead. From her trunk, she selected undergarments and a stylish muslin dress with a lace collar. She wanted to look her best when they went to the theater.

Her waist was so small that she never wore a corset. She slipped into a chemise with a fitted bodice and three petticoats that fell below the knees. Silk hose, ankle-high shoes of soft calfskin, and the muslin dress completed her outfit. On the spur of the moment, she took from the trunk her prize possession, a light paisley shawl purchased at Lord & Taylor in New York. The shawl, exorbitantly expensive, had been a present from her mother their last Christmas together. Lillian wore it only on special occasions.

Shortly after three o'clock the Fontaines entered the Comique Variety Theater. The theater was a pleasant surprise, with a small orchestra pit, a proscenium stage, and seating for 400 people. Lou Gordon, the owner, was a beefy man with a walrus mustache and the dour look of a mortician. He greeted the men with a perfunctory handshake and a curt nod. His eyes lingered on Lillian.

"High time you're here," he said brusquely. "You open tomorrow night."

Fontaine smiled. "Perfect timing, my dear chap."

"Hope for your sake your booking agent was right. His wire said you put on a good show."

"I have every confidence you will be pleased. We present a range of entertainment for everyone."

"Such as?"

"All the world's a stage." Fontaine gestured grandly. "And all the men and women merely players. They have their exits and their entrances. And one man in his time plays many parts."

Gordon frowned. "What's that?"

"Shakespeare," Fontaine said lightly. *"As You Like It."*

"Cowhands aren't much on culture. Your agent said you do first-rate melodrama."

"Why, yes, of course, that, too. We're quite versatile."

"Glad to hear it." Gordon paused, glanced at Lillian. "What's the girl do?"

"Lillian is a fine actress," Fontaine observed proudly. "And I might add, she has a very nice voice. She opens our show with a ballad."

"Cowhands like a pretty songbird. Just don't overdo the Shakespeare."

"Have no fear, old chap. We'll leave them thoroughly entertained."

"You know Eddie Foy?" Gordon asked. "Tonight's his closing night."

"We've not had the pleasure," Fontaine said. "Headliners rarely share the same bill."

"Come on by for the show. You'll get an idea what these Texans like."

"I wouldn't miss an opportunity to see Eddie Foy."

Fontaine led the way out of the theater. He set off at a brisk pace toward the hotel. "The nerve of the man!" he said indignantly. "Instructing me on Shakespeare."

Lillian hurried to stay up. "He was only telling you about the audience, Papa."

"We shall see, my dear. We shall indeed!"

*   *   *

The chorus line kicked and squealed. They pranced offstage, flashing their legs, to thunderous applause from the crowd. The house was packed with Texans, most of them already juiced on rotgut liquor. Their lusty shouts rose in pitch as the girls disappeared into the wings.

The orchestra segued into a sprightly tune. The horns were muted, the strings more pronounced, and the audience quieted in anticipation. Eddie Foy skipped onstage, tipping his derby to the crowd, and went into a shuffling soft-shoe routine. The sound of his light feet on the floor was like velvety sandpaper.

Foy was short and wiry, with ginger hair and an infectious smile. Halfway through the routine, he began singing a bawdy ballad that brought bursts of laughter from the trailhands. The title of the song was *Such a Delicate Duck*.

> *I took her out one night for a walk*
> *We indulged in all sports of pleasantry and talk*
> *We came to a potato patch; she wouldn't go*
>   *across*
> *The potatoes had eyes and she didn't wear no*
>   *drawers!*

Lillian blushed a bright crimson. She was seated between her father and brother, three rows back from the orchestra. The lyrics of the song were far more ribald than anything she'd ever heard in a variety theater. Secretly, she thought the tune was indecently amusing, and wondered if she had no shame. Her blush deepened.

Foy ended the soft-shoe number. The orchestra fell silent with a last note of the strings as he moved to center stage. Framed in the footlights, he walked back and forth with herky-jerky gestures, delivering a rapid comedic patter that was at once risque and hilarious. The Texans honked and hooted with rolling waves of laughter.

On the heels of a last riotous joke, the orchestra suddenly blared to life. Foy nimbly sprang into a high-stepping buck-and-wing dance routine that took him cavorting around the stage. His voice raised in a madcap shout, he belted out a naughty tune. The lyrics involved a girl and her one-legged lover.

Toward the end of the number, Foy's rubbery face stretched wide in a clownish grin. He whirled, clicking his heels in midair, and skipped offstage with a final tip of his derby. The audience whistled and cheered, on their feet, rocking the walls with shrill ovation. Foy, bouncing merrily onto the stage, took three curtain calls.

The crowd, still laughing, began filing out of the theater. Fontaine waited for the aisle to clear, then led Lillian and Chester backstage. They found Foy seated before a mirror in his dressing room, wiping off greasepaint. He rose, turning to greet them, as Fontaine performed the introductions. His mouth split in a broad smile.

"Welcome to Abilene," he said jauntily. "Lou Gordon told me you're opening tomorrow night."

"Indeed we are," Fontaine affirmed. "Though I have to say, you'll be a hard act to follow. You're quite the showman."

"Same goes both ways. The Fontaines have some classy reputation on the circuit back East."

"The question is, will East meet West? We certainly had an education on Texans tonight."

Foy laughed. "Hey, you'll do swell. Just remember they're a bunch of rowdies at heart."

"Not to mention uncouth," Fontaine amended. "I'm afraid we haven't your gift for humor, Eddie. Gordon warned us that culture wouldn't play well in Abilene."

"You think I'd try the material you heard tonight in New York? No sir, I wouldn't, not on your tintype! You have to tailor your material to suit your audience. Westerners just like it a little . . . raunchy."

"Perhaps it's herding all those cows. Hardly what would be termed a genteel endeavor."

"That's a good one!" Foy said with a moonlike grin. "Nothing genteel about cowboys. Nosiree."

"Well, in any event," Fontaine said, offering a warm handshake. "A distinct pleasure meeting you, Eddie. We enjoyed the show."

"All the luck in the world to you! Hope you knock'em in the aisles."

"We'll certainly do our very best."

Fontaine found the way to the stage door. They emerged into a narrow alley that opened onto Texas Street. Lillian fell in between the men and glanced furtively at her father. She could tell he was in a dark mood.

"How enlightening," he said sourly. "I hardly think we'll follow Mr. Foy's advice."

"What would it harm, Papa?" Lillian suggested. "Melodrama with a few laughs might play well."

"I will not pander to vulgarians! Let's hear no more of it."

On the street, they turned toward the hotel. A group of cowhands, ossified on whiskey, lurched into them on the boardwalk. The Texans stopped, blocking their way, and one of them pushed forward. He was a burly man, thick through the shoulders, with mean eyes. He leered drunkenly at Lillian.

"Lookee here," he said in a rough voice. "Where'd you come from, little miss puss? How about we have ourselves a drink?"

"How dare you!" Fontaine demanded. "I'll thank you to move aside."

"Old man, don't gimme none of yore sass. I'm talkin' to the little darlin' here."

Chester stepped between them "Do as you're told, and quickly. I won't ask again."

"Hear that, boys?" the cowhand said, glancing at the other Texans. "Way he talks, he's from Boston or somewheres. We done treed a gawddamn Yankee."

"Out of our way."

Chester shoved him and the cowhand launched a murderous haymaker. The blow caught Chester flush on the jaw and he dropped to his knees. The Texan cocked a fist to finish him off.

A man bulled through the knot of trailhands. He was tall, with hawklike features, a badge pinned to his coat. His pistol rose and fell, and he thunked the troublemaker over the head with the barrel. The Texan went down and out, sprawled on the boardwalk.

"You boys skedaddle," the lawman said, motioning with the pistol. "Take your friend along and sober him up."

The cowboys jumped to obey. None of them said a word, and they avoided the lawman's eyes, fear written across their faces. They grabbed the fallen Texan under the arms and dragged him off down the street. The lawman watched them a moment, then turned to the Fontaines. He knuckled the brim of his low-crowned hat.

"I'm Marshal Hickok," he said. "Them drunks won't bother you no more."

Lillian was fascinated. His auburn hair was long, spilling down over his shoulders. He wore a frock coat, with a scarlet sash around his waist, a brace of Colt pistols tucked cross-draw fashion into the sash. His sweeping mustache curled slightly at the ends.

Hickok helped Chester to his feet. Fontaine introduced himself, as well as Lillian and Chester. The marshal nodded politely.

"I reckon you're the actors," he said. "Heard you start at the Comique tomorrow."

"Yes indeed," Fontaine acknowledged. "I do hope you will attend, Marshal."

"Wouldn't miss it for all the tea in China."

"Allow me to express our most sincere thanks for your assistance tonight."

"Never yet met a Texan worth a tinker's damn. Pleasure was all mine."

Hickok again tipped his hat. He walked off upstreet, broad shoulders straining against the fabric of his coat. Fontaine chuckled softly to himself.

"Do you know who he is?"

"No," Lillian said. "Who?"

"Only the deadliest marshal in the West. I read about him in *Harper's Magazine*."

"Yes, but who is he, Papa?"

"My dear, they call him Wild Bill Hickok."

CHAPTER 3

A JUGGLER dressed in tights flung three bowie knives in a blinding circle. The steel of the heavy blades glittered in the footlights as he kept them spinning in mid-air. His face was a study in concentration.

The Comique was sold out. Tonight was opening night for *The Fontaines*, and every seat in the house was taken. The crowd, mostly Texas cowhands, watched the juggler with rapt interest. They thought he might slip and lose a finger.

The juggler suddenly flipped all three knives high in the air. He stood perfectly still as the knives rotated once, then twice, and plummeted downward. The points of the blades struck the floor, embedded deep in the wood, quivering not an inch from his shoes. The Texans broke out in rollicking applause for his death-defying stunt.

The orchestra blared as the juggler bowed, collecting his knives, and skipped off the stage. A chorus line of eight girls exploded out of the wings, squealing and kicking as the orchestra thumped louder. The girls were scantily clad, bosoms heaving, skirts flashing to reveal their legs. They bounded exuberantly around the stage in a high-stepping dance routine.

Lillian stood in the wings at stage right. She was dressed in a gown of teal silk, with a high collar and a hemline that swept the floor. Her heart fluttered and her throat felt dry, a nervous state she invariably experi-

enced before a performance. Her father appeared from
backstage, attired in the period costume of a Danish
nobleman. His hands lightly touched her shoulders.

"You look beautiful," he said softly. "Your mother
would have been proud of you."

"If only I had Mama's voice. I feel so . . . inade-
quate."

"Simply remember what your mother taught you.
You'll do fine, my dear. I know you will."

Her mother had had an operatic voice, with the range
of a soprano. Lillian's voice was lower, a husky alto,
and her mother had taught her how to stay within her
range, lend deeper emotion to the lyrics. Yet she never
failed to draw the comparison with her mother, and in
her mind she fell short. On her best nights, she was
merely adequate.

The chorus line came romping offstage. The curtain
swished closed, and Lou Gordon stepped before the
footlights, briefly introducing his new headliner act.
When the curtain opened, Lillian was positioned center
stage, her hands folded at her waist. By contrast with
the chorus girls, she looked innocent, somehow virginal.
The orchestra came up softly as she opened with *Darling Nelly Gray.*

> *There's a low green valley*
> *On the old Kentucky shore*
> *There I've whiled happy hours away*
> *Sitting and singing by the cottage door*
> *Where lived my darling Nelly Gray*

Something extraordinary happened. A hushed silence
fell over the audience as her clear alto, pitched low and

intimate, filled the hall. She acted out the song with poignant emotion, and her sultry voice somehow gave the lyrics a haunting quality. She sensed the cowhands were captivated, and she saw Wild Bill Hickok watching intently from the back of the theater. She played it for all it was worth.

> *Oh, my darling Nelly Gray*
> *Up in heaven there they say*
> *They'll take you from me no more*
> *I'm coming as angels clear the way*
> *Farewell now to the old Kentucky shore*

There was hardly a dry eye in the house. The Texans were Southerners, many having served under the Confederate flag during the late war. They were caught up in a melancholy tale that was all the more sorrowful because of Lillian's striking good looks. She held them enthralled to the last note, and then the theater vibrated to rolling applause. She took a bow and bowed a final time before disappearing into the wings. The Texans chanted their approval.

"Lilly! Lilly! Lilly!"

The curtain closed as the clamor died down. Gordon again appeared before the footlights, announcing that the famed thespian Alistair Fontaine would now render a soliloquy from Shakespeare's masterpiece *Hamlet*. A moment later the curtain opened with Fontaine at center stage, bathed in the cider glow of a spotlight from the rear of the theater. He struck a classic profile, arresting in the costume of a Danish prince. His voice floated over the hall in a tragic baritone.

> *To be, or not to be: that is the question:*
> *Whether 'tis nobler in the mind to suffer*
> *The slings and arrows of outrageous fortune,*
> *Or to take arms against a sea of troubles,*
> *And by opposing end them? To die, to sleep . . .*

The cowhands in the audience traded puzzled glances. They knew little of Shakespeare and even less of some strangely dressed character called Hamlet. Though they tried to follow the odd cadence of his words, the meaning eluded them. Fontaine doggedly plowed on, aware that they were restive and quickly losing interest. He ended the passage with a dramatic gesture, his features grimly stark in the spotlight. The Texans gave him a smattering of polite applause.

The finale of the show was a one-act melodrama titled *A Husband's Vengeance*. Chester played the husband and Lillian, attired in a cheap print dress, the attractive wife. Fontaine, following a quick change from Danish prince to top-hatted villain, played a lecherous landlord. In Scene 1, Chester and Lillian's love-struggling-against-poverty was established for the audience. In Scene 2, with the husband off at work, the lustful landlord demanded that the wife surrender her virtue for the overdue rent or be evicted. The crowd hissed and booed the villain for the cad he was.

Scene 3 brought the denouement. Chester returned from work to discover the landlord stalking his wife around the set, with the bed the most prominent item of furniture in the shabby apartment. The husband, properly infuriated, flattened Fontaine with a mighty punch and bodily tossed him out the door. The cowhands jumped to their feet, whooping and hollering, cheering the valorous conquest of good over evil. Then, to even greater cheers, the curtain closed with Chester and Lillian clinched in a loving embrace. The crowd went wild.

The show might have ended there. But the Texans almost immediately resumed their chant. They stood, shouting and stomping, the jingle of their spurs like musical chimes. Their voices were raised in a collective roar.

"We want Lilly! We want Lilly! We want Lilly!"

Lou Gordon hastily improvised an encore. After a hurried backstage conference with Lillian, he ran out to distribute sheet music to the orchestra. Some minutes later the curtain opened with Lillian center stage, still costumed in the cheap print dress. A hush settled over the audience as violins' from the orchestra came up on *Take Back the Heart*. Her dulcet voice throbbed with emotion.

> *Take back the heart that thou gavest*
> *What is my anguish to thee?*
> *Take back the freedom thou cravest*
> *Leaving the fetters to me*
> *Take back the vows thou hast spoken*
> *Fling them aside and be free*
> *Smile o'er each pitiful token*
> *Leaving the sorrow for me*

The ballad went on with the story of unrequited love. By the time she finished the last stanza, hardened Texans were sniffling noisily and swiping at tears. Their thoughts were on mothers and sisters, and girlfriends left behind, and there was no shame among grown men that night. Lillian bowed off the stage to tumultuous applause.

Gordon caught her as she stepped into the wings. "Little lady, from now on you're Lilly Fontaine! You hear what I'm saying—*Lilly Fontaine!*"

Lillian was in a daze. Her father was waiting as she turned backstage. He enfolded her into his arms, holding her close. His voice was a whisper.

"Thou art thy mother's glass, and she in thee calls back the lovely April of her prime."

"Oh, Papa!" She hugged him tightly. "You know that's my favorite of all the sonnets."

Fontaine grinned. "Your mother and the Bard would be proud of you."

She desperately hoped it was true.

Hickok was waiting at the stage door. The alleyway was deep in shadow, faintly lighted by a lamppost from the street. He knuckled the brim of his hat.

"Evenin'," he said pleasantly. "You folks put on a mighty good show. Liked it a lot."

"Why, thank you, Marshal," Fontaine said. "We're delighted you enjoyed yourself."

Hickok shrugged. "Figured I'd see you back to your hotel. Things get a little testy on the streets this late at night."

"How kind of you, Marshal. As it happens, Mayor McCoy invited Chester and myself for a drink. Perhaps you wouldn't mind escorting Lillian."

Joseph McCoy, the town founder, was also Abilene's mayor. His invitation, extended backstage following the show, did not include Lillian. Women of moral character never patronized saloons.

"Be an honor, ma'am," Hickok said, nodding to Lillian. "A lawman don't often get such pleasurable duty."

Lillian batted her eyelashes. "How very gallant, Marshal."

On the street, Fontaine and Chester turned north toward the Alamo Saloon. The Alamo catered to wealthy Texas cattlemen and local citizens of means. Lillian and Hickok walked south along the boardwalk.

"Tell me, Marshal," Lillian said, making conversation. "Have you been a peace officer very long?"

"A spell," Hickok allowed. "I was sheriff over at Hays City before I came here. How about you?"

"Pardon?"

"How long you been in variety work?"

"Oh, goodness, all of my life. I was born in the theater."

Hickok looked at her. "You was *born* in a theater?"

"A figure of speech," Lillian said gaily. "I started on the stage when I was five. The theater's all I've ever known."

"Well, now, don't that beat all."

A young man stopped in front of them. He was dressed in cowboy gear, a pistol holstered at his side. His eyes were cold slate blue, and Lillian placed him at about her own age. He gave Hickok a lopsided smile.

"How's tricks, Wild Bill?"

"Tolerable, Wes," Hickok said shortly. "You stayin' out of trouble?"

"Yeah, I'm on my good behavior. Wouldn't do to get on your bad side, would it now?"

"Never figured you any other way."

"Well, I'll see you around, Marshal. Don't take any wooden nickels."

The young man stepped around them, never once looking at Lillian. As they moved on, she darted a glance at Hickok. His expression was somber.

"How strange," she said. "I really don't think he likes you."

"Miss Lillian, the feeling's mutual."

"Who is he?"

"John Wesley Hardin," Hickok said. "Got himself a reputation as a gunman down in Texas. I warned him to mind his manners here in Abilene."

"Gunman?" Lillian said, shocked. "You mean he killed someone?"

"More'n one, so folks say."

"He doesn't look old enough."

"They raise'em quick in Texas."

Hickok bid her good night in the lobby of the Drover's Cottage. From her father she knew that Hickok himself was a notorious gunman. Apparently, a raft of dime novels had been written about his exploits on the frontier, dubbing him the "Prince of Pistoleers." She wondered how many men he had killed.

Upstairs, she undressed and changed into a nightgown. She got into bed, too exhilarated for sleep, remembering the applause. In her most fanciful dreams, she would never have imagined the reception she'd received tonight. The thought of men shedding tears at the sound of her voice made her shiver. She closed her eyes and fervently prayed it would last. An image of her mother formed. . . .

A gunshot brought her out of bed. She realized she'd fallen asleep, dreaming of her mother. There was no noise from the street, and she thought it must be late.

She went to the window, still confused by the gunshot, and looked out. Three rooms down from hers, she saw a man leap from the window and land heavily on the boardwalk. He jumped to his feet.

The spill of light from a lamppost momentarily froze his features. She recognized him as the young man she'd seen earlier, John Wesley Hardin. She saw now that he appeared disheveled, shirttail flapping, boots in one hand, his pistol in the other. He searched the street in both directions, spotting no one, and then sprinted off in his stocking feet. He disappeared around the corner.

Some minutes later she heard voices in the hall. She opened the door a crack and saw her father and Chester, barefoot, their nightshirts stuffed into their trousers. Other men, similarly awakened from sleep, were gathered before a door two rooms down from hers. They all turned as Hickok pounded up the stairs into the hall, his gun drawn. He brushed past them, entering the darkened room. A moment later lamplight glowed from the doorway.

"Good Lord!" her father exclaimed. "He's been shot."

Hickok stepped out of the room. His features were grim as he looked around at the men. "Anybody see what went on here?"

There were murmurs of bewilderment, men shaking their heads. Then, stuffing his pistol back in his sash, Hickok saw Lillian peering out of her door. He walked down the hall.

"Miss Lillian," he said. "Some poor devil's been shot and killed in his own bed. You hear anything unusual?"

"I saw him," Lillian said on an indrawn breath. "The gunshot awoke me and I went to my window. It was the young Texan you and I met on the street earlier. He leapt out the window of his room."

"You talkin' about Wes Hardin?"

"Yes, the one you said was a gunman."

"Where'd he go?"

"Why, he ran away," Lillian replied. "Around the corner, by the mercantile store."

"I'm most obliged for your help."

Hickok hurried to the stairwell. Fontaine and Chester, who were listening to the conversation, entered her room. She explained how she'd met Hardin and later recognized him as he fled the hotel. Fontaine slowly wagged his head.

"I'm sorry, my dear," he said, clearly shaken. "I've brought you to a place where murderers lodge just down the hall."

"Oh, Papa," she said quickly. "You mustn't blame yourself. It might have happened anywhere."

"I am reminded of the Bard by this dreadful affair. 'As flies to wanton boys, are we to the gods; they kill us for their sport.' "

Chester snorted. "Shakespeare should have seen Abilene!"

Several days later they learned the truth. John Wesley Hardin, after a drunken night on the town, was annoyed by the rumbling snores of a hotel guest in the next room. Hardin fired through the wall and killed the man where he lay fast asleep. Then, rather than face Hickok, he fled on foot to a cowcamp outside Abilene. From there, he made good his escape to Texas. He was eighteen years old.

Lillian, thinking back on it, was struck by how very little changed with time. Shakespeare, nearly three centuries before, had penned an axiom for all time.

Wanton boys, like the gods, still killed for sport.

CHAPTER 4

A BRILLIANT sun stood fixed at its zenith. The weather was moderate for late September, with cottony clouds drifting westward against an azure sky. The bawling of cows was constant from the stockyards near the railroad siding.

Hickok arrived at the hotel shortly before one o'clock. Lillian was waiting in the lobby, wearing a corded cotton dress with delicate stripes worked into the fabric. She carried a parasol and wore a chambray bonnet that accentuated her features. She gave him a fetching smile as he tipped his hat.

"I see you're punctual, as always."

"Never keep a lady waiting," Hickok said smoothly. "All ready to see the sights?"

"Oh, yes, I'm so looking forward to it."

Outside, on the boardwalk, she took his arm. They drew stares from passersby as they walked south along Texas Street. After a fortnight at the Comique, Lillian was the talk of the town. The *Abilene Courier* referred to her as a "chanteuse," and beguiled cowhands flocked to her performances. The theater was sold out every night.

The town was no less interested in her curious relationship with Hickok. He was a womanizer of some renown, having carried on liaisons with several ladies since arriving in Abilene. Even more, at thirty-four, he was fifteen years Lillian's senior, and the difference was the source of considerable gossip. Yet, for all anyone could tell, it was a benign relationship. Hickok appeared the perfect gentleman.

Lillian was attracted to him in the way a moth flirts with flame. She knew he was dangerous, having been informed by her father that he had killed at least a dozen men, not including Indians. He was a former army scout and deputy U.S. marshal and lionized by the press as the West's foremost "shootist." The term was peculiar to the frontier, reserved for those considered to be mankillers of some distinction. Other men crossed him at their own peril.

For all that, Lillian found him to be considerate and thoughtful, gentle in a roughhewn sort of way. Her father at first forbade her to see Hickok, and she deflected his protests with kittenish artifice. She was intrigued as well by Hickok's reputation as a womanizer, for she had never known a lothario, apart from Shakespeare's plays. One of the chorus girls at the Comique told her Hickok had lost his most recent lady friend to a Texas gambler named Phil Coe. Lillian thought, perhaps, the loss accounted for his courtly manner. He was, she sensed, a lonely man.

Every night, Hickok escorted her from the theater back to the Drover's Cottage. There, assured she was safe, he left her in the lobby and went about his duties as marshal. On three occasions, before the evening show at the Comique, he had invited her to dinner at the restaurant in the hotel. Today, leaving his deputy, Mike Williams, to police Abilene, he had invited her for an afternoon ride in the country. They had never been alone together or far from her father's sight, and she somehow relished the experience. She felt breathlessly close to the flame.

The owner of the livery stable was a paunchy man, bald as a bullet. He greeted Hickok with a nervous grin and led them to the rig, hired for the afternoon. Hickok assisted her into the buggy, which was drawn by a coal black mare with ginger in her step. He had a good hand with horses, lightly popping the reins, urging the mare along at a brisk clip. They drove east from town, on a wagon trace skirting the Smoky Hill and the Kansas Pacific tracks. Dappled sunlight filtered through tall cottonwoods bordering the river.

On the southeast corner of the town limits, they passed what was derisively known as the Devil's Addition. Abilene, with hordes of randy cowhands roaming the streets, attracted prostitutes in large numbers. The decent women of the community, offended by the revelry, demanded that the mayor close down the bordellos. Joseph McCoy, ever the pragmatist and fearful of inciting the Texans, banished the soiled doves instead to an isolated red-light district. The cowhands simply had to walk a little farther to slake their lust.

Lillian stared straight ahead as they drove past the brothels. She was no innocent, even though she had managed to retain her virginity despite the advances of handsome and persuasive admirers on the variety circuit. She knew men consorted with prostitutes and that the world's oldest profession could be traced to biblical times. Sometimes, wakeful in the dark of night, she tried to imagine what services the girls provided to their clientele. She often wished she could be a fly on the wall, just for a moment. She thought she might learn wicked and exotic secrets.

One secret she already knew. Her mother had taught her that the way to a man's heart was through his vanity. Men loved nothing quite so much as talking about themselves and their feats, imagined or otherwise. A woman who was a good listener and expressed interest captivated men by the sound of their own voices. Lillian had found what seemed an eternal axiom to be no less true with Wild Bill Hickok. She turned to him now.

"I've been wondering," she said with an engaging smile. "Why do people call you Wild Bill?"

"Well," Hickok said, clearly pleased by her interest. "One time durin' the war I had to fight off a passel of Rebs and swim a river to make my escape. The Federal boys watchin' from the other side was plumb amazed. They up and dubbed me Wild Bill."

"What a marvelous story!"

"Yeah, ceptin' my name's not Bill. It's James."

"James?" Lillian said, looking properly confused. "Why didn't they call you Wild *Jim?*"

"Never rightly knew," Hickok said. "The name stuck and I've been tagged with it ever since. Finally got wore out tryin' to set folks straight."

"I think James is a fine name."

"So'd my ma and pa."

Lillian urged him on. "So you were with the Union army?"

"Worked mostly as a scout behind enemy lines. The Rebs would've shot me for a spy if I'd ever got caught."

"How exciting!"

Hickok brought the buggy to a halt. They were stopped on a low bluff, overlooking the river and the prairie. The grasslands stretched endlessly in the distance, broken only by the churned earth of the Chisholm

Trail. A herd of longhorns, choused along by cowhands, plodded north toward Abilene.

"How beautiful!" she said. "I wish I were a painter."

"You're mighty pretty yourself." Hickok casually placed his arm on top of the seat behind her. "Somebody ought to paint you."

Lillian felt his fingers brush her shoulder. She thought she might allow him to kiss her, and then, just as quickly, she changed her mind. She knew he wouldn't be satisfied with a kiss.

"I'm simply fascinated by your work," she said, shifting slightly in the seat. "Do you enjoy being a peace officer?"

The question distracted Hickok. She seemed genuinely interested, and young as she was, she was probably impressionable. Talking about himself might lead to more than a kiss.

"Guess every man's got his callin'," he said with a tinge of bravado. "Turns out I'm good at enforcin' the law."

"Yes, but everyone out here carries a gun. Aren't you sometimes afraid . . . just a little?"

Hickok explained the code of the West. There were no rules that governed conduct in a shootout, except the rule of fairness: A man could not fire on an unarmed opponent or open fire without warning. Apart from that, every man looked for an edge, some slight advantage. The idea was to survive with honor intact.

"Not likely I'll ever be beat," he bragged. "Don't you see, I've already got the edge over other men. I'm Wild Bill."

Lillian at first thought he was joking. But then she realized he was serious, deadly serious. She wished her mother were there, for how they would have laughed. Wild Bill Hickok proved the point.

No man, given an attentive female, could resist tooting his own horn.

The spotlight bathed Lillian in an umber glow. She stood poised at center stage, the light caressing her features, the audience still. The house was again sold out, and every cowhand in the theater stared at her with a look of moony adoration. The orchestra glided into *The Rose of Killarney* as her voice filled the hall.

> *There's a spot in old Ireland still dear to my*
>   *heart*
> *Thousands of miles 'cross the sea tho I'm*
>   *forced to part*
> *I've a place now in the land of the free*
> *Tho the home there I shall never forget*
> *It brings a tear for thoughts I so regret*
> *When I bid goodbye to the rose of Killarney*

Her eyes roved over the audience. At the rear of the hall, she saw Hickok in his usual post by the door. Even in the midst of the song, she wondered if he regretted the loss of a kiss, having talked about himself all the way back to town. When she finished the last stanza, the crowd whooped and shouted, their hands pounding in applause. The spotlight followed her as she bowed her way offstage.

Fontaine came on next with a piece from *The Merchant of Venice*. The audience slumped into their seats, murmuring their displeasure, as though Shakespeare were an unwelcome guest at an otherwise festive occasion. Then, suddenly, the door at the rear of the hall burst open with a resounding whack. A cowboy, mounted on a sorrel gelding, ducked low through the door and rode down the center aisle. He caterwauled a loud, screeching Rebel yell.

Hickok was only a step behind. He levered himself over the horse's rump with one hand, grabbed a fistful of shirt with the other, and yanked the cowboy out of the saddle. The Texan hit the floor on his back, and as he scrambled to his feet, Hickok thumped him across the head with a pistol. The impact of metal on bone sounded with a mushy *splat*, and a welter of blood geysered out from the cowboy's scalp. He dropped into the arms of a man seated directly beside the aisle.

The horse reared at the railing of the orchestra pit. Terrified, the members of the orchestra dived in every direction, scattering horns and violins. By now thoroughly spooked, the gelding whirled around, wall eyed with fright, and started up the aisle. Hickok stepped aside, whacking him across the rump, and the horse bolted out of the theater. As he went through the door, the Texans in the audience erupted from their seats, angered that Hickok had spoiled the fun. All the more, they were outraged by his treatment of the cowboy.

"You sorry sonovabitch!" someone yelled. "You got yours comin' now!"

A knot of cowhands jammed into the aisle. Hickok backed to the orchestra pit, pulling his other Colt. He leveled the pistols on the crowd.

"Stop right there!" he ordered. "I'll drill the first man that comes any closer."

"You cain't get us all!" one of the cowhands in the front rank shouted. "C'mon, boys, let's rush the Yankee bastard."

A shotgun boomed from the rear of the theater. The Texans turned and saw Hickok's deputy, Mike Williams, standing in the doorway. Plaster rained down from a hole in the ceiling, and he swung the double-barrel scattergun in a wide arc, covering the crowd. Hickok rapped out a command.

"Everybody back in your seats!" he barked. "Any more nonsense and I'll march the whole bunch of you off to jail."

"Yore jail ain't that big, Hickok!"

"Who wants to try me and find out?"

No one seemed inclined to accept the offer. Order was restored within minutes, and the Texans, still muttering, slowly resumed their seats. Hickok walked up the aisle, both pistols trained on the audience, and stopped at the door. Mike Williams, who was a beefy man with a thatch of red hair, gave him a peg-toothed grin. They stood watching as the crowd settled down.

The Fontaines went directly into a melodrama titled *A Dastardly Deed.* When the play was over, Lillian came back onstage alone, for her nightly encore was by now part of the show. In an effort to further dampen the cowhands' temper, she sang their favorite song, *Dixie.* She sang it not as a stirring marching ballad but rather as a plaintive melody. Her voice was pitched low and sad, almost mournful.

> *I wish I was in the land of cotton*
> *Old times there are not forgotten*
> *Look away! Look away! Look away, Dixieland!*

The Texans, unrepentant Confederates to a man, trooped out of the theater in weepy silence. They jammed into saloons along the street, drinking maudlin toasts to the Bonnie Blue Flag and blessing the gracious sentiment of Lilly Fontaine. Some of them, after a few snorts of popskull, wandered off to the Devil's Addition. There they found solace in the arms of whores.

Hickok escorted Lillian, as well as Fontaine and Chester, back to the hotel. He bid them a solemn good night, his features grave, and rejoined Mike Williams on the street. His manner was that of a man off to do battle, and the Fontaines fully expected to hear gunshots before the night was done. They went to their rooms wondering if the Texans would leave well enough alone.

Later, lying awake in the dark, Lillian was reminded of Abilene's former marshal. One of the chorus girls had related the gory end of Hickok's predecessor, Tom Smith. By all accounts a respected peace officer, Smith had gone to arrest a homesteader, Andrew McConnell, on a murder warrant. McConnell waylaid the marshal, grievously wounding him with a Winchester rifle. As Smith lay helpless, McConnell hefted an ax and chopped off his head. Abilene gave the slain lawman a stately funeral.

Lillian shuddered at the image. Still, the grisly death of Tom Smith helped her to better understand Hickok. Tonight's incident at the theater was part and parcel of what he'd tried to explain on their buggy ride that afternoon.

Wild Bill Hickok lived by a code ancient even in olden times: Do unto them before they do unto you.

CHAPTER 5

THE EVENING of October 5 was brisk and clear. A full moon washed the town in spectral light and stars dotted the sky like diamond dust. Texas Street was all but deserted.

A last contingent of cowhands wandered from saloon to saloon. Earlier that day the final herd of longhorns had been loaded at the stockyards and shipped east by train. The trailing season was officially over, for the onset of winter was only weeks away. Two months, perhaps less, would see the plains adrift with snow.

The mood was glum at the Comique. Abilene, the first of the western cowtowns, was sounding the death knell. The railroad had laid track a hundred miles south to Wichita, a burgeoning center of commerce located on the Arkansas River. By next spring, when the herds came north on the Chisholm Trail, Wichita would be the nearest railhead. Abilene would be a ghost town.

Lou Gordon planned to move his operation to Wichita. With the coming of spring, he would reopen the Comique on the banks of the Arkansas and welcome the Texans with yet another variety show. He had offered the Fontaines headliner billing, for Lillian was now a star attraction with a loyal following. But that left the problem of where they would spend the winter and how they would subsist in the months ahead. So far, he'd uncovered only one likely alternative.

Alistair Fontaine was deeply troubled. Though he usually managed a cheery facade, he was all but despondent over their bleak turn of fortune. Upon traveling West, he had anticipated a bravura engagement in Abilene and a triumphant return to New York. Yet his booking agent, despite solid notices in the *Abilene Courier,* had been unable to secure a spot for them on the Eastern variety circuit. A hit show in Kansas kindled little enthusiasm among impresarios on Broadway.

Fontaine saw it as a descent into obscurity. To climb so high and fall so far had about it the bitter taste of ignominy. He'd begun life as John Hagerty, an Irish ragamuffin from the Hell's Kitchen district of New York. Brash and ambitious, he fled poverty by working his way up in the theater, from stagehand to actor. Almost twenty-five years ago, he had adopted the stage name Alistair Fontaine, lending himself an air of culture and refinement. Then, seemingly graced, he had married Estell.

Yet now, after thirty years in the theater, he was reduced to a vagabond. The descent began with Estell's untimely death and the realization that he was, at best, a modest Shakespearian. In Abilene came the discovery that his daughter, though a lesser talent than her mother, nonetheless brought that indefinable magic to the stage. But he hadn't foreseen the vagaries of a celebrated return to New York or the growth of the railroad and the abrupt demise of Abilene. He wasn't prepared to winter in some primitive outpost called Dodge City.

The crowd for tonight's show was sparse. There were fewer than a hundred cowhands still in Abilene and perhaps half that number in the audience. The melodrama finished only moments ago, Fontaine and Chester stood in the wings, watching Lillian perform her encore. For their last night in Abilene, she had selected as her final number a poignant ballad titled *The Wayfarer*. She thought it would appeal to the Texans on their long journey home, south along the Chisholm Trail. Her voice gave the lyrics a sorrowful quality.

> *The sun is in the west,*
> *The stars are on the sea,*
> *Each kindly hand I've pres't,*
> *And now, farewell to thee.*
> *The cup of parting done,*
> *'Tis the darkest I can sip.*
> *I have pledg'd them ev'ry one*
> *With my heart and with my lip.*
> *But I came to thee the last,*
> *That together we might throw*
> *One look upon the past*
> *In sadness ere I go*

On the final note, the cowhands gave her a rousing ovation. They rose, calling out her name, waving good-bye with their broad-brimmed hats. She smiled wistfully, waving in return as the curtain closed, throwing them a kiss at the last moment. Her eyes were misty as she moved into the wings, where Fontaine and Chester waited. She swiped at a tear.

"Oh, just look at me," she said with a catch in her throat. "Crying over a bunch of cowboys."

"Well, it's closing night," Chester consoled her. "You're entitled to a few tears."

"I feel like crying myself," Fontaine grumped. "We've certainly nothing to celebrate."

"Papa!" Lillian scolded gently. "I'm surprised at you. What's wrong?"

"We are not traveling to New York, my dear. To paraphrase Robert Burns, the best laid schemes of mice and men often go awry."

"Yes, but Lou felt almost certain he could arrange a booking in Dodge City. It's not as though we're out of work."

"Dodge City!" Fontaine scoffed. "Gordon seemed quite chary with information about the place. Other than to say it is somewhere—*somewhere*—in western Kansas."

Chester grinned. "Dad, you were talking about a grand adventure when we came out here. This way, we get to see a little more of the West."

"And it's only for the winter," Lillian added. "Lou promised an engagement in Wichita in the spring."

Fontaine considered a moment. "I've no wish to see more of the West. But your point is well taken." He paused, nodding sagely. "Any engagement is better than no engagement a'tall."

Lou Gordon appeared from backstage. Over the course of their month in Abilene, he had become a friend, particularly where Lillian was concerned. He felt she was destined for big things on the variety stage. He extended a telegram to Fontaine.

"Got a wire from Frank Murphy just before the show. He's agreed to book you for the winter."

"Has he indeed?"

Fontaine scanned the telegram. His eyes narrowed. "Two hundred dollars a month! I refuse to work for a pauper's wages."

"Lodging and meals are included," Gordon pointed out. "Besides, Alistair, it's not like you've got a better offer."

"Papa, please," Lillian interceded. "Do we really have a choice?"

"I appear to be outnumbered," Fontaine said. "Very well, Lou, we will accept Mr. Murphy's parsimonious offer. How are we to accomplish this pilgrimage?"

Gordon quickly explained that railroad tracks had not yet been laid into western Kansas. He went on to say that he'd arranged for them to accompany a caravan of freight wagons bound for Dodge City. He felt sure they could make an excellent deal for a buggy and team at the livery stable. With the loss of the cattle trade, everything in Abilene was for sale at bargain prices.

"A buggy!" Fontaine parroted. "Good Lord, I'd given it no thought until now. We'll be sleeping on the *ground*."

"Afraid so," Gordon acknowledged. "You'll be cooking your own meals, too. The hardware store can supply you with camp gear."

"Is there no end to it?" Fontaine said in a wounded voice. "We are to travel like . . . Mongols."

Chester laughed. "No adventure as grand as an expedition. Nostradamus has nothing on you, Dad."

"I hardly predicted a sojourn into the wilderness."

"How marvelous!" Lillian clapped her hands with excitement. "We'll have such fun."

Fontaine arched an eyebrow. He thought perhaps her mother had missed something in her training. There was, after all, a certain limit to hardship.

Overland travel was hardly his idea of fun.

* * *

Hickok checked his pocket watch. He rose from behind his desk in the jailhouse and went out the door. He walked toward the theater.

All evening he'd been expecting trouble. As he passed the Lone Star Saloon, he glanced through the plate glass window. Phil Coe and several cowhands were standing at the bar, swilling whiskey. He wondered if Coe would at last find courage in a bottle.

Their mutual antagonism went back over the summer. Coe was a tinhorn gambler who preyed on guileless cowhands by duping them with friendship and liquor. Hickok, sometime in early July, put out the word that Coe was a cardsharp, the worst kind of cheat. He gulled fellow Texans in crooked games.

The charge brought no immediate confrontation. Hickok heard through the grapevine that Coe had threatened his life, but he suspected the gambler had no stomach for a fight. Coe retaliated instead by charming a saloon girl widely considered to be Hickok's woman and stealing away her affections. The animosity between the men deepened even more.

Word on the street was that the last of the Texans planned to depart town tomorrow. Coe, whose home was in Austin, would likely join them on the long trek down the Chisholm Trail. Without cowhands for him to fleece, there was nothing to hold Coe in Abilene any longer. So it made sense to Hickok that trouble, if it came at all, would come tonight. Coe, to all appearances, was fueling his courage with alcohol.

Hickok turned into the alley beside the Comique. He intended to see Lillian safely back to the hotel, just as he'd done every night since she arrived in Abilene. He planned to apply for the job of marshal in Wichita, and he thought that might have some bearing on their future. Lou Gordon was opening a variety theater there, and Hickok assumed the Fontaines would tag along. He would arrange to talk with her about it in the next day or so. Tonight, given the slightest pretext, he would attend to Phil Coe.

The stage door opened as he moved into the alleyway. Lillian stepped outside, accompanied by her father and brother. He greeted Fontaine and Chester as she waited for him by the door. Her features were animated.

"Aren't you the tardy one," she said with a teasing lilt. "You missed my last performance."

"Not by choice," Hickok begged off. "Had some business that needed tendin'."

"Wait till you hear our news!"

Lillian was eager to tell him about their plans. She fantasized that he would join them on the trip, perhaps become the marshal of Dodge City. She wasn't sure she loved him, for she still had no idea of what love was supposed to feel like. But she was attracted to him, and she knew the feeling was mutual, and she thought there was a good man beneath the rough exterior. A trip west together would make it even more of an adventure.

"What news is that?" Hickok asked.

"Well, we just found out tonight we're going—"

A gunshot sounded from the street. Then, in rapid succession, two more shots bracketed through the still night. Hickok was moving even as the echoes died away.

"Stay here!" he ordered. "Don't go out on the street."

"Where are you—"

"Just stay put!"

Hickok rushed off into the darkness. He moved to the far end of the alley, turning the corner of the building across from the Comique. Headed north, he walked quickly to the rear of the third building and entered the back door of the Alamo Saloon. He hurried through the saloon, startled customers frozen in place as he drew both pistols. He stepped through the front door onto the boardwalk.

Phil Coe stood in the middle of the street. A dead dog lay on the ground at his feet, the earth puddled with blood. He had a bottle in one hand and a gun in the other, bantering in a loud voice with four Texans who were gathered around. He idly waved the bottle at the dog.

"Boys, there lies one tough scutter. Never thought it'd take me three shots to kill a dog."

"Hell, it didn't," one of the cowhands cackled. "You done missed him twice."

"What's going on here, Coe?"

The men turned at the sound of Hickok's voice. He was framed in a shaft of light from the door, the pistols held loosely at his sides. Coe separated from the Texans, a tall man with handsome features, his mouth quirked in a tight smile. He gestured with the bottle.

"No harm done, Marshal," he said. "Just shot myself a dog, that's all."

"Drop your gun," Hickok told him. "You're under arrest."

"What the hell for?"

"Discharging firearms within the town limits."

"Bullshit!" Coe flared. "You're not arresting me for shootin' a goddamn dog."

"I won't tell you again—drop it."

Coe raised his pistol and fired. The slug plucked the sleeve of Hickok's coat and thunked into the saloon door. He extended his right arm at shoulder level and the Colt spat a sheet of flame. Coe staggered backward, firing another round that shattered the Alamo's window. Hickok shot him again.

A crimson starburst spread over the breast of Coe's jacket. His legs tangled in a nerveless dance, and he slumped to the ground, eyes fixed on the starry sky. Footsteps clattered on the boardwalk as a man bulled through a crowd of onlookers, gun in hand, and hurried forward. Hickok caught movement from the corner of his eye, the glint of metal in silvery moonlight. He whirled, reflexes strung tight, and fired.

The man faltered, clutching at his chest, and tumbled off the boardwalk into the street. One of the onlookers, a railroad worker, eased from the crowd and peered down at the body. His face went taut and he turned to Hickok with an accusing stare. "It's Mike Williams!" he shouted. "You've killed your own deputy."

A look of disbelief clouded Hickok's features. He walked to the body and knelt down, pistols dangling from his hands. His hard visage seemed to crack, and he bowed his head, shoulders slumped. The onlookers stared at him in stony silence.

The Fontaines watched from the alleyway. They had witnessed the gunfight, then the senseless death of a man rushing to help his friend. Fontaine was reminded of a Greek tragedy, played out on the dusty street of a cowtown, and Chester seemed struck dumb. Lillian had a hand pressed to her mouth in horror.

Fontaine took her arm. She glanced one last time at Hickok as her father led her away. Chester followed along, still mute, and they angled across the street to the Drover's Cottage. The desk clerk was standing in the door, drawn by the gunshots, on the verge of questioning them. He moved aside as they entered the lobby, reduced to silence by the expression on their faces. They mounted the stairs to their rooms.

Some while later, changed into her nightgown, Lillian crawled in bed. She felt numb with shock, her insides gone cold, and she pulled the covers to her chin. She had never seen a man killed, much less two in a matter of seconds, and the image of it kept flashing through her mind. The spectacle of it, random violence and death, was suddenly too much to bear. She closed her eyes to the terror.

A thought came to her in a moment of revelation. She could never love a man who so readily dealt in killing. The fantasy she had concocted was born of girlish dreams, silly notions about honor and knights of the plains. She saw now that it was all foolish whimsy.

Tomorrow, she would say goodbye to Wild Bill Hickok.

Chapter 6

THE CARAVAN stretched nearly a mile along the river. The broad, rushing waters of the Arkansas tumbled over a rocky streambed that curved southwestward across the plains. A fiery sun tilted lower toward the distant horizon.

Lillian was seated between her father and Chester. She wore a linsey-woolsey dress with a fitted mantle coat that fell below her knees. The men were attired in whipcord trousers, plaid mackinaws, and wide-brimmed slouch hats. They looked like reluctant city folk cast in the role of pioneers.

Their buckboard, purchased in Abilene, was a stout four-wheeled vehicle designed for overland travel. The rig was drawn by a team of horses, one sorrel and one dun, plodding along as though hitched to a plow. The storage bed behind the seat was loaded with camp gear, food crates, and their steamer trunks. The goods were lashed securely and covered with a tarpaulin.

"Ah, for the outdoor life," Fontaine said in a sardonic tone. "My backsides feel as though I have been flailed with cane rods."

Chester, who was driving the buckboard, chuckled aloud. "Dad, you have to look on the bright side. We're almost there."

"How would you know that?"

"One of the teamsters told me this morning."

"Well then, we have it from an unimpeachable source."

"Honestly!" Lillian said with a perky smile. "Why do you complain so, Papa? I've never seen anything so wonderful in my life." She suddenly stopped, pointing at the sky. "There, look!"

A hawk floated past on smothered wings. Beyond, distant on the rolling plains, a small herd of buffalo grazed placidly beneath wads of puffy clouds. The hawk caught an updraft, soaring higher into the sun. Lillian watched it fade away against a lucent sky.

"Oooo," she said softly, her eyes round with wonder. "I think it's all so . . . so magnificent."

"Do you really?" Chester said all too casually. "I'll wager you don't think so when you have to do your business. You sure look mortified, then."

"You're such a ninny, Chester. I sometimes wonder you're my brother."

Her indignation hardly covered her embarrassment. There were fifty-three wagons in the caravan and more than a hundred men, including teamsters, laborers, and scouts. The upshot, when she needed to relieve herself, was scant privacy and a desperate search for bushes along the river. She absolutely dreaded the urge to pee.

Yet, apart from the matter of privacy, she was content with their journey. Fifteen days ago, south of Abilene, they had joined the freight caravan on the Santa Fe Trail. The muleskinners were a rough lot, unaccustomed to having a woman in their company, and at first standoffish. But Josh Ingram, the wagon master, welcomed them into the caravan. He worked for a trading firm headquartered in Independence, Missouri.

The Santa Fe Trail, pioneered in 1821, was a major trading route with the far southwest. The trail began in Independence, crossing the Missouri line, and meandered a hundred-fifty miles across Kansas to the great northern bend of the Arkansas. The trail then followed the serpentine course of the river for another hundred-twenty miles to Fort Dodge and the nearby civilian outpost, Dodge City. From there, the trail wound southwest for some five hundred miles before terminating in Santa Fe, the capital of New Mexico Territory. Hundreds of wagons made the yearly trek over a vast wilderness where no railroads yet existed.

Lillian was fascinated by the grand scheme of the venture. One aspect in particular, the Conestoga wagons, attracted her immediate attention. Over the campfire their first night with the caravan, Josh Ingram explained that the wagons dated back to the early eighteenth century. Developed in the Conestoga River Valley of Pennsylvania, the wagons bore the distinctive touch of Dutch craftsmen. The design, still much the same after a hundred and fifty years, had moved westward with the expansion of the frontier.

The wagon bed, as Ingram later showed her, was almost four feet wide, bowed downward like the hull of a ship. Overall, the wagon was sixteen feet in length, with immense wheels bound by tire irons for navigating rough terrain. The wagon box was fitted with oval wooden bows covered by sturdy canvas, which resulted in the nickname prairie schooner. Drawn by a six-hitch of mules, the wagons regularly carried up to 4,000 pounds in freight. The trade goods ran the gamut from needles and thread to axes and shovels and household furniture.

Late every afternoon, on Ingram's signal, the wagons were drawn into a four-sided defensive square. So far west, there was the constant threat of Indian attack and the imperative to protect the crew as well as the livestock. There were army posts scattered about Kansas, and west of Fort Dodge, where warlike tribes roamed at will, cavalry patrols accompanied the caravan. But an experienced wagon master looked to the defense of his own outfit, and before sundown the livestock was grazed and watered. Then everyone, man and beast, settled down for the night within the improvised stockade.

The Fontaines made their own small campfire every evening. They could have eaten with the crew, for the caravan employed a full-time cook. But the food was only passable, and Lillian, anxious to experience life on the trial, had taught herself to cook over open coals. The company scouts, who killed a couple of buffalo every day to provision the men, always gave Lillian the choice cuts from the hump meat. Chester took care of the horses, and Fontaine, adverse to menial chores of any nature, humbled himself to collect firewood along the river. He then treated himself to a dram from his stock of Irish whiskey.

By sundown, Lillian had the cooking under way. She worked over a shallow pit, ringed with rocks and aglow with coals scooped from the fire. Her battery of cast-iron cookware turned out stews and steaks and sourdough biscuits and an occasional cobbler made from dried fruit. Fontaine, who had appointed himself armorer, displayed a surprising aptitude for the care and cleaning of weapons. In Abilene, the hardware store owner had convinced him that no sane man went unarmed on the plains, and he'd bought two Henry .44

lever-action repeaters. His evening ritual included wiping trail dust from the rifles.

"Fate has many twists," he said, posing with a rifle as he looked around at the camp enclosed by wagons. "I am reminded of a passage from *King Lear*."

Lillian glanced up from a skillet of sizzling steaks. She knew he was performing and she was his audience. "Which passage is that, Papa?"

" 'When we are born we cry that we are come to this great stage of fools.' "

"You believe our journey is foolhardy?"

"We shall discover that by the by," Fontaine said, playing the oracle. "Some harbinger tells me that our lives will never again be the same."

"Evenin', folks."

Josh Ingram stepped into the circle of firelight. He was a large man with weathered features and a soup-strainer mustache. He nodded soberly to Fontaine.

"Figgered I'd best let you know. Our scouts cut Injun sign just before we camped. Wouldn't hurt to be on guard tonight."

Fontaine frowned. "Are we in danger of attack?"

"Never know," Ingram said. "Cheyenne and Kiowa get pretty thick out this way. They're partial to the trade goods we haul."

"Would they attack a caravan with so many men?"

"They have before and they doubtless will again. Don't mean to alarm you overly much. Just wanted you to know."

"We very much appreciate your concern."

Ingram touched his hat, a shy smile directed at Lillian. "Ma'am."

When he walked off, Fontaine stood for a moment with the rifle cradled over his arm. At length, he turned to Lillian and Chester. "I daresay we are in for a long night."

Chester took the other Henry repeater from the buckboard. He levered a shell into the chamber and lowered the hammer. "Wish we had practiced more with these rifles. I'd hate to miss when it counts."

"As the commander at Bunker Hill told his men, wait until you see the whites of their eyes. What worked on British Red Coats applies equally well to redskins."

Lillian thought it a witty pun. She knew her father's levity was meant to allay their fears. She was suddenly quite proud of him.

Alistair Fontaine was truly a man of many parts.

A noonday sun was lodged like a brass ball in the sky. The caravan followed a rutted track almost due west along the river. Scouts rode posted to the cardinal points of the compass.

The Fontaines' buckboard was near the front of the column. Josh Ingram, mounted on a blaze-faced roan, had stopped by not quite an hour ago with a piece of welcome news. He'd told them the caravan, by his reckoning, was less than twenty miles from Fort Dodge. He expected to sight the garrison by the next afternoon.

Lillian breathed a sigh of relief. The likelihood of confronting Indians seemed remote so close to a military post. Even more, from a personal standpoint, she would no longer have to suffer the indignity of squatting behind bushes to relieve herself. Her spirits brightened as she began thinking about the civilized comforts—

A scout galloped hell for leather over a low knoll to the north. He was waving his hat in the air and his bellow carried on the wind. *"Injuns! Injuns!"*

Ingram roared a command at the lead wagon. The teamster sawed hard on the reins and swung his mules off the trail. The wagons behind followed along, the drivers popping their whips, and the column maneuvered between the river and the rutted trace. The lead wagon spliced into the rear wagon minutes later, forming a defensive ring. Chester halted the Fontaines' buckboard in the center of the encircled caravan.

A war party boiled over the knoll even as the men jumped from their wagons. The massed Indians appeared to number a hundred or more, and they charged down the slope, whipping their ponies, at a dead run. The warriors rapidly deployed into a V-shaped formation and fanned out into two wings. They thundered toward the caravan whooping shrill battle cries.

The men behind the barricaded wagons opened fire. Before them, the buckskin-clad horde swirled back and forth, the wings simultaneously moving left and right, individual horsemen passing one another in opposite directions. The warriors were armed for the most part with bows and arrows, perhaps one in five carrying an ancient musket or a modern repeater. A cloud of arrows whizzed into the embattled defenders.

Ingram rushed about the wagons shouting orders. Fontaine instructed Lillian to remain crouched on the far side of the buckboard, where she would be protected from stray arrows. He left her armed with a Colt .32 pocket pistol he'd bought in Abilene, quickly showing her how to cock the hammer. She watched as he and Chester joined the men behind the barricade, shouldering their rifles. Here and there mules fell, kicking in the traces, pincushioned with feathered shafts. The din of gunfire quickly became general.

Ten minutes into the battle the warriors suddenly retreated out of rifle range. Several teamsters lay sprawled on the ground, dead or wounded, and beyond the wagons Lillian saw the bodies of dark-skinned braves. She thought the attack was over and prayed it was so, for neither her father nor Chester had suffered any wounds. Then, with hardly a respite, the Indians tore down off the knoll, again splitting into two formations. Lillian ducked behind the buckboard, peering over the seat, racked with shame and yet mesmerized at the same time. She was struck by something splendid and noble in the savage courage of the Indians.

A man stumbled away from one of the wagons, an arrow protruding from his chest. In the next instant, a lone brave separated from the horde and galloped directly toward the wagons. He vaulted his pony over a team of mules, steel-tipped lance in hand, and landed in the encirclement. All along the line men were firing at him, and Lillian, breath-taken, thought it was the most magnificent act of daring she'd ever seen. Suddenly he spotted her, and without a moment's hesitation he charged the buckboard, lance raised overhead. She froze, ready to crawl beneath the buckboard, and then, witless with fear, cocked the hammer on the small Colt. She closed her eyes and fired as he hurled the lance.

The warrior was flung forward off the back of his pony. He crashed onto the seat of the buckboard, a feather in his hair and a hole in his forehead, staring with dead eyes at Lillian. She backed away, oddly fixated on the war paint covering his face, her hands shaking uncontrollably. She couldn't credit that she had shot him—between the eyes—actually killed a man. The lance quivered in the ground at her side, and she knew she'd been extraordinarily lucky. A mote of guilt drifted through her mind even as she lowered the pistol. Yet she had never felt so exhilarated, so giddy. She was alive.

The Indians seemed emboldened by the one warrior's suicidal charge. Their ponies edged closer to the wagons, and the sky rained wave upon wave of arrows. Here and there a brave would break ranks and charge the defenders, whooping defiance, only to be shot down. But it appeared the Indians were working themselves into a fever pitch, probing for a weak spot in the defenses. There was little doubt that they would attempt to overrun the wagons and slaughter everyone in savage struggle. Then, so abruptly that it confounded defenders and attackers alike, the din of gunfire swelled to a drumming rattle. A bugle sounded over the roar of battle.

The Indians were enveloped from the rear by massed cavalry. Fully two troops of horseback soldiers delivered a withering volley as they closed on the warriors at a gallop. The lines collided in a fearsome clash, and the screams of dying men rose eerily above the clatter of gunfire. Lillian saw a cavalry officer with long golden ringlets, attired in a buckskin jacket, wielding a saber slick with blood. The warriors were caught between the soldiers and a wall of gunfire from the wagons, and scores of red men toppled dead from their ponies. Others broke through the line of blue coats and fled across the plains in disorganized retreat. A small group, surrounded at the center of the fight, was quickly taken prisoner.

One of the captured warriors was tall and powerfully built. His features were broad and coarse, as though adzed from dark wood, and his eyes glittered with menace. Lillian watched, almost transfixed, as the cavalry officer with the golden hair reined through the milling horses and stopped near the tall warrior. He saluted with his bloody saber.

"*Hao,* Santana," he said crisply. "We have you now."

The warrior stared at him with a stoic expression. After a moment, the officer wiped the blood from his saber with a kerchief and sheathed the blade in his saddle scabbard. He spun his horse, a magnificent bay stallion, and rode toward Josh Ingram and the men at the wagons. He reined to a halt, touched the brim of his hat with a casual salute. His grin was that of Caesar triumphant.

"Gentlemen," he said smartly. "The Seventh Cavalry at your service."

"The Seventh!" someone yelled. "You're Custer!"

"I am indeed."

Ingram stepped over a dead mule. "General, I'm the wagon master, Josh Ingram. We're damned glad to see you and your boys. How'd you happen on this here fracas?"

Custer idly waved at the tall warrior. "Mr. Ingram, you are looking at Santana, chief of the Kiowa. We've been trailing him and his war party for near on a week." He paused with an indulgent smile. "You are fortunate we were not far behind. We rode to the sound of gunfire."

"Mighty glad you did, General. We might've lost our scalps."

"Yes, where Santana's concerned, you're entirely correct. He keeps his scalping knife sharply honed."

Lillian had joined her father and Chester. She listened to the conversation while studying the dashing cavalry officer. Finally, unable to contain herself, she whispered to Fontaine, "Who is he, Papa?"

"The greatest Indian fighter of them all, my dear. George Armstrong Custer."

"Thank God he came along when he did."

Fontaine smiled. "Thank God and the Seventh Cavalry."

CHAPTER 7

THE FONTAINES were quartered in a billet normally reserved for visiting officers. There were two bedrooms and a sitting room, appointed in what Lillian assumed was military-issue furniture. She stood looking out the door at the garrison.

Fort Dodge was situated on a bluff overlooking the Arkansas. To her immediate front was the parade ground, and beyond that the post headquarters. Close by were the hospital and the quartermaster's depot and farther on the quarters for married officers. The enlisted men's barracks and the stables bordered a creek that emptied into the river. Everything looked spruce and well tended, orderly.

The caravan, accompanied by the cavalry, had arrived earlier that afternoon. The wagons were now encamped by the river, preparations under way to continue tomorrow on the Santa Fe Trail. Colonel Custer, courteous to a fault, had arranged for the Fontaines to stay the night in the officers' billet. Upon discovering they were actors, he had invited them to his quarters for dinner that evening. He seemed particularly taken with Fontaine's mastery of Shakespeare.

Fontaine, on the way to the fort, had spoken at length about the man many called the Boy General. He informed Lillian and Chester that their host was the most highly decorated soldier of the late Civil War. A graduate of West Point, his gift for tactics and warfare resulted in an extraordinary series of battlefield promotions. From 1862 to 1865, a mere three years, he leaped from first lieutenant to major general. He was twenty-five years old when the war ended.

Gen. Philip Sheridan personally posted Custer to the West following the Civil War. Though his peacetime rank was that of lieutenant colonel, he retained the brevet rank of major general. A splendid figure of a man, he was six feet tall, with a sweeping golden mustache, and wore his hair in curls that fell to his shoulders. He had participated in campaigns against the Plains Tribes throughout Kansas and Nebraska, culminating in a great victory in Indian Territory. There, on the Washita River, Custer and the Seventh Cavalry had routed the fabled Cheyenne.

Josh Ingram, listening to Fontaine's dissertation on Custer, had pointed out a parallel with Santana, the Kiowa war chief. His Indian name, *Se-Tain-te*, meant White Bear, bestowed on him after a vision quest. A blooded warrior at twenty, he began leading raids along the Santa Fe Trail and as far south as Mexico. He ranged across the frontier, burning and pillaging, leaving in his path a legion of scalped settlers and dead soldiers. What Custer was to the army Santana was to the Kiowa: a bold, fearless leader who dared anything, no matter the odds.

Lillian, reflecting on it as the sun went down over the parade ground, thought there was a stark difference. Santana, with his four followers who were captured in yesterday's battle, was in chains in the post stockade. George Armstrong Custer, victorious in every battle he'd ever fought, was yet again lauded for his courage in the field. She recalled him saying that he "rode to the sound of gunfire," and she mused that he was a man who thrived on war. She wouldn't be surprised if he one day replaced William Tecumseh Sherman as General of the Army. Custer, too, was a leader who never reckoned the odds.

Capt. Terrance Clark, Custer's adjutant, called for the Fontaines as twilight settled over the post. He was a strikingly handsome man, tall and muscular, resplendent in a tailored uniform. He shook hands with Fontaine and Chester and bowed politely to Lillian. Outside, he offered her his arm and led them across the parade ground in the quickening dusk. His manner somehow reminded her of Adonis, the young hero of Greek mythology. A warrior too handsome for words.

Custer's home was a military-style Victorian, with a pitched roof, square towers, and arched windows. The furniture in the parlor was French Victorian, with a rosewood piano against one wall flanked by a matching harp. The study was clearly a man's room, the walls decorated with mounted heads of antelope and deer and framed portraits of Custer and Gen. Philip Sheridan. The bookshelves were lined with classics, from Homer, to Shakespeare, to James Fenimore Cooper.

Elizabeth Custer was a small, attractive woman, with dark hair and delicate features. She insisted on being called Libbie and welcomed the Fontaines as though she'd never met a stranger in her life. She informed them that she was thrilled to have a troupe of professional actors in her home. Hardly catching her breath, she went on to say that she and the general were amateur thespians themselves. Lillian gathered that Libbie Custer, at least in public, referred to her husband only by rank.

"We have such fun," she rattled on. "Our last playlet was one written by the General himself. And he starred in it as well!"

"Libbie makes too much of it," Custer said with an air of modesty. "We stage amateur theatricals for the officers and their wives. Life on an army post requires that we provide our own entertainment."

"How very interesting," Fontaine observed. "And what was the subject of your production, General?"

Custer squared his shoulders. "I played the part of a Cheyenne war chief and one of the officers' wives played my . . . bride." He paused, suddenly aware of their curious stares. "We depicted a traditional Indian wedding ceremony. All quite authentic."

"I must say that sounds fascinating."

"Hardly in your league, Mr. Fontaine. Perhaps, after dinner, you would favor us with a reading from Shakespeare. We thirst for culture here on the frontier."

Fontaine preened. "I would be honored, General."

"By the by, I forgot to ask," Custer said. "Where will you be performing in Dodge City?"

"We are booked for the winter at Murphy's Exchange."

Fontaine caught the look that passed between Custer and his wife. Lillian saw it as well, and in the prolonged silence that followed she rushed to fill the void. Her expression was light and gay.

"We so wanted to see something of the frontier. And the timing is perfect, since we're between engagements until next spring. We open then at the Comique Theater in Wichita."

A manservant saved the moment. He appeared in the doorway of the dining room, dressed in a white jacket and blue uniform trousers, and announced dinner. Libbie, ever the gracious hostess, tactfully arranged the seating. Fontaine and Chester were placed on one side of the table, and Lillian was seated on the other, beside Captain Clark. Custer and Libbie occupied opposite ends of the table.

Dinner opened with terrapin soup, followed by a main course of prairie quail simmered in wine sauce. Throughout the meal, the Custers peppered their guests with questions about their life in the theater. Fontaine, though flattered, gradually steered the discussion to Custer's military campaigns against the warlike tribes. The conversation eventually touched on yesterday's engagement with the Kiowa.

"A sight to behold!" Fontaine announced, nodding to Libbie. "Your husband and the Seventh Cavalry at a full charge. I shan't soon forget the spectacle."

"*Au contraire*," Libbie said, displaying her grasp of French. "The General tells me your daughter was the heroine of the day." She cast an almost envious glance at Lillian. "Did you really shoot an Indian, my dear?"

Lillian blushed. "I'll never know how," she said with open wonder. "I closed my eyes when I fired the gun— and then . . . he practically fell in my lap."

Everyone laughed appreciatively at her candid amazement. Lillian was all too aware of Captain Clark's look of undisguised infatuation. He stared at her as if she were a ripe and creamy éclair and he wished he had a spoon. She noted as well that he wore no wedding ring.

After dinner, the men retired to the study for cigars and brandy. Lillian and Libbie conversed about New York and the latest fashions, discreetly avoiding any mention of the Fontaines' upcoming appearance at Murphy's Exchange. A short while later, the men joined them in the parlor. Captain Clark, rather too casually, took a seat beside Lillian on the sofa.

Fontaine required no great coaxing to perform. He positioned himself by the piano, his gaze fixed on infinity, and delivered a soliloquy from *King Richard II*. Custer and Libbie applauded exuberantly when he finished, congratulating him on the nuance of his interpretation. Then, with Libbie playing the piano, Lillian sang one of the day's most popular ballads. Her voice filled the parlor with *'Tis Sweet to Be Remembered*.

Terrance Clark watched her as though he'd seen a vision.

Dodge City was five miles west of Fort Dodge. A sprawling hodgepodge of buildings, it was inhabited principally by traders, teamsters, and buffalo hunters. Thousands of flint hides awaited shipment by wagon to the nearest railhead.

Late the next morning, when the Fontaines drove into town, they were dismayed by what they saw. Nothing had prepared them for a ramshackle outpost that looked as though it had been slapped together with spit and poster glue. Abilene, by comparsion, seemed like a megalopolis.

"To paraphrase the Bard," Fontaine said in a dazed voice. "I have ventured like wanton boys that swim on bladders. Far beyond my depth, my high-blown pride at length broke under me."

Chester nodded glumly. "Dad, no one could have said it better. We'll be lucky if we don't drown in this sinkhole."

The permanent population of the Dodge City looked to be something less than 500. At one end of Front Street, the main thoroughfare, were the Dodge House Hotel and Zimmerman's Hardware, flanked by a livery stable. Up the other way was a scattering of saloons, two trading companies, a mercantile store, and a whorehouse. The town's economy was fueled by buffalo hunters and troopers of the Seventh Cavalry. Whiskey and whores were a profitable enterprise on the edge of the frontier.

Fontaine directed Chester to the Dodge House. There were no porters, and they were forced to unload the buckboard themselves. Fortunately, it was a one-story building, and after registering with the desk clerk, they were able to slide their steamer trunks through the hall. Their rooms were little more than cubicles, furnished with a bed, a washstand, one chair, and a johnny pot. The clerk informed them the johnny pots would be emptied every morning.

Still shaking his head, Fontaine instructed Chester to take the buckboard to the livery stable. He expressed the view that it would not be prudent as yet to sell the horses and the buckboard. Their escape from Gomorrah, he noted dryly, might well depend on a ready source of transport. An hour or so later, after unpacking and changing from their trail clothes, they emerged from the hotel with their trepidation still intact. The men were attired in conservative three-piece suits and the Western headgear they had adopted while in Abilene. Lillian wore a demure day dress and a dark woolen shawl.

Murphy's Exchange was located across from one of the trading companies. Three buffalo hunters, lounging out front, gave them a squinted once-over as they

moved through the door. The establishment was a combination saloon, dance hall, and gaming dive. Opposite
a long mahogany bar were faro layouts and poker tables. A small stage at the rear overlooked a dance floor,
with a piano player and a fiddler providing the music.
Saloon girls in full war paint mingled with the crowd.

All conversation ceased as the soldiers and hide hunters treated Lillian to a slow inspection. She had the
sinking sensation that they were undressing her with
their eyes, layer by layer. Frank Murphy, the proprietor,
walked forward from the end of the bar. He was a toadish man, short and stout, with jowls covered by mut-
tonchop whiskers. His jaw cranked in a horsey smile,
revealing a gold tooth, as he stopped in front of them.
He regarded the finery of their clothes.

"From your duds," he said, flashing his gold tooth,
"I'd say you're the Fontaines. Welcome to Dodge City."

"Thank you so much," Fontaine replied. "Our arrival
was delayed by a slight skirmish with Kiowa brigands."

"Yeah, the word's all over town. Custer and his boys
pulled your fat out of the fire, huh?"

"An apt if somewhat colloquial description."

"Well, you're here now and that's all that counts."

"Indeed we are."

Fontaine stared a moment at the miniature stage. His
arm swept the room with a patrician gesture. "There is
no sin but to be rich; there is no vice but beggary."

"Uh-huh," Murphy said, stroking his whiskers. "That
wire I got about you folks, from Lou Gordon? He said
you was partial to Shakespeare."

"Yes, I understand, Mr. Murphy. For the sake of your
clientele, tread lightly with the verse."

"I guess it's sort of like bitin' into a green persimmon. A little bit goes a long ways."

"A green persimmon?" Fontaine said thoughtfully. "I've not heard the expression before. Is it a bitter fruit?"

"Right tasty when they're ripe," Murphy said. "A green one'll make your mouth pucker up worse'n wormwood."

"I have no doubt you dispense sound advice, Mr. Murphy. However, from the look of your customers, a dab of culture and a hot bath would do wonders. Charity demands that I acquaint them with the Bard."

"Don't say I didn't warn you."

"Consider your duty done."

Murphy turned his attention to Lillian. "You must be Lilly, the singer Gordon told me about. His wire said you're better'n good."

"How nice of him," Lillian said with a dimpled smile. "I'll certainly do my best, Mr. Murphy."

"Hope you've got some racy numbers in your songbook. The boys don't come here for church hymns."

"I sing all the popular ballads. The audiences in Abilene weren't disappointed."

"Hide hunters are a rougher lot than cowhands. Maybe just a little something off-color?"

"No, I'm afraid not."

"Too bad." Murphy examined her outfit. "Maybe you've got a dress that don't dust the floor. The boys like to see some ankle."

Lillian glanced at her father, clearly uncomfortable. Fontaine quickly intervened. "We are what we are, Mr. Murphy. Neither ribald nor risqué is included in our repertoire."

Murphy considered a moment. He thought he'd made a bad deal but saw no practical remedy. October was almost gone, and the chances of importing another act for the winter were somewhere between slim and none. He decided there was nothing for it.

"Guess we'll have to make do," he grouched. "I'm a man of my word, so I'll still pick up the tab for your lodging and your eats. Just try to gimme a good show."

"Have no fear," Fontaine said stiffly. "We never fail to entertain."

Outside, Fontaine led the way back toward the hotel. Lillian and Chester were silent, aware that his dour mood had turned even darker. He finally grunted a saturnine laugh. His expression was stolid.

"I believe our employer lacks confidence."

"Who cares?" Chester said. "We're a far cry from Broadway."

"You miss the point entirely, my boy."

"What point is that?"

"We are the Fontaines, and we thrive on challenge. Need I say more?"

Lillian thought that said it all.

CHAPTER 8

FONTAINE PROVED to a prophet. By the end of the week, Murphy's Exchange was the most popular spot in town. The other saloons were all but empty.

Every night, at show time, the house was packed. The audience, mainly buffalo hunters and soldiers, suffered through Shakespeare with only occasional jeers. The melodrama usually held their interest, though that was hardly the reason for their presence. They were there to see Lilly Fontaine.

Frank Murphy was the most amazed man in town. To his profound shock, he discovered that burly cavalrymen and rancid-smelling hide hunters all had a soft spot. A tender ballad, sung by a young innocent with the face of an angel, left them a-sea in memories of lost and long-ago yesterdays. Even the saloon girls wept.

The nature of the men made it all the more astounding. Buffalo hunters, who traveled where others feared to tread, lived from day to day. They wandered the plains, constantly under the threat of Indian attack, for they killed the beasts that were the very sustenance of nomadic tribes. The horse soldiers, even more inured to brutality, were in the business of killing Indians. Sentiment seemed lost in the scheme of things.

Yet none among them was so hardened that memory of gentler times failed. All of which made Frank Murphy the happiest saloonkeeper in Dodge City. Winters were harsh on the plains, with blizzards that sometimes left the land impassable, locked in snow and ice. The freezing cold drove men into town, often for weeks on end, seeking sanctuary from polar winds howling out of the north. The longer they stayed, the more they spent, and Murphy saw it as the winter of great fortune. He'd cornered the trade with Lilly Fontaine.

Lillian sometimes felt guilty. She was flattered by all the attention and adored the appreciative cheers of men who watched her perform. But she was saddened for her father, whose love of Shakespeare played to an unreceptive audience. He jokingly referred to them as "buffoons and jackanapes" and tried to slough off their indifference with nonchalant humor. Still, she knew he was disheartened, often embittered, while at the same time he gloried in her success. Her father's pride merely served to underscore her guilt.

On Monday morning, Fontaine's pride was put to the test. They were in his room, rehearsing the lines of a new melodrama he'd written, when someone knocked on the door. Fontaine moved across the room, opening the door, freshly inked script still in hand. A portly man in a checkered suit stood in the hallway.

"Mr. Fontaine," he said, "I'm Joe Porter. I own the Lucky Star Saloon and I'd like to talk to you."

"May I inquire the purpose of your call, Mr. Porter?"

"Let's just say it's a private matter. I'd sooner not discuss it standin' here in the hall. Could I come in a minute?"

"Of course."

Fontaine held the door. Porter entered, hat in hand, nodding mechanically to Chester. He smiled warmly at Lillian. "Miss Fontaine, a pleasure to see you."

"How may we assist you?" Fontaine asked. "I believe you said it was a private matter."

"Well, sir, just to be truthful, it's a business matter. I'd like to hire you folks over to the Lucky Star."

"As you must know, we are currently engaged."

"Yessir," Porter confirmed. "Everybody in a hundred miles knows about your daughter. And you and your boy, too, naturally."

Fontaine pursed his mouth. "I believe that rather nicely covers it, Mr. Porter."

"No, not just exactly it don't. What would you say if I was to offer you twice what Frank Murphy's payin' you?"

"I would have to say . . . no, thank you."

"Then name your price, if that ain't enough. I'd pay pretty near anything to have your girl singin' at the Lucky Star."

"Mr. Porter."

"Yeah?"

"We are not available," Fontaine said firmly. "We accepted a winter's engagement at Murphy's Exchange. We intend to honor our commitment."

"Look here," Porter insisted. "Your girl's runnin' the rest of us saloon owners out of business. We don't get no trade till your show's over every night. It just ain't fair."

"I most sincerely regret the inconvenience."

"Hell's bells, you gotta have a price! Name it!"

"Good day, Mr. Porter."

Fontaine opened the door. Porter gave him a look of bewildered disbelief, then marched out with a muttered curse. When the door closed, Fontaine turned back into the room. His gaze settled on Lillian.

"You appear to have the town bedazzled, my dear."

"I'm sorry, Papa," she said, genuinely contrite. "So very sorry."

"Never apologize for your talent. You deserve all the accolades one might imagine."

"What about the money?" Chester interjected. "Porter would have paid through the nose. We may never get another offer like that."

Fontaine smiled. "I daresay Mr. Murphy will be open to renegotiation. He most certainly will not be pleased, but then . . . business is business."

There were no secrets in a small town. Joe Porter made the mistake of grumbling about his unsatisfactory meeting with the Fontaines. The news spread on the moccasin telegraph, and Frank Murphy heard of it long before the noon hour. He took it as a personal affront.

"Tryin' to steal away my trade!" he huffed to one of the bartenders. "I always knew Joe Porter was a no-good sonovabitch."

Murphy's Exchange and the Lucky Star were located catty-corner from each other on Front Street. Porter, as was his custom, took his noon meal at the Silver Dollar Café, three doors down from his establishment. Shortly before one o'clock, he emerged from the café and turned upstreet. He had a toothpick wedged in the corner of his mouth.

Murphy stepped from the door of his saloon. He held a Colt Navy revolver at his side, and cognizant of the rules in such affairs, he prudently avoided being tagged a bushwhacker. He issued the proper warning to his opponent.

"Porter!" he shouted. *"Defend yourself!"*

Porter, taken by surprise, nonetheless reacted with dispatch. His stout legs pumping, he sprinted along the boardwalk as he drew a pistol from his waistband. Murphy fired, imploding a storefront window, and Porter winged a wild shot in return. He barreled through the door of the Lucky Star, diving for cover. Murphy wisely retreated within his own saloon.

The gunfight soon evolved into siege warfare. Murphy and Porter, after emptying their revolvers, switched to repeating rifles. They banged away at one another with more spirit than accuracy, bullets whizzing back and forth across the intersection. All along Front Street people took cover in saloons and dance halls, watching the duel as though it were some new and titillating spectator sport. By two o'clock, the windows in both Murphy's Exchange and the Lucky Star were reduced to shards of glass.

There was no law in Dodge City. The town was not incorporated and lacked either a city council or a town marshal. Law enforcement was the province of deputy U.S. marshals, who only occasionally wandered into western Kansas. An hour or so into the siege, someone decided a stray bullet would eventually claim the life of an innocent bystander. The military seemed the most likely solution, and a rider was dispatched to Fort Dodge. The onlookers settled down to await developments.

Capt. Terrance Clark, at the head of a cavalry troop, rode into town late that afternoon. He dismounted the company, stationing troopers armed with Springfield rifles around the intersection. The sight of fifty soldiers and the threat of military reprisal got the attention of Murphy and Porter. Clark arranged a cease-fire and then, ordering the saloonkeepers to lay down their arms, coaxed them into the street. There he negotiated a truce, which concluded with the two men reluctantly shaking hands. The onlookers applauded the end of what would later be called the Darlin' Lilly War.

Before departing town, Captain Clark seized the opportunity to call on Lillian at the hotel. She was already aware of the reason for the shooting and highly embarrassed rather than flattered. Yet her spirits were restored when he invited her to a military ball, two weeks hence at Fort Dodge. She was planning her wardrobe before he was out the door.

Terrance Clark, for his part, felt like clicking his heels. He'd taken the first step in his campaign to capture Lilly Fontaine.

> *I have done the state some service, and they*
>   *know 't;*
> *No more of that. I pray you, in your letters,*
> *When you shall these unlucky deeds relate,*
> *Speak of me as I am; nothing extenuate,*
> *Nor set down aught in malice: then, must you*
>   *speak*
> *Of one that lov'd not wisely but too well.*

The lines from *Othello* fell on deaf ears. Fontaine, in blackface and costumed as a Moorish nobleman, wrung agony from every word. The buffalo hunters and soldiers in the audience stared at him as if he were a field slave, strangely dressed and speaking in foreign tongues. He slogged on through the soliloquy.

There were times, alone on the stage, when Fontaine despaired that the majesty of the words had the least effect. He wondered now if the men watching him had any comprehension that he—Othello—had murdered Desdemona, a faithful wife falsely accused of betrayal. He despaired even more that he was acting out the tragedy for an audience of one. Himself.

The crude stage in Murphy's Exchange had no curtain. When he completed his oration, Fontaine paused with dramatic flair and then bowed his way offstage. The crowd, by now resigned to his nightly histrionics, gave him a smattering of applause. The fiddler and the piano player struck up a sprightly tune, allowing him time to run backstage and hurriedly scrub off the blackface. Saloon girls circulated with bee-stung smiles, pushing drinks.

The windows fronting the saloon, now empty holes, had been boarded over. The pitched battle that afternoon was all the talk, and Frank Murphy found himself something of a celebrity. He had, after all, defended what was rightfully his, and other men admired a man who would not tolerate insult. The crowd tonight was even larger than normal, standing-room-only and spilling out onto the boardwalk. Everyone wanted to see the sweet young temptress now known as Darlin' Lilly.

Lillian was repulsed by the whole affair. She thought it sordid and tawdry, and she felt soiled by the nickname bestowed on her just that afternoon. Earlier, when she performed her first number, she'd fixed her gaze on the front wall, ignoring the crowd. Where before she had given them the benefit of the doubt, she suddenly found the men brutish and coarse, rough vulgarians. She felt they stripped her naked with their loutish stares.

The melodrama that evening was titled *The Dying Kiss*. Fontaine, who recognized his limitations as a playwright, had plagiarized freely from Shakespeare's *Romeo and Juliet*. Lillian and Chester played the tragic young lovers, and Fontaine, casting himself as the villain of the piece, played the girl's father. The buffalo hunters and soldiers, caught up in what was a soppy tearjerker, roundly booed Fontaine off the stage. The final scene, when the lovers' suicide left them in eternal embrace, made tough men honk into their kerchiefs. Saloon girls wept so copiously they spoiled their war paint.

The audience gave the cast three curtain calls, albeit sans the curtain. Then, as though the brotherhood of men were of a single mind, they began chanting, *"Lilly! Lilly! Lilly!"* Lillian performed a quick change of costume, slipping into one of her two silk gowns, royal blue with white piping. The piano player and the fiddler, by now thoroughly rehearsed on her numbers, segued into Stephen Foster's immortal classic, *Beautiful Dreamer*. Her voice resonated poignantly through the saloon.

> *Beautiful dreamer, wake unto me*
> *Starlight and dew drops are waiting for thee*
> *Sounds of the rude world heard in the day*
> *Lulled by the moonlight have all passed away*

The crowd hung on her every word. The saloon was still as a church, the men and saloon girls a hushed tableau. Her face was turned as to the heavens and her eyes shone with emotion. On the last note there was an instant of impassioned silence, and then the audience erupted in raucous adulation and cheers. She bowed low, her features radiant.

A buffalo hunter lurched forward from the front of the crowd. His eyes were bloodshot with liquor and he drunkenly hoisted himself onto the stage. He spread his arms wide, reaching for her, and like a bull in rut bellowed, "Darlin' Lilly!" She backed away, unnerved and frightened, moving toward the wings. He lumbered after her.

She saw another man leap over the footlights. His features were wind-seamed, ruggedly forceful under a thatch of sandy hair and a bristling mustache. Though he wasn't a tall man, he was full-spanned through the shoulders, his wrists thick as a singletree. He grabbed the hide hunter by the collar, jerked him around, and lashed out with a splintering blow to the jaw. Clubbed off his feet, the hunter crashed to the floor.

The man stooped down, lifting the drunk by the collar and the seat of the pants. He walked to the footlights, carrying his load like a sack of potatoes, and hurled the buffalo hunter off the stage. Saloon girls squealed and men scattered as the inert form tumbled across the dance floor and skidded to a halt. The crowd roared with laughter as the man on the stage grinned and neatly dusted his hands. Their voices raised in a rowdy chant.

"Cimarron! Cimarron! Cimarron!"

Waving them off, the man turned and strode across the stage. Lillian noted he was dressed in the rough work clothes worn by the other buffalo hunters. But unlike them, his clothing was clean and freshly pressed and he smelled faintly of barber's lotion. His eyes crinkled with amusement as he stopped in front of her. He doffed his hat.

"Sorry for the trouble," he said, holding her gaze. "Some of these boys get liquored up and lose their heads." He paused, still grinning. "I'm Cimarron Jordan."

"How do you do," Lillian said warmly. "You saved me from a most unpleasant experience. Thank you so much."

"Why, anybody would've done the same for a pretty lady like yourself. No thanks necessary."

"Are you a buffalo hunter, Mr. Jordan?"

"That I am," Jordan said with amiable good humor. "Hope you haven't got nothin' against hunters."

"Oh, no, apart from the anarchy of Dodge City. I've never lived in a place where there isn't any law."

"Miss Lilly, you just whistle and I'll be your lawdog. Anytime a'tall."

Lillian sensed the magnetism of the man. He seemed to radiate strength and a quiet, but certain, force of character. She was amazed at herself that she found him attractive, although somewhat rough around the edges. She amazed herself even more by inviting him backstage to meet her father and brother. His unusual name intrigued her as well. Cimarron!

She thought she would ask him about that later.

CHAPTER 9

"I won't have it! Goddammit, it's Saturday night!"

"Lower your voice," Fontaine said curtly. "I will not permit you to curse at my daughter."

Murphy glowered at him. "Why'd she wait till tonight to tell me? I'd like to hear you answer that."

"For the very reason we see exhibited in your behavior. You are an intemperate man."

"You and your highfalutin words. What's that mean?"

"Quite simply, it means you are a hothead. You lack civility."

The Friday night show had concluded only moments ago. Lillian, with her father and Chester still in their melodrama costumes, had caught Murphy backstage. She explained as politely as possible that she had been invited to a military ball tomorrow night, Saturday night, at Fort Dodge. She asked for the night off.

"Tell me this," Murphy said gruffly. "When'd you get this invitation?"

"Two weeks ago," Lillian replied. "The day Captain Clark stopped you from killing Mr. Porter. He asked me while he was in town."

"And you waited till now to tell me?"

"Father has already explained that. I knew you wouldn't be . . . pleased."

"*Pleased!*" Murphy echoed. "You know good and well, Lilly—"

Lillian interrupted him. "I've told you over and over. I will not be called Lilly."

"All right then, Lillian, you know Saturday night's the biggest night of the week. And everybody in town turns out to hear you sing."

"I still have to have the night off."

Lillian was determined. After three weeks in Dodge City, she longed for the refinement and decorum that could be found only at Fort Dodge. Terrance Clark and sometimes Cimarron Jordan occasionally took her for afternoon buggy rides in the country. But she hadn't had a free night since she'd arrived in town. She meant to stand her ground.

"Let's be reasonable," Fontaine interceded. "We have performed every night—including Sunday, I might add—for three weeks running. Lillian deserves a night to herself."

Murphy laughed derisively. "You just don't get it, do you? Lillian's pipes are what draws the crowd. No songs, no crowd, no business!"

"On the contrary," Fontaine said indignantly. "Chester and I are perfectly capable of providing the entertainment for one night. We are, after all, actors."

Chester nodded eagerly. "I can even do a soft-shoe routine. I started practicing after we saw Eddie Foy in Abilene. I'm pretty good."

Fontaine and Lillian looked at him. Neither of them was aware that he had the slightest interest in dance routines. He had never once alluded to it, and so far as they knew, he had no talent as a hoofer. They could only conclude he'd been practicing secretly in his room at the hotel.

"There you have it," Fontaine jumped in with a confident air. "Chester will perform a soft-shoe number, with accompaniment from the piano. I will present a special rendering from Shakespeare. Perhaps something from *Macbeth*."

"You're cracked, the both of you," Murphy growled. "You think anybody's gonna stick around to watch a couple of hams trod the boards? Lillian goes on and that's that!"

"No," Lillian said adamantly. "I insist on a night off."

"Well, insist all you want, little lady, but the answer's no. That's final."

"Then I quit."

Murphy looked as though his hearing had failed him. Fontaine and Chester, equally shocked, appeared speechless. The three men stared at her in startled apprehension.

"You leave us no choice," Lillian said, her eyes on Murphy. "We are forced to give you notice as of tonight. I feel quite sure Mr. Porter will welcome us to the Lucky Star."

"You'd do that to me!" Murphy exploded. "You'd take it across the street to that four-flusher—after I made you a star?"

"You made nothing," Lillian informed him. "We were The Fontaines long before we arrived in Dodge City."

Fontaine and Chester were struck dumb. The girl they'd known all their lives seemed to have stepped over the threshold into womanhood. She sounded eerily like her mother, quiet and strong and utterly certain of herself. They knew she wasn't bluffing.

Frank Murphy knew it as well. His toadish features mottled, and for a moment it appeared he would strangle before he recovered his voice. But he finally got his wits about him and recognized who was who in the scheme of things. He offered her a lame smile.

"Don't blame me if we have a riot on our hands. Hope you enjoy yourself."

"I'm sure I shall."

The officers' mess had been cleared of furniture for the occasion. Gaudy streamers festooned the ceiling, and several coats of wax, buffed since early morning by enlisted men, had brought the floor to a mirror polish. The regimental band, attired in gold-frogged uniforms, thumped sedately under the baton of a stern-eyed master sergeant.

Terrance Clark held Lillian at arm's length. He stiffly pushed her around the dance floor, neither light on his feet nor an accomplished dancer. Although perfectly tailored, splendid in a uniform bedecked with sash and medals, he was nonetheless overshadowed by his partner. As they moved about the floor, other men kept darting hidden glances at her. The women, more direct than their husbands, stared openly.

Lillian had dressed carefully for the ball. Her hair was arranged in an *en revanche* coiffure of ribbons and silk flowers, a French style she had copied from a ladies' periodical. Her svelte figure was stunningly displayed in the better of her two gowns, the teal silk with dark lace at the throat. Draped around her neck was her most prized possession, a string of black deep-sea pearls presented to her mother by her father on their tenth wedding anniversary. Lillian thought her mother would approve.

Tonight was her first formal ball. She'd never before kept company with a man, her mother wisely shielding her from the many Don Juans who populated variety theaters. Captain Clark, an officer and a gentleman, had assured her father she would be properly chaperoned during her stay at Fort Dodge. Arrangements had been made for her to spend the night with Colonel and Mrs. Custer, and Clark would drive her back to town Sunday morning. Still, chaperone or not, she wasn't worried about Terry Clark. His intentions were perhaps too honorable.

The band segued into a waltz. Custer claimed the dance while Libbie glided away on the arms of Clark. Lillian discovered that Custer was nimble of foot, clearly a veteran of ballroom engagements. He held her lightly, his golden ringlets bobbing as they floated off in time to the music. His mustache lifted in a foxy smile.

"I trust you are enjoying yourself."

"Oh, yes, very much."

"Excellent." Custer stared directly into her eyes. "Permit me to say you look ravishing tonight."

"Why, thank you," she said with a shy smile. "You're much too kind, General."

"A beautiful woman needs to be told so on occasion. Don't you agree?"

"You flatter me."

"Hardly more than you deserve."

By now, Lillian knew from gossips in town that Custer has an eye for the ladies. There were rumors he kept an Indian mistress tucked away somewhere, though he was circumspect around Fort Dodge. She'd also heard that his great victory over the Cheyenne was actually the massacre of a harmless band led by the peace chief Black Kettle. She chose not to believe the latter, for she remembered his valor the day he had rescued her from the Kiowa war party. But she accepted the story about his roving ways with women.

Long ago, her mother had warned her about smooth-talking men who could charm the birds out of the trees. She understood, though her mother had deftly employed a metaphor, that it was girls who were too often charmed out of their drawers. The world was full of glib, sweet-talking flatterers—George Armstrong Custer not being the first one she'd met—and she had long since taken her mother's lesson to heart. She would not be charmed out of her drawers.

Yet, on a moment's reflection, she realized that Custer was simply flirting. She was in no danger tonight, for Libbie rarely let her husband out of her sight. To put a point on it, Libbie reclaimed him as soon as the waltz ended. The foursome stood talking awhile, and then Custer, with Libbie on his arm, wandered off to mingle with the other guests. Clark suggested the refreshment table.

A grizzled sergeant served them punch from a crystal bowl. Their cups in hand, Clark led her across the room, where a row of chairs lined the dance floor. He chose a section with mostly empty chairs and courteously waited for her to be seated. She knew he wanted to be alone with her and sensed he had something on his mind. But Terry, as he insisted she call him, was not one of the smooth talkers and usually took the time to organize his thoughts. He finally got his tongue untied.

"Are you happy in Dodge City?" he asked. "I mean, do you enjoy theater work?"

Clark had only attended one show, and she'd intuited that he was disturbed by her working conditions. "I enjoy singing," she replied, pausing to take a sip of her punch. "I can't say I enjoy performing in a saloon."

"Army life is a good deal different." Clark seemed unaware of his awkward non sequitur. "Probably the main reason I chose a career as a soldier."

"Oh?" She wondered where he was trying to lead the conversation. "How is the army different?"

"Well, take this ball, for example. There's never a dull moment, and always something cultural to hold your interest. Do you see what I mean?"

"Like the ball?"

"Yes, and the theatricals we put on for ourselves. Not to mention our discussion groups on classical literature. And picnics in the summer and the evenings we get together for sing-alongs. You'd really enjoy that."

"I'm sure I would."

"The army's a fine life," he said with conviction. "Wonderful people, educated and intelligent, a stimulating culture. You couldn't ask for a better life."

All in a rush, Lillian realized he was trying to sell her on the army life. Or more to the point, the joys of the life of an army *wife*. He was, she saw in sudden comprehension, working himself around to a proposal. She thought it was a marvelous compliment, unbelievably flattering. He was so earnest, so handsome—and yet . . .

"Oh!" She sprang to her feet as the band swung into a lively tune. "Don't you just love a Virginia Reel!"

Before Clark knew what hit him, she had set their punch cups on an empty chair. She laughed, taking his hands, and pulled him onto the dance floor. There seemed no alternative but that she keep him dancing all night.

She wasn't yet ready to hear his proposal.

A warm sun flooded the streets of Dodge City. The weather was nonetheless brisk, for it was the middle of November and a chilly breeze drifted across the plains. Lillian wore her linsey-woolsey dress with a heavy shawl.

Jordan called for her at one o'clock. She'd arrived at the hotel with only enough time to change clothes. The drive back from Fort Dodge had required artifice and a good deal of chatter on her part. Terrance Clark had yet to complete the thought he'd started last night.

Fontaine had gently chided her about being a social butterfly. Out with the army last night, he slyly teased, and off with the buffalo hunter today. Still, he trusted her to do what was right and offered no real objection. He was secure in the knowledge that her mother had raised her to be a lady.

Today, with a buggy rented from the livery, Jordan drove west along the Arkansas. He and his crew of skinners returned to town every ten days or so with a load of hides. Lillian had learned that his nickname—Cimarron—derived from the fact that he was the only buffalo man willing to cross the Cimarron River and hunt in Indian Territory. His given name was Samuel.

She knew as well, from talking with the saloon girls, that he was widely admired by the other buffalo hunters. His daring had made him a legend of sorts, for he had returned time and again with his scalp intact from a land jealously guarded by hostile tribes. He was no less a legend for his ferocity in saloon brawls, though the girls vowed he'd never been known to start a fight. His temper, once unleashed, quickly ended any dispute.

Lillian found him different than his reputation. With her, he was quiet and gently spoken and always a gentleman. Today was their third ride into the country, and he'd never attempted to make advances, not even a kiss. He went armed with a pistol, and he carried his Sharps buffalo rifle whenever they traveled outside Dodge City. But she had never seen his violent side, and she sometimes wished he would try to kiss her. She found him a very attractive man.

Jordan stopped the buggy on a low rise some ten miles west of town. Off in the distance, a herd of buffalo numbering in the thousands slowly grazed southward against the umber plains. He explained that the herds migrated south for the winter, taking refuge in Palo Duro Canyon or on the vast uncharted wilderness known as the Staked Plains. At length, his explanation finished, he turned to her with a quizzical smile.

"How'd you enjoy the dance last night?"

"Very much," she said, taken aback. "How did you know where I went?"

"Well, I got to town expectin' to see you in the show. I asked your dad about it, thinkin' maybe you was sick. He told me you was sweet on that soldier-boy, Clark."

"Oh, that's just like Papa! He knows very well it's not true."

"Simmer down," Jordan said with an amused chuckle. "I was only funnin' you."

Lillian looked at him. "You don't care much for the army, do you? I've noticed you never speak to the soldiers in Murphy's. Why is that?"

"The cavalry tries to stop me from crossin' into Injun country. There's some treaty or another that says nobody's supposed to hunt down there."

"But you do it anyway?"

"I reckon somebody's got to keep the soldier-boys on their toes."

"You're shameless."

Her tone was light. Still, his casual manner made her wonder again at the violence of the frontier. The army fought the Indians, and the Indians pillaged settlements, and the buffalo hunters provoked the tribes even more with the slaughter of the herds. Hardly a night went by that hide hunters and soldiers weren't evolved in a brawl, just for the sheer deviltry of it. Everyone, white and red, fought everyone else.

First in Abilene, and now in Dodge City, it seemed to her that men fought without any great rhyme or reason. There was no real effort on anyone's part to live in peace, and the hostility inevitably led to more bloodshed. Of course, she had killed a Kiowa warrior—who thought he was justified in trying to kill her—so she had no right to be critical. But it all struck her as such a waste.

"Where'd you go?" Jordan asked. "You look like you're a million miles away."

"Oh, just daydreaming," Lillian fibbed. "Nothing important really."

"Thinking about that fancy ball last night?"

"No, actually, I was thinking about you. Am I the only one who calls you Samuel?"

"Most folks don't even know my real name."

"Then I want to know even more. How did you become a buffalo hunter?"

"That's a long story."

"We have all afternoon."

Jordan, like most men, was easily prompted to talk about himself. She listened, nodding with interest, seemingly all attention. Yet her mind was a world away, another time and another place. A time of gentler memory.

She longed again for the sight of New York.

CHAPTER 10

THE PLAINS were blanketed with snow. The air crackled with cold, and there were patches of ice along the banks of the Arkansas. Clouds the color of pewter hung low in the sky.

The Fontaines arrived shortly after eleven o'clock. They were bundled in heavy coats and lap robes, their breath like frosty puffs of smoke. An orderly rushed out to take charge of the buckboard and team as they stopped before the house. Libbie Custer met them at the door.

"Merry Christmas!" she cried gaily. "Come in out of the cold."

"Yes, Merry Christmas," Lillian replied, hugging her fondly. "Thank you so much for having us."

"Indeed," Fontaine added heartily. "You are the very spirit of the season for strangers far from home. We feel blessed by your charity."

"Don't be silly," Libbie fussed. "Now, get out of those coats and come into the parlor. Everyone's waiting."

Their coats were hung in the vestibule. Libbie led them into the parlor, where a cheery blaze snapped in the fireplace. Custer moved forward, his hand outstretched, followed by Clark. His manner was jovial.

"Here you are!" he said, shaking their hands. "To quote our friend Dickens, 'God bless us every one!' Welcome to our home."

Chester went to warm himself by the fire. Custer nodded to a manservant, who shortly returned with a tray of hot toddies in porcelain mugs. The mix of brandy, water, and sugar, heated with a red-hot poker, brought a flush to Lillian's face. Clark raised his mug in a toast.

"Merry Christmas," he said cordially. "You look lovely today."

"You're being gallant," she said with a smile. "I'm sure my nose is red as an apple. I thought I would freeze before we got here."

"I'm afraid it will be even colder when you drive back."

"Yes, but as you know, there's no rest for actors. The show must go on, even on Christmas night."

"We could change that easily enough. All you have to do is say the word."

Lillian avoided a reply. Over the past month Clark had proposed on several occasions, and each time she had gently turned him down. She was still attracted to him, just as she was to Jordan, who continued to court her whenever he was in town. But the thought of being stranded in Kansas, marriage or not, made her shudder. She looked for a way to change the subject.

"Oh, what a marvelous tree!" she said, turning to Libbie. "Why, it's absolutely gorgeous."

Libbie brightened. "I sent all the way to Chicago for some of the ornaments. I'm so happy you like it."

George Armstrong Custer was not a man to do things by half-measure. In mid-December, he'd had a fir tree imported from Missouri, freighted overland with a consignment of military stores. Libbie had decorated the tree with cranberries and popcorn strung together on thread and gaily-colored ribbon bows. Her most treasured ornaments, ordered from Chicago, were white satin angels with gossamer wings and shiny glass balls. The tree was crowned with a silver papier-mâché star.

The Custers were childless, but Christmas was nonetheless a time of celebration. Watching them, it occurred to Lillian that there was something childlike about the couple. They were forever inventing reasons for gala parties, amateur theatricals, or nature outings that often involved a dozen or more officers and their wives. Yet Christmas was clearly their favorite festivity of the year, eclipsing even the Fourth of July. The tree, imported all the way from Missouri, stood as testament to their Yuletide spirit.

The hot toddies were apparently a tradition in the Custer household. Apart from wine with dinner, women seldom drank hard liquor in the company of men. But Custer insisted, and before an hour was out Lillian felt as though her head would float away from her shoulders. Libbie coaxed her into singing a Christmas carol, and she managed to get through it without missing a note. She was giddy with delight.

Fontaine, who needed little prompting, was then asked to perform. To their surprise, he selected a poem written by Clement C. Moore, one that had gained enormous popularity in recent years. He positioned himself beside the tree and recited the poem with a Shakespearean flair for the dramatic. His silken baritone filled the parlor.

> *Twas the night before Christmas, when all*
> *through the house*
> *Not a creature was stirring—not even a mouse;*

> *The stockings were hung by the chimney with*
> *   care,*
> *In hopes that St. Nicholas soon would be*
> *   there . . .*

"Bravo!" Custer yelled when Fontaine finished the last line. "Never have I heard it done better. Never!"

Libbie was reduced to tears. Lillian, still lightheaded from the hot toddies, was amazed. Apart from Shakespeare, she had no idea that her father had ever committed anything to memory. She glanced at Chester, who offered her an elaborate shrug. He seemed equally nonplussed.

The manservant, with impeccable timing, announced dinner. The table was decorated with greenery, bight red berries, and tall colored candles. A roasted goose, its legs tied with red and green bows, lay cooked to a crisp on a large serving platter. Custer, wielding a carving knife as though it were a cavalry saber, adeptly trimmed the bird. After loading their plates, he waited for the manservant to pour wine. He hoisted his glass.

"You honor Libbie and I with your presence on the day of Our Lord's birth. Merry Christmas!"

Everyone clinked glasses and echoed the sentiment. The serving bowls were passed and their plates were soon heaped with stuffing, winter squash, cranberry sauce, mashed potatoes, and a rich oyster gravy. Fontaine offered his compliments to the chef, though the army cook in the kitchen had never been seen on any of their visits to the house. The manservant kept their wineglasses full.

Lillian was acutely conscious of Clark seated on her right. He hadn't spoken since their earlier conversation in the parlor, when she'd blithely evaded his reference to marriage. His manner was sullen, and while the others ate with gusto, he merely picked at his food. No one else seemed to notice, but she saw Libbie glance at him several times during the meal. He drained his wineglass every time it was replenished.

Later, after dessert, the men retired to the study for cigars and brandy. Clark was bleary-eyed with wine on top of hot toddies and scarcely looked at Lillian as he walked from the room. Libbie led her into the parlor, where they seated themselves on a sofa before the fireplace. The gaiety of the party seemed diminished for Lillian, and she scolded herself for having hurt Clark with an unintentional rebuff. There was an awkward silence as she stared into the flames.

"I couldn't help but notice," Libbie finally said. "Did you and Terrance have words?"

Lillian smiled wanly. "I'm sure you knew he asked me to marry him."

"Yes, he mentioned it to the general."

"I've told him no any number of times. I think he realized today it's really final."

"What a shame," Libbie said sadly. "Terrance would make a fine husband."

"I know," Lillian said, a tear at the corner of her eye. "I just hate it, but I'm not ready for marriage. I haven't yet sorted out my own life."

"How do you mean?"

"Oh, it seems I'll never see New York again. And I so wanted a stage career."

"Aren't you scheduled to play Wichita next spring?"

"Wichita isn't New York," Lillian said fiercely. "I really loathe performing for cowboys and buffalo hunters, and drunken, brawling men. Everything in the West is so crude and . . . uncivilized."

"Yes, unfortunately, it is," Libbie agreed. "I often have those same feelings myself." She hesitated, considering. "Tell me, have you given any thought to Denver?"

"Denver?" Lillian looked at her. "Isn't that somewhere in Colorado? The mountains?"

"My dear, you have never seen anything like it. The Rockies are absolutely stunning, and Denver itself is really quite cosmopolitan. A very sophisticated city."

"Honestly?"

"Oh, goodness yes," Libbie said earnestly. "Theater, and opera, and shops with all the latest fashions. And scads of wealthy men. Just scads!"

Lillian's face lit up. "It sounds like the answer to a dream."

"Well, for someone who wants a career on the stage, it's perfect. I just know you would be a sensation there."

"Would you tell Father about it? Would you, please?"

"You mean, how grand and sophisticated it is? Perhaps a little hyperbole?"

"Yes! Yes!"

"Why, of course. What are friends for?"

The men trooped in from the study. Lillian caught Chester's eye and warned him to silence with a sharp look. Then, artful as a pickpocket, she got her father seated on the sofa. She gave the general's wife a conspiratorial wink.

Libbie Custer began her pitch on the wonders of Denver.

*　　*　　*

Murphy's Exchange was mobbed. The blizzard a few days past had driven every buffalo hunter on the plains into Dodge City. They decided to stay and celebrate Christmas.

Their idea of celebrating the Christ Child's birth was little short of heathen. The first stop was a saloon, where they got modestly tanked on rotgut whiskey. The second was a whorehouse, where the girls baptized them in ways unknown to practicing Christians. After a carnage of drinking, gambling, and whoring, they were ready at last for Christmas night. They came, en masse, to see Darlin' Lilly.

Lillian was beside herself with excitement. On the drive back from Fort Dodge, her father had spoken of little else but Denver. Libbie Custer's glowing account had left him intrigued by the thought of a cosmopolitan oasis in the heart of the mountains. The general, not to be outdone by his wife, had embellished the Mile High City with an aura of elegance second to none. His comments added authority to an already dazzling portrait.

The marvelous thing was that Alistair Fontaine adopted the idea as his own. New York was a tattered dream, and Wichita was yet another cowtown quagmire, hardly better than Dodge City. But Denver, he declared after the Custers' stirring narrative, was the affirmation of an actor's prayer. He hadn't committed to a journey into the Rockies, but Lillian told herself it was only a matter of time. A gentle nudge here and there and he would talk himself into it.

Tonight's show was almost ended. Lillian was waiting in the wings for the finale, her last song of the evening. Her father was farther backstage, involved in a discussion with Frank Murphy. Chester approached

her, glancing over his shoulder to make sure the conversation was still in progress. He gave her a dour look.

"Dad's back there grilling Murphy about Denver.
You sure put a bee in his bonnet."

"*Me?*" Lillian said innocently. "The Custers got him
started on it, not me."

"Yeah, sure," Chester scoffed, "and the moon's made
of green cheese."

"Listen to me, Chester. However much Papa talks,
we're never going back to New York. Denver is our
only hope for a decent life."

"I know."

"You do?"

"Of course I do," Chester said. "The chances are nil
of our ever getting a booking back East. Either we go
to Wichita or we take a crack at Denver."

"Well . . ." Lillian was relieved. "I hope you favor
Denver."

"Don't worry, we'll talk Dad into it."

"No, he thinks it's his own idea. Let him talk himself
into it."

Chester smiled. "I can almost hear Mom saying the
same thing. You remind me more and more of her
lately."

"Oh, Chet . . ."

The piano player opened with her introduction. She
gave Chester a quick kiss on the cheek and moved out
of the wings. The fiddler joined the piano, and the
crowd of drunken buffalo hunters greeted her with
rowdy applause. She walked to the footlights, hoping
they would appreciate her selection. She thought it a
fitting end to the Christmas season. On the musicians'
cue, her voice seemed to fill the night.

Hark! the herald angels sing
Glory to the newborn King;
Peace on earth and mercy mild,
God and sinners reconciled!
Joyful all ye nations rise,
Join the triumph of the skies;
With th' angelic host proclaim
Christ is born in Bethlehem

The saloon went silent. She saw Cimarron Jordan at the bar, and he nodded with an approving smile. The hide hunters, heathen or not, stared at her as though suddenly touched by memories past. To a man, their thoughts slipped from whiskey and whores to long-gone times of Christmas trees and family. Many snuffled, their noses runny, and one blubbered without shame, his features slack with emotion. A carol sung in a saloon took them back to better days, gentler times.

The hush held until her voice faded on the last note. Then they recovered themselves, and a roar went up, whistles and cheers and drumming applause. She curtsied, warmed by their reaction, and made her way offstage. They brought her back for another ovation, and then another, and she thought there was, after all, some glimmer of hope for buffalo hunters. Yet it was a passing thought, and one quickly gone. Her mind was fixed on Denver.

Later, after she'd changed, Jordan took her to a café for a late supper. The food was greasy, thick slabs of buffalo fried in a skillet, and she hardly ate a bite. But she chattered on with growing excitement as she related her conspiracy with Libbie Custer. Her eyes sparkled whenever she mentioned Denver, and she could scarcely contain herself. She bubbled with the thrill of it all.

"What about your pa?" Jordan asked, when she paused for breath. "Think he'll go for the idea?"

"Oh, I know he will. I just know it! He's talked of nothing else."

"Well, I'm pleased for you. Mighty pleased."

Lillian saw his downcast expression. She knew he was taken with her and chided herself for not being more sensitive. She touched his hand.

"You could always come visit me in Denver."

"Suppose I could," Jordan said, studying on it. "Course, they'll turn you into a big-city girl with fancy notions. Likely you wouldn't have time for a rough old cob like me."

"That simply isn't true," she said, squeezing his hand. "I'll always have time for you, Samuel. Always."

Cimarron Jordan wanted to believe it. But he was a pragmatist, and he told himself there was a greater truth in what he'd heard tonight. Come spring, there was no doubt in his mind.

Dodge City would see the last of Darlin' Lilly.

CHAPTER 11

SPRING LAY across the land. The plains stretched onward to infinity, an emerald ocean of grass sprinkled
with a riotous profusion of wildflowers. A late-
afternoon sun heeled over toward the horizon.

Fontaine rode a bloodbay gelding. A Henry repeater
was balanced behind the saddlehorn, and he wore a light
doeskin jacket with fringe on the sleeves. Chester drove
the buckboard, drawn by the mismatched sorrel and dun
team, fat from a winter in the livery stable. Lillian was
seated beside him, the brim of her bonnet lowered
against the glare of the sun. They were three days west
of Dodge City.

Lillian thought her father was in his glory. She
glanced at him from beneath her bonnet, forced to smile
at the striking figure he cut on the gelding. He rather
fancied himself the intrepid plainsman and looked like
he was playing a role that borrowed assorted traits from
Daniel Boone and Kit Carson. She was amused that he
played the part of stalwart scout with such élan.

Their immediate destination was Pueblo, Colorado.
By her reckoning, she marked the date at April 18, and
she hoped 1872 would prove more rewarding than the
year just past. She had celebrated her twentieth birthday
in February, and she felt immensely matured by her
experiences in Abilene and Dodge City. So much so
that she seldom fell into reverie about some grand and

joyous return to New York. Her thoughts were on Denver.

By New Year's Day, Alistair Fontaine had sold himself on the idea. Over the next three months he'd devoted his time to planning their artistic assault on the Mile High City. The top nightspot in Denver was the Alcazar Variety Theater, and he had arranged for their New York booking agent to forward their notices and a glowing report on the show. The owner of the Alcazar had sent a lukewarm response, stating he was interested but offering no firm commitment. Fontaine, undeterred by details, went ahead with his plans. He was confident they would take Denver by storm.

George Armstrong Custer became their unofficial adviser. The Kansas Pacific railroad was laying track westward but had not completed the line into Colorado. The nearest railhead was Wichita, a week's journey to the east, and at least another week by train to Denver. The better route, Custer suggested, was to follow the Arkansas River overland, which would bring them to Pueblo within two weeks' time. From there, it was a short hop by train to Denver.

Cimarron Jordan considered the overland route to be foolhardy. He told Lillian, and then Fontaine, that Custer was playing daredevil with their lives. The country west of Dodge City, he explained, was a hunting ground for the Cheyenne, the Comanche, and other tribes. A strip of unsettled territory bordering their route, known as No Man's Land, was also haven to outlaws from throughout the West. He firmly believed they would be placing themselves in jeopardy.

Fontaine blithely ignored the warning. General Custer was a distinguished soldier and the greatest Indian fighter in the West. Jordan was a common buffalo hunter and, in the end, a man who lacked the wisdom of a military commander. To no small degree, Fontaine was influenced by Custer's derring-do and quixotic spirit. He saw the journey as another step in their westward adventure, and he cast himself in the role of trailblazer and scout. He declared they would take the overland route.

Their final week in Dodge City was spent in provisioning for the trip. Fontaine stocked all manner of victuals, including buffalo jerky, dried fruit, and four quarts of Irish whiskey. He purchased a ten-gauge shotgun, with powder and shot, announcing it was suitable for wild fowl or wild Indians. Then, in a picaresque moment, he bought a bloodbay gelding with fire in its eye and a quick, prancing gait. Custer, after seeing the horse, gave Fontaine a doeskin jacket taken in the spoils of war. He looked like a centaur with fringe on his sleeves.

Their departure brought out all of Dodge City in a rousing farewell. Custer was there, along with Libbie, who hugged Lillian with teary-eyed fondness and good wishes for the journey. Jordan and his crew of skinners accompanied them west for the first day and then turned south for the Cimarron River. Before they separated, Jordan again cautioned them to be wary at all times and to mount a guard over their livestock every night. Indians, he observed, might steal your horses and, rather than kill, leave you to a crueler fate. A man on foot would never survive the limitless plains.

Fontaine consulted his compass an hour or so before sundown. Encased in brass, indicating direction and azimuth without fail, the compass was largely a showpiece. The Arkansas River wound due west like a silver ribbon, and simply following its course would bring them to Pueblo. But Fontaine, immersed in his role as scout, wanted all the props to fit the part, and he'd bought a compass. After snapping the lid closed, he signaled Chester to a stand of cottonwoods along the riverbank. He announced they would stop for the night.

By now, they went about their assigned tasks with little conversation. Chester hobbled the horses and put them to graze on a grassy swale that bordered the river. Later, he would water them for the night and then place them on a picket line by the buckboard. Fontaine gathered deadwood from beneath the trees and kindled a fire with a mound of twigs. Lillian removed her cast-iron cookware and foodstuffs from the buckboard and began preparing supper. She planned to serve buffalo jerky, softened and fried, with beans and biscuits left over from breakfast.

Twilight settled over the land as she dished out the meal. The fire was like a beacon in the night, and they gathered around with tin plates and mugs of steaming coffee. She thought the scene was curiously atavistic, not unlike a primordial tribe, hunkered before a fire, sharing the end of another day. Three days on the trail had already toughened them, and though her father and Chester religiously shaved every morning, they appeared somehow leaner and harder. Every time she looked in her little vanity mirror, she got a fright. She was afraid the harsh plains sun would freckle her nose.

"Westerners do like their beans," Fontaine said, holding a bean to the firelight on the tines of his fork. "I've always found it amusing that they call them whistleberries."

"Oh, Papa," Lillian said, shocked. "That's disgusting."

"A natural function of the body, my dear. Beans produce wind."

"I really don't care to discuss it."

Lillian was still embarrassed by aspects of life on the trail. A call of nature required that she hunt down thick brush or hide behind a tree. Even then, she thought there was scarcely any privacy. She always felt exposed.

"Your modesty becomes you," Fontaine said understandingly. "In fact, it provides a lesson for us all. We mustn't allow ourselves to be coarsened by the demands of nomadic travel."

Chester laughed. "Buffalo jerky and beans are coarse all right. I'd give anything for a good steak."

"Capital idea!" Fontaine said. "The land fairly teams with wildlife. I'll set out on a hunt tomorrow."

Lillian was alarmed. Her father knew virtually nothing about hunting and even less about negotiating his way on the plains. She had visions of him becoming hopelessly lost on the sea of grass.

"Do you think that's wise, Papa?" she asked uneasily. "Shouldn't we stay together?"

"Have no fear," Fontaine said with a bold air. "I shan't stray too far from the river. Besides, I have my trusty compass."

Chester looked worried. "Lillian has a point. If we were separated somehow, we might never get back together. I can do without fresh meat."

"Nonsense," Fontaine said stubbornly. "You concern yourselves for no reason. The matter is settled."

Later, after the horses were picketed, they spread their bedrolls around the fire. Chester took the first shift of guarding the camp, stationed with his rifle near the buckboard. Fontaine would relieve him in two hours, and they would alternate shifts throughout the night. Neither of them would hear of Lillian standing guard. She was, after all, a girl.

Lillian was less offended than amused. They seemed to have forgotten that she'd killed a Kiowa warrior on the Santa Fe Trail last fall. But then, male vanity was as prevalent in the Fontaine family as any other. She was to be protected simply because she was a woman. Or in their minds, still a girl.

She snuggled into her bedroll. The sky was purest indigo, flecked with stars scattered about the heavens like shards of ice. She stared up at the Big Dipper, filled with wonder that they were here, roughing it on the plains, sleeping on the ground. Her father their scout and hunter.

She thought her mother would have been beyond laughter.

Fontaine rode out of camp at false dawn. He reined the bloodbay gelding north, toward a distant copse of trees bordering a tributary creek. He reasoned that deer would water there before sunrise.

Chester and Lillian, following his instructions, were to continue westward along the banks of the Arkansas. Fontaine was still touched by their concern for his welfare but nonetheless determined that plains travel was largely an exercise of the intellect. He planned to have his deer and rejoin them long before midday.

Hunting, he told himself, was a matter of intellect as well. He recalled reading somewhere—possibly Thoreau—that deer were by nature nocturnal creatures. So it made sense, after a night of foraging, they would water before bedding down for the day. He felt confident a fat buck awaited him even now at the creek.

The tree line was farther than he'd estimated. He reminded himself again that the vastness of the plains was deceptive; everything was more distant than it appeared to the eye. The sun burst free from the edge of the earth, a blinding globe of vermilion, just as he rode into the shade of the trees. He dismounted, tying the gelding to a stout limb. He moved into the shadows with the Henry repeater.

Fontaine was immensely pleased with himself. He'd taken equestrian lessons many years ago, and the rhythm of it had come back to him after a day or so in the saddle. He was armed with a rifle that shot true and perfectly capable of navigating across the vistas of open grassland. Everything considered, he felt the dime-novel exploits of Buffalo Bill and his ilk were greatly overrated, more myth than fact. Any man with a modicum of intelligence could become a plainsman, and the same was true of a hunter. All he needed was to spot—

A buck stepped out of the shadows across the creek, some fifty yards upstream. Streamers of sunlight filtered through the trees, glinting on antlers as the buck lowered his nose to the water. Fontaine thumbed the hammer on his rifle, slowly tucking the butt into his shoulder. His arms were shaking with excitement, and it took him a moment to steady the sights. He recalled a conversation with Cimarron Jordan, about the cleanest way to kill an animal. He aimed slightly behind the foreleg.

The gunshot reverberated like a kettledrum. The buck jerked back from the water, then whirled about and bounded off through the trees. Fontaine was too astounded to move, roundly cursing himself for having missed the shot. Before he could lever another cartridge into the chamber, the buck disappeared into a thicket far upstream. He lowered the rifle, still baffled by his poor marksmanship and struck by a vagrant, if somewhat unsavory, thought. There would be no fresh meat in the pot tonight.

The thud of hoofbeats sounded off to the east. Fontaine wondered if a herd of buffalo was headed his way, and in the next instant the notion was dispelled. Five Indians, drawn by the gunshot, topped the rise that sloped down to the creek and reined to a halt. Their eyes found him almost immediately, and for a moment he felt paralyzed, rooted to the ground. Then they gigged their ponies, whooping and screeching as they tore down the slope, and he scrambled to unhitch his horse. He flung himself into the saddle.

The Indians splashed across the creek. Fontaine had perhaps a hundred yards' head start, and he booted his horse hard in the ribs. The gelding responded, stretching out into a dead gallop, and he thanked the gods he'd bought a spirited mount. A quick glance over his shoulder brought reassurance that he was extending his lead, and he bent low in the saddle. Something fried the air past his ear, and a split second later he heard the report of a rifle from far behind. He thundered southwest toward the river.

Some twenty minutes into the chase Fontaine had widened the gap to a quarter-mile. He silently offered up a prayer that the gelding had stamina as well as speed, for if he faltered now all was lost. Then, as he rounded a bend in the river, he saw the buckboard not far ahead. Chester and Lillian turned in the seat as he pounded closer, and by the expression on their faces, he knew they'd seen the Indians. He frantically motioned them toward the riverbank.

"Get down!" he shouted. *"Take cover!"*

Chester sawed on the reins. He whipped the team off the grassy prairie and brought the buckboard to a skidding halt where a brush-choked overhang sheltered the streambed. He jumped to the ground, rifle in hand, as Lillian hopped out on the other side with the shotgun. Fontaine reined the gelding to a dust-smothered stop and vaulted from the saddle. His eyes were wild.

"Open fire!" he ordered. "Don't let them overrun us!"

The Indians galloped toward them at a full charge. The sight of a white woman and a buckboard full of supplies merely galvanized them to action. Fontaine and Chester commenced firing, working the levers on their rifles in a rolling staccato roar. The breakneck speed of the ponies made it difficult to center on a target, and none of their shots took effect. The warriors clearly intended to overrun their position.

Lillian finally joined the fight. After a struggle to cock both hammers on the shotgun, she found it required all her strength to raise the heavy weapon. She brought it to shoulder level, trying to steady the long barrels, and accidentally tripped both triggers. The shotgun boomed, the double hammers dropping almost simultaneously, and a hail of buckshot sizzled into the charging Indians. The brutal kick of the recoil knocked Lillian off her feet.

A warrior flung out his arms and toppled dead from his pony. The others swerved aside as buckshot simmered through their ranks like angry hornets. Their

charge was broken not ten feet from the overhang, and
Fontaine and Chester continued to blast away with their
Henry repeaters. None of the slugs found a mark, but
the Indians retreated to a stand of cottonwoods some
thirty yards from the riverbank. They dismounted in the
cover of the tree line.

"Help your sister," Fontaine said sharply. "I'll keep
an eye on the red devils."

Lillian lay sprawled on the rocky shoreline. Her
shoulder throbbed and her head ached, and there was a
loud ringing in her ears. Chester lifted her off the
ground and set her on her feet, supporting her until she
recovered her balance. He grinned at her.

"You got one!"

"I did?"

"Look for yourself."

A gunshot from the trees sent a slug whizzing over
their heads. They ducked beneath the overhang and
quickly crouched beside their father. Fontaine gave
them a doleful look.

"There are four left," he said. "They have only one
rifle, but that is sufficient to keep us pinned down. I fear
we're in for a siege."

"A siege?" Chester questioned. "You don't think
they'll rush us again?"

"Not until nightfall," Fontaine remarked. "I daresay
they are wary of Lillian's shotgun. You saved the day,
my dear."

Lillian was still dazed. "Will they come after us tonight, Papa?"

"Yes, I believe they will. Chester, reload your sister's
shotgun. We'll have need of our artillery."

Fontaine bent low behind the buckboard and tied his gelding to a wheel rim. He knew the Indians were as interested in their horses as in their scalps. A live horse was of equal value as a dead man.

He thought they were in for a long night.

CHAPTER 12

A BALL of orange flame rose over the eastern horizon. The heat of the sun slowly burned off a pallid mist that hung across the river. Somewhere in the distance a bird twittered, then fell silent.

The clearing between the riverbank and the cottonwoods was ghostly still. Fontaine was crouched at the right of the overhang, with Lillian in the middle and Chester at the opposite end. Lillian's shoulder was sore and bruised, and Chester had relieved her of the shotgun. She was now armed with a Henry repeater.

They were exhausted. Three times in the course of the night the Indians had attempted to infiltrate their position. Twice, using stealth and the cover of darkness, the warriors had crept in from the flanks. The last time had been an abortive assault from the river, floating downstream and trying to take them from behind. They had fought off every attack.

A starlit sky proved to be their salvation. The light was murky but nonetheless adequate to discern movement and form. Fontaine's instructions were to fire at the first sign of danger, and Lillian and Chester, their nerves on edge, were alert to the slightest sound. Accuracy was difficult in the dim light, and yet it did nothing to hamper volley after volley of rapid fire. The Indians beat a hasty retreat in the face of flying lead.

The horses reared and pitched with every skirmish. But Chester, exhibiting foresight long before darkness fell, had secured the team to thick, ancient roots jutting out from the overhang. The bloodbay gelding, tied to the near wheel of the buckboard, kicked and squealed with a ferocity that threatened to snap the reins. Still, with the coming of daylight, the horses dozed off standing up, as if calmed by the relative quiet. The only sound was a bird that twittered now and again.

Fontaine removed his hat. He cautiously edged his head around the side of the overhang and peered across the clearing. He saw no movement in the stand of cottonwoods and wondered if the Indians had pulled out under cover of darkness. His eyes narrowed as he realized that, sometime during the night they had recovered the body of the warrior killed by Lillian. A spurt of smoke blossomed from the tree line and a slug kicked dirt in his face. He jerked his head back.

"How depressing," he said with a mild attempt at humor. "Our friends are a determined lot."

Chester grunted. "Hope we killed some of them last night."

"I rather doubt it, my boy. Unless they still had us outnumbered, I suspect they would have given up the fight."

"So what do we do now?"

"Well, it is somewhat like a game of cat and mouse, isn't it? We have no option but to wait them out."

"Some option," Chester said dourly. "We could be here forever."

"Isn't there another way, Papa?" Lillian asked. "I dread the thought of another night like last night."

Fontaine smiled. "My dear, you are the only soldier among us. Chet and I have yet to kill our first savage."

"I can't say I'm proud of it. Besides, it was an accident with that stupid old shotgun anyway. It's a wonder I didn't break my shoulder."

"Or your *derriere*," Chester added with a sly grin. "You hit the ground so hard the earth shook."

Lillian was too tired to bandy words. Her face was smudged with dirt and the smoke of gunpowder, and stray locks of hair spilled down over her forehead. She was scared to death and felt as though she hadn't slept in a week. She wondered if they would live to see Denver.

Fontaine stuck his rifle around the edge of the overhang and fired. He turned back to them with a crafty smile. "A reminder for our friends," he said. "We musn't let them think we're not alert."

"I don't feel very alert," Lillian said. "I honestly believe I could close my eyes and go to sleep right now."

"Excellent idea, my dear. We need to be fresh for tonight's war of wits. You and Chet try to catch a nap. I'll keep watch for a while."

"You must be exhausted, too, Papa."

"On the contrary, I've never felt more—"

A herd of horses thundered around the bend in the river. At first glance, Fontaine estimated there were fifty or more, their manes streaming in the wind. Then, looking closer, he was never more heartened in his life. There were six men driving the horses. Six *white* men.

The four remaining Indians exploded out of the cottonwoods. They whipped their ponies, galloping north from the river, clearly no less startled by the sudden appearance of the herd. Several of the drovers pulled their pistols, jolted by the sight of Indians, and prepared to open fire. A man on a magnificent roan stallion raised his hand.

"Hold off!" he bellowed. "You'll spook the gawd-damn herd!"

The men obediently holstered their pistols. They circled the herd and brought the horses to a milling standstill. One of them gestured off at the fleeing Indians.

"Them there's Comanche," he said in a puzzled voice. "Think they was fixin' to jump us, Rufe?"

"Tend to doubt it," the one named Rufe said. "Not the way they're hightailin' it outta here."

"Then what the blue-billy hell was they doin' here?"

Fontaine stepped around the overhang. Lillian and Chester followed him, all of them still armed. The six men stared at them as though a flock of doves had burst from a magician's hat. Fontaine nodded to the man named Rufe, the one who appeared to be the leader. He smiled amiably.

"Those heathens"—he motioned casually at the fast-departing Indians—"were here attempting to collect our scalps. You gentlemen arrived in the very nick of time."

"Who are you?"

"Alistair Fontaine. May I present my daughter, Lillian, and my son, Chester. And whom do I have the honor of addressing?"

"The name's Rufe Stroud."

"Well, sir," Fontaine said, the rifle nestled in the crook of his arm. "Never have I been more delighted to see anyone, Mr. Stroud. You are a welcome sight indeed."

Stroud squinted. "What brings you to this neck of the woods?"

"We are on our way to Denver."

"You picked a helluva way to get there. Them Comanche would've roasted you alive."

"All too true," Fontaine conceded. "You are, in every sense of the word, our deliverance."

"Mebbe so," Stroud said. "You folks on foot, are you?"

"Our buckboard is there on the riverbank."

One of the men rode to the overhang for a look. He turned in the saddle to Stroud. "Buckboard and three horses, Rufe. Got a bay gelding that's purty nice."

Stroud nodded. "I'm a mite curious," he said to Fontaine. "Why're you headed to Denver?"

"We are actors," Fontaine said in his best baritone. "We plan to play the Alcazar Theater."

"Your girl an actor, too?"

"Yes indeed, a fine actress. And a singer of exceptional merit, I might add."

"That a fact?"

Lillian felt uncomfortable under his stare. Fontaine smiled amicably. "From the size of your herd, I take it you are a horse rancher, Mr. Stroud."

"You take it wrong," Stroud said. "I'm a horse thief."

"I beg you pardon?"

"Drop them guns."

The men pulled their pistols as though on command. Fontaine looked at them, suddenly aware he was in the company of desperadoes. He dropped his rifle on the ground, nodding to Lillian and Chester, who quickly followed his lead. Then, ever so slowly, he fished the Colt .32 revolver from his jacket pocket and tossed it on the ground. He looked at Stroud.

"Those are all of our weapons. May I ask your intentions, Mr. Stroud?"

Stroud ignored him. "Shorty," he said to one of the men. "Get them into the buckboard and let's make tracks. Them Comanche might have friends hereabouts."

Shorty Martin was well named. He was hardly taller than a stump post, a thickset man with beady eyes. "Whyn't we kill'em now?" he said flatly. "They're just gonna slow us down."

Lillian's heart skipped a beat. She seemed unable to catch her breath as Stroud inspected them as if they were lame horses that might slow his progress. His eyes suddenly locked onto her and held her in a gaze that was at once assessment and raw lust. The look lasted a mere instant, though she felt stripped naked, and his eyes again went cold. He glanced at Martin.

"Do like you're told."

Martin knew an order when he heard one. Within minutes, the outfit proceeded west along the river. The Fontaines were in the buckboard, and the bloodbay gelding, now unsaddled, ran with the herd. Fontaine, nagged by a worrisome thought, wished he had kept the pistol.

He'd seen the way Stroud looked at Lillian.

The sun was high when they crossed the Arkansas. At a wide spot in the river, where the water ran shallow, they forded through a rocky streambed. Their direction was now almost due southwest.

Fontaine watched the operation with increasing vigilance. His mind was already exploring how they might escape, and he was committing the terrain and their direction to memory. Yet he discerned that the gang functioned like a military unit, relentlessly on guard and with an economy of commands. The men clearly knew what was expected of them.

The chain of command was clear as well. Stroud was the leader, and his orders were not open to question. The other men, though a rough lot, seemed wary of incurring his anger. Shorty Martin was apparently Stroud's lieutenant and nominally the second in command. But there was little doubt as to his place in the scheme of things. Every order originated with Stroud.

Lillian was frightened into stony silence. Her intuition told her that these men were far more dangerous than the Comanche warriors they'd fought off just last night. Their abductors were callous and openly cold-blooded, evidenced by the one who had so calmly suggested that killing them was the better alternative. Only by the whim of the gang leader were they still alive.

Their deliverance from the Indians seemed to her a harsher fate. She knew lust when she saw it, and she'd seen it all too plainly in Stroud's cool gaze. She thought they'd jumped from the frying pan into the fire, and all because of her. Some inner voice warned her that the lives of her father and Chester were hostage to how she behaved. She sensed it was only a matter of time until her virtue was tested.

Stroud called a halt at noon. A narrow creek lay across their path, and he ordered the horses watered. The men took turns watching the herd, some rolling themselves smokes while the horses crowded around the stream. Others dismounted, pulling their puds as if there weren't a woman within a hundred miles, and relieved themselves on the ground. Lillian kept her eyes averted.

Stroud rode over to the buckboard. Chester, whose face was white with fury, erupted in anger. "Don't your men have any decency? How can you let them. . . . do that! . . . in front of a woman?"

"Sonny, you'd best shut your mouth. I won't be barked at by pups."

"Listen here—"

"That's enough!" Fontaine broke in. "Do as he says, Chet. Say nothing more."

"Good advice," Stroud said. "Don't speak till you're spoke to. Savvy?"

"We understand," Fontaine assured him. "It won't happen again."

Stroud nodded. He hooked one leg around the saddlehorn and pulled the makings from his shirt pocket. After spilling tobacco from a sack into the paper, he licked the edges and rolled it tight. He popped a sulphurhead on his thumbnail and lit up in a haze of smoke. His gaze lingered on Lillian a moment as he exhaled. Then he looked back at Fontaine.

"I never met an actor," he said. "Go ahead, do something."

"Pardon me?"

"Let's see you act."

"Seated in a buckboard?"

"I ain't in the habit of repeatin' myself. Show me your stuff."

Fontaine realized it was a crude test of some sort. He knew he would have only one chance to make good and decided to give it his all. The other men, drawn by the spectacle, moved closer to the buckboard. His voice rose in a booming baritone.

The quality of mercy is not strained,
It droppeth as the gentle rain from heaven

Upon the place beneath: it is twice bless'd;
It blesseth him that gives and him that takes:
'Tis mightest in the mightiest; it becomes
The throned monarch better than his crown;
His scepter shows the force of temporal power,
The attribute to awe and majesty,
Wherein doth sit the dread and fear of kings

Stroud was silent a moment. He took a drag and exhaled a wad of smoke. Then he smiled. "I like that," he said. " 'The dread and fear of kings.' You just pick that out of thin air?"

Fontaine spread his hands. "I thought it appropriate to the occasion."

"The part about mercy wasn't bad, either. I can see you've got a sly way about you."

"A supplicant often petitions mercy. Under the circumstances, it seemed fitting."

Stroud turned to the men. "You boys ever hear Shakespeare before?"

The men traded sheepish glances, shook their heads. "Thought not," he said, flicking an ash off his cigarette. "Well, Mr. Fontaine, mebbe we won't have to kill you, after all. We're plumb shy on entertainment out our way."

Lillian thought he was evil incarnate. He was lithe and muscular, with square features and a bristly ginger mustache. His eyes were hooded and seemed to emanate menace. She found herself staring into them now.

"Your pa says you're—how'd he put it?—an exceptional singer."

"I try," she replied softly. "Some people think I have a nice voice."

"You be thinkin' up a good tune for when we camp tonight. I'll let you sing for the boys."

Stroud shifted his gaze to Chester. "What is it you do, sonny?"

Chester reddened. "I act in melodramas. And I do a soft-shoe routine."

"You'll be dancin' for your supper before we're done. Just don't gimme no more of your sass."

"We understand perfectly," Fontaine interjected. "You may depend on us for the spirit of cooperation."

Stroud snuffed his cigarette between thumb and forefinger. He gestured to his men. "Awright, we been jawbonin' long enough. Let's get them horses on the trail."

The men jumped to obey. Stroud swung his leg over the saddlehorn and jammed his boot in the stirrup. Fontaine cleared his throat.

"May I ask you something, Mr. Stroud?"

"Try me and see."

"Where, exactly, are you taking us?"

Stroud smiled. "Folks call it No Man's Land."

CHAPTER 13

THREE DAYS later they crossed into No Man's Land. Their line of march was due southwest, through desolate country parched by wind and sun. On the fourth day, they sighted Wild Horse Lake.

Rufe Stroud seemed to unwind a little when they neared the outlaw camp. He rode beside the buckboard, suddenly talkative, almost genial, chatting with Fontaine. Lillian got the impression that it was all for her benefit, meant to impress her with the man and the place. He was in a bragging mood.

The remote strip of wilderness, Stroud told them, was all but uninhabited. Centuries ago Spanish explorers had called it *Cimarron*, which loosely translated meant "wild and unruly." Through a hodgepodge of confused and poorly written treaties, it now belonged to none of the Western states or territories. So it was aptly dubbed No Man's Land.

Despite the name, there was nothing confusing about its borders. Texas and Kansas were separated by its depth of some thirty-five miles, while its breadth extended nearly two hundred miles westward from Indian Territory to New Mexico Territory. Along its northwestern fringe, the isolated strip of grasslands formed a juncture with Colorado as well. To a large degree, the raw expanse of wilderness had been forgotten by God and government alike. There was no law, Stroud idly warned them, but his law.

Wild Horse Lake was his headquarters. Known to few white men, the spot was situated on the divide between the Beaver and Cimarron Rivers. A prominent landmark, it was the haunt of renegades and desperadoes from across the West. Those who came there were predators, wanted men on the dodge, and the law of the gun prevailed. A man survived on cunning and nerve and by minding his own business. Too much curiosity, Stroud explained, could get a man killed.

The lake itself was centered in a large basin. Somewhat like a deep bowl, it served as a reservoir for thunderstorms that whipped across the plains. Above the basin, sweeping away on all sides, was a limitless prairie where the grasses grew thick and tall. Wild things, the mustangs that gave the lake its name, no longer came there to feed and water. The basin was now the domain of men.

Outlaws found refuge there. A sanctuary where those who rode the owlhoot could retreat with no fear of pursuit. Not even U.S. marshals dared venture into the isolated stronghold, for lawmen were considered a form of prey anywhere in No Man's Land. Discretion being the better part of valor, peace officers stayed away, and a man on the run could find no safer place. There was absolute immunity from the law at Wild Horse Lake.

Several cabins dotted the perimeter of the lake. A trail from the east dropped off the plains and followed an incline into the basin. Lillian counted seven cabins and upward of ten men lounging about in the late-afternoon sunshine. Three men on hoseback were watering a herd of longhorns, and she noticed that the cattle wore fresh brands, the hair and hide still singed. She knew nothing of such matters, but it appeared to her that the old brands had somehow been altered. The men watched her with interest as the buckboard rolled past.

Stroud's headquarters was on the west side of the lake. There were three cabins, one larger than the others, and off on the south side a corral constructed of stout poles. The men hazed the horses into the corral, and a woman came running to slam and bolt the gate. Lillian saw two other women standing outside the larger cabin, and for a moment her spirits soared. But then, looking closer, she was reminded of the prostitutes she'd seen in Dodge City. She would find no friends at Wild Horse Lake.

One of the women walked forward. She was plump and curvaceous, with a mound of dark hair and bold amber eyes. Her gaze touched on Lillian with an instant's appraisal and then moved to Stroud. Her mouth ovaled in a saucy smile.

"Hello there, lover," she said. "Glad to see you back."

"Glad to be back."

Stroud stepped down from the saddle. The woman put her arms around his neck and kissed him full on the mouth. After a moment, she disengaged and nodded to the buckboard. "What've you got here?"

"They're actors," Stroud said, his arm around her waist. "The old man's pure hell on Shakespeare. The boy dances a little and the girl's a singer. Got a real nice voice."

"You plan to keep them here?"

"Don't see why not. We could stand some entertainment. Liven up the place."

She poked him in the ribs. "Thought I was lively enough for you."

"Course you are," Stroud said quickly. "Wait'll you hear the girl sing, though. She's damn good."

"Just make sure singing's all she does."

"C'mon now, Sally, don't get started on me. I'm in no mood for it."

She laughed a bawdy laugh. "I guess I know how to change your mood."

The order of things soon became apparent. Stroud and his woman, Sally Keogh, shared one of the smaller cabins. The other small cabin was occupied by Shorty Martin and a frowsy woman with broad hips and red hair. The largest of the cabins was a combination mess hall and bunkhouse for the remaining four men. The third woman appeared to be their communal harlot.

Martin quickly got a rude surprise. Stroud motioned him over to the buckboard. "The actors," he said, jerking a thumb at the Fontaines, "are takin' over your place. You and Mae move your stuff into the big cabin."

"For chrissake!" Martin howled. "You got no call to do that, Rufe."

"Don't gimme no argument. Get'em settled and quit your bellyachin'."

"There ain't no extra bunk in the big cabin!"

"Work out your own sleepin' arrangements. Just get it done."

"Yeah, awright," Martin grumped. "Still ain't fair."

Stroud turned to the buckboard. "Listen to me real good," he said, staring hard at Fontaine. "You mixin' with my men—'specially the girl—that's liable to cause trouble. So I'm givin' you a cabin to yourselves."

Fontaine nodded. "We appreciate the courtesy, Mr. Stroud."

"You're gonna see we don't have no padlock to put on your door. Before long, you might get it in your head to steal some horses and make a run for it."

"I assure you—"

"Lemme finish," Stroud said coldly. "You run, I'll let Shorty have his way with you. Get my drift?"

"Yes, I do."

"Then don't do nothin' stupid."

By sundown, the Fontaines were settled in the small cabin. Not long afterward, Fontaine and Chester were ordered to carry armloads of firewood into the big cabin. Lillian was assigned to the kitchen, which consisted of a woodburning cookstove and a crude table for preparing food. The other women, who were frying antelope steaks and a huge skillet of potatoes, gave her the silent treatment. But as the men trooped in, taking seats on long benches at a dining table, Sally Keogh sidled up to her. The woman's features were contorted.

"Stay away from Rufe," she hissed. "You mess with him and I'll slit your gullet."

"Why not tell him that?" Lillian said, suddenly angry. "All I want is to be left alone."

"Just remember you were warned."

Stroud broke out the whiskey. He waved Fontaine and Chester to the table and poured them drinks in enamel mugs. His amiable mood left them puzzled until they realized he wanted to celebrate a successful horse raid. He once again began bragging about his operation.

The whiskey and other essentials, he informed them, were imported to Wild Horse Lake from a distant trading post. There were three gangs who made the basin their headquarters, and his was the largest of the bunch. Some rustled cattle, others robbed banks and stage-coaches, but none dealt in stolen horses. Stroud reserved that right to himself, and the other gangs went along, aware that he would fight to protect his interests. No one cared to tangle with him or his outfit.

Fontaine mentioned he'd been told that the Comanche and Cheyenne tribes were active in this part of the country. He alluded specifically to Stroud and his men saving them from certain death at the hands of the Comanche raiding party. He asked how Stroud and the other gangs managed to operate so openly in a land where warlike tribes traveled at will. Stroud laughed loudly.

"We buy 'em off," he said. "Injuns would trade their souls for repeatin' rifles. Bastards think we hung the moon."

Lillian listened as she worked at the stove. She knew all his bragging was like the sounding of their death knell. He would never have brought them here or expounded at such length on his operation if there was any chance they would be released. Or any chance they might escape.

He was telling them that they would never leave Wild Horse Lake.

Stroud threw a party that night. He invited all the members of the other gangs headquartered at Wild Horse Lake. By eight o'clock, some twenty people were jammed into the big cabin.

The announced purpose of the shindig was celebration of still another profitable horse raid. Yet it was apparent to all who attended that Stroud was eager to show off his captives, the Fontaines. Or as he insisted on referring to them in a loud, boastful manner: The Actors.

Jugs of whiskey were liberally dispensed to the revelers. Stroud and the other gang leaders were seated at the head of the long dining table, the position of honor. Their followers were left to stand for the most part, though some took seats on the bunks. The party steadily became more boisterous as they swilled popskull liquor.

One of Stroud's men whanged away on a Jew's harp. With the metal instrument clamped between his teeth, he plucked musical tones that were surprisingly melodious. A member of another gang was no less proficient on a harmonica, and the sounds produced on the mouth organ complemented those from the Jew's harp. They soon had the cabin rollicking with sprightly tunes.

Fontaine felt like he was attending some mad festivity hosted by an ancient feudal lord. The only difference in his mind was that the men were armed with pistols rather than broadswords and crossbows. Somewhat sequestered, he stood watching with Lillian and Chester by the woodstove as liquor flowed and the party got rowdier. He sensed they were about to become the court jesters of Wild Horse Lake.

Not quite an hour into the revelry Stroud rose to his feet. His face was flushed with whiskey and his mouth stretched wide in a drunken grin. He pounded on the table with a thorny fist until the Jew's harp and the harmonica trailed off in a final note. The crowd fell silent.

"I got a treat for you boys," he said with a broad gesture directed at the Fontaines. "These here folks are professional actors, come all the way from Dodge City.

Song and dance and, believe it or not, Shakespeare!"

Monte Dunn, the leader of a band of robbers, guffawed loudly. He was lean, the welt of an old scar across his eyebrow, with muddy eyes and buttered hair. He gave Stroud a scornful look.

"Shakespeare?" he said caustically. "Who the hell wants to hear Shakespeare? Ain't no swells in this bunch."

Stroud glowered at him. "Don't gimme none of your bullshit, Monte. This here's my show and I'll run it any damn way I see fit. Got it?"

"Don't get your bowels in an uproar. I was just sayin' it ain't my cup of tea."

"Like it or lump it, you're gonna hear it."

Stroud nodded to Fontaine, motioning him forward. Fontaine walked to a cleared area at the end of the table and bowed with a grandiose air. "For your edification," he said, glancing about the room, "I shall present the most famous passage from *Julius Caesar*."

The outlaws stared back at him with blank expressions. The thought crossed his mind that he might as well be a minister preaching to a congregation of deaf imbeciles. Yet he knew that his audience was Stroud alone, a man with the power of life and death. His eloquent baritone lifted with emotion.

> *Friends, Romans, countrymen, lend me your*
> *ears;*
> *I come to bury Caesar, not to praise him.*
> *The evil that men do lives after them,*
> *The good is oft interred with their bones;*
> *So let it be with Caesar . . .*

Fontaine labored on to the end of the soliloquy. When he finished, the crowd swapped baffled glances, as though he'd spoken in Mandarin Chinese. But Stroud laughed and pounded the table with hearty exuberance. "You hear that!" he whooped. "That there's art!"

No one appeared to share the sentiment. Chester was the next to perform, accompanied by the Jew's harp and the harmonica. He went into a soft-shoe routine, which was made all the more effective by the sandpaper scrape of his soles against dirt on the floor. He shuffled in place, executed a few lazy whirls, and ended with legs extended and arms spread wide. The outlaws whistled and hooted their approval.

Lillian was to close with a song. She asked the men on the Jew's harp and harmonica if they knew the ballad *Molly Bawn*. When they shook their heads, she suggested they follow her lead and try to catch the melody as she went along. She moved to the end of the table, hands folded at her waist, and avoided the leering stares of a crowd now gone quiet. Her husky alto flooded the room.

> *Oh, Molly Bawn, why leave me pining,*
> *All lonely, waiting here for you?*
> *The stars above are brightly shining,*
> *Because they've nothing else to do.*
> *The flowers so gay were keeping,*
> *To try a rival blush with you;*
> *But Mother Nature set them sleeping,*
> *Their rosy faces washed with dew.*
> *Oh, Molly Bawn! Oh, Molly Bawn!*

The ballad ended on a heartrending note. There was a moment's silence; then the outlaws rocked the cabin with applause and cheers. Stroud looked proud enough to bust his buttons, grinning and nodding until the commotion died down. He climbed to his feet.

"Listen here, Lilly," he said expansively. "Let's give these boys a real show. What say?"

"I don't understand," Lillian said.

"That old rag you're wearin' don't do you justice. Go change into one of them pretty silk gowns. The ones I saw in your trunk."

"Now?"

"Yeah, right now," Stroud said. "Get dolled up and come give us another song."

Lillian looked at Fontaine, who shrugged helplessly. She turned away from the table, unwilling to anger Stroud, and moved toward the door, As she went out, the Jew's harp twanged and the harmonica chimed in on *The Tenderfoot*. The men poured a fresh round of drinks, clapping in time to the music.

"Good-lookin' gal," Monte Dunn said, glancing at Stroud. "How'd you like to sell that little buttercup, Rufe? I'd pay you a handsome price."

"What d'you think I am?" Stroud said indignantly. "I don't sell humans like some gawddamn slave trader."

"Well, I don't know why not. You stole her just like you stole them horses out in the corral. You're gonna sell them horses for a profit. Why not her?"

"She ain't for sale."

Dunn laughed. "Hell, anything's for sale. Name a price."

"Monte, you stink up a place worse'n a polecat. Think I'll get myself some fresh air."

Stroud walked to the door. Sally started after him and he waved her off. She'd overheard his conversation with Dunn, and she didn't believe a word of it. She thought he was after more than fresh air.

Outside, Stroud hurried off in the direction of the Fontaines' cabin. A coal-oil lamp lighted the window, and he paused, darting a look over his shoulder, before he opened the door. Lillian was clothed only in her chemise, about to slip into her blue silk gown. She backed away, holding the gown to cover her breasts. He closed the door behind him.

"Well, looky here," he said, advancing on her. "I knew you was hidin' something special under that dress."

"Get out!" Lillian backed up against the wall. "Get out or I'll scream."

"Naw, you ain't gonna scream. That'd bring your pa runnin' and I'd have to kill him."

"Please don't do this, I beg you. I'm not that kind of woman."

"You're my kind of woman," Stroud said, reaching for her. "You and me are gonna have some good times."

Lillian swatted his hand away. "Leave me alone! Don't touch me!"

"I'm gonna do more'n touch you."

The door burst open. Before Stroud could turn, Sally whapped him over the head with a gnarled stick of firewood. The blow drove him to his knees, and he saved himself from falling by planting a hand against the floor. She shook the log in his face.

"You son-of-a-bitch!" she screeched. "You try any strange pussy and I'll cut your balls off. You hear me?"

Stroud wobbled to his feet. "You ought'nt have hit me like that, Sal. I was just talkin' to her, that's all."

"You're a lying no-good two-timin' bastard!"

She shoved him out the door and slammed it behind her. Lillian sat down on the bunk, the gown still clutched to her breasts. Her heart was in her throat, and she had to gulp to get her breath. Yet a small vixenish smile dimpled the corner of her mouth.

She thought Sally really would cut off his balls.

CHAPTER 14

LATE THE next morning, the first of the stolen horses was led to the branding fire. Outside the corral, thick stakes were driven into the ground several feet apart, and laid out near the fire were lengths of heavy-gauge wire and a lip twist. A wooden bucket, with a rag dauber fastened to a stick, was positioned off to the side.

The horse was thrown and the men swarmed over him. Within seconds, his legs, front and rear, were lashed to the stakes. One man held the gelding's head down, while two others kept his hindquarters from thrashing. The fourth man stepped into the fray with the twist. He attached the rope loop to the horse's lower lip, then began twisting it like a tourniquet. The pain, intensifying with every turn, quickly distracted the horse from all else.

Stroud stood watching with Fontaine and Chester. His eyes were bloodshot from last night's party, and his head pounded with a dull hangover. But he was proud of his operation, and he'd invited them to observe the crew in action. He wanted them to see how a stolen horse was transformed into a salable horse.

"Watch close now," he said. "Shorty's a regular brand doctor."

"Pardon me?" Fontaine said, curious despite himself. "A brand doctor?"

"Yeah, somebody that makes a new brand out of the old brand. He's a gawddamn wizard."

Shorty Martin walked to the fire. He studied the brand on the gelding's flank—Bar C—then selected a piece of wire. His hands worked the metal the way a sculptor fashions clay; with a twist here and a curl there, he shaped one end of the wire into a graceful but oddly patterned design. A quick measurement against the old brand apparently satisfied him.

"You gotta pay attention," Stroud urged. "Shorty works fast once't he gets started."

Martin pulled the length of wire, now cherry red, out of the fire. With a critical eye, he positioned the wire and laid it over the old brand. The smell of burnt hair and scorched flesh filled the air, and an instant later he stepped back, inspecting his handiwork. As if by magic, the original C had been transformed into a △.

"Ever see the like!" Stroud crowed. "Touch here and a touch there, and we got a Triangle O."

"Amazing," Fontaine said, truly impressed. "Mr. Martin is something of an artist."

Chester's brow furrowed. "I don't mean to question his work, Mr. Stroud. But isn't the burning and the redness something of a tip-off?"

Stroud chuckled. "Keep your eyes peeled, sonny. You're fixin' to see why Shorty's a sure-enough doctor."

Martin hefted the bucket. He stirred the contents, which appeared thick as axle grease and had the faint odor of liniment. Then he turned to the horse, and with a quick stroke of the dauber he spread a dark, pasty layer across the new brand. The entire operation had taken less than five minutes.

"I'm still at a loss," Chester said. "What does that do?"

"Shorty's secret recipe," Stroud announced. "Heals the brand natural as all get-out in a couple of days. Jesus Christ himself couldn't tell it'd ever been worked over."

The gelding was released and choused back into the corral. One of the men roped another horse and led it toward the fire. Fontaine wagged his head.

"I must say, you have it down to a science. Very impressive indeed."

"Tricks of the trade," Stroud said. "Stealin' horses takes a sight of know-how."

"I'm curious," Fontaine said in a musing tone. "How do you sell the rebranded horses?"

"You'll recollect I told you curiosity could get you killed around here."

"I withdraw the question."

"No, come to think of it, what's the difference? You gents are gonna be with us till hell freezes over. It ain't like you'll ever be tellin' anybody."

"I take your point," Fontaine said. "We are, in a manner of speaking, residents of Wild Horse Lake."

"Like I said, you won't be tellin' tales out of school."

Stroud was in an expansive mood. He went on to liken his operation to a thimblerigger's shell game. Several livestock dealers, spread throughout surrounding states and territories, represented the pea under the pod. Every week or so the gang would conduct a raid into Kansas, Colorado, New Mexico, or Texas. The stolen horses were then trailed back to No Man's Land, where the brands were altered with Shorty's magic wire.

The stolen stock, Stroud elaborated, was never sold on home ground. Horses from Kansas were trailed to Colorado and those from Texas to New Mexico. To muddy the waters further, the order of the raids was rotated among the states and territories. Local ranchers were never able to establish any pattern to the random nature of the raids. Yet it was all very methodical, nearly impossible to defend against.

The shell game was played out on many fronts. After being trailed to different locations, never on home ground, the horses were sold by livestock dealers over a widespread area. Usually, there was a mix of altered brands, and to all appearances, the stock had been bought here and there by an itinerant horse trader. In the end, horses stolen in random order were the shells of the game, sold across the breadth of four states. The livestock dealers, the pea under the pod, were known only to Stroud and his gang. Not one had ever been caught selling stolen stock.

"Nothin's foolproof," Stroud concluded, "but this here's mighty damn close. Them horses are scattered to hell and gone, and nobody the wiser."

Fontaine could hardly argue the point. There was a logistical genius to the operation, which virtually eliminated any chance of being detected. Yet Stroud had revealed the inner workings of the scheme with what amounted to a veiled threat. The Fontaines would never leave Wild Horse Lake. Not alive.

Lillian was watching them from the kitchen window. She and the other women were preparing the noon meal, and she wondered why her father and Stroud were involved in such lengthy discussion. As she turned from the window, she saw that Sally had taken a break, seated at the table with a mug of coffee. She decided now was the time.

"May I speak with you?" she asked, moving to the table. "We haven't talked about last night and perhaps we should."

Sally looked at her. "What's on your mind?"

"Well . . ." Lillian seated herself. "I wanted to apologize for what happened. I was as surprised as you were."

"Wasn't any surprise to me. Rufe never could keep his pecker in his pants."

"Do you think he'll try again?"

"Damn sure better not," Sally said evenly. "If he does, I won't stop with his balls. I'll lop his tally-whacker off."

The term was new to Lillian. She considered a moment and suddenly blushed with understanding. Her mother had always referred to that part of a man's anatomy as his "dingus." She mentally committed *tally-whacker* to her vocabulary.

"You sound unsure," she said. "Does he really believe you would—you know . . . do that?"

"Oh, he believes it," Sally said with a wicked smile. "Trouble is, he'd risk it if he caught you off alone somewhere. He knows you'd never talk."

"Why on earth wouldn't I?"

"Did you tell your pa about last night?"

"No . . . I didn't."

"Because you knew he'd get riled and start trouble and Rufe would kill him. That about cover it?"

"Yes."

"Well, dearie, Rufe figures it the same way."

Lillian was silent a moment. She glanced quickly at the kitchen area, to make sure they wouldn't be overheard by the other women. Then, lowering her voice, she took a chance. "Will you help us escape?"

"You're off your rocker!" Sally said, flummoxed by the very thought. "Why would I do a fool thing like that?"

"You know why we were brought here. It has nothing to do with my father or my brother, or with the fact that we're entertainers. It has only to do with me."

"So?"

"So where will it end?" Lillian coaxed her. "Will you kill him when he finally manages to . . . to rape me? Will you kill me just to remove the temptation?"

"You're some piece of work. Either I help you escape, or somebody—you, Rufe, maybe even me—winds up dead. That the general idea?"

"Yes, exactly."

"Wish to hell you'd stayed in Dodge City."

"So you'll help us get away?"

Sally sighed wearily. "I'll think about it . . . no promises."

The cabin was cramped. There was a single bunk, wedged into a corner, and wall pegs for hanging clothes. Last night Fontaine had insisted that Lillian take the bunk while he and Chester made do with pallets on the floor. Yet it was their only haven from Stroud and the gang. The one place they could talk in privacy.

By early afternoon all the horses had been doctored with new brands. Stroud, finally tired by a morning of braggadocio on the stratagems of a horse thief, had dismissed Fontaine and Chester. Lillian helped the women clean up in the kitchen following the noon meal and afterward was left to her own devices as well. The family gathered in the relative security of the cabin.

Fontaine related the details of Stroud's windy discourse on the triumphs of the gang. His tone was one of grudging admiration, and he admitted that the outlaw chieftain had a natural gift for organization. He readily

admitted as well that Stroud's garrulous revelations of
how the operation worked had come at a high price.
They were, for all practical purposes, consigned to
spend the rest of their lives at Wild Horse Lake. Stroud
would never release them.

"You should have heard him," Chester added, looking at Lillian. "He as much as said he was confiding in
us because we would never be able to tell anyone. He
would kill us before he'd let that happen."

"Not in those exact words," Fontaine amended. "He
has a clever way of issuing a threat without stating it
openly. But you are nonetheless correct, Chet. Our lives
are at peril."

"I had the feeling that we were being sworn in as
members of the gang."

"With the proviso, of course, that anyone who be-
trays the trust signs his own death warrant. I feel sure
Mr. Martin would gladly carry out the sentence."

"Huh!" Chester grunted dismally. "Shorty Martin
would kill us just to get this cabin back."

Fontaine nodded. "I daresay you're right."

Lillian listened with growing concern. She desperately wanted to tell them of her conversation with Sally
Keogh. But she wondered how to do it without revealing last night's failed assault by Stroud. She decided to
shade the truth.

"We may have an ally," she said. "I spoke with Sally
this morning. She might help us."

"Oh?" Fontaine inquired. "Help us in what way?"

"To escape."

Fontaine stared at her, and Chester's mouth dropped
open. A moment elapsed before Fontaine recovered his
composure. "Why in God's name would you ever raise

the subject with her? She is Stroud's woman."

"That was exactly the reason," Lillian said with more confidence than she felt. "Sally thinks Stroud is attracted to me and she's worried. She told me so herself."

"One moment." Fontaine stopped her with an upraised palm. "Are you saying she is concerned Stroud would turn her out for you? She would lose his . . . affections?"

"Yes, Papa, that's what I'm saying."

"And she broached the matter with you?"

"Not about the escape," Lillian said evasively. "She expressed her concern that she might lose Stroud. I suggested the way around that was to help us escape. She promised to think about it."

"Extraordinary," Fontaine muttered. "Wouldn't that rather place her in jeopardy with Stroud?"

"Not unless she's caught."

"What if *we're* caught?" Chester interjected. "We already know what Stroud would do to us. He'd kill us!"

Fontaine thought that was only partially true. He suspected Stroud would kill Chester and himself without a moment's hesitation. Lillian, on the other hand, would be spared only to become Stroud's concubine. But all of that might happen anyway, for he'd seen Stroud's covetous attitude toward his daughter. He told himself that escape was their only option.

"Let me understand," he said. "Do you have reason to believe Sally will help us? Did she say anything to that effect?"

"Nothing definite," Lillian admitted. "But I really do believe she will, Papa. She loves Stroud very much."

"Talk about a revolting thought," Chester said. "She certainly has poor taste in men."

Fontaine crossed to the door. He stood staring out at the bleak landscape, trying to puzzle through all of the ramifications. A movement caught his eye and he saw a rider approaching from the northwest. The man rode into the compound, dismounted, and left his horse hitched at the corral. He walked toward the big cabin.

Lost in his own thoughts, Fontaine dismissed the man from mind. Some while later, as the sun dropped steadily westward, he suggested they leave for the main cabin. The women would be preparing supper, he noted, and their appearance would be expected at the dinner table. He cautioned Lillian and Chester to act as normal as possible, particularly around Sally Keogh. The slightest misstep might alert Stroud.

On the way across the compound, they saw Sally stagger around the corner of the cabin. Her lip was split, blood leaking out of her mouth, and her left eye was almost swollen shut. She lurched, all but losing her balance, and managed to recover herself. Lillian rushed forward.

"Sally, my God, what happened?"

"Watch yourself, kiddo," Sally mumbled. "I tried, but it got nasty. Rufe's on a tear."

"He hit you?"

"Slugged me a couple of times. Knocked me flat on my ass."

"That's terrible!" Lillian said angrily. "Why would he hit you?"

"Ed Farley's here," Sally said. "He's always had a thing for me and I thought I could trust him. Turns out I was wrong."

"Wait, you aren't making sense. Who's Ed Farley?"

"Ed's a livestock dealer. He buys all the horses Rufe trails to Colorado."

"And you told him about us?"

Sally, dabbing at her split lip, briefly explained. She'd gotten Farley aside and told him what great entertainers the Fontaines were. She suggested that he buy them from Stroud and make them sign a contract appointing him their manager. She convinced him there was money to be made on the variety circuit.

"Wasn't a bad idea," she concluded. "I figured you could escape lots easier in Colorado than here. Trouble is, Rufe popped his cork and Ed lost his nerve. He told Rufe it was my idea."

Lillian gently touched her arm. "I'm so sorry I got you into this."

"Worry about yourself," Sally warned her. "Rufe's never gonna let you go. He's like a madman."

"Yes, but what about you? Will you be all right?"

"Honey, that's anybody's guess. Rufe knows I'll kill him if he touches you or any other woman. Maybe he'll be cooled down by the time he comes to bed."

Sally tottered off toward her cabin. Fontaine appeared unsettled by what he'd heard. He finally squared his shoulders. "We'll have to have our wits about us tonight. Under the circumstances, we cannot afforded to provoke Stroud."

There was a moment of turgid silence when they entered the cabin. The women busied themselves in the kitchen, their eyes fixed on their tasks. Stroud was seated at the table with Ed Farley and the other gang members. His features were set in a sphinxlike mask.

"Well, here's the actors," he said curtly. "Look 'em over real good, Ed. Make me an offer."

Farley was a heavyset man with a full beard. He shook his head. "Rufe, I think I'll stick to horses."

Stroud studied Lillian as if trying to read her mind. His gaze abruptly shifted to Fontaine. "Don't matter which one of you put Sally up to that nonsense. It was a dumb move."

"Yes, it was," Fontaine agreed. "Very foolish indeed."

"I warned you twice about tryin' to escape. There's not gonna be a third time. You follow me?"

"Implicitly, Mr. Stroud."

"You and your fancy words," Stroud said with a tight smile. "Tell you what, actor; let's see you act. Show Ed some of your Shakespeare."

"I would be honored to do so."

Fontaine felt like an organ grinder's monkey. Yet he knew there was no choice but to perform on command. He struck a dramatic pose.

"O, what a rogue and peasant slave am I . . ."

Chapter 15

THE LAKE was molten with sunlight. Stroud stood in the door of the main cabin with a mug of coffee. His gaze was fixed on the corral.

Four men, one of them Ed Farley, were saddling their horses. Farley finished tightening the cinch on his chestnut gelding and spoke to the men. One of them racked back the bolt on the gate while the others swung into the saddle. He led his horse toward the cabin.

"We're ready," he said. "Didn't forget to pay you, did I?"

"That'll be the day," Stroud said with a crooked grin. "You're off to an early start."

"Well, Rufe, I'm not a man of leisure. I've got a ways to go before those horses turn a profit."

"Don't give me no sob stories. You make out like a Mexican bandit."

Farley shrugged. "Guess I've got no complaints."

"Course you ain't." Stroud drained his coffee mug. "Make sure them boys head on back here when the job's done. I don't want'em lollygaggin' around whorehouses and such."

The men choused the stolen horses out of the corral. The herd now included Fontaine's bloodbay gelding and the team that had once pulled the buckboard. One of the men turned the lead horse, while the others circled from behind, and they drove the herd west from the cabins. Farley stepped into the saddle.

"Always good doing business with you, Rufe. See you in about a month."

"I'll be here."

Stroud moved back into the cabin. As the door closed, Farley and the three gang members pushed the herd up the western slope of the basin. Fontaine, watching from the door of his cabin, waited until the horses disappeared over the rim onto the plains. He shook his head with a frown.

"A pity," he said, almost to himself. "They've taken my horse and the buckboard team. We are, quite literally, afoot."

Chester laughed sourly. "Dad, that's how Stroud intended it all along. He knows we're not about to walk out of here."

"Quite so," Fontaine concurred. "Somehow, though, it makes me feel all the more a prisoner. I rather liked that horse."

Lillian was seated on the bunk. "We musn't despair, Papa. There has to be a way."

"Yes, of course, my dear. Spirits bright, for we are nothing without hope. I'm sure we will find a way."

Fontaine tried to sound optimistic. Still, given the circumstances, his spirits had never been lower. Last night, Stroud had made them perform until even the men grew bored. The lengthy show was punishment for their abortive escape attempt and a message as well. Their next attempt to flee would be their last.

For all that, Fontaine saw no alternative. Stroud, before too long, would try to force himself on Lillian. When that happened, Fontaine would resist, as would Chester, and they would both be killed. Even worse, Lillian would be doomed to a life of depravity and unremitting torment. Fontaine thought it preferable, if death was inevitable, to die trying to escape.

Lillian scooted off the bunk. "I think I'll go talk to Sally. Maybe she'll have another idea."

"Be very careful," Fontaine admonished. "We have no way of knowing what transpired overnight. She may report anything you say to Stroud."

"Oh, I doubt that very much, Papa. Not after the way he abused her."

"Exactly the point I'm trying to make. After last night, she may well fear for her own life."

"Don't worry, I'll be careful. I promise."

Lillian stepped out the door. Sally had failed to appear at breakfast that morning, and she was concerned about her. She was no less concerned about a means of escape, for she knew the stalemate with Stroud would not last much longer. Time was running out.

Sally was huddled in the bunk of her cabin. When Lillian entered, a bright shaft of sunlight filled the dim interior. Sally winced, her left eye swollen shut, bruised in a rosette of black and purple, and her lip caked with dried blood. She looked worse than last night.

"Close the door," she said. "I'm a sight not fit to see."

Lillian sat on the edge of the bunk. "I was worried when you didn't come to breakfast. Is there anything I can do to help?"

"No, thanks just the same. Time's the only thing that'll heal what I've got."

"Sometimes I wish I were a man. I'd give him a lesson he wouldn't forget."

"Honey, a half-dozen men sat there last night and watched him beat me. None of them said a damn word."

"Yes, but they're afraid of him."

"And you aren't?"

"Actually, I'm terrified," Lillian admitted. "I didn't sleep a wink worrying he might come for me."

Sally sniffed. "Rufe won't be comin' for you till he kills me. Not that he wouldn't, you understand."

"What happened?"

"I waited for him last night. Minute he got in bed, I put a knife to his throat. Told him if he ever hit me again I'd slit his gullet."

"You didn't!"

"Yeah, I did, too," Sally said hotly. "Told him it was him and me, or nothin'. I won't be thrown over for another woman . . . meanin' you, of course."

"Good heavens," Lillian breathed. "What did he say?"

"Oh, he tried to play lovey-dovey. Longer I held that knife to his throat, the more promises I got. But that don't mean a lot for either you or me."

"Why not?"

Sally went solemn. "Rufe's a born liar, that's why not. He might kill me to get at you." Her voice dropped. "Or he might turn you over to the men . . . just to spite me."

"The men?"

"Toss you to that pack of wolves in the big cabin. Way he thinks, that'd still give him the last laugh."

Lillian paled. She had been too worried about Stroud to conjure an even worse fate. The thought had never occurred to her that she might be forced to submit to the horror of several men, night after night. As she considered it now, she felt queasy and the bitter taste of bile flooded her throat. She silently swore she would kill herself first.

"Do you . . ." She faltered, groping for words. "There has to be some way we can escape from here. Do you know of anything that might have a chance?"

Sally looked defeated. "Wish I did. Trouble is, if I try anything else, Rufe *will* kill me. And it'd all be for nothing. He'd still get you."

"Oh, God, Sally, I feel so helpless."

"Honey, I've felt that way most of my life."

A distant gunshot brought their heads around. Then, in the space of a heartbeat, a rattling volley of gunfire echoed through the basin. Lillian rushed to the window, with Sally only a step behind. Across the way, they saw three columns of horsemen fanning out around Wild Horse Lake. One column was galloping directly toward Stroud's compound.

The attack caught everyone by surprise. Monte Dunn and his men, as well as the gang of cattle rustlers, were lounging in the sunshine outside their cabins. The men tried to put up a fight, but they were overwhelmed by sheer numbers. There appeared to be ten or more horsemen in each column, their pistols popping as they came on at a gallop. The outlaws were cut down in a withering maelstrom of lead.

Stroud ran out of the big cabin as the attack started from the southern rim of the basin. Shorty Martin and the other men followed him outside, guns drawn, their women watching from the door. They opened fire on the column headed toward the cabin, and then, too late, realized they were outnumbered. As they turned back to the cabin, Martin took a slug between the shoulders and pitched to the ground. The other men, riddled, dropped on the doorstep.

A swarm of bullets sizzled all around Stroud. His hat went flying and a slug clipped his bootheel, but somehow, miraculously, he was otherwise unscathed. Some visceral instinct told him he would be killed if he tried to make it into the cabin, and he abruptly gave up the fight. He flung his pistol into the dirt and stopped, still as a statue, his hands high overhead. He waited for a shot in the back, then the gunfire suddenly ceased. The riders reined to a halt before the cabin.

"My God," Lillian whispered. "Who are they?"

Sally swallowed hard. "I think you've just been saved."

"What do you mean?"

"I mean they're wearin' badges."

Capt. Ben Tuttle held court in front of the cabin. He was a large man, with the jaw of a bulldog and eyes the color of dead coals. The star of a Texas Ranger was pinned to his shirt.

Tuttle had been a Ranger for almost twenty years. He'd fought Comanche marauders who raided south of the Brazos and Mexican *banditos* who struck north of the Rio Grande. In his time, he had seen some strange things and yet nothing as strange as what he'd found at Wild Horse Lake. He thought it beggared belief.

The dining table had been brought outside and positioned before the cabin. Tuttle was seated behind the table, having adopted the role of judge and jury in today's hearings. The Rangers, throughout the organization's history, were notorious for dispensing summary justice in the field. Wild Horse Lake was no exception.

There were thirty Rangers in Tuttle's company. In the course of the raid, they had killed nine outlaws without suffering a casualty. They were now guarding the survivors, who were ranked before Tuttle's impromptu courtroom. Stroud waited with Sally and the other women off to one side. Monte Dunn, whose gang had been wiped out, was held with the two cattle rustlers. His left arm dripped blood from a bullet wound.

The Fontaines stood before the bench. Alistair Fontaine had just finished telling their saga of escaping wild Indians only to be taken captive by a band of outlaws. Lillian and Chester had said nothing, merely nodding affirmation as their father related one hair-raising exploit after another. Capt. Ben Tuttle, who knew a whopper when he heard one, considered them with a skeptical eye. He thought it was all a load of hogwash.

"Let me get this straight," he said. "You're being held here prisoner and forced to entertain this bunch, or they'd kill you. That about the gist of it?"

"Indeed so," Fontaine acknowledged. "You and your men were our very salvation. You have delivered us from certain death."

Tuttle scowled. "You never stole a horse, or rustled a cow, or robbed nobody. Have I got it right?"

"Never!" Fontaine intoned. "We are actors."

"And you're from New York City?"

"By way of Abilene and Dodge City."

"And George Armstrong Custer advised you to take the overland route to Denver."

"None other," Fontaine said. "General Custer and his wife Libbie are our very good friends."

Tuttle rolled his eyes. "That's the damnedest story I ever heard."

"Captain, I assure you every word of it is true."

"Your word don't count for much in this neck of the woods. I'll need some proof."

Fontaine assumed a classic profile. " 'O, I have passed a miserable night. So full of ugly sights, of ghastly dreams. That, as I am a Christian faithful man, I would not spend another such a night.' You may recognize a passage from *King Richard the Third*."

"That ain't exactly proof," Tuttle said cynically. "Any dimdot might memorize himself some Shakespeare."

"Lillian, step forward," Fontaine prompted. "Sing something for the captain, my dear."

"Without music, Papa?"

"A cappella will do quite nicely."

Lillian composed herself. She knew all Texans were former Confederates, and she sang *The Bonnie Blue Flag*. Her clear alto voice finished on a stirring note.

> *Hurrah, hurrah, for Southern rights, hurrah!*
> *Hurrah for the Bonnie Blue Flag that bears the*
>   *single star!*

"You sing right good," Tuttle complimented her. "Course, that don't mean you're a stage actress. I've heard near as good in a church choir."

"Like hell!" Sally interrupted loudly. "Not unless you're deaf as a post. She's the real article."

Tuttle squinted. "Who might you be?"

"Sally Keogh."

"You a singer, too, are you?"

"I'm his woman," she said, pointing at Stroud. "That's Rufe Stroud, all-round horse thief and woman beater. He abducted these folks, just like they told you."

Stroud blanched with rage. "You gawddamn lyin' bitch! Shut your mouth!"

Tuttle nodded to one of his Rangers. "Teach that rowdy some manners."

The Ranger whacked Stroud upside the jaw with a rifle butt. Stroud went down as though poleaxed, spitting blood and teeth. Tuttle looked pleased with the result.

"Mind your tongue," he said. "I won't have nobody takin' the Lord's name in vain in my courtroom."

"This ain't Texas!" Stroud said, levering himself to his knees. "This here's No Man's Land. You ain't got no . . . no . . ."

"Jurisdiction?"

"Yeah, you ain't got no jurisdiction here. You can't do nothin' to us."

"Don't bet on it," Tuttle said. "Time or two, I've taken jurisdiction across the border into Old Mexico. I reckon No Man's Land ain't no different."

"That's a crock!" Stroud sputtered, his front teeth missing. "You're breakin' the law yourself!"

"Have me arrested." Tuttle turned back to Fontaine. "Appears you folks was tellin' the truth, and this court won't hold you. You're free to go."

"Thank you, Captain."

Fontaine motioned Lillian and Chester away from the table. Tuttle riveted the outlaws with a look. "Rufe Stroud," he said, "we been huntin' you a long time now. Like your woman says, you're a top-notch horse thief."

"Go to hell," Stroud spat through bloody gums. "You ain't got nothin' on me."

"Monte Dunn." Tuttle fixed his gaze on Dunn. "Your name's pretty well known in Texas, too. Heard your description so often I would've knowed you in a crowd."

"You got the wrong man," Dunn blustered. "I never been in Texas in my life."

"There's many a stagecoach driver that would dispute that. You've robbed your last one."

"I'm tellin' you, I'm not your man!"

Tuttle straightened in his chair. "This here court sentences you gents to be hung by the neck till you're dead." He looked at the two cattle rustlers. "You boys are found guilty by the company you keep."

"You sorry sonovabitch!" Stroud roared. "You can't hang us without a trial!"

"Objection overruled." Tuttle got to his feet. "Let's get on with this business. Time's awastin'."

A lone oak tree stood between the cabin and the lake. Within minutes, the four men were bound, mounted on horses, and positioned beneath a stout limb. The Rangers tossed ropes over the limb and snugged them firmly to the trunk of the tree. The nooses were cinched around the necks of the doomed men.

Lillian turned away, unable to watch. Tuttle walked forward, staring up at the men. "You boys got any last words?"

"I do," Stroud said, glowering down at Sally. "Hope you're satisfied, you dumb slut. You got me hung."

"No, Rufe," she said in a teary voice. "You got yourself hung."

Tuttle motioned with his hand. The Rangers cracked the horses across the rumps, and the outlaws were jerked into the air. When the nooses snapped tight, their eyes seemed to burst from the sockets, growing huge and distended. They thrashed and kicked, their legs dancing, as though trying to gain a foothold. A full minute passed before their bodies went limp.

"We're done here," Tuttle called to his Rangers. "Get ready to move out!"

Fontaine was aghast. "Aren't you going to bury them?"

"We rode ten days to catch this bunch. I reckon we'll leave 'em as warnin' to anybody that thinks they're safe in No Man's Land."

"I daresay that would be warning enough."

Tuttle studied him a moment. "You still set on headin' for Denver?"

"Yes, we are," Fontaine said. "Why do you ask?"

"Stroud's woman and them other two floozies. We don't take prisoners, specially women. You might want to cart 'em along to Denver."

"Good God!"

"Life's hell sometimes, ain't it?"

Lillian took Sally in her arms. She watched the Rangers mount, forming in a column, and ride out over the southern rim of the basin. In the silence, the creak of rope caught her attention, and she turned, staring at the bodies swaying beneath the tree. The brutal suddenness of it still left her in shock.

She prayed as she'd never prayed before for the bright lights of Denver.

CHAPTER 16

THE ARKANSAS River brought them at last to Pueblo. They had been on the trail twelve days, and the tale of the journey was told in their appearance. They looked worn and weary, somewhat bedraggled.

Fontaine was mounted astride Rufe Stroud's roan stallion. Beside him, Chester rode the frisky gelding formerly owned by Shorty Martin. They thought it only fitting that they had appropriated the horses of their now-deceased captors. The irony of it had a certain appeal.

The buckboard was drawn by two saddle horses, drafted into service as a team. Lillian drove the buckboard, with Sally seated beside her and the other two women in the rear. Fontaine promised himself that he would never again undertake overland travel with four women. He felt somewhat like the headmaster of a seminary on wheels.

Pueblo was situated in the southern foothills of the Rockies. The surrounding countryside was arid, despite the proximity of the Arkansas River to the town. Eastward lay a vista of broken plains, and to the west towering summits were still capped with snow. The mountains marched northward like an unbroken column of sentinels.

By 1872, Pueblo was the railway center of Southern Colorado. The road into town crossed the Denver & Rio Grande tracks, which extended some ninety miles northward to Denver. Directly past the tracks, Pueblo's main thoroughfare was clogged with wagons and buggies and the boardwalks were crowded with shoppers. The street was jammed with stores, and a block away the new courthouse was under construction. The arrival of the railroad had transformed a once-isolated outpost into a bustling mecca of commerce.

Lillian was all eyes. She hadn't seen anything so civilized since they departed New York almost nine months ago. Abilene, then Dodge City and No Man's Land seemed to her a journey through a wasteland most memorable for its bloodshed and violence. Several times she'd had nightmares about the brutal hangings, bodies dangling with crooked necks beneath a tree limb. She was determined never again to stray far from a city.

Sally asked her to stop as they neared the edge of the business district. She reined the team to a halt by the boardwalk, wondering why Sally wanted to stop short of the uptown area. Over the past twelve days they had become friends, confiding in each other and sharing secrets. She called out to her father and Chester, who rode back to the buckboard. Sally faced them with a sober expression.

"We'll leave you here," she said, nodding to the other women. "We're obliged for everything you've done."

"Why?" Lillian asked, openly surprised. "We've only just arrived."

"You don't want to be seen with the likes of us. Wouldn't do much for your reputation."

"Who cares about reputation? You're as new to Pueblo as we are. How will you manage?"

"Don't worry about us," Sally said with a rueful smile. "We'll do lots better here than we did at Wild Horse Lake."

"I won't hear of it!" Lillian said adamantly. "At least wait until we get settled."

"No, trust me, it's best this way. We'll likely see you before you leave for Denver."

Sally gave her an affectionate hug. Lillian's eyes puddled with tears as the women crawled out of the buckboard. They were poorly dressed, and their belongings, brought from Wild Horse Lake, were hardly any better. She knew they would become prostitutes or, if they were lucky, kept women. She knew as well that Sally was fibbing about getting together. She would never see them again.

The women walked away, Sally waving back over her shoulder. Fontaine waited a moment for Lillian to collect herself, then reined his horse around. Uptown, he quickly surveyed the street and led them toward the Manitou House Hotel. An imposing brick structure, three stories high, the hotel had two bellmen. They wrestled the steamer trunks off the buckboard and carried them inside. Fontaine turned to Chester.

"Lillian and I will register," he said. "Find the nearest livery stable and sell the lot. Horses, buckboard, everything."

"All right," Chester said. "What price should I ask?"

"Take whatever you're offered. I'm happy to say we have completed our last overland expedition. We will travel by train from now on."

"Dad, that sounds good to me. Hope I never see a horse again."

"I devoutly second the motion."

Fontaine engaged a suite on the third floor. After their travails, he informed Lillian, they were due some modicum of comfort. The suite contained a sitting room and two bedrooms, with windows overlooking the street. Lillian would take one bedroom, and Fontaine would share the other one with Chester. He ordered the bellmen to bring corrugated metal tubs for each bedroom and loads of hot water.

Lillian thought it grand enough for royalty. By the time she unpacked her trunk, the tub and hot water arrived. She spent the next hour luxuriating in steamy bliss, unable to remember when she'd been so content. Her very soul seemed encrusted with grime from No Man's Land and the overland trek, and she gave herself over to the cleansing of a good scrub and washing her hair. She stepped from the tub reborn.

Some while later she wandered into the sitting room. She was barefoot, wearing a fluffy robe, her hair wrapped in a towel. Fontaine, already bathed, shaved, and dressed, was attired in a suit he'd had pressed while he was in the tub. He was standing by the windows, staring out over the town, and turned when she entered the room. Before he could speak, Chester came through the door.

"I was becoming concerned," Fontaine said. "What took you so long, Chet?"

Chester grinned, pulling a leather pouch from his coat pocket. He dumped a mound of gold coins on a table by the sofa. "I finally talked them out of three hundred dollars."

"Three hundred!" Lillian yelped excitedly. "We're rich!"

"Bravo, my boy," Fontaine congratulated him. "You obviously have a gift for finance."

"I don't know about that." Chester shrugged modestly. "But I have to say, I enjoyed the dickering. It's fun to get the better of the deal."

"Yes, of course," Fontaine said. "Now, hurry along and have your bath. Lillian will be ready before you are."

"Where are we going?"

"Why, we're off to see the town. I'm looking forward to a decent meal."

Early that evening they emerged from an Italian restaurant recommended by the hotel. Fontaine was impressed by the service and, even more so, the food; they were stuffed on fresh garden salad, beef cannelloni, and a rich assortment of pastries. On the street, Fontaine suggested they have a look at some of Pueblo's variety theaters. He was interested to see what played well in the Rockies.

The sporting district was south of the business center. There, as in most western towns, the stage shows were mingled among saloons and gambling establishments. The largest, and by far the most crowded, was the Tivoli Variety Theater. A barnlike structure, the Tivoli boasted the longest bar in Pueblo, assorted games of chance, and a wide stage at the rear of the room. Fontaine arranged for a table near the orchestra.

A waiter seated them as a magician produced a rabbit from a top hat. Then, playing to the audience, he brought forth a pair of doves from a silk scarf. By the time Fontaine and Chester were served drinks, the headline act, billed as the Ethiopian Minstrels, pranced onstage. The troupe of twelve men, all in blackface, proceeded to rattle their tambourines while they sang and ribbed one another with colorful badinage. Fontaine was fascinated.

"I know this act," he said. "They played many of the theaters we did on the circuit back East."

"By golly, you're right," Chester remarked. "I remember we followed them into Syracuse one time. I forget the name of the theater."

"The Rialto."

Fontaine fell silent. He watched the minstrels clown and trade barbs, but his thoughts seemed elsewhere. His features were a study in concentration, and when the curtain came down, he scarcely bothered to applaud. He looked around at Lillian and Chester with a buoyant expression.

"I've just had a marvelous idea," he said. "Do you recall the roundabout message we got from the owner of the Alcazar Theater in Denver? That we would have to audition before he would consider booking us?"

"Yes, I do," Lillian replied. "You thought it was awfully stuffy of him."

"Well, a better plan occurs to me now. We will make our name here and then storm the gates of Denver."

"You mean . . . here . . . in Pueblo?"

"Exactly!"

"Oh, Papa, I so wanted to go on to Denver. Libbie Custer said it is absolutely cosmopolitan."

"Think a moment, my dear," Fontaine said earnestly. "We haven't yet made our name on the Western circuit. A short time here and we enter Denver with headliner billing."

"Listen to him," Chester encouraged her. "Pueblo may not be cosmopolitan, but it's the right place to start.

We need good notices going into Denver."

"No question of it!" Fontaine said vigorously. "We will make them *beg* for The Fontaines!"

Lillian knew she'd been outvoted. However disappointing, her father was wise in the ways of the theater. Pueblo really was the place to start.

Denver would have to wait.

Late the following morning they returned to the Tivoli. Bartenders were busy stocking the shelves, and one of them pointed toward the rear. The office was off to one side of the stage.

Nate Varnum, the owner, was a sparrow of a man. He was short and slight, with thinning hair and a reedy voice. At their knock, he invited them into the office and offered them seats. Fontaine went straight to the point.

"Mr. Varnum, I'm quite confident you are familiar with The Fontaines. We have been a headline act back East for many years."

"No, can't say as I am," Varnum commented. "How'd you wind up in Pueblo?"

"We decided to come West," Fontaine said evasively. "Naturally, we've heard a good deal about you and your theater. All of it quite complimentary, I might add."

"Hottest spot in town, that's for sure."

"And the very reason we are here. I see by the billboard that the Ethiopian Minstrels are closing tonight."

Varnum grimaced. "You know Foster and Davis, the comedy act?"

"Indeed we do," Fontaine said. "They were on the undercard when we played the Orpheum in New York."

"Well, they were supposed to open tomorrow night. But I got a wire from Burt Tully, he owns the Alcazar in Denver. Davis dropped dead last night in the middle of the act. Heart attack."

"I am most distressed to hear that, Mr. Varnum. Phil Davis was a consummate performer."

"Well, anyway, your timing's good," Varnum said. "I need an act and you pop up out of nowhere. What is it you folks do, exactly?"

Fontaine explained the nature of their show. Varnum listened, his birdlike features revealing very little. He gave them a pensive look when Fontaine finished.

"I'll have to see it," he said. "We're not open for business till noon. You got any objection to doing it now?"

"Not at all, my dear fellow. We would be delighted, absolutely delighted."

Varnum led them out to the theater. He was a middling piano player and offered to accompany Lillian. She sang *Wondrous Love* as her opening number, and then Fontaine delivered a soliloquy from *Hamlet*. Working as an ensemble, they next performed the melodrama *A Husband's Vengeance*. Lillian closed the show with an evocative rendition of *Molly Bawn*.

On the last note, Varnum smiled at her, nodding his approval. He swung around on the piano stool, facing Fontaine and Chester, who were seated at one of the tables. His expression was neutral.

"Lillian's a natural," he said. "Great voice, good looks, lots of emotion. Anybody ever think of calling her Lilly?"

"Yes, they have," Lillian said, descending a short flight of stairs beside the stage. "I was billed that way at our last two engagements."

"Good, that's what we'll use." Varnum rose from the piano stool. "Now, let's talk about your material. You can hold an audience only so long with love ballads. Don't you know any snappy tunes?"

"I usually sing selections similar to what you heard."

"Little lady, you have to be versatile to get to the top. So let me put it another way. Do you want to be a star?"

"Mr. Varnum, if you please," Fontaine interrupted. "My daughter will not lower herself to the vulgarian."

"Hush, Papa," Lillian said sharply. "Let him talk."

Fontaine was stunned into silence by her tone. Varnum glanced from one to the other, then turned to Lillian. He spread his hands in a conciliatory gesture.

"I don't mean dirty stuff," he said. "I'm talking about songs with some spirit, a little oomph. You want to leave the audience feeling good. End it on an upnote."

"Could you give me an illustration?"

"How about *Buffalo Gals*? Or maybe *Sweet Betsy from Pike*? Do you know songs like that?"

"Yes, I know them."

"Well?"

Lillian considered it, slowly nodded. "I could open the show with a ballad and close with something more lively. Would that work?"

"You bet it would!"

"Then it's settled."

"Not just exactly." Varnum's gaze swung around to Fontaine. "Lilly's fine and the melodrama ought to play well. But I can't use the Shakespeare."

Fontaine stiffened. "May I ask why not?"

"Shakespeare's too highbrow for our crowd. They want to be entertained."

"For your information, Shakespeare has been entertaining audiences for almost three hundred years. I rather think it will play well in your . . . establishment."

"Don't try to teach me my business, Fontaine. I said it's out and that's final. No Shakespeare."

"Then we've wasted your time," Lillian said forcefully. "Our act is as you've seen it, Mr. Varnum. All or nothing."

"There's no place for you in Pueblo but the Tivoli. I doubt the other joints would even take the melodrama."

"Yes, but that leaves you without a headliner tomorrow night . . . doesn't it?"

"You'd do that to save ten minutes of Shakespeare?"

"I believe I just have."

Varnum clenched his teeth. "You're tougher than you look, Lilly. I'll give you fifty a week for the whole act."

"A hundred," Lillian countered. "Not a penny less."

"You know, it's a good thing you sing as well as you do. Otherwise the whole bunch of you would be out on the street. All right, a hundred it is."

"Thank you very much, Mr. Varnum."

Arrangements were made for Lillian to rehearse with the orchestra the next morning. Then, after a cursory round of handshakes, Fontaine stalked out of the theater. Lillian and Chester followed along, and they turned back toward the hotel. Fontaine let go a bitter laugh.

"Shakespeare has no currency with our new employer. As he said, it is a good thing you sing so well, my dear."

"Oh, Papa," Lillian said, taking his arm. "You'll be just wonderful, wait and see. You always are."

"To quote the Bard," Fontaine replied. " 'When he had occasion to be seen, he was but as the cuckoo in

June. Heard, not regarded.' I am about to become the cuckoo of Pueblo."

Fontaine began drinking that afternoon. The more he drank, the more his perception of things became clear. He realized that, but for Lillian's voice, they would not open at the Tivoli tomorrow night. Even more, he toyed with the idea that the West was no place for a thespian and thought perhaps it was true. He felt as though he'd lost control of some essential part of his life and wondered where and how. By early evening, he was too drunk to stand.

Chester put him to bed shortly before seven o'clock. Lillian was waiting when he returned, seated on the sofa. Her features were taut with worry, and she looked on the verge of tears. She waited until he sat down.

"I feel like I'm responsible. Why didn't I let Father deal with Varnum? He must resent me terribly."

"No, you're wrong," Chester said. "It's something else entirely."

"What?"

"You're the only thing keeping this act together. Varnum was right when he said we'd be out on the street except for you. Dad finally saw it for himself today."

"Oh, that simply isn't true! I don't believe it for a minute."

"Yeah, it was true in Abilene and Dodge City, and it's true here. Like it or not, you'd better get used to the idea. You're the star of the show."

A tear rolled down Lillian's cheek. Her father was so proud and dignified, so defined by his years in the theater. A Shakespearean who had devoted his life to his art. She swore herself to an oath.

She wouldn't let him become the cuckoo of Pueblo.

CHAPTER 17

A TEAM of acrobats gyrated around the stage. The Tivoli was packed for the opening night of the new headliners. Handbills had been plastered around town and an advertisement had appeared in the *Pueblo Sentinel*. The boldest line left no question as to the star of the show:

LILLY FONTAINE & THE FONTAINES

Lillian waited in the wings. She watched the acrobats as she prepared to go on with her opening number. Her hair was stylishly arranged in a chignon, and overnight she'd sponged and pressed her gowns. She looked radiant, her checks flushed with excitement.

Yet, appearances aside, she was worried. The Tivoli was the largest theater they'd played since leaving New York, and hopefully, their entrée to bigger things in Denver. Her father had read the ad in the newspaper and passed it along with no comment whatever about his second billing. She was deeply troubled by his silence.

The audience rewarded the acrobats with modest applause. The curtains swished closed as they bounded into the wings, and Lillian moved to center stage. As the curtains opened, she stood bathed in the glow of the footlights, and the orchestra segued into *We Parted By*

The River Side. Her voice sent a hush through the crowd.

The lyrics told the story of lovers biding fond adieu until they could be reunited. Lillian sang the ballad with ardent emotion, her eyes lingering here and there on members of the audience. Down front, seated at separate tables, she noticed two men dressed in frock coats and expensive silk cravats. Their attire set them apart from the other men in the crowd.

On the last note of the ballad, the audience exploded with applause. She bowed her way offstage, aware that the two well-dressed men were on their feet, trying to outclap one another. Her father was waiting in the wings, dressed in costume for *Macbeth*, and she gave him an encouraging kiss on the cheek. She smelled liquor on his breath.

Fontaine walked to center stage. He had been nipping at whiskey all day, and it had taken the edge off his hangover from last night. The liquor had dulled his dismal mood as well, for he was still unsettled by the ad in the morning newspaper. But he was determined that his sudden demotion to a supporting role would not affect his performance. His voice boomed out over the theater.

> *Tomorrow, and tomorrow, and tomorrow,*
> *Creeps in this petty pace from day to day,*
> *To the last syllable of recorded time;*
> *And all our yesterdays have lighted fools*
> *The way to dusty death. Out, out, brief candle!*
> *Life's but a walking shadow, a poor player*
> *That struts and frets his hour upon the stage,*
> *And then is heard no more; it is a tale*

Told by an idiot, full of sound and fury,
Signifying nothing. . . .

Lillian was overcome with emotion. Her eyes teared as she watched from the wings, never prouder of him than at this moment. She prayed there would be no catcalls or jeers from the crowd, and her eyes quickly scanned the theater. The two men she'd noted before, seated close to the stage, were following the performance with respectful interest. She got the impression that the audience, though restless, was looking to the men to set the example.

After a moment, she hurried backstage. She'd been given a tiny dressing room, and she began changing into her costume for the melodrama. She hung her teal gown on a hanger and slipped into the clinging cotton frock she would wear as a love-stricken young maiden. As she was brushed her hair to shoulder length, one of the chorus girls stopped in the doorway. Her name was Lulu Banes.

"Sweetie, I hafta tell you," she said with a bee-stung smile. "You got a real nice set of pipes."

"Why, thank you, Lulu."

Lillian had met her at rehearsal earlier in the day. Some of the chorus girls kept their distance, waiting to see if Lillian thought herself a prima donna. But Lulu was bubbly and outgoing, and they'd immediately hit it off. Lillian looked at her now in the mirror.

"Do you really think the audience enjoyed it?"

"Are you kiddin'?" Lulu said brightly. "You had those jokers eating out of your hand. They love you!"

"Oh, I hope so." Lillian paused with her hairbrush. "Did you see those nicely dressed gentlemen down near the front? The ones who look like bankers?"

"Spotted them, did you? That's Jake Tallant and Hank Warner, the biggest ranchers in these parts. And, sweetie, they're both rich as Midas!"

"I thought the crowd was watching them with unusual interest. Now I know why."

"No, that's not it," Lulu said archly. "Everybody was waiting to see which one pulled a gun. The crowd probably had bets down."

"Are you serious?" Lillian asked. "Do they dislike each other that much?"

"Hate would be more like it. Those two have been fighting a range war for almost a year. They're sworn enemies."

"Well, I must say I'm surprised. They look so refined."

"Not so refined they wouldn't shoot one another. They're on their good behavior tonight."

The stage manager called Lillian. She joined her father and Chester onstage for the melodrama *The Dying Kiss*. During the performance, she kept sneaking peeks at the two ranchers and found it difficult to concentrate on her lines. They were both handsome in their own way, one dark and the other fair, their mustaches neatly trimmed. She thought it a shame they were enemies.

The crowd applauded politely at the end of the melodrama. A juggler kept them entertained while Lillian rushed backstage and changed into her royal blue gown. She had rehearsed a new number most of the afternoon, and when the curtain opened her demeanor was totally changed. Hands on her hips, she gave the audience a saucy look as the orchestra launched into a sprightly melody. She belted out the tune.

Oh, don't you remember sweet Besty from Pike
Crossed the great mountains with her lover Ike
With two yoke of oxen, a large yellow dog
A tall Shanghai rooster and one spotted hog!

The lyrics about Betsy and Ike became suggestive, though never openly risqué. Lillian danced about the stage, with a wink here and a sassy grin there. She was enjoying herself immensely, and the audience, caught up in her performance, began clapping in time to the music. She ended with a pirouette, revealing a dainty ankle, her arms spread wide. The crowd went wild.

Lillian took four curtain calls. Finally, with the audience still cheering, she waved and skipped into the wings. Fontaine and Chester, along with Nate Varnum and the rest of the cast, were waiting backstage and broke out in applause. Her features were flushed with the thrill of it all—the freedom of letting go with a snappy, foot-stomping number—and she threw herself into her father's arms. His eyes were misty with pride.

"You were magnificent," he said softly. "How I wish your mother could have seen you tonight."

"Do you think she would have liked it, Papa?"

"My dear, she would have adored it."

A waiter appeared from the stairs by the stage. He nodded to Lillian. "Ma'am," he said formally. "Mr. Jacob Tallant sends his compliments. He requests you have champagne with him at his table."

A second waiter appeared. "Miss Lillian," he said, beaming. "Mr. Henry Warner extends his most sincere congratulations. He's asked you to join him and celebrate with champagne."

"Good God!" Varnum howled. "You can't pick one over the other, Lilly. We'll have a riot on our hands!"

Lillian shrugged. "Perhaps I should accept both invitations. The three of us could share a bottle of champagne."

"Never work," Varnum told her. "Jake Tallant and Hank Warner at the same table would be like lighting the fuse on a powder keg. They'd kill one another."

Fontaine stepped forward. "May I make a suggestion, my dear?"

"Yes, of course, Papa."

"There is no reason for you to become involved in other people's problems. Politely refuse both invitations."

"That'll work," Varnum quickly added. "Gets them off the premises without a fight. Smart thinking, Fontaine."

"You should read the Bard," Fontaine said with a mocking smile. "His plays are a treatise on the art of masterful scheming."

Lillian turned to the waiters. "Please inform Mr. Tallant and Mr. Warner that I decline their invitations—with sincere regrets."

Varnum heaved a sigh of relief. "Thank God."

"No, old chap," Fontaine reminded him. "Thank Shakespeare."

The *Pueblo Sentinel* gave the show rave notices. Fontaine and Chester were mentioned in passing, but Lillian was the centerpiece of the review. The editor rhapsodized at length on her voice, her stage presence, and her ethereal beauty. As though anointing a saint, he dubbed her the Colorado Nightingale.

Fontaine read the paper over breakfast. He'd arranged with the hotel to have room service in the suite every morning. The waiter brought the paper along with a serving cart loaded with eggs, ham, fluffy buttermilk biscuits, and coffee. The article was on the bottom fold of the front page.

Lillian wandered into the sitting room, still dressed in her robe and nightgown. Her face was freshly scrubbed, and her hair, cascading about her shoulders, was lustrous and tawny. Fontaine never ceased to marvel that she had the gift of awakening so exquisitely attractive that it took a man's breath. She was her mother's daughter.

Chester, who had finished reading the article, was slathering butter on a biscuit. He looked up as Lillian poured herself a cup of coffee. "Here she is," he said with a broad grin. "The Colorado Nightingale."

"Chet, really, it's too early for jokes."

"No joke," he said, spearing a hunk of ham with his fork. "Have a look at the paper."

Lillian sat down on the sofa. She placed her cup on the table and scanned the newspaper article. Then she read it again, more slowly. Her expression was pensive.

"Well, it's very nice," she said, folding the paper. "But I wasn't *that* good."

"Indeed you were," Fontaine corrected her. "I believe adding a number with quicker tempo inspirited your performance. You've found your true mêtier, my dear."

"Oh, Papa!" Her face was suddenly suffused with joy. "I'm so happy you think so. I felt so . . . so alive."

Fontaine nodded. "There is no question you held the audience enthralled. They would have listened to you sing all night."

"Why not!" Chester said, grinning around a mouthful of biscuit. "She's the Colorado Nightingale."

"I rather like it," Fontaine observed. "There's a certain ring to it, and it's catchy. Not to mention the metaphoric symmetry—the nightingale."

Lillian laughed. "I only wish it were true. I'd love to sound like a nightingale."

"Never underestimate yourself," Fontaine said, wagging his finger. "You have a lovely voice, and a range few singers ever attain. I see no limit to your career."

Lillian felt a stab of pain. She knew he was speaking as her father, and the pride was evident in his voice. Yet the newspaper article had scarcely mentioned his name or Chester's, and she sensed her father's hurt, the wound to his dignity. She sensed as well that she could offer no comfort, nothing to soothe his hurt. Anything she said would only make it worse.

"Aren't you going to eat?" Chester asked, buttering another biscuit. "A singer needs to keep up her strength. We're sure to pack the house tonight."

"Oh, nothing for me," Lillian said. "I'm having lunch with Lulu Banes. She's such a nice girl."

"Yes, I thought so, too," Fontaine remarked. "She struck me as a cut above the other girls. I'm delighted you've found a friend."

"She's really quite—"

A knock sounded at the door. Fontaine rose, crossed the room, and opened it to find a bellman in the hallway. The bellman gave him a sheepish smile.

"Sorry to bother you, Mr. Fontaine. We've got sort of a problem."

"Yes?"

"Well, sir, there's two cowhands downstairs. One sent here by Jake Tallant and the other from Hank Warner."

"How does that concern me?"

"Not you, your daughter," the bellman said nervously. "They've both got horses for Miss Fontaine."

Fontaine frowned. "Horses?"

"Yessir, outside on the street. Appears like Mr. Tallant and Mr. Warner both sent your daughter a present. Couple of real nice horses."

"One from each, is that it?"

"Yessir, and those cowhands are down there fit to fight. I mean to say, both of them showing up with horses at the same time. They're hot under the collar."

"Wait here a moment, young man."

Fontaine turned back into the suite. He looked at Lillian with a wry smile. "I believe you are being courted, my dear. Did you hear what was said?"

Lillian walked to the window. Fontaine and Chester followed, and they stared down at the street. Outside the hotel were two cowhands, studiously trying to ignore each other. One held the reins of a glossy sorrel gelding and the other those of a chocolate-spotted pinto mare.

"Horses!" Lillian said uncertainly. "What kind of gift is that?"

"Hardly the question," Fontaine advised. "More to the point, do you wish to accept gifts from men you've never met—albeit admirers?"

"No, I don't," Lillian said, after a moment's thought. "I think it would be inappropriate."

"Quite so."

Fontaine returned to the door. "If you will be so kind," he said to the bellman. "Inform the gentlemen downstairs that Miss Fontaine declines the gifts. They may so advise Mr. Tallant and Mr. Warner."

"Yessir, Mr. Fontaine," the bellman replied. "I'll tell'em just what you said."

"Thank you so much."

Lillian was flattered but nonetheless embarrassed. Chester attempted to josh with her about her new beaux, and she went to her bedroom. She stayed there the rest of the morning, emerging shortly before noon in a fitted cotton dress and carrying a parasol. She smiled at her father.

"I'm going to meet Lulu for lunch, Papa."

"Enjoy yourself, my dear."

"Take care, little sister," Chester called out. "Don't talk to men with strange horses."

"I wonder that I talk to you, Chester Fontaine!"

Lillian slammed the door. She was still steaming when she joined Lulu at a restaurant some ten minutes later. After a waiter took their orders, she told Lulu about the horses and how upset she was by the entire affair. Lulu was of a different opinion.

"Sugar, you ought to count your blessings. I wish I had those two scamps after me."

"Oh, honestly!" Lillian said. "Whoever heard of offering a lady *horses?* Everyone in town will be talking!"

"Who cares?" Lulu scoffed. "If they're wearing a skirt, they're just jealous. They'd give their eyeteeth to catch Jake Tallant or Hank Warner."

"Money isn't everything."

"A good-looking man with money is *definitely* every-thing. Take my word for it, sweetheart."

Lillian was silent a moment. "Tell me about them, will you? Why are they such enemies?"

Lulu quickly warmed to the subject. Jake Tallant was a widower, with two children, who owned an enormous ranch on the south side of the Arkansas River. Hank Warner, a bachelor, owned an equally large cattle spread on the north side of the river. For years, they had disputed water rights where the river curled through their separate spreads. Then, just within the last year, it had developed into a range war.

"I don't know all the details," Lulu concluded. "Something to do with one of those old Spanish land grants. You'd think either one had enough land for one man."

"How did the range war start?"

"Warner sued Tallant in court, and don't ask me what for. All that legal stuff makes me dizzy."

"How rich are they?"

"Sugar, they've both got more money than God!"

Lillian vaguely wondered why she'd even asked the question. She was still somewhat offended by the incident with the horses. Lulu finally uttered a sly laugh. "One thing's for sure."

"Oh?"

"Those two aren't through with you yet. The game has just started."

"What game?"

"Why, the game to see who wins your favor. You're the prize."

Lillian sniffed. "I have no intention of being any-one's prize."

"We'll see."

"What do you mean by that?"

Lulu smiled. "Get ready for the whirlwind, sugar. It's headed your way."

CHAPTER 18

THE FONTAINES' second night at the Tivoli was standing-room-only. The crowd spilled out of the theater into the barroom and onto the street. Everyone wanted to see the Colorado Nightingale.

Jake Tallant and Hank Warner were again seated at tables in the front row. Neither of them appeared in the least daunted by the unceremonious refusal of their gifts. Their eyes were glued to Lillian every moment she was onstage.

Bouquets of wildflowers from both men were delivered backstage following the show. There were cards with the flowers, the script tactfully phrased, requesting the honor of calling on Lillian. She was flattered by their perseverance but again declined the invitations. Still, she considered flowers a more appropriate gift than horses. She put them in a vase in her dressing room.

The next morning she awoke expecting some new enticement to appear at the hotel. She was oddly disappointed when nothing was delivered to the suite and no messages were left at the desk. There was something titillating about being courted by suitors who were not only handsome but also enormously wealthy. She wondered if she had offended them by her seeming lack of interest. She wondered even more why she cared.

Early that afternoon there was a knock at the door. Chester admitted a man who wore the dog collar of a minister and, in fact, introduced himself as the Reverend Buford Blackburn. He was portly, with a thatch of hair the color of a pumpkin and the ever-ready smile of a preacher. His manner indicated that he was the very soul of discretion.

Fontaine was seated in an easy chair, reading the paper. Lillian came out of her bedroom, curious as to who might be calling. Chester ushered the minister into the sitting room and performed the introductions. There was an awkward moment while everyone got themselves arranged, Fontaine and Blackburn in overstuffed chairs and Lillian and Chester on the sofa. Fontaine opened the conversation.

"Well now, Reverend, a man of God is always welcome in our humble abode. To what do we owe the pleasure?"

"I am here on a mission," Blackburn ventured in an orotund voice. "One might say at the behest of Jacob Tallant and Henry Warner."

"Indeed?" Fontaine arched an eyebrow. "I take it this has to do with my daughter."

"Mr. Fontaine, I am the pastor of the First Methodist Church. Jake Tallant and Hank Warner are among my most loyal and devoted parishioners. They have asked me to act as their emissary."

"In what regard?"

"A truce keeper," Blackburn said with a small shrug. "Jake and Hank are fine, honorable men, true servants of Christ. Unfortunately, they are also the bitterest of enemies."

"So we are told," Fontaine allowed. "And what, precisely, is your mission with respect to Lillian?"

"These gentlemen hold your daughter in the highest esteem. They wish to call on her, and I am here to plead their case."

"A jolly plot indeed, Reverend. Shakespeare might have written it himself."

Blackburn smiled. "These are men of honorable intentions. In the most formal sense of the word, they wish to court your daughter."

"I see," Fontaine said. "Perhaps your remarks should be addressed to Lillian. She is, after all, the purpose of your mission."

"Yes, of course." Blackburn turned to her with a benign expression. "Miss Fontaine, let me assure you most earnestly that Mr. Tallant and Mr. Warner are sincere in their admiration of you. They wish only to be given the opportunity to call on you in person."

Lillian felt like hugging herself. She was all the more flattered that the men had sent a minister as their emissary. Their persistence as well spoke to the matter of sincerity and a guileless, rather unaffected admiration. Yet she was still wary.

"May I be frank, Reverend?" She waited until he nodded. "I understand Mr. Tallant and Mr. Warner are involved in what's known as a 'range war.' I have no interest in associating with violent men."

"Your fears are unjustified, Miss Fontaine. The range war you speak of is being fought in a court of law. Nothing of a violent nature has occurred."

"Everyone I've spoken with believes they might shoot one another on a moment's notice. You said yourself they are the bitterest enemies."

"And so they are," Blackburn conceded. "But these men are good Christians, and despite their differences, neither of them has resorted to violence. I have utmost confidence they will settle the matter in a peaceful fashion."

Lillian considered a moment. "Very well," she said at length. "You may tell them I will be most happy to have them call on me. You might also tell them of my aversion to violent men."

"I shall faithfully follow your wishes, Miss Fontaine."

"How will I decide which one to see first?"

"Oh, yes, that is a problem," Blackburn confessed. "Neither of them would want to feel slighted."

"That's simple enough," Chester broke in with an amused laugh. "Draw straws for the lucky man."

"Bully!" Blackburn exclaimed in quick agreement. "Certainly no one could object to a random draw."

Fontaine thought the Bard would have written it as a farce. Lillian went along, even though she felt somewhat the object of a lottery. Rev. Buford Blackburn, intent on his mission, would have agreed to anything short of blasphemy. A cleaning maid provided the broom straws.

Jake Tallant, his luck running strong, won the draw.

Lillian bought a new dress for the occasion. She was a perfect size 4, and the clerk at Mendel's Mercantile was delighted with her patronage. By now, she was something of a celebrity, and virtually every man in Pueblo knew her on sight. Her visit to the store caused a minor sensation.

The fabric of the dress was sateen, snugly fitted to complement her figure. Her black pearls against the dove gray material made the outfit all the more spectacular. Her hair was upswept and she wore a hat adorned with feathers the color of her dress. She looked stunning.

Tallant called for her at six o'clock. The plan was to have an early get-acquainted dinner and deliver her to the theater in time for the eight o'clock curtain. Fontaine and Chester greeted the rancher with cordiality and made small talk until Lillian swept into the sitting room. Her entrance, Fontaine wryly noted, was staged for maximum effect.

The restaurant Tallant chose was the finest in Pueblo. With impeccable service and an atmosphere of decorum, it was where men of influence and wealth took their wives for a night out. The tables were covered with linen, appointed with crystal and silver and the finest china. The owner greeted Tallant effusively, bowing to Lillian, and personally escorted them to their table. A waiter materialized with menus.

Lillian was charmed by all the attention. Tallant was a man of impressive bearing with a leonine head of dark hair, somewhere in his early thirties. His features were angular, set off by a sweeping mustache, and he wore a tailored charcoal suit with a patterned cravat. His manner was soft-spoken, though commanding, and he was gentlemanly in an old-world sort of way. She thought he was even more handsome up close.

Over dinner, he tried to draw her out about her life in the theater. She entertained him with a brief but amusing account of her adventures in the West. Ever so deftly, she then turned the conversation to his life and interests. He quietly explained that he was a widower and that his wife, a woman of Mexican heritage, had died of influenza just over a year ago. He had two children, a son and a daughter, ages nine and ten.

"How wonderful you had children," Lillian said, trying for a cheerful tone. "You have something of your wife in them. I'm sure they're adorable."

"Yeah, they're a pair," Tallant said proudly. "I'd like you to meet them sometime. Maybe you could come to Sunday dinner."

"I think that would be very nice."

"Don't let Hank Warner sour you on the idea. He won't have anything good to say about me."

"Oh?" Lillian was momentarily flustered by his directness. "You apparently know I'm having dinner with Mr. Warner tomorrow night."

"Reverend Blackburn told me," Tallant said with a faint smile. "He's keeping us both informed."

"Yes, I can understand that he would. He's very concerned about the difficulty between you and Mr. Warner."

"Well, that's a long story. Not a pretty one, either."

Lillian sensed he was dying to tell his version. She thought he'd raised Hank Warner's name for that very reason. Tonight was his night to impress on her the justness of his cause and the strength of his character. With only a little coaxing, she got him talking. She found it a fascinating story.

All land north of the Rio Grande had been ceded to the United States following the 1846 war with Mexico. By the Treaty of Guadalupe Hidalgo, the U.S. government agreed to respect the holdings of Mexican land-owners. Yet the title to all property in the ceded zone had evolved from ancient land grants; the issue of who owned what was clouded by a convoluted maze of documents. To compound the problem, many of the grants overlapped one another.

Nowhere was the issue more confused than in Southern Colorado. Some Mexican landowners claimed that their holdings spilled over the New Mexico line into the southern reaches of the Rockies. At various times, land grants had been awarded by the king of Spain, the Republic of Mexico, and provincial governors who haphazardly drew a line on a map. Ownership was often nine points physical possession and one point law. For generations, the force to back the claim overrode legal technicalities.

"Maria, my wife, was the last of her line," Tallant explained. "The land had been in her family for over a hundred years, and when we were married, it became our land. No one disputed that until Warner filed his lawsuit."

"Good heavens," Lillian sympathized. "Are you saying his lawsuit is frivolous?"

"Well, he contends that the Treaty of Guadalupe Hidalgo didn't cover land grants in Colorado. Nobody ever questioned it before, so why now? He's just greedy, that's all."

"Does he have any chance of winning?"

"Not according to my lawyers," Tallant said. "They think he's plumb loco."

"And if they're wrong?" Lillian asked "What would you do then?"

"I won't be thrown off the land my wife's ancestors worked to build. Not by some scoundrel like Hank Warner."

"Yes, that would be terrible."

Lillian felt sorry for him. From what she'd just heard, there was every reason for bad blood between the two men. She halfway hoped Warner wouldn't appear at the theater for tonight's performance. But that was wishful thinking.

She knew he would be seated front and center.

Lillian was prepared to dislike Henry Warner. All she'd heard last night led her to believe he was an out-and-out rogue. But to her surprise, he was a very engaging rogue.

Warner was lithe and muscular, with sandy hair and a neatly groomed mustache. He was so personable that he charmed her father and Chester in a matter of moments. His magnetism all but took her breath.

They went to the restaurant where she'd dined last night. The owner was equally effusive in his greeting of Warner and made a production of escorting them to their table. The waiter was the same as last night, and he gave Lillian a conspiratorial smile. She hardly knew what to think.

Warner took charge. He ordered braised squab with wild rice for both of them. Then he selected a delicate white wine with a marvelous bouquet. When they clinked glasses, Lillian only sipped, but the taste was like some heady nectar. His vivid blue eyes pinned her like a butterfly to a board.

"Before anything else," he said in a deep voice, "I want to say you are the most beautiful woman I've ever seen. I intend to marry you."

Lillian was aghast. "Mr. Warner, you're frightening me."

"Call me Hank," he said jovially. "And no, Lillian—you prefer that to Lilly, don't you?—no, Lillian, I'm not frightening you. Am I?"

"How did you know I prefer Lillian?"

"Nate Varnum told me everything about you. I think he's in love with you himself."

"I somehow doubt that," Lillian said. "Do you always sweep the ladies off their feet?"

Warner chuckled, a low rumble. "As they say, the race goes to the swiftest. Jake Tallant probably convinced you I'm an immoral bounder." He paused, looking deep into her eyes. "Get to know me and you'll know better. I never toy with a lady's affections—especially yours."

Lillian tried to deflect his onslaught. "What Mr. Tallant and I discussed was your lawsuit. He is very disturbed you're attempting to take his ranch."

The remark seemed to amuse Warner. He wagged his head with a satiric smile. "Did Jake tell you about his wife?"

"Yes, as a matter of fact, he did. He said the land had been in her family for generations."

"Did he tell you that I was in love with her, too?"

"No." Lillian was visibly startled. "You were in love with another man's wife?"

"A long time ago." Warner hesitated, sipping his wine. "Jake and me were both courting Maria back in '61. Her folks were still alive then. Best people you'd ever hope to meet."

"And she married Mr. Tallant . . . Jake."

"Well, don't you see, I wasn't the lighthearted rascal that I am now. Jake beat me out."

Lillian suddenly realized it was all an act. Beneath the glib manner, there was nothing lighthearted about Henry Warner. She felt an outrush of sympathy.

"And having lost Maria, you never married?"

"Never saw her match," Warner said with a debonair grin. "Leastways, not till the night I saw you. I'm liable to propose any moment now."

The waiter appeared with a serving tray. He set their plates before them, succulent squab on beds of brown rice. Their conversation momentarily dwindled off as they took cutlery in hand and began dissecting the plump birds. Lillian savored her first bite.

"It's wonderful!" she marveled. "I've never had squab before."

"Stick with me and I'll show you a whole new world. How'd you like to go to Paris on our honeymoon?"

"I do believe you're an incorrigible flirt."

"A gentleman never lies," Warner said with a contagious smile. "You're the girl for me and no two ways about. I'm plumb smitten."

Lillian was silent for a moment. "May I ask you a personal question?"

"Darlin', for you, I'm an open book."

"Why did you wait until Maria died to sue Jake Tallant?"

Warner stopped eating. "You're a regular little firecracker. Don't miss much, do you?"

"I don't mean to pry," Lillian said with guileful innocence. "I was just curious."

"Well, what with you and me practically at the altar, I've got no secrets. I waited because I'd never have done anything to hurt Maria."

"What does that have to do with Jake's ranch?"

"Couple of things," Warner said, more serious now. "For openers, the river corkscrews all through our boundary lines. We've been fightin' over water rights for years."

Lillian looked at him. "But that isn't the main issue . . . is it?"

"No, it's not. There's an old Spanish land grant handed down through Maria. Did Jake tell you about it?"

"Yes, last night."

"Thing is, it'll never stand up in court. Jake knows it and I know it. He's just burned I opened his can of worms."

"Do you really want his ranch that badly?"

Warner grinned. "I don't want his ranch at all. I've got enough land of my own."

"I—" Lillian was shocked. "Why have you sued him, then?"

"Take a guess."

"Maria?"

"None other," Warner acknowledged. "Jake stole her away from me. Laughed about it for ten years to anybody that'd listen. I figure to have the last laugh."

Lillian thought she had never heard of anything so vindictive. But then, on second thought, she knew she'd heard a deeper truth. Henry Warner was a victim of the most powerful emotion imaginable. He had lived with a broken heart until the day Maria Tallant died. She felt his sorrow beneath the veneer of devil-may-care nonchalance.

"Do you still love her . . . even now?"

"No, ma'am," Warner said with a bold smile. "You are the light of my life. I hear the wedding bells ringing!"

Lillian wondered if he saw in her the ghost of a dead woman. She hoped not.

CHAPTER 19

LILLIAN'S DRESSING room was scarcely more than a cubicle. She was stripped to her chemise, seated before a tiny mirror lighted by small coal-oil lamps. She began applying kohl to her eyelids.

Following dinner, Hank Warner had dropped her off at the stage-door entrance. Her first number was usually around eight-thirty, after the juggler, the fire-eater, and a comic who told risqué jokes. That gave her an hour or so to finish her makeup.

Decent women never wore makeup in public. Lillian wished social conventions were different; she thought pinching one's cheeks to give them color was prudish and outmoded. She liked the way kohl enhanced her eyes and how nicely rouge accentuated her features. Still, she had to limit herself to nightly appearances on-stage. Only prostitutes wore makeup on the street.

There was a light rap at the door. She slipped into a smock she'd bought to cover herself backstage. She was proud of her figure but cautious around stagehands and male performers of any variety. Her mother had taught her that a girl's physical assets, if kept a mystery, were all the more a temptation. She tightened the belt on the smock. "Come in!" she called out. "I'm decent."

Lulu Banes stepped into the dressing room. She was in full war paint, wearing a skimpy peekaboo gown that left little to the imagination. The chorus line always opened the show, and the girls were usually costumed before anyone else. She paused inside the door.

"I couldn't wait till later," she said with a bee-stung smile. "How'd it go with Handsome Hank?"

"Oh, very nice," Lillian said, seating herself before the mirror. "He was a perfect gentleman."

"Honey, they all are till they get their way. C'mon, skip straight to the hot stuff."

By now, Lulu was her confidante. Last night, Lillian had related the details of her dinner with Jake Tallant. She'd never before had a close woman friend, and she was pleased to have someone to talk to. She knew Lulu thrived on gossip.

"You have to remember," she said, "everything is in confidence. You can't repeat a word to anyone."

"Cross my heart." Lulu drew a sign over her breast. "My lips are sealed."

"Well . . ." Lillian patted rouge on her cheekbones. "I know it will be hard to believe. . . ."

"Uh-oh, here it comes. What'd he say?"

"Hank was really quite open. He told me he doesn't want Jake's ranch. That isn't why he sued."

"Nooo," Lulu said slowly, with a look of undisguised amusement. "And you bought that?"

Lillian nodded. "I most certainly did."

"Sounds like malarkey to me."

"Not when you know the reason. Hank was in love with Maria Tallant, Jake's wife. He waited until she died to bring legal action."

"Omigod!" Lulu's eyes went round. "He was having an affair with Tallant's wife?"

"No, no," Lillian said dismissively. "They were rivals for her affections long before she married Jake. Hank has loved her all this time."

"You lost me there, kiddo. What's that got to do with the lawsuit?"

"Hank wants Jake to suffer the way he's suffered. How tragic that they both loved the same woman . . . and lost her."

"Uh-huh." Lulu raised a skeptical eyebrow. "Sounds to me like Hank is after revenge. Don't you think?"

"Yes, perhaps a little," Lillian admitted. "But only because he'd loved her all these years. I mean, think about it, he never married!"

"Sweetie, I hate to say it, but you're a soft touch. That's the most cockamamy story I ever heard."

"I think it's rather romantic."

Lulu *humphed.* "Are you going to see him again?"

"Saturday," Lillian said. "He invited me to see his ranch. I accepted."

"And you're having Sunday dinner at Jake Tallant's ranch? You're an awfully busy little bee."

"Yes, but they're both such nice men. How could I refuse?"

"Far be it from me to give you advice. . . ."

"Oh, don't be silly, go ahead."

"Whatever sad tale they tell you . . . ?"

"Yes?"

"Forget a grain of salt, honey. Take it with a spoon."

Later that evening, Lillian went on for her opening number. Tallant and Warner, as usual, were seated at tables down front. They applauded mightily even as she stood bathed in the footlights, each trying to outdo the other. She blushed, avoiding their eyes, as the maestro lifted his baton and led the orchestra into *Aura Lee*. Her voice floated dreamily across the theater.

Aura Lee, Aura Lee
Maid of golden hair
Sunshine came along with thee
And took my heart for fair

Lillian thought the song was suitable to the moment. Never before had she had two such handsome and pleasantly wealthy men vying for her attention. She told herself that Lulu was simply too protective, perhaps too cynical. There was no need for a grain of salt.

No need for salt at all.

Hank Warner called for her the next morning. He was attired in range clothes, whipcord trousers stuffed in his boots and a dark placket shirt. His hat was tall-crowned, roweled spurs on his boots and a Colt pistol strapped on his hip. He looked every inch the cattleman.

Lillian wore a muslin day dress, a gay little bonnet atop her mound of curls. She carried her parasol and snapped it open as he assisted her into a buckboard drawn by a matched team of sorrel mares. The sun was in their faces as they drove east from town.

"I'm so excited," she said happily. "I've never seen an honest-to-goodness ranch."

Warner smiled secretly. "Well, you're in for a treat today. I arranged a surprise."

"Oh, I love surprises! What is it?"

"Wouldn't be a surprise if I told you, would it? You'll just have to wait and see."

"Will it be worth the wait?"

"I've got a notion you'll approve."

Near the edge of town, they had to wait until a train pulled out of the railroad station. As they crossed the tracks, she gave him a quick sideways inspection. He caught the look.

"What?" he said. "Something wrong?"

"Nothing really." Lillian titled her parasol against the glare of the sun. "It's just that I've never seen you wear a gun before."

"You've never seen it because I was wearing a suit. I carry it tucked in my waistband. You shy of guns?"

"No, not in the right hands."

"Well, I have to say, I'm right handy."

"I think you are making fun of me."

"You're too pretty to make fun of. I'm plumb struck blind."

"In that event"—Lillian playfully batted her eyelashes—"I insist you tell me your surprise."

Warner laughed, "Now that would spoil the fun. Wait till we get there."

The ranch was located some five miles east of Pueblo. Warner explained that he owned nearly a hundred thousand acres of grazeland, all of it north of the Arkansas River. The range was well watered, sheltered from plains blizzards by the walls of a canyon, and covered with lush grama grass that fattened steers. He ran about ten thousand head of cattle.

Lillian was stunned into silence. She couldn't imagine anyone owning so much land, and as the road wound along the canyon, she was mesmerized by vast herds of cattle grazing beneath a forenoon sun. The headquarters compound, situated leeward of the canyon walls, consisted of a main house, a large bunkhouse, and a corral. The buildings were stout log structures.

"Not the grandest in the world," Warner said, halting the buckboard in front of the main house. "But it's warm in the winter and cool in the summer. Built to last, too."

"Yes, I can see." Lillian thought it looked like a fort with windows. "It's really very nice."

She realized he was trying to impress her. The land, the cattle, the house, an empire built on an ocean of grass. There were at least thirty men gathered outside the bunkhouse, and Warner explained that they were some of the cowhands on his payroll. A whole steer, cleaved down the middle, was being roasted over a bed of coals. The day, he told her, had been planned to honor her visit to the ranch. Later they would celebrate with a traditional Western feast.

The festivities started with an exhibition by Warner's top broncbuster. A buckskin renegade was blindfolded with a gunnysack while Alvin Johnson, the broncbuster, got himself mounted. When the sack was removed, the horse exploded at both ends, like a stick of dynamite bursting within itself. All four feet left the ground as the buckskin swapped ends in midair and sunfished across the corral in a series of bounding catlike leaps. The battle went on for what seemed an eternity, with the men whooping and shouting as the horse whirled and kicked with squeals of outrage. Johnson rode the bronc to a standstill.

"Bravo! Bravo!" Lillian cried, clapping loudly when it was over. "I've never seen anything so exciting in my life. It was just wonderful!"

Warner seemed pleased. "No doubt about it, Alvin's the best. Glad you liked it."

"Your surprise really was worth waiting for."

"There's more to come, lots more. All for you."

The men took turns aboard pitching broncs. None of them were as good as Alvin Johnson, and most got thrown off. But there was a spirit of camaraderie about it, and everyone hooted and cheered when a rider got dumped. After the broncbusting, there was a demonstration of fancy work with a lariat. Longhorns were hazed onto open ground near the corral, and horsemen would cast loops at a dead run, snaring the steers' horns and hind legs, and neatly drop them in midstride. Lillian applauded the men's feats like a young girl at her first circus.

Late that afternoon the feast was served. Cooks sliced choice cuts off the roasted steer and loaded plates with beef, beans, and sourdough biscuits fresh from a Dutch oven. The men scattered about the compound, wolfing down their food, while Lillian and Warner were served at a table in the shade of a leafy oak tree. Afterward, Warner gave her a tour of the house, which, much as she expected, was a masculine domain. The parlor was dominated by a huge stone fireplace with a bearskin rug and lots of leather furniture.

Warner drove her back into town as sunset fired the sky beyond distant mountains. Lillian was exhilarated, still bubbling with excitement, and yet oddly reflective. She had the feeling she'd spent the day auditioning for a role. Mistress of the manor or perhaps queen of the cowboys.

She wasn't sure it was the part for her.

The Fontaines were invited to Jacob Tallant's for dinner the following day. The noon meal on Sunday, commonly called dinner by country folk, was considered the occasion of the week. Fontaine rented a buggy and team at the livery stable.

The ranch headquarters was located some three miles east of Pueblo. On the drive out, Lillian thought Jake Tallant was playing the diplomat by inviting her father and Chester. His intent, clearly, was to win over the entire Fontaine family. His designs on her would only be furthered by her father's blessing.

The *casa grande* reflected its Mexican heritage. The main house was one-story, constructed of native adobe, with broad wings extending off the central living quarters. Beneath a tile roof, hewn beams protruded from walls four feet thick. The window casements gleamed of tallowed oak, and the double doors were wider than a man's outspanned arms. The effect was one of old-world gentility.

The house, which overlooked the river to the north, commanded the ranch compound. The buildings formed a quadrangle, grouped with a symmetry that was at once functional and pleasing to the eye. Corrals and stables, flanked by storage sheds, angled off to the south. A commissary and an open-sided blacksmith forge were situated on a plot central to a compound that covered several acres. It looked like a small but prosperous village.

Fontaine brought the team to a halt in front of the house. Tallant hurried outside and assisted Lillian from the buggy. "Welcome to my home," he said cordially. "I trust you had a good drive from town."

"Yes, we did," Lillian replied. "The views are simply marvelous along the river."

"Quite an operation," Fontaine said, gesturing about the compound. "How large is your ranch?"

"Just over a hundred thousand acres. We run in the neighborhood of ten thousand head."

"How do you keep up with that many cows?"

"Mr. Fontaine, I often wonder myself. Please, won't you come inside?"

The interior of the house was even more impressive than the outside. The floors were tiled, and off the foyer was an immense parlor with furniture crafted of rich hardwood. Waiting in the parlor were Tallant's children, dressed in their Sunday best. The girl was nine, with the olive complexion of her mother and hair the color of a raven's wing. The boy, who was ten, favored his father, with dark, curly hair. Their eyes fixed immediately on Lillian.

"This is Jennifer," Tallant introduced them, "and this is Robert. And I warn you, they're dying of curiosity."

Lillian smiled warmly. "I'm so happy to meet you, Jennifer and Robert. Thank you for having us to your home."

"Father says you're a singer," Jennifer said, overcome with curiosity. "Will you sing something for us?"

"Why, yes, of course I will. Do you have a favorite song?"

"Father likes *Aura Lee*," Robert said with boyish enthusiasm. "He told us how you sang it the other night. He likes it a lot."

"Mind your manners," Tallant broke in. "Perhaps Miss Fontaine will favor us with a song after dinner. Although I'm afraid we don't have a piano."

"Miguel plays the guitar," Robert reminded him. "Want me to run down to the bunkhouse?"

"Not just yet, Son. I think it'll wait till we've eaten."

Dinner was served in a spacious dining room. There were two servants, a man and a woman, and they brought from the kitchen platters of spicy Mexican dishes. Fontaine, as well as Lillian and Chester, found the food delicious, if somewhat zesty to the palate. Jennifer and Robert peppered them with questions throughout the meal, eager to learn everything about their life in the theater. Fontaine, playing to a wide-eyed audience, gave them a running discourse on the wonders of Shakespeare.

After dinner, Miguel was summoned from the bunkhouse. Lillian hummed the melody for him, and he quickly found the chords on his guitar. Everyone got themselves seated in the parlor, and with Miguel strumming softly, she sang *Aura Lee*. The children were fascinated, watching her intently, and applauded wildly on the last note. When they clamored for more, Fontaine stepped into the breech, delivering a stirring passage from *Hamlet*. As her father's baritone filled the room, Lillian joined Tallant, who was standing behind the sofa. He gave her an apologetic shrug.

"I hope you don't mind," he said. "They get carried away sometimes."

"I think they're wonderful," Lillian said graciously. "You should encourage them in the arts. They enjoy it so much."

"Well, I don't have to encourage them about you. I've never seen them take to anyone so fast."

"Jennifer is so beautiful, and Robert is the very image of you. You must be very proud."

"Never more so than today, Lillian."

The afternoon sped past. Tallant gave them a tour of the compound, explaining the many facets of how a ranch operates. The children clung to Lillian, and she sensed they were starved for a woman's affection. Before anyone quite knew it, the sun heeled over to the west, and it was time to leave. Fontaine told them that actors, unlike the Lord, were allowed no rest on the Sabbath. The show, he noted jovially, must go on.

Tallant and the children saw them off. Jennifer and Robert hugged Lillian, begging her to return, and ran alongside until the buggy picked up speed. On the way into town, Lillian was silent, playing the afternoon back in her mind. Fontaine finally broke into her reverie, looking at her with an amused expression. He shook his head.

"I believe the Bard said it all," he observed wryly. " 'She's beautiful and therefore to be wooed. She is a woman, therefore to be won.' You have captured their hearts, my dear."

Lillian ignored the jest. She stared off into the fading sun and suddenly felt the race was too swift for her liking. All the more so after a visit to the Tallant ranch.

She thought she was too young to be a mother. Perhaps too young to be a wife.

CHAPTER 20

LILLIAN WRESTLED with her uncertainty all through Sunday night. Neither Tallant nor Warner attended the evening performance, and she was relieved by their absence. She needed time to sort out her feelings.

Her ambivalence was unsettling. She genuinely liked both men, though they were as different as night and day. One lived like an old-world Spanish *grandee* and the other like a devil-may-care plains buccaneer. She'd never known two men so dissimilar.

All of which was part of a larger problem. She had never been courted, and she'd never known any man intimately. Her experiences with men were of a flirtatious nature, a stolen kiss that never led to anything more. Her mother had imparted wisdom about men, but Lillian had no actual experience. She felt oddly like a vestal virgin in ancient Rome. Chaste, even wise, but nonetheless ignorant.

She wasn't sure she wanted to lose that ignorance to either of them. Jake Tallant was a gentleman of the old school, kind and considerate, almost chivalrous in manner. Yet his children, however delightful, posed the worrisome question of overnight motherhood. Hank Warner was perhaps more debonair, a puckish bon vivant with a devilish sense of humor. Still, for all his protests, he lived with the memory of a dead woman. A wife would never displace the ghost of Maria Tallant.

Lillian's ambivalence was underscored by an even more personal dilemma. Over the course of her Western odyssey, she had found some essential part of herself in the theater. She loved the audiences and the thrill of it all, the wave of adulation that came to her over the footlights. She thought she loved it more than she might ever love a man, and she wasn't willing to trade one for the other. Her stage career was, at least for now, her life.

By Monday morning, she had arrived at a partial solution. She wrote discreet notes to both Tallant and Warner, explaining that she felt overwhelmed by their attentions. The notes were identical except for the salutations, tactfully phrased word-for-word appeals for patience. She emphasized that she needed time, needed to be alone with her thoughts, for it had all happened too fast, too quickly. She asked that they not contact her until she was able to reconcile her own feelings.

The notes were secretly delivered to each of the men by Chester. He caught them separately, as they were entering the Tivoli Monday evening, and slipped them the notes in the course of a handshake. That night, and for the three days following, the men honored her wishes. They attended her performances every evening, seated at their usual tables, following her about the stage with the eyes of infatuated schoolboys. True to her request, neither of them attempted to contact her.

Friday morning she awoke with a vague sense of disquiet. Her father and Chester went out to attend to personal errands, and she was left alone with her thoughts. She couldn't identify the source of her unease, apart from the fact that she somehow felt lonely. She inwardly admitted that she missed the company of the men, Tallant for his courtly manner and Warner for his waggish humor. She wondered if a woman, after all, needed a man in her life.

Fontaine returned shortly before noon. He found her moping about, still dressed in her housecoat, staring listlessly out the window. She didn't move as he crossed the sitting room and stopped at her side. Her expression was pensive, vaguely sad. He tried for a light note.

"What's this?" he said. "I planned to take you out for lunch. Why aren't you dressed?"

"I just haven't gotten around to it."

"Come now, my dear, that is hardly an answer. What's wrong?"

"Oh, Papa." Her voice wavered. "I'm so confused."

Fontaine studied her with concern. "Need I ask the source of your confusion? Something to do with men, is it?"

"I was standing here thinking I miss them. And then I thought how perfectly ingenuous. How naive."

"No one would ever accuse you of naïveté. You are much more the sophisticate than you realize."

"Am I?" Lillian said with a tinge of melancholy. "One minute I want them out of my life, and the next I wish they were knocking on the door. How sophisticated is that, Papa?"

"You punish yourself unnecessarily," Fontaine said. "Quite often logic dictates one thing while the heart dictates another. Are you in love with either of these men?"

"No, of course not."

"And the stage is still your beacon?"

"Yes, more than anything."

"Then logic prevails, my dear. There are simpler ways to resolve matters of the heart."

Lillian turned from the window. "I'm not sure I understand, Papa. What is it you're suggesting?"

"Nothing unseemly," Fontaine assured her. "You are lonely for male companionship and nothing could be more natural. Amuse yourself without becoming involved."

"Wouldn't that be unfair to them?"

"I'm sure your mother educated you about the whys and wherefores of men. A woman need not worry about trifling with their affections."

"Yes, but how would—"

Chester burst through the door. His face was flushed and he looked as though he'd just run a marathon. He hurried across the room, gesturing wildly.

"Your gentleman friends just shot it out! Not five minutes ago in front of the bank."

Lillian appeared to stagger. "Hank and Jake?"

"None other," Chester said. "I saw it myself."

"Are they . . . dead?"

"Warner got it in the arm and Tallant lost a piece of his ear. They're both lousy shots."

Fontaine put an arm around Lillian's shoulders. He looked at Chester. "How did it happen?"

"Warner started it," Chester said. "Tallant was coming out of the bank and Warner stopped him on the street. They exchanged insults, and next thing you know, they pulled their guns. Wounded one another with the first shot."

"Unfortunate," Fontaine remarked. "I assume it had to do with Warner's lawsuit?"

"No, Dad, it was literally an *affaire de coeur.* They were fighting over Lillian."

"Me!" Lillian was nonplussed. "Why would they fight over me?"

Chester suppressed a grin. "Warner used some dirty language. Accused Tallant of stealing your affections."

"That's ridiculous!"

"You haven't heard the rest of it. Tallant cursed Warner out and accused him of the same thing. That's when they went for their guns."

"How dare they!" Lillian fumed. "I never gave either of them reason to believe I favored one over the other. I asked both of them to leave me alone!"

"Not to hear them tell it," Chester informed her. "They each think the other one stole your heart away. Talk about jealousy."

"I feel like a common streetwalker. Men fighting over me, for mercy's sake! It's disgusting."

A knock sounded at the door. Chester opened it and admitted Lulu Banes. She rushed across the room to Lillian.

"Have you heard?"

"Chester just finished telling me. I can't believe it."

"Believe it," Lulu said archly. "Lucky the fools didn't kill one another."

"I wrote each of them notes," Lillian said with a dazed expression. "And they weren't love notes, either. I told them to stay away."

"Honey, you think they compare dance cards?"

"What do you mean?"

"I mean your notes had the opposite effect. They both thought you ditched one for the other."

"Well, that's absurd," Lillian protested. "Neither of them has any claim on me. I made that very clear."

Lulu chuckled. "Not clear enough, sugar. They just got through fighting a duel for you. How's it feel to be fought over?"

"Absolutely revolting! I wish I'd never met either of them."

"And I'd give anything in the world to be in your place. How I wish, I wish, I wish."

Lillian sniffed. "You're welcome to them."

"Not in this lifetime," Lulu said woefully. "They've only got eyes for you, kiddo."

"Then I'll have to persuade them otherwise, won't I?"

"What are you talking about?"

"Lulu, I mean to put an end to it—permanently!"

*   *   *

For God's sake, let us sit upon the ground
And tell sad stories of the death of kings:
How some have been depos'd, some slain in
    war,
Some haunted by the ghosts they have deposed,
Some poison'd by their wives, some sleeping
    kill'd;
All murder'd: for within the hollow crown
That rounds the mortal temples of a king
Keeps Death his court . . .

Fontaine plowed on with the soliloquy from *King Richard II*. The patrons of the Tivoli were by now resigned to his nightly orations from Shakespeare. For the most part, they ignored him, milling about and carrying on conversations interspersed with laughter. He might have been playing to an empty house.

Two members of the audience were nonetheless attentive. Jake Tallant was seated at his usual table, his right ear heavily bandaged with gauze. Across the aisle, Hank Warner sat with his left arm cradled in a dark sling that matched the color of his suit. Fontaine was surprised to find them in the crowd, for their wounds were still fresh from the morning gunfight. He suspected their attendance had little to do with Shakepeare.

The magician kept the audience entertained between acts. The curtain then opened on the melodrama of the evening, *The Dying Kiss*. Lillian was all too aware of Tallant and Warner, for their tables were just beyond the orchestra, near the stage. She noted that they studiously ignored each other, but she thought their presence was scandalous. The eyes of every man in the room were on her, and she knew what they were thinking. She was the temptress who provoked men to gunfights.

After the melodrama, she hurried backstage to change for her final number. She was still seething as she slipped into her teal gown and tried to repair her makeup. When she went on, her face was scarlet and she had little doubt that everyone in the theater looked upon her as a scarlet woman. She was, in all likelihood, branded the lover of the two men seated down front. The orchestra led her into a lively tune.

> *I came from Alabama*
> *With a banjo on my knee*
> *I'm going to Louisiana*
> *My true love for to see*

It rained all night the day I left
The weather it was dry
The sun so hot I froze to death
Susanna, don't you cry
Oh! Susanna, oh don't you cry for me
I've come from Alabama with a banjo on my
    knee

The crowd gave her a rousing ovation. Tallant, undeterred by his mangled ear, applauded mightily. Warner, limited to one good arm, pounded the table with the flat of his hand. She took three curtain calls, then bowed offstage into the wings. Nate Varnum was standing nearby, and she asked him to invite Tallant and Warner backstage. Her look was such that he restrained himself from questioning her judgment. He hurried off.

Fontaine and Chester were finished removing their greasepaint. They exchanged glances, having overheard her conversation with Varnum, and joined her near her dressing room. Fontaine appeared troubled.

"Do you think this is wise?" he asked. "Bringing them together so soon after their altercation?"

"Their welfare doesn't concern me," Lillian said. "I intend to put an end to it here—tonight."

"I hope you know what you're doing, my dear."

"Yes, I know very well, Papa."

Varnum came through the door at the side of the stage. Warner was directly behind him, followed by Tallant. Everything came to a standstill as the cast—chorus girls, acrobats, jugglers, and the magician—paused to watch. Varnum led the ranchers backstage and stopped outside Lillian's dressing room. The men seemed disconcerted by her summons, nodding to her with weak smiles. Her eyes flashed with anger.

"Look at you!" she said in a stinging voice. "You should be ashamed of yourselves."

Tallant and Warner ducked their heads like naughty urchins. Lillian felt a momentary pang of sympathy, for they were proud men being humbled in public. But she was determined to see it end. She lashed out at them.

"Do you have any idea how you've humiliated me? Fighting like common thugs in the street. And all in my name!"

"Lillian, listen," Warner said, thoroughly abashed. "I wouldn't offend you for anything in the world. I just wasn't thinking straight."

Tallant nodded his head rapidly. "That goes double for me. I'm as much to blame as Hank."

"Yes, you are," Lillian said shortly. "Now, I want you both to shake hands. Let it end here."

Warner and Tallant swapped a quick glance. After a moment, Tallant stuck out his hand and Warner clasped it in a firm grip. Lillian allowed herself a tight smile.

"I hope you can behave like gentlemen from now on. You might even become friends."

"I tend to doubt it," Warner said.

Tallant grunted. "Yeah, not too likely."

"Well, you won't have me as an excuse." Lillian looked from one to the other. "I am leaving Pueblo and I never want to see you again. Either of you."

"Hold on!" Warner barked, and Tallant added a hasty, "Let's talk about this!"

Fontaine stepped forward. "Gentlemen, I believe my daughter—"

"Please, Papa," Lillian cut him off. "I have to do this myself."

"Of course, my dear."

"Goodbye, Hank. Goodbye, Jake." Lillian permitted herself a softer smile. "Please don't say anything to make it more difficult. Just leave now. Please."

Tallant and Warner seemed on the verge of arguing it further. But then, under her cool stare, they mumbled their goodbyes and turned away. No one said anything as they crossed backstage and went out the door. Fontaine looked at Lillian.

"Leaving Pueblo?" he said. "Wasn't that what you told them? I recall no discussion to that effect."

"Yes, Papa, we are leaving."

"You might have consulted me first."

"I'm sorry," Lillian said evenly. "I've had my fill of ruffians, Papa. It's time to go on to Denver."

Fontaine nodded judiciously. "Certainly our notices merit moving onward and upward. You may have a point."

"Just a damn minute!" Varnum jumped in. "You can't run off and leave me high and dry."

"Indeed?" Fontaine said, suddenly testy. "For a man who dislikes Shakespeare, you take umbrage rather too quickly. Do we have a contract with you, Mr. Varnum?"

"I gave you your start!" Varnum objected loudly. "And besides, it's not professional."

"Hmmn." Fontaine feigned deep consideration. "Never let it be said that the Fontaines are less than professional. What say, my dear, shall we give him another week?"

Lillian sighed. "One week, Papa, but no more. I'm anxious to see Denver."

"I concur," Fontaine said, gesturing idly in Varnum's direction. "There you have it, my good man. One week and we bid you *adieu*."

"Godalmighty," Varnum groaned. "I'll never find a headliner act in a week."

"Nor will you find one to replace The Fontaines, my dear fellow. We are, in a word, singular."

Lillian turned toward her dressing room. Lulu was waiting by the door and gave her Kewpie-doll smile. "Sugar, you sure know how to end a romance. I never saw two chumps dusted off so fast."

"I hope I wasn't too harsh on them. Although I must say they deserved it."

"Well, who knows, maybe I'll snag one of them while he's sobbin' in his beer. But whether I do or don't, I'm gonna miss you, kiddo."

"Oh, Lulu, I'll miss you, too."

"Yeah, but I can always say I knew you when. You're on your way to the big time now."

"Do you think so, honestly?"

"Sugar, I'd lay odds on it."

Theatrical people were superstitious and rarely counted their good fortune until it came true. Yet Lillian, who was caught up in the moment, cast her superstitions aside. She already knew it was true.

She saw her name in lights.

CHAPTER 21

THE ENGINEER set the brakes with a racketing squeal. A moment later the train rocked to a halt before the Denver stationhouse. Towering skyward, the Rockies rose majestically under a noonday sun, the snowcapped spires touching the clouds. Lillian thought it was a scene of unimaginable grandeur.

Passengers began deboarding the train. Fontaine signaled one of the porters who waited outside the stationhouse. When the baggage car was unloaded, the porter muscled their steamer trunks onto a cart and led them across the platform. In front of the depot, Fontaine engaged a carriage and told the cabbie to take them to the Brown Palace Hotel. From all he'd heard, the hotel was an institution, the finest in Denver. He planned to establish residence in proper style.

On the way uptown Lillian noted that the streets were cobbled and many of the buildings were constructed of brick masonry. She recalled Libbie Custer telling her that a town founded on a gold strike had become a center of finance and commerce. Over the years, the mining camp reproduced itself a hundredfold, until finally a modern metropolis rose along the banks of Cherry Creek and the South Platte River. Denver was transformed into a cosmopolitan beehive, with opera and a stock exchange and a population approaching 20,000. The city was unrivaled on the Western plains.

The Brown Palace was all they'd been led to expect. Thick carpets covered the marble floor of the lobby, and a central seating area was furnished with leather chairs and sofas. The whole of the lobby ceiling glittered with an ornate mural, and a wide, sweeping staircase ascended to the upper floors. The place had the look and smell of wealth, home away from home for the upper class. At the reception desk, Fontaine noted a calendar with the date May 25, and he marked it as an auspicious day. Their journey had at last brought them to Denver.

"Good afternoon," he said, nodding to the clerk. "You have a suite reserved for Alistair Fontaine."

"Yes, sir," the clerk replied. "How long will you be staying with us, Mr. Fontaine?"

"Indefinitely."

"Welcome to the Brown Palace."

"Thank you so much."

Fontaine signed the register with a flourish. Upstairs, led by a bellman, they were shown into a lavish suite. A lush Persian carpet covered the sitting room floor, and grouped before a marble fireplace were several chairs and a chesterfield divan. There were connecting doors to the bedrooms, both of which were appointed in Victorian style and equipped with a private lavatory. A series of handsomely draped windows overlooked the city.

Lillian whirled around the sitting room. "I can hardly believe we're here. It's like a dream come true."

"Indeed, my dear," Fontaine said. "Far more civilized than anything we've seen in our travels, hmmm?"

"And running water," Chester added, returning from the bedroom. "I think I'm going to like Denver."

"I'm going to *love* it!" Lillian said gaily. "Papa, when will we see the theater? Could we go this afternoon?"

"Tonight, I believe," Fontaine said. "We'll take in the show and get a feel for the crowd. No need to rush."

"I'm just so anxious, that's all. I wish we were opening tonight."

"What is one night more or less? We will have a long run in Denver, my dear. You may depend on it."

Fontaine exuded confidence. By telegraph, he'd spent the last week negotiating with Burt Tully, owner of the Alcazar Variety Theater. Their notices from Pueblo, just as he'd predicted, had made Tully eager to offer them headliner billing. Though Tully's principal interest was in Lillian, Fontaine had nonetheless struck a lucrative deal for the entire act. Their salary was $300 a week, with a four-week guarantee.

Early that evening, they took a stroll through the sporting district. For reasons lost to time, the district was known locally as the Tenderloin. There, within a few square blocks of Blake Street, gaming dives and variety theaters provided a circus of nightlife. Saloons and gambling, mixed with top-drawer entertainment, presented an enticing lure. Sporting men were attracted from all across the West.

One block over was Denver's infamous red-light district. Known simply as the Row, Holladay Street was a lusty fleshpot, with a veritable crush of dollar cribs. Yet while hook shops dominated the row, there was no scarcity of high-class bordellos. The parlor houses offered exotic tarts, usually younger and prettier, all at steeper prices. Something over a thousand soiled doves plied their trade on Holladay Street.

Hop Alley satisfied the more bizarre tastes. A narrow passageway off Holladay, it was Denver's version of Lotus Land. Chinese fan-tan parlors vied with the faint sweet odor of opium dens, and those addicted to the Orient's heady delights beat a steady path to this backstreet world of pipe dreams. To a select clientele, dainty China dolls were available day or night. Vice in every form was available at a price.

Fontaine cut short their tour of Holladay Street. He realized within a block that they had strayed from the more respectable section of the sporting district. Lillian kept her gaze averted, though she felt shamelessly intrigued by the sight of so much sin for sale. Chester, on the other hand, oogled the girls and mentally marked a few bordellos that looked worthy of a visit. They quickly found themselves back on Blake Street.

The Alcazar Variety Theater was the liveliest spot in town. A two-story structure with leaded-glass windows, if offered diverse forms of entertainment for the sporting crowd. On the first floor was the bar and, through an arched doorway at the rear, the theater. The stage was centered on the room, with seating for 400, and a gallery of private booths circled the mezzanine. The upper floor of the club was devoted exclusively to gambling.

Their entrance was not altogether unnoticed. Lillian, though she was dressed in a simple gown, drew admiring stares from men at the bar. Fontaine purchased tickets to the theater and slipped the doorman a gold eagle, which resulted in a table near the orchestra. The audience was composed primarily of men, and waiters scurried back and forth serving drinks. As they were seated,

Fontaine saw a man emerge from a door leading backstage. He nodded at Lillian.

"Unless I'm mistaken," he said, "there goes our employer, Mr. Tully."

Lillian followed his look. The man was stoutly built, with salt-and-pepper hair and a handlebar mustache, attired in a dark suit and a colorful brocade vest. He stopped here and there, greeting customers seated at tables, and slowly made his way to the rear of the theater. She glanced back at her father.

"Shouldn't we introduce ourselves, Papa?"

"No need, my dear," Fontaine said idly. "We aren't expected until tomorrow. Time enough, then."

"Yes, I suppose," Lillian said. "He certainly has a nice theater."

"Let us hope he's a good showman as well."

The orchestra thumped into a spirited dance number. As the curtain opened, a line of chorus girls went high-stepping across the stage. The lead dancer raised her skirts, revealing a shapely leg, and joined them in a prancing cakewalk. The dance routine was followed by a comic, a sword swallower and his pretty assistant, a contortionist who tied himself in knots, and a team of nimble acrobats dressed in tights. The audience applauded appreciatively after every act.

The headliner was billed as The Flying Nymph. A trapeze bar flew out of the stage loft with a woman hanging by her knees. She was identified on the program as Darlene LaRue, and she wore abbreviated tights covered by flowing veils. She performed daring flips and at one point hung by her heels, all the while divesting herself of a veil at a time. The orchestra built to a cresendo as she swung by one hand, tossing the last veil into the audience, her buxom figure revealed in the footlights. The curtain swished closed to applause and cheers.

"Good Lord!" Fontaine muttered. "I thought I'd seen everything. That is positively bizarre."

Chester laughed. "Dad, it's the show business. You have to admit she's different."

"So are dancing elephants," Fontaine said. "That doesn't mean it is art." He turned to Lillian. "Don't you agree, my dear?"

Lillian thought Denver was no different than Pueblo. Or for that matter, Abilene and Dodge City. Men were men, and they wanted to be entertained rather than enlightened. Opera would never play on a variety stage.

"Yes, Papa, I agree," she said. "No dancing elephants."

Fontaine gave her a strange look. "Pardon me?"

"I won't sing from a trapeze, either."

"I should think not!"

She decided to humor him. His art was his life and not a subject for jest. Alistair Fontaine was who he was.

She hoped Shakespeare would play in Denver.

Springtime was the best of times in the Rockies. The air was invigorating, and on the mountains green-leafed aspens fluttered on gentle breezes. The slopes sparkled below the timberline with a kaleidoscope of wildflowers.

A horse-drawn streetcar trundled past as the Fontaines emerged from the hotel. The sun was directly overhead, fixed like a copper ball in a cloudless sky. Fontaine, who was in a chipper mood, filled his lungs with air. He exhaled with gusto.

"I do believe I'm going to like it here. There's something bracing about the mountain air."

"Not to mention the streetcars," Chester said. "Give me a city anytime, all the time."

"I endorse the sentiment, my boy."

Lillian shared their spirited manner. The sidewalks were crowded with smartly dressed men and women attired in the latest fashions. Everywhere she looked there were shops and stores, and the city seemed to pulse with an energy that was all but palpable. She thought she'd already fallen in love with Denver.

Fontaine set off briskly down the street. They were on their way to meet with Burt Tully, the owner of the Alcazar. Fontaine and Chester looked dapper in their three-piece suits, freshly pressed for the occasion. Lillian wore her dove gray taffeta gown, her hair upswept, a parasol over her shoulder. She had never felt so alive, or more eager to get on with anything. She was excited by their prospects.

"I'm looking forward to this," Fontaine said, waiting for a streetcar to pass. "From what we saw last night, Tully's establishment needs a touch of class. That is to say, The Fontaines."

Lillian took his arm. "Papa, will you do something for me?"

"Why, of course, my dear. What is it?"

"Try not to lecture Mr. Tully."

"Lecture?" Fontaine said in a bemused tone. "Why on earth would I lecture him?"

"You know," Lillian gently reminded. "What we were talking about last night? Dancing elephants and trapeze ladies."

"I see no reason to raise topics of an unpleasant nature. After all, we have Mr. Tully exactly where we want him."

"We do?"

"Yes indeed," Fontaine said confidently. "Three hundred a week speaks to the fact that we have the upper hand. His first offer, as you will recall, was rather niggardly."

"Papa, we mustn't let him think we're overbearing. Won't you be tactful . . . for me?"

"I shall be the very soul of discretion. You may depend on it."

Lillian exchanged a look with Chester. He tipped his head in an imperceptible nod. "Listen to her, Dad," he urged. "Denver's our big break and we don't want to spoil it. We might end up in Pueblo again."

Fontaine laughed it off. "Never fear, my boy, we have seen the last of Pueblo. Leave everything to me."

Some ten minutes later they entered the Alcazar. A bartender told them that Tully's office was on the second floor, at the rear of the gaming room. Upstairs, they found a plushly appointed room with faro layouts, twenty-one, chuck-a-luck, roulette, and several poker tables. Though it was scarcely past the noon hour, there were men gathered around the various gaming devices. The girls serving drinks wore peekaboo gowns that displayed their cleavage to maximum effect.

The office looked more suited to a railroad mogul. A lush carpet covered the floor, the furniture was oxblood leather, and the walls were paneled in dark hardwood. Burt Tully was seated at a massive walnut desk; a large painting of sunset over the Rockies hung behind his chair. He rose after they knocked and came through the door. His mouth lifted in a pleasant smile.

"Let me guess," he said, extending his hand. "You're the Fontaines."

Fontaine accepted his handshake. "A distinct pleasure to meet you at last, Mr. Tully. May I introduce my daughter, Lillian, and my son, Chester."

"An honor, Miss Fontaine," Tully said, gently taking her hand. "I've heard a good deal about the Colorado Nightingale. Welcome to the Alcazar."

Lillian smiled winningly. "Thank you so much, Mr. Tully. We're delighted to be here."

"Please, won't you folks have a seat?"

There were two wingback chairs before the desk. Fontaine took one and Chester stepped back, motioning Lillian to the other. He seated himself on a leather sofa against the wall, casually crossing his legs. Tully dropped into his chair behind the desk.

"Allow me to congratulate you," Fontaine said. "You have a very impressive operation here."

"I don't mean to brag—" Tully spread his hands with a modest grin. "The Alcazar is the top spot in the Tenderloin. We pack them in seven nights a week."

"And well you should, my dear fellow. You offer the finest in entertainment."

"All the more reason you're here. Darlene LaRue closes tonight and you open tomorrow night."

"Indeed!" Fontaine said jovially. "I'm sure we will fill the house."

"No doubt you will." Tully paused, his gaze shifting to Lillian. "I have ads starting in all the papers tomorrow. Everyone in town will want to see the Colorado Nightingale."

Lillian detected an unspoken message. There was no mention of The Fontaines but instead a rather subtle reference to the Colorado Nightingale. She returned his look.

"Are you familiar with the way we present our act?"

"Yes, of course he is," Fontaine interrupted. "I covered all that in our telegrams. Didn't I, dear fellow?"

"Let's talk about that," Tully said seriously. "You realize your daughter is the attraction? The real headliner?"

"I—" Fontaine seemed taken aback. "I would be the first to admit that Lillian draws the crowds. Was there some other point?"

Tully steepled his hands. "I have no objection to the melodrama. We haven't held one in a while and it ought to play pretty well." He hesitated, his features solemn. "I'd like you to consider dropping the Shakespeare."

"Nate Varnum said the same thing in Pueblo. Shakespeare played well enough there."

"No, Mr. Fontaine, it didn't. I exchanged telegrams with Nate, and he told me—you'll pardon my saying so—the crowd sat on their hands. The same thing will happen here."

Fontaine reddened. "You signed The Fontaines to an engagement, and The Fontaines are here. I expect you to honor the terms of our agreement."

"Think about it," Tully suggested. "Your daughter has a great career ahead of her. She's doing two songs a show, and she should be doing three or four. Without the Shakespeare, she could."

"Mr. Tully."

Their heads snapped around at the tone in Lillian's voice. She shifted forward in her chair. "Father speaks for The Fontaines. You have to accept us as we are . . . or not at all."

There was a moment of intense silence. Tully finally shook his head. "You're doing yourself a disservice, Miss Fontaine. Your father knows it and I know it. And you know it, too, don't you?"

"As I said, we are The Fontaines. Shakespeare is part of our act."

"Just as you wish," Tully said in a resigned voice. "I'll go along only because I want the Colorado Nightingale at the Alcazar. For you, personally, I think it's a big mistake."

Lillian smiled. "You won't think so tomorrow night. We'll fill the house."

"Yes, I'm sure *you* will, Miss Fontaine."

Tully arranged a rehersal schedule for her the next morning. After a perfunctory round of handshakes, they left his office. Outside, walking along Blake Street, it was apparent that Fontaine's chipper mood had vanished. He appeared somehow diminished, head bowed and shoulders hunched. Lillian knew he was crushed.

"Papa—"

"Later, my dear."

"Are you all right?"

"I think I need a drink."

CHAPTER 22

LILLIAN STROLLED along Larimer Street. The central thoroughfare of Denver, it was lined with shops and stores, banks and newspaper offices, and all manner of business establishments. She turned into Mlle. Tourneau's Dress Shop.

The shop was airy and pleasantly appointed, with a large plate glass window fronting Larimer Street. Dresses were displayed on mannequins, and from the rear, behind a partition, she heard the whir of sewing machines. A small woman with pince-nez glasses walked forward as the bell over the door jingled. She nodded amiably.

"Good afternoon," she said with a trace of an accent. "May I help you?"

"Are you Mademoiselle Tourneau?" Lillian asked.

"*Oui.*"

Lillian thought the accent was slightly off and wondered if the woman was really French. She smiled politely. "The manager at the Brown Palace told me you are the finest dressmaker in Denver."

"M'sieur Clark is very kind," Mlle. Tourneau said. "And whom do I have the privilege of addressing?"

"My name is Lillian Fontaine."

"*Enchanté*, Mademoiselle Fontaine. How may I serve you?"

"I'm in desperate need of some gowns. I hoped you might design them for me."

"But of course, with pleasure. What type of gowns do you require?"

"Stage gowns," Lillian replied. "I'm an actress and a singer. I open tomorrow night at the Alcazar Variety Theater."

Mlle. Tourneau laughed coyly. "There is much talk about you, I believe. You are the one called the Colorado Nightingale. *Non?*"

"Well, yes, that is how they have me billed."

"How very exciting! I will be honored to design your gowns."

Mlle. Tourneau began spreading bolts of cloth on a large table. As she prattled on about the quality of the fabrics, Lillian ran her fingers over the material, pausing to study various colors and textures. Finally, hardly able to choose from the delicate fabrics, she made three selections. The bolts were set aside.

Scarcely drawing a breath, Mlle. Tourneau pulled out a large pad of paper and a stick of charcoal shaved to a point. She began sketching gowns, rapidly filling in details as the charcoal flew across the paper. One was to be done in embroidered yellow tulle, another in Lyon silk with white lace trim, and the third in pleated ivory satin with guipure lace. She completed the last sketch with a flourish.

"*Voilà!*" she announced dramatically. "*C'est magnifique!*"

Lillian studied the sketches. She had given considerable thought to remarks made by both theater owners and stage performers over the last several months. The more discreet had alluded to the aura of innocence she projected onstage and how irresistible that was to men. The more plainspoken advised naughty but nice, a peek here and a peek there to heighten the sense of mystery. She decided now that some of both would enhance the overall effect.

"Here," she said, a fingernail on the sketch. "Perhaps we could lower it slightly . . . to here."

"Ahhh!" Mlle. Tourneau peered over her pince-nez. "You wish to accentuate the décolletage. *Tres bien*!"

"And here." Lillian pointed to the bottom of the gown. "Perhaps we could raise this just a . . . touch."

"*Mais oui!* You wish a tiny display of the ankle. How very daring."

"Nothing vulgar, you understand."

"*Non, non!* Never!"

Mlle. Tourneau led her to the fitting room. Lillian disrobed to her chemise and the dressmaker began taking measurements. She ran the tape around hips, waist, and bust, and her eyes went round. She clucked appreciatively.

"*Extraordinaire!*" she said merrily. "You will look absolutely lovely in these gowns. I predict you will break hearts. Many hearts."

"Well . . ." Lillian studied herself in the full-length mirror and giggled. "I'll certainly try."

"*Fait accompli, mon cher.* Men will fall at your feet."

"I have to ask you a favor, mademoiselle."

"Anything in my power."

"The ivory gown . . ." Lillian waited until she nodded. "I'll need it by tomorrow evening. I just have to have it for my opening show."

"*Sacre bleu!*" Mlle. Tourneau exclaimed. "Tomorrow?"

"Won't you please?"

Lillian looked at her with a beseeching gaze. Mlle. Tourneau's stern expression slowly gave way to a resigned smile. Her eyes blinked behind her pince-nez.

"How could I refuse you? I will work my girls throughout the night. You must be here first thing in the morning for a fitting. But you will have your gown. *Certainment!*"

"Oh, thank you! Thank you!"

The measurements completed, Mlle. Tourneau suggested an accessory to complement the outfit. She carried a line of low-cut slippers with a medium heel, which she could cover in the same fabric as the gown. She laughed a wicked little laugh.

"Show the shoe, show the ankle. Eh?"

"I think it's perfect!"

A short while later Lillian left the shop. She returned to the hotel, tingling with excitement at the thought of her new gown. When she entered the suite, her father was slumped in an easy chair, a bottle of whiskey at hand on a side table. His jaw was slack and his eyes appeared glazed. He lifted his glass in a mock toast.

"Welcome back to our cheery abode, my dear. How went the shopping?"

Chester was seated on the divan. As she crossed the room, he looked at her with an expression of rueful concern, wagging his head from side to side. She stopped by the fireplace. "I ordered a lovely gown," she said, forcing herself to smile. "I'll have it for the opening tomorrow night."

"Marvelous!" Fontaine pronounced in a slurred voice. "Never disappoint your public."

Lillian saw that he was already drunk. He laughed as though amused by some private joke and poured himself another drink. The bottle wobbled when he set it back on the table, and he watched it with an indifferent stare. He took a slug of whiskey.

"Papa," Lillian said tentatively. "Don't you think you've had enough to drink?"

Fontaine waved her off with an idle gesture. "Have no fear," he said. "John Barleycorn and I are old friends. He treats me gently."

"I worry anyway. Too much liquor isn't good for you."

"I am indestructible, my dear. A rock upon which a sea of troubles doth scatter to the winds."

Lillian knew he was trying to escape into a bottle. His optimism about their prospects in Denver and his pride in negotiating such a lucrative engagement at the Alcazar—all that had been dashed by their meeting with Burt Tully. Her father had heard all over again that no one was interested in Shakespeare. Or Alistair Fontaine.

She felt guilty about her own good fortune. The accolades accorded the Colorado Nightingale, first in Pueblo and now in Denver, had pushed her father out of the limelight and ever deeper into the shadows. She suddenly felt guilty about her new gowns, for while she was happy, her father was drunk and disconsolate. She simply didn't know how to erase his pain.

"Papa, listen to me," she temporized. "You're only hurting yourself, and I hate to see you like this. Won't you please stop . . . for me?"

Fontaine grunted. " 'Men's evil manners live in brass; their virtues we write in water.' I believe the Bard penned the line for me. Yes, indeed, quite apropos."

Lillian was reduced to silence. She looked at Chester, and he again shook his head in dull defeat. Fontaine

downed the glass of whiskey, muttering something unintelligible, and slumped deeper in the chair. His eyes
went blank, then slowly closed, and his chin sank lower
on his chest. The glass dropped from his hand onto the
carpet.

Lillian took a seat on the divan. She stared at her
father a moment, listening to his light snore. "I feel so
terrible," she said, tears welling up in her eyes. "Surely
there's something we can do."

"Like what?" Chester said. "You know yourself, he
lives and breathes Shakespeare. Tully might as well
have hit him over the head with a hammer."

"Yes, you're right, he was just devastated. He
thought Denver would be so much more cultured. His
hopes were so high."

"Maybe he'll sleep it off and come to his senses.
He's always bounced back before."

"I'm not sure sleep will solve anything."

"You tell me then, what will?"

"Perhaps Tully was wrong about the audiences. Perhaps they will appreciate Shakespeare."

"Anything's possible," Chester said with no great
confidence. "I guess we'll find out tomorrow night."

"Oh, Chet, I feel so helpless."

"Let's cross our fingers and hope for the best."

Lillian thought they would need more than luck.

Denver turned out for opening night. The theater was
full by seven o'clock, and men were wedged tight in
the barroom. The crowd spilled out onto the sidewalk,
and a police squad was brought in to maintain order.
The backlit marquee blazed outside the Alcazar.

LILLY FONTAINE
THE COLORADO NIGHTINGALE

Lillian complained to Burt Tully. The marquee made no reference to her father or Chester, and she was upset by the oversight. Her father had sloughed it off, but she knew he was offended and hurt. Tully told her it was no oversight and then repeated what he'd said the day before. The crowd was there to see her, not The Fontaines. She was the headliner.

Before her opening number, she stopped by the dressing room her father shared with Chester. Fontaine was attired in the costume of a Danish nobleman, and his breath reeked of alcohol. His eyes were bloodshot, and though he tried to hide a tremor in his hand, he seemed in rare form. He nodded affably and inspected her outfit, the teal gown with the black pearls. He arched an eyebrow.

"What's this?" he said. "Not wearing your new gown?"

Lillian smiled. "I'm saving it for the closing number."

"Excellent thinking, my dear. Contrary to common wisdom, the last impression is the one most remembered."

"Are you all right, Papa?"

"I am in fine fettle," Fontaine said grandly. "I shall acquit myself admirably indeed."

Lillian kissed him on the cheek. "You will always be my Hamlet."

"And you the sweet voice in the darkness of my night."

"I have to go."

"Leave them enraptured, my dear. Hearts in their throats!"

A juggler came offstage as she moved into the wings. She walked to center stage, composing herself, hands clasped at her waist. The orchestra glided smoothly into *Nobody's Darling* as the curtain opened to reveal her awash in a rose-hued spotlight. Her voice brought an expectant hush over the audience.

> *They say I am nobody's darling*
> *Nobody cares for me*
> *While others are radiant and joyful*
> *I'm lonely as lonely can be*
> *I'm lonely indeed without you*
> *But I know what I know in my heart*
> *Dreaming at morning and evening*
> *Of meeting, oh never to part*

On the last note there was a moment of almost reverent silence. Then the crowd stood, everyone in the theater on their feet, their applause vibrating off the walls. She curtsied, her eyes radiant, and slowly bowed her way offstage. The uproar went on unabated, and the audience brought her back for four curtain calls. Her face was flushed with joy when at last the commotion subsided.

Fontaine was waiting in the wings. His eyes were misty and he hugged her in a fierce outpouring of pride. She again smelled liquor on his breath, and then he marched, shoulders squared, to the center of the stage. The curtain swished open, and he raised one hand in a dramatic gesture, caught in the glow of a cider spotlight.

He hesitated an instant, staring out over the audience, and launched into a soliloquy from *Hamlet*. His rich baritone resonated across the theater.

> *Neither a borrower, nor a lender be;*
> *For loan oft loses both itself and friend,*
> *And borrowing dulls the edge of husbandry,*
> *This above all: to thine own self be true,*
> *And it must follow, as the night the day,*
> *Thou canst not then be false to any man . . .*

The crowd watched him with a look of dumb bemusement. There was a sense of some misguided gathering come upon a man speaking in a tongue foreign to the ear. When he delivered the last line, they stared at him as though waiting for a summation that would make it all comprehensible. Then, just as Burt Tully had predicted, they sat on their hands. Their applause was scattered, quickly gone.

Fontaine took no curtain calls. The acrobats bounded onstage as he walked, head bowed, to his dressing room to change costumes. A few minutes later he joined Lillian and Chester in the presentation of the melodrama *A Husband's Vengeance*. All through the performance Lillian's concentration was on her father rather than on the play. She knew, even if the audience never would, why he had selected that particular passage from *Hamlet*. He wanted to deliver the one line that personified Alistair Fontaine.

To thine own self be true.

The crowd responded favorably to the melodrama. Following the performance, Fontaine's spirits seemed somewhat restored. He changed into his street clothes, leaving Chester backstage, and moved quickly to the door leading to the theater. Lillian came out of her dressing room just as he went through the door. She was wearing her new gown, resplendent in ivory, her hair loose to her shoulders. She saw Chester standing outside his dressing room, his face screwed up in a puzzled frown. She hurried forward.

"Chet?" she said anxiously. "Where did Papa go?"

"To the bar." Chester appeared troubled. "He said he'd watch your performance from there. He just rushed off."

"I'm worried about his drinking. Will you find him and stay with him?"

"The way he acted, I'm not sure he wants company. He didn't invite me along."

"Yes, but he shouldn't be left alone. Not tonight."

"You're right. I'll go find him."

Chester walked away. The stage manager motioned frantically to Lillian as the chorus line pranced offstage. She moved through the wings, taking her position at center stage, and struck a coquettish pose. The curtain opened as the orchestra swung into *Buffalo Gals* and the spotlight made her a vision in ivory. Her cleavage and the sight of a dainty ankle brought shouts from the audience. She performed a cheeky dance routine as she zestfully banged out the lyrics.

> *Buffalo gals, won't you come out tonight*
> *Come out tonight, come out tonight*

Buffalo gals, won't you come out tonight
And we'll dance by the light of the moon

Lillian twirled around the stage, her ivory slippers lightly skipping in time to the music. Her voice was animated and strong, every mirthful stanza of the song followed by the rollicking chorus. She spun about in a playful pirouette on the last line and ended with her arms flung wide and her hip cocked at a saucy angle. The uproar from the crowd rocked the theater with applause and cheers and shrill whistles of exuberance. A standing ovation drummed on through five curtain calls.

The cast surrounded her backstage. She was jubilant with the wild reception from the audience, and congratulations from the other performers made it all the more heady. Burt Tully pulled her into a smothering bear hug and told her she would play the Alcazar forever. As he let her go, she saw her father and Chester, followed by another man, come through the door from the theater. She threw herself into her father's arms.

"Oh, Papa!" she cried. "Wasn't it just wonderful!"

Fontaine was glassy-eyed with liquor. He kissed her with drunken affection. "You bedazzled them, my dear. You were magical."

"I could have sung forever and ever! And Papa, five curtain calls!"

"Yes, indeed, you brought the house down."

"Oooo, I'm so excited!"

"I'd like you to meet someone." Fontaine motioned the other man forward. "Permit me to introduce Otis Gaylord. I've invited him to join us for supper."

Gaylord was a man of imposing stature. He was tall, lithely built, with sandy hair and pale blue eyes. He took her hand in his and lifted it to his lips. He caressed it with a kiss.

"I am your most ardent admirer, Miss Fontaine. Your performance left me thoroughly bewitched."

Lillian smiled graciously. He wasn't the handsomest man she'd ever seen. But he was devilishly good-looking, strongly virile, with a cleft chin and rugged features. She thought she might drown in his pale blue eyes.

"Otis favors Irish whiskey," Fontaine said with a tipsy chortle. "I can think of no finer attribute in a friend. And lest I betray a secret, my dear—he is smitten with you."

Gaylord laughed. "I would be a liar if I said otherwise."

Lillian sensed they would celebrate more than her triumph tonight.

CHAPTER 23

LILLIAN WAS the toast of Denver. Her first week at the Alcazar Variety Theater was a sellout every night. The Colorado Nightingale was front-page news.

Articles appeared in the *Denver Tribune* and the *Rocky Mountain News*. The stories gushed with accolades and adjectives, unanimous agreement that she was a sensation, a singer with the voice of an angel. She was the talk of the town.

The response was overwhelming. Loads of flowers were delivered to her dressing room every night, with notes expressing adulation and all but begging her attention. Every man in Denver was seemingly a rabid admirer and intent on becoming a suitor. She was an object of adoration, the stuff of men's dreams.

Otis Gaylord was the envy of her many admirers. He managed to monopolize her time and squired her around town at every opportunity. Today, she joined him for lunch in the restaurant at the Brown Palace, and the maître d' greeted them with the fanfare reserved for the hotel's resident celebrity. Heads turned as they were led to their table.

Lillian was taken with Gaylord's urbane manner. He was courteous, thoughtful, and attentive to her every wish. His wit amused her, and if he was not the handsomest man she'd ever known, he was nonetheless the most attractive. So much so that she declined dozens of invitations every night, for she was drawn to him by an emotional affinity she'd never before felt. And apart from all that, he was enormously wealthy.

Gaylord was a mining investor. As he explained it, he owned blocks of stock in several gold mines in Central City, which was located some thirty miles west of Denver. The mining camp was called the richest square mile on earth, and upward of a hundred thousand dollars a week was gouged from the mountainous terrain. A shrewd financier might easily quadruple his investment in a year or less.

For Lillian, Otis Gaylord seemed the answer to a girl's prayers. Nor was she alone in that sense, for fortune had smiled on Chester as well. Earlier in the week he'd met Ethel Weaver, who kept the books at her father's store, Weaver's Mercantile. The girl was cute as a button, and to hear Chester tell it, she was one in a million. He spent every spare moment in her company, and he acted like a man who had fallen hard. He talked of nothing else.

Lillian's one concern was her father. His spirit seemed broken by the theater crowd's yawning indifference to Shakespeare and to him as an actor. His drinking had grown worse over the past week, starting in the morning and ending only when he fell into bed at night. His mind was fogged with alcohol, and on two occasions he'd forgotten his lines in the course of the melodrama. His escape into a bottle, just as Lillian had feared, was sapping him mentally and physically. He seemed a shell of his former self.

Gaylord tried to write it off as a momentary lapse. He enjoyed Fontaine's sardonic wit, and even more, he respected his integrity as an actor. Gaylord counseled Lillian to patience, and today, when she seemed particularly distressed, he assured her that her father, given time, would come to grips with the problem. No more had he offered his assurances than James Clark, the manager of the Brown Palace, interrupted their luncheon. He rushed into the dining room.

"Pardon the intrusion," he said earnestly. "Miss Fontaine, your father has been injured. Your brother asked that you come immediately to the suite."

Lillian pushed back her chair. "What kind of injury?"

"I'm afraid I haven't any details. I saw your brother and several men carry your father in from the street. He asked me to find you."

Lillian hurried from the restaurant. Gaylord escorted her upstairs, and three men came out of the suite as they arrived. They found Chester nervously pacing around the sitting room. He turned as they entered.

"Thank God you're here," he said. "Dad got run over by a lumber wagon. I was on the way to lunch with Ethel and I saw it. He just stepped off the curb into the path of the horses."

"How bad is he?" Lillian demanded. "Have you sent for a doctor?"

"There was a doctor there. On the street, on his way to lunch, I mean. He and some other men helped me carry Dad back here."

"The doctor's here, now?"

"Dr. Macquire." Chester motioned to the closed bedroom door. "Dad was unconscious when we brought him in. He didn't look good."

Lillian sagged and Gaylord put his arm around her shoulders. "Steady now," he said. "No need to think the worst."

"Oh, Otis, I feel so terrible. Drinking the way he does, he shouldn't have been on the street. I should have known better."

Chester grimaced. "We would have to keep him under lock and key. Or hide the whiskey."

The bedroom door opened. Dr. Thomas Macquire moved into the sitting room, his features solemn. He nodded to Lillian and Chester. "Your father has the constitution of an ox. Of course, in a way, being drunk was a lucky thing. Drunks can absorb more damage than a sober man."

Lillian stepped forward. "Are you saying he'll be all right?"

"There are no broken bones, and so far as I can tell, there's no internal injuries. I'll have to keep an eye on him for a few days."

"Has he regained consciousness?"

"Miss Fontaine, not only is he awake, he asked for a drink."

Lillian walked to the bedroom. Her father's features were ashen, a discolored bruise on his jaw and a large knot on his forehead. His eyes were rheumy and his breathing raspy. He looked at her with a forlorn expression.

" 'If I must die,' " he said in a slurred voice, " 'I will encounter darkness as a bride, and hug it in mine arms.' Send for a priest, my dear."

"You aren't going to die, Papa. Not as long as you can quote Shakespeare."

" 'The stroke of death is as a lover's pinch'! I could quote the Bard from my grave."

"Dr. Macquire says you'll live."

"What do doctors know?" Fontaine said dismissively. "I need a drink and a priest. Would you oblige me, my dear?"

"Try to get some rest," Lillian said, turning away. "We'll talk later, Papa."

She closed the door on her way out.

Lillian carried on the show by herself. She was forced to cancel the melodrama, as well as the Shakespearean act, for the immediate future. Neither could be performed without her father.

Burt Tully was almost deliriously happy. The crowds jamming the Alcazar shared the sentiment to a man. Lillian was now singing five songs a night, and the theater was sold out a week in advance. A cottage industry sprang up with street hustlers hawking tickets for triple the box office price.

Chester, much to Lillian's surprise, took it all in stride. He told her he was available to resume stage work whenever their father recovered. But he promptly obtained a job as a clerk in Weaver's Mercantile and seemed content to spend his days in close proximity to Ethel Weaver. His nights were spent in her company as well.

Dr. Macquire, at Fontaine's insistence, got the clergy involved. The Reverend Titus Hunnicut, pastor of the First Baptist Church, became a regular at Fontaine's bedside. The actor and the minister sequestered themselves, talking for hours at a time. A male nurse was hired to tend to Fontaine's physical needs, and Reverend Hunnicut tended to his spiritual needs. Fontaine, to Lillian's utter shock, stopped drinking.

Three days after the accident, Fontaine was on the mend. Dr. Macquire pronounced his recovery remarkable, for he'd been trampled by the horses and the lumber wagon had passed over his right leg. He was alert and sober, his cheeks glowing with health, and positively reveling in all the attention. Even more remarkable, he'd taken a vow of abstinence, swearing off demon rum forever. He basked in the glory of the Lord.

Lillian returned from rehearsing a new number late that afternoon. Reverend Hunnicut was on his way out and stopped to chat with her for a moment. A slight man, with oily hair and an unctuous manner, he seemed forever on the pulpit. He nodded as though angels were whispering in his ear.

"Praise the Lord," he said in a sepulchral voice. "Your father has been delivered from the damnation of hell's fires. He is truly blessed."

"How wonderful," Lillian demurred. "Thank you for all your concern, Reverend."

"I am but a humble servant of Christ, Miss Fontaine. God's will be done!"

"Yes, of course."

Lillian showed him to the door. The male nurse, who was seated on the divan reading a newspaper, started to his feet. She waved him down with a smile and proceeded on into the bedroom. Her father was propped up against a bank of pillows.

"Hello, Papa," she said, bussing him on the cheek. "How are you feeling?"

"Quite well." Fontaine studied her with an eager look. "I have something to tell you, my dear. Reverend Hunnicut convinced me it was time."

"Oh?"

"The day the wagon ran over me—actually it was that evening—God spoke to me in the moment of my death."

"You weren't dying, Papa. And since when have you become so devout?"

" 'Ye of little faith,' " Fontaine chided her. " 'They that wait upon the Lord shall renew their strength; they shall mount up with wings as eagles.' " He paused, holding her gaze. "I have been spared death for a greater mission in life."

"A greater mission?"

"Yes indeed, my dear. I shall carry the word of our Lord to the infidels in the mining camps. Their immortal souls are but a step away from perdition."

Lillian was never more stunned in her life. "Are you serious, Papa?"

"I most certainly am."

"What about the stage?"

"All the world's a stage." Fontaine's eyes burned with a fervent light. "I shall be an actor for our Lord Jesus Christ."

"Really?" Lillian said dubiously. "You intend to give up Shakespeare to become a preacher?"

" 'To every thing there is a season, and a time to every purpose under the heaven.' That comes from Ecclesiastes, not Shakespeare."

"Yes, but how can you forsake the stage?"

"On the contrary, the stage has forsaken me. I go now to spread the word of Him who so oft inspired the Bard."

"Are you certain about this, Papa?"

"I have been called," Fontaine said with conviction. "The Gospel will light my way."

Lillian returned to the sitting room in a daze. The male nurse rose from the divan and went past her into the bedroom. As she sat down, the door opened and Chester entered the suite. She gave him a look of baffled consternation.

"Papa has decided to become a preacher."

"I know," Chester said, crossing to the divan. "He's been working himself up to telling you. I found out last night."

"And you didn't say anything?" Lillian was astounded. "Do you think he's lost his mind? I have to talk to the doctor."

"Think about it a minute and you'll understand. What he lost was his faith in himself as a Shakespearean. He's adopted a new role in life—a man of God."

"Oh, Chet, how can you say that? He's an actor, not a preacher."

"As the Bard said," Chester quoted, " 'one man in his time plays many parts.' I'm taking on a new part myself."

"You?" Lillian said. "What are you talking about?"

"I've decided to quit the stage."

"I don't believe it!"

Chester sat down beside her. "You know yourself I was never much of an actor. I stayed with it because it was sort of the family tradition. I think it's time to move on."

Lillian's head was reeling. "Move on to what?"

"I really believe I was cut out to be a merchant. I can't tell you how much I enjoy working in the store. Ethel's father says I have a head for business."

"For business or for Ethel?"

"Well, her, too," Chester said with a goofy smile. "But the point is, what with the act breaking up, I have no future on the stage. Time to make a new career for myself."

"I'm speechless." Lillian felt dizzy and somehow saddened. "Papa a preacher and you a merchant. Where will it end?"

"As for Dad and myself, who's to say? You're the only sure bet in the family."

"I'd so much rather have you and Papa onstage with me."

"You don't need us where you're going, little sister. You never did."

Lillian snuggled close in his arms, her head on his shoulder. A tear ran down her cheek and she wondered how they'd come so far to have it end this way. So abruptly, so unforeseen. So final.

The end of The Fontaines.

*   *   *

> *My wild Irish Rose*
> *The sweetest flower that grows*
> *You may search everywhere*
> *But none can compare*
> *With my wild Irish Rose*

Lillian's voice was particularly poignant that night. She was thinking not of the lyrics but of her father and Chester. Her eyes shone with tears, and the emotion she felt inside gave the song a haunting quality. She got hold of herself for the last refrain.

> *My wild Irish Rose*
> *The dearest flower that grows*

And someday for my sake
She may let me take
The bloom from my wild Irish Rose

A momentary lull held the audience in thrall as the last note faded away. Then the house rocked with applause, men swiping at their noses, their eyes moist with memories evoked by her performance. The noise quickened, went on unabated, the crowd on their feet, bellowing their approval. She left them wanting more with a fifth curtain call.

Some while later Otis Gaylord met her at the stage-door entrance. She was dressed in a gossamer satin gown, a fashionable Eton jacket thrown over her shoulders, her hair pulled back in a lustrous chignon. A carriage took them to Delmonico's, one of the finer restaurants in Denver. The owner personally escorted them to their table.

"That was some performance," Gaylord said when they were seated. "You had the boys crying in their beer."

"I feel like crying myself."

"What's wrong?"

Lillian told him about her afternoon. Gaylord was no less amazed to hear that her father was to become a preacher. The news of her brother was no great surprise, for he'd always felt Chester was the least talented of the family. She ended on a rueful note.

"Nothing will ever be the same again. We've been an act since I was a little girl."

"Yeah, it's a shame," Gaylord agreed. "Of course, maybe it's the best thing for Alistair, and Chester, too. You have to look on the bright side."

"What bright side?" Lillian said. "We'll be separated now."

"Only on the stage. Sounds to me like Alistair and Chester will be doing something that makes them lots happier. Think of it that way."

The waiter appeared with menus. Lillian thought about Gaylord's advice, and after they ordered, she looked at him. Her eyes crinkled with a smile.

"I was being selfish," she said. "If they're happy, why should I be sad? Isn't that what you meant?"

Gaylord chuckled. "I think I put it a little more tactfully. But yeah, that's the general idea."

"Well, you were right, and I feel like a ninny I didn't see it for myself. No more tears."

"Maybe this will cheer you up even more."

Gaylord took a small box from his pocket. He set it before her on the table, his expression unreadable, and eased back in his chair. She opened it and saw a gold heart-shaped locket bordered with tiny diamonds, strung on a delicate chain. Her mouth ovaled with surprise.

"Oh, it's beautiful!" she said merrily. "No one ever gave me anything so nice!"

"We'll have to correct that," Gaylord said. "Lots of pretty presents for a pretty lady. I like it when you laugh."

Lillian batted her eyelashes. "Are you trying to ply me with favors, Mr. Gaylord?"

"I'll ply you any way I can, Miss Fontaine. I intend to be the object of your affections."

"Do you?"

"No question about it."

"Well . . ." She gave him a sultry look. "We'll see."

Gaylord ordered champagne. Lillian strung the locket around her neck, aware that he was watching her. She wondered if tonight was the beginning of what would lead to a proposal. She certainly wasn't going to surrender herself without a wedding band on her finger. But then, on second thought, she wasn't at all sure that love and marriage were the same thing. She felt awfully old to still be a virgin. Too old.

The waiter poured champagne, then moved away. Gaylord lifted his glass, staring at her over the rim. "To us," he said in a seductive voice. "And the future."

Lillian laughed vivaciously. "Yes, to the future."

CHAPTER 24

SOME DAYS mark a passage in time. Lillian was never to forget June 12, 1872, the day her world turned topsy-turvy. She felt alone for the first time in her life.

Alistair Fontaine stood at the curb in front of the Brown Palace Hotel. He was dressed in a black frock coat, with dark trousers and a white shirt, the crown of his hat rounded in a dome. His horse, a swaybacked gelding donated by the church, was black as well. Fontaine looked every inch the part of an itinerant preacher.

Lillian and Chester waited while he checked his saddlebags. Over the past week he had recovered fully from his encounter with the lumber wagon. By now, after daily sessions with Reverend Hunnicut, he virtually had the Bible memorized, and the paperwork, properly endorsed, had been submitted to have him ordained. He was a man of God.

Watching him, Lillian thought he'd never looked so fit. He held himself tall and straight, and there was fire in his eyes, the zealotry of a man reborn in faith. The saddlebags held all his worldly possessions, and he pulled the strap tight with a firm hand. He turned to face them with an expression that was beatific, at peace with himself.

"Come now," he said, looking from one to the other. "Will you send me off with dreary faces?"

"Oh, Papa!" Lillian sniffled, on the verge of tears. "We'll miss you so."

"The Spirit of the Lord God is upon me. I go forth to give light to them that sit in darkness. I am blessed among men, my dear."

"Dad, I'd like to hear your first sermon," Chester said, grinning. "You'll probably convert those miners in droves."

Fontaine chortled. "I will try to save my first wedding ceremony for you and Ethel."

Chester was himself like a man with a new lease on life. After a whirlwind courtship, he'd announced that morning his betrothal to Ethel Weaver. Her father, who knew a natural-born tradesman when he saw one, welcomed Chester into the family. They were to be married in October.

"God bless you both and keep you safe until I return."

Fontaine hugged Lillian and shook hands with Chester. He stepped into the saddle, tipping his hat with a jaunty air, and rode off along Larimer Street. They stood watching until he rounded the corner and turned west toward the distant mountains. Lillian dabbed at her eyes with a hankie.

"How things change," she said. "I expected him to leave us with a quote from Shakespeare. Something properly dashing, or adventurous."

"Actually . . ." Chester paused, nodding to himself. "I was thinking of Cervantes. A line he wrote in *Don Quixote* strikes me as perfect: 'Many are the ways by which God leads His children home.' "

"For a storekeeper, you're still very much the actor. Are you sure you've given up on the stage?"

"Never more sure of anything. And speaking of the store, I have to get back. I'll see you later."

Chester hurried off down the street. Lillian turned into the hotel, feeling lonely and blue. Upstairs, she wandered through the empty suite, reminded of her father everywhere she looked. She wished she had a rehearsal, or a dress fitting, anything to take her mind off the overwhelming loneliness. She thought she might go to the theater early tonight.

A short while later there was a knock at the door. Lillian was staring out the window, brooding, and she welcomed the distraction. She moved across the sitting room, opening the door, and found two men standing in the hall. One was short and stocky, the other one tall and lean, both attired in conservative suits. She nodded pleasantly.

"May I help you?"

"Miss Fontaine?"

"Yes."

"I'm David Cook," the short one said, "and this is my associate, Jeff Carr. I wonder if we might speak with you a moment."

"May I ask what it regards?"

"A personal matter involving Otis Gaylord."

Lillian invited them inside. Once they were seated, Cook explained that he was head of the Rocky Mountain Detective Association, located in Denver, and currently retained by Wells Fargo. Jeff Carr, he went on, was the county sheriff from Cheyenne, Wyoming. They wanted to ask her a few questions about Otis Gaylord.

"I don't understand," she said. "Why are you interested in Mr. Gaylord?"

Lillian would later discover that David Cook and Jeff Carr were renowned manhunters. Cook, the chief operative of the Rocky Mountain Detective Association, had tracked fugitives all across the West. Carr, who had killed several men in gunfights, was reputed to be the only lawman who had ridden into Hole-in-the-Wall, the outlaw sanctuary, and ridden out alive. Cook looked at her now.

"We have reason to believe that Gaylord's real name is Earl Miller. He's wanted for robbery and murder."

"You're mistaken," Lillian said tersely. "Mr. Gaylord is a mining investor. He's quite wealthy."

"Guess he oughta be," Jeff Carr said. "He robbed a Wells Fargo stagecoach outside of Cheyenne. Got forty-three thousand in gold bullion and killed the express guard."

"And those investments?" Cook added. "We checked out the story he uses, about owning mines in Central City. Nobody there ever heard of him."

Lillian sniffed. "That isn't proof. There could be any number of explanations."

"How's this for proof?" Cook said. "Gaylord sold almost forty thousand in gold bullion to Ed Chase for seventy cents on the dollar. Our informant saw the transaction."

Everyone in Denver knew the name Ed Chase. He was the underworld czar who controlled the rackets and ruled the Tenderloin with a gang of thugs. One of his sidelines was operating as a fence for stolen goods.

"I don't believe you," Lillian said tartly. "If you have evidence, why haven't you arrested Mr. Gaylord? Why come to me?"

Cook informed her that the gold bars, once in the hands of Ed Chase, were untraceable. As for Earl Miller, the robber and murderer, he always wore a bandanna mask and had yet to be positively identified. The break in the case came when they were informed of the underworld sale of the gold.

"We know of your relationship with Gaylord," Cook went on discreetly. "We hoped to solicit your assistance in identifying him."

"Really?" Lillian countered. "Why would I help you?"

"The man's a killer," Carr said bluntly. "Because of him that express guard left a widow and three kids. How's that for a reason?"

"And you might be doing Gaylord a service," Cook argued. "If he's not Earl Miller, you could clear his name. Prove we've got the wrong suspect."

Lillian was less certain of herself than a moment ago. Yet she couldn't believe that Otis Gaylord was a robber, not to mention a murderer. Still, the lawmen were determined, and unless he was cleared, they might very well destroy his reputation. She decided to cooperate.

"What do you want me to do?"

Cook told her what they had in mind.

Gaylord maintained rooms at the Windsor Hotel. Lillian sent a note by messenger, asking that their usual late supper be changed to an early dinner. She suggested their favorite restaurant, Delmonico's.

All afternoon she fretted over what seemed to her a conspiracy. For more than two weeks now, Gaylord had been her lone suitor and her constant companion. She wasn't in love with him, but she thought that might come with time. He was immensely attractive, and she'd even had wicked dreams about him. Wild, delicious dreams.

By five o'clock, she had all but convinced herself that she was betraying him. However much she rationalized it, the plot hatched with Cook and Carr left a bitter taste in her mouth. She went over it again as she was dressing for dinner and forced herself to justify it as a means to an end. Tonight, she would clear Gaylord's name!

Gaylord called for her at six. As they walked to the restaurant, she excused the early dinner by saying she was lonely. She told him about her father's departure that morning and Chester's announcement of his impending marriage. She was happy for them, for one had found salvation in God and the other with the girl of his dreams. But she'd never felt so alone, and a little lost. She missed her father terribly.

Over dinner, Gaylord sympathized with her sense of loss. She felt all the more guilty because he was so considerate and understanding, hardly the traits of a robber and murderer. Finally, when she declined dessert and Gaylord ordered chokecherry pie she knew she was unable to avoid it any longer. She waited until he was served, then leaned forward on her elbows. She lowered her voice.

"Today, two men called on me at the hotel . . . a detective and a sheriff."

"Oh?" Gaylord said curiously. "What was the purpose of their call?"

Lillian composed herself. "The detective works for Wells Fargo and the sheriff is from Wyoming. They're searching for a robber."

"That's the strangest thing I ever heard of. Why would they ask you about a robber?"

"I'm afraid they were asking about you. They said your name is really Earl Miller."

Gaylord's fork paused in midair. She saw something flicker in his eyes, and then he recovered himself. He forked the bite of pie into his mouth and looked at her with an open expression. He chewed away, seemingly puzzled.

"Well, I've been called many things, but never a robber. It must be a case of mistaken identity."

Lillian held his gaze. "They have a witness."

"A witness to what?"

"Someone who saw you sell the gold from the robbery to Ed Chase. And they know you haven't any mining properties in Central City."

"Lillian—"

"You are Earl Miller, aren't you?"

Gaylord placed his fork on his plate. "I'm sorry, more sorry than you'll ever know. I'd hoped to start fresh here in Denver."

"Omigod," Lillian whispered. "I wasn't sure until just now. I prayed it wasn't so."

"And I forgot what a good actress you are. They sent you here to get a confession, didn't they?"

"I thought I could clear your name. How silly of me."

"Where are they now?"

"Sitting right over there."

David Cook and Jeff Carr were seated at a table across the room. Gaylord looked at them and they returned his look with flat stares. He glanced back at Lillian.

"Time to go," he said with an ironic smile. "Wish I could stick around and see how we made out. I think it would've worked."

"Wait, please!" Lillian pleaded. "You musn't try to run."

"Didn't they tell you I killed a man?"

"Yes—"

"I won't be hung."

"Otis, please—"

"So long, Lillian."

Gaylord swung out of his chair. He walked quickly toward the front of the restaurant, snaring his hat off a wall rack. As he neared the door, Cook and Carr got to their feet. Carr pushed a waiter aside.

"Earl Miller!" he commanded. "Halt right there!"

Miller, alias Otis Gaylord, stopped at the door. His hand snaked inside his jacket and came out with a Colt Navy revolver. He whirled, bringing the Colt to bear, and found himself a beat behind. Jeff Carr, pistol extended at shoulder level, fired.

The slug struck Miller dead-center in the chest. His shirt colored as though a small rosebud had been painted on the cloth by an invisible brush. A look of mild surprise came over his face, and he staggered back, dropping the Colt, slamming into the door. His knees buckled and he slumped to the floor.

Lillian stared at him as though she'd been shot herself. Her mouth opened in a soundless scream and for a moment she couldn't get her breath. She buried her head in her hands.

Her low, choking sob was the only sound in Delmonico's.

The theater was mobbed. Within the hour, the news of the shooting had spread throughout the Tenderloin, and the star of the Alcazar became even more sensational.

Everyone wanted a glimpse of the woman assumed to be the dead man's paramour. The Colorado Nightingale.

Lillian somehow got through her first four numbers. She felt wretched about Gaylord's death and oddly guilty for having exposed him as an outlaw. But she kept reminding herself of what her father—and her mother—had always taught as the cardinal tenet of the theater. No matter what, the show must go on.

The oldest bromide in the business was her lodestone. A trouper, barring earthquake or flood, went out on the stage and performed. She sang the ballads with heartfelt emotion for Gaylord (she still couldn't think of him as Earl Miller, robber and murderer). And she belted out the snappy tunes with an insouciance that belied her sorrow.

A comic came offstage as she waited in the wings. Her final number for the evening was *Lily of the West*, which played well off her own billing. She walked to center stage, steeling herself to hold it all together and close out the night on a high note. She put on a happy face as the curtain opened and the orchestra swung into the tune. Her voice was bubbly and spirited.

> *When first I came to Denver*
> *Some pleasure here to find*
> *A damsel fresh from Durango*
> *Was laughter to my mind*
> *Her rosy cheeks, her ruby lips*
> *Set things aflutter in my chest*
> *Her name so sweet and dear was Dora*
> *The Lily of the West . . .*

The audience began clapping in time to the music. Her ivory gown shone in the spotlight as she whirled and skipped about the stage, revealing her ankles in a sprightly dance routine. She finished the song with a winsome smile and playfully threw kisses to the crowd, bowing low when she curtsied for a mischievous display of cleavage. The applause swelled into a standing ovation that brought her on for five—then six—curtain calls.

Backstage, she nodded politely to congratulations from the other performers. Burt Tully had earlier offered his condolences about Gaylord, and she hoped she'd seen the last of him for the night. She wanted nothing more than to hurry back to the hotel and climb into bed and hide. She thought she might burst into tears at any moment.

Before she could undo her gown, there was a light rap on the door. She sighed, thinking it was Tully, or Chester come to express his sympathy, and sulked across the room. When she opened the door, a man in his early thirties, dressed in an impeccably tailored suit, stood outside. His mouth flashed in an engaging smile.

"Miss Fontaine," he said in a modulated voice. "I'm Victor Stanton, from San Francisco. May I speak with you a moment?"

Lillian held her ground. "What is it you want, Mr. Stanton? How did you get backstage?"

"I talked my way past Burt Tully. As to my purpose, I own the Bella Union Theater. Perhaps you've heard of it."

Everyone in show business had heard of the Bella Union. Even in New York, which was considered the center of the universe for theater, the Bella Union was fabled for its opulent productions. Victor Stanton, the impresario, was considered a showman second to none. Lillian suddenly placed the man with the name.

"Yes, of course," she said pleasantly. "Won't you please come in?"

There was a small, sagging sofa against the wall. Lillian got him seated and took her chair by the dressing table. "How nice of you to drop by," she said, trying to gather her wits. "What brings you to Denver?"

"I come here once or twice a year," Stanton said amiably. "I'm always scouting for new acts, and I must say, tonight was my lucky night. You were absolutely brilliant, Miss Fontaine."

"Why, thank you!" Lillian gushed. "I'm very flattered you would say so."

"Let me ask, are you familiar with San Francisco?"

"Well, no, not really."

"We like to think of it as the Paris of North America. Even more cosmopolitan than New York."

Stanton went on like a civic booster, extolling the virtues of the City by the Bay. As he talked, Lillian noticed his dapper attire, his polished manner and his chiseled features, and the fact that he wore no wedding ring. A fleeting thought crossed her mind about the rotten luck she'd had with men on her odyssey through the West. She wondered if her fortunes might change.

"There you have it," Stanton said. "A city worthy of your remarkable talent."

Lillian realized she was focused on the man rather than his words. "Pardon me?"

"Miss Fontaine, I'm offering you star billing at the Bella Union. How much is Tully paying you?"

"Why . . . three hundred a week."

"I'll make it five hundred," Stanton said without hesitation. "With a one-year contract and my personal guarantee of fame beyond your wildest expectations. What do you say?"

"I . . ." Lillian thought she might faint. "I have almost two weeks left on my engagement here."

"Then you'll open at the Bella Union on Independence Day. We'll introduce you to San Francisco with fireworks on July Fourth! I couldn't think of anything more fitting."

Lillian felt a sudden rush of memory. Abilene and the Comique and Wild Bill Hickok. Dodge City and George Armstrong Custer and Cimarron Jordan. Pueblo and Denver and her long run as the Colorado Nightingale. And now, her name in lights in the City by the Bay.

"You'll love it there," Stanton said, staring directly into her eyes. "I can't wait to show you all the sights, Telegraph Hill and the Golden Gate. I predict you'll never leave."

"I've always heard it's very nice."

"Do you prefer to be called Lilly or Lillian?"

"All my friends call me Lillian."

"And mine call me Victor. I think this is the start of something big, Lillian. Do you feel it, too?"

Lillian all but melted under the warmth of his gaze. The Bella Union, her name in lights, and maybe, with just a little luck, Victor Stanton. Yes, she told herself with the wonder of it all . . .

San Francisco, here I come.

Epilogue

Victor Stanton made good on his promise. Lillian was billed simply as *The Nightingale*, and she quickly became the star of the Bella Union. By early summer of 1873, she was the sweetheart of stage and song.

Lillian loved San Francisco. The city was wondrously nestled in a natural amphitheater, with steep hills surrounding the center of the community. The bay was the finest landlocked harbor on the continent, and westward along the peninsula, through the Golden Gate, sailed tall-masted clippers and oceangoing steamers from around the world. The trade had transformed the City by the Bay into one of the richest ports on earth.

A profusion of cultures, it was also the premier city of the West. Along the waterfront was the infamous Barbary Coast, a wild carnival of dance halls and brothels where sailors were shanghaied onto ships bound for the Orient. Chinatown, an exotic city within a city, was like being transported backward in time to Old Cathay, where ancient customs still prevailed. The Uptown Tenderloin, a district reserved for society swells, was filled with theaters and cabarets and plush casinos. To Lillian, it was all a storybook come to life.

The Bella Union, located in the heart of the Uptown Tenderloin, was on O'Farrel Street. There was a casino for affluent high rollers upstairs and on the ground floor an ornate barroom fronting the building. Beyond the bar was a spacious theater, with a sunken orchestra pit and the largest proscenium stage west of Chicago. The floor was jammed with linen-covered tables for 500, and a horseshoe balcony was partitioned into private boxes for wealthy patrons. Crowds flocked there every night of the week to see The Nightingale.

Lillian's dressing room was decorated in pale blue. The furnishings were expensive and tasteful, a Louis XIV sofa and chairs and a lush Persian carpet. Victor Stanton, as was his custom, lounged on the sofa while she changed behind a silk screen that was all but translucent. For her last number of the night, she slipped into a bead-embroidered gown of lavender crepe de chine. When she stepped from behind the screen, Stanton stared at her as though spellbound. The gown clung like silken skin to her sumptuous figure.

"Do you like it?" she said, posing for him. "I ordered it especially for you."

Stanton seemed short of breath. "You have never looked lovelier," he said, his eyes glued to her. "I deeply regret I must share you with the audience."

"How gallant!" She laughed a minxish little laugh. "Perhaps I'll wear it only for you."

"No, no," Stanton said, ever the showman. "You owe it to your public, my dear. You are, after all, The Nightingale."

"Then you won't mind sharing me with the audience?"

"I smother my desires to the good of the show."

"Sweet Victor, you really are a naughty man. I somehow doubt your resolve will hold after the show."

Lillian was a very chic and sophisticated twenty-one. She was not a maiden any longer, but neither was she a fallen woman. Any number of times, Victor had asked